MORE THAN FRIENDS

Tessa had just finished dressing after a long, cool shower when Jed knocked, then walked in, calling her name. He met her at the bottom of the stairs.

"You smell nice," he said. "Soapy."

"Soapy, hell. It's a very pricey cologne the kids gave me for my birthday."

"Okay, expensive soapy. Spicy but sweet."

"If you were thinking of adding 'just like you,' you can forget it, pal," Tessa said.

Jed's eyebrows rose. "Never crossed my mind," he said. He moved closer to her, placed his hand on her shoulder. Her eyes, he realized, matched the color of her shirt—clear, vibrant, and very blue.

"Thanks for being such a good friend," she said, reaching up to kiss his cheek.

Friend. Could be worse, he thought wryly. Could be better, though, too.

He gathered her into his arms. Instead of resisting, she clung to him, her hands clutching his shoulders, then slipping around his neck. Then her lips met his, joined with his, as if it were the most natural thing in the world . . .

COLORADO HIGH

JOYCE C. WARE

ZEBRA BOOKS
KENSINGTON PUBLISHING CORP.

ZEBRA BOOKS are published by

Kensington Publishing Corp.
850 Third Avenue
New York, NY 10022

Zebra, the Z logo, and To Love Again Reg. U.S. Pat. & TM
Off.

First Printing: April, 1995

Printed in the United States of America

For Wilson
And for the ten halcyon summers spent gawking at the San Juans from our little cabin at the foot of Log Hill Mesa

One

By ten o'clock Friday morning, Tessa Wagner had already received three phone calls telling her Scott Shelby was back in town. The fourth came from Jeannie Disbrow.

"Shoot, Tessa!" She sounded real pissed. Jeannie never did like being low man on the totem pole.

"Well, I'm sorry, Jeannie. Of course, the others didn't actually *see* him—"

"See him? Gawd, I could *smell* him! He passed right by the door of the shop, and I don't mind telling you that cologne of his is a nice change from aroma de cow flop we get from most of the guys around here. I swear he turned every female head in the whole entire town square."

The "whole entire town square" being about a third the size of Cottonwood's 4H rodeo arena, Tessa figured that didn't add up to a whole lot of women, especially on a morning when most of them were up in Montrose at the City Market stocking up for the weekend.

She hesitated before asking the obvious next

question. It had, after all, been a lot of years. "Umm-mm, how does he look?"

"Fabulous. I mean really fabulous. He's still got that gold brush cut. By now he's gotta be having it touched up, but that's to be expected, right? I mean it *is* his trademark, after all. Super job, though. Bright but not brassy. And that cut . . . whoever did that never got his training in a Marine boot camp."

Tessa knew that in this case Jeannie's remarks stemmed as much from professional interest as common garden curiosity. "Think you could duplicate it?" she asked, amused.

"Gawd, I dunno, Tessa. I'd sure like the opportunity. But a guy like that . . . I bet he could tell Bill Clinton a thing or two about the price of haircuts!"

A guy like that.

Twenty years ago Scott Shelby had seen Tessa barrel-racing at Cottonwood's annual Labor Day rodeo. An exhibition, actually, since she'd long since won every prize and title going. Sweaty and disheveled, she was leading her quarter horse towards the van where Barry, her husband, awaited them, when this classy-looking man walked up and told her she was the answer to his prayers.

His fashion prayers, it turned out. As Tessa tried later to explain to Barry, Scott Shelby was neither a designer nor a glorified dressmaker. He'd never sketched the shape of a sleeve; he didn't know what a gusset was, much less ever sewn one. What he did have was an unerring sense of style coupled with an ego-driven ability to think large. Articles in magazines like *Vanity Fair* and *Vogue* would soon describe him as an entrepreneur; in *Cosmo,* the noun was preceded by sexy.

Tessa, a high-energy person herself, had been astounded by him. "What the hell are you after?" she had asked.

She remembered his lips twisting up in that cocky little smile of his. Smirk, Barry called it.

"Not much. Winning the fashion loyalty of the American woman, for starters."

Starters being the huge, growing, largely overlooked market represented by women edging out of the miniskirt and hotpants age but not yet ready to throw in the towel. Successful professional women, and women married to success. Women who preferred tweed and denim to sequins.

Scott's entering bid, the one he signed her up for, was a line of cowpoke chic, pricey playclothes for expensive playgrounds. Aspen, Vail, Sundance, Telluride. He'd already registered the name, Wild Westerns; what he lacked, until he saw Tessa, was the image.

That first afternoon, after declaring her as dashing and authentic as the leather split skirts and hand-tooled boots he already had in production, be had hooked his arm cozily through hers, cut her glowering spouse dead, and continued crooning his siren's song into her dazed ear.

"In this business, it's package or die," he said, "and I want *you* to deliver mine tied up in a big luscious, long-legged, streaked-blond bow."

He paused to sweep his hand towards the high grasslands nudging the jag of peaks spread out against the blue September sky. "My range-riding Valkyrie!" he exclaimed. Then, peering down into her face, his fingers tapping apologetically on her forearm, she recalled him murmuring something about her name escaping him.

"Tessa?" he echoed. "Tessa *Wagner?* Oh my God." His ecstatic smile had dazzled her.

"Do you still have that leather split skirt?" Jeannie was asking.

"I have it," Tessa said, "but Garland wears it. My size eight days are long gone, my friend."

Jeannie, whose weren't, clicked her tongue. To Tessa, it conveyed a smugness she tried not to resent.

"These days, seeing Garland— and Gavin, too, of course— it's like looking in our high school yearbook," Jeannie said. "Those twins of yours sure are chips off their daddy's block. Barry had to be blind not to see it."

"Barry saw only what he chose to see."

There was a brief awkward silence.

"Uh, did I tell you I saw Jed meet up with Scott Shelby? They went and sat at that broken-down table under the cottonwoods across from the shop, heads together, yammering away. Wouldn't of thought those two'd have much to yammer about."

"Jed leases his grazing land, Jeannie."

"Oh, yeah, I forgot. That Jed. What a waste. How's his daddy these days?"

"Cranky."

"That old man was *born* cranky, Tessa."

"Well, crankier then. Still thinks of himself as top bull."

"And Jed keeps letting him get away with it." Jeannie sighed. "What a waste."

After Tessa hung up, she glanced out the window to see shreds of gray rapidly moving in high overhead. Even as she watched, they lowered and thickened, robbing the sky of its earlier cobalt hue and flattening the crags spiking up beyond the horse pasture into shadowless two-dimensionality.

She rose from the well-scrubbed kitchen table and stood, undecided, her strong hands tightening on the back of the oak kitchen chair. God knows she'd worked up on Hayden's Bald in weather a lot worse than this. In fact, this wasn't "weather" at all, just a passing front . . . unexpected maybe, but nothing out of the ordinary for this time of year. She remained standing, seized by an inexplicable dismay that deepened as she caught sight of herself in the cracked mirror next to the sink. Her hair was still a streaky blond, thanks to Jeannie's ministrations, but the lines radiating from the corners of her eyes . . .

She narrowed them, blurring the tell-tale signs of the passing years into temporary oblivion. *Damn Jeannie and her nattering on about Scott Shelby and split skirts and high school yearbooks* . . .

Tessa plucked Barry's torn, stained, down-filled vest from the line of wooden hooks on the back of the door and shrugged into it. She snatched her lined leather gloves from the counter, slammed out into the late spring rawness, strode to the corral, and whistled up Turnip with the help of a measure of oats.

The big rangy roan didn't much like being saddled; he liked being mounted and ridden even less. But Tessa hadn't chosen him for his disposition, and no one would choose him for his looks: with his ears flattened against his oddly lumpy head, his resemblance to his vegetable namesake was striking. What she needed was diversion, and Turnip always provided plenty of that.

By the time they neared the top of the hill, Turnip had confined his antics to an occasional sideways scuttling, like the crabs Tessa had seen on her sole trip to the East Coast, North Carolina to be exact, where Scott had wanted her photographed in his Western gear on a rented, showy-looking horse galloping through the breaking surf with the Cape Hatteras lighthouse rearing up behind them. It hadn't made any sense to her, but not much about the fashion industry did.

As they topped the rise, she saw Jed Bradburn's tall, rangy figure silhouetted against the cloud-shrouded peaks. Turnip whinnied; Jed turned from the fence he was mending, waved, and leaned back against a battered pickup bristling with posts and barbed-wire, his lean frame assuming the familiar hipshot slouch her father had wryly characterized as the patience of Jed.

Tessa frowned. *Long-suffering is more like it.*

Jed grinned at her as she pulled Turnip up in front of him. He tilted his Stetson back on his head. Even this early in the season, his face was bronzy save for the white strip just below his hairline. "What made you choose that sorry excuse for a horse? I'd forgotten how ugly he is. Never could figure why Barry gave him grazing room."

"Barry used to say he was the ugliest son of a bitch he'd ever clamped onto. Ornery as hell, and not about to change his ways. That's why Barry liked him . . . well, maybe 'liked' is the wrong word . . ."

"Tolerated?"

"No-o-o, not exactly; Turnip tolerated *him*, maybe, but Barry . . . well, I think he sort of envied Turnip's in-your-face meanness."

Jed's eyebrows rose. "You're saying Barry *en-*

joyed being bitten and kicked at? I never thought of him as being a glutton for punishment."

"He stayed married to me, didn't he?"

Jed dropped his eyes; his fingers rubbed along the worn edge of the Stetson's brim. "Lot of water's flowed under the bridge in two years," Jed said softly.

"I swear, if you tell me not to speak ill of the dead—"

Jed's eyes snapped up. "Don't patronize me, Tessa."

They glared at each other.

"Spilt milk, flowing water, whatever," Tessa muttered. "We came up here to work; guess we'd best get at it."

Hayden's Bald had been divided long ago into two unequal parts: Tessa had inherited the larger part of it on her parents' untimely death; Jed's adoptive parents owned the lesser, but the Hattons and the Bradburns had always shared the upkeep, and despite Barry's grumbles about the inequities, Tessa had no wish to alter the arrangement, either then or now.

They worked in silent practiced tandem at a chore shared for so many years it could be accomplished, if not quite in their sleep, with an ease as automatic as the making of the morning pot of coffee.

"Garland's coming home next week," Tessa said. "Thursday, I think. Any chance of your coming to dinner? She asked especially."

Jed turned to look up at her. His hat brim

hid his eyes, but she saw the corners of his mouth curve up. "Thursday?"

"I think that's what her letter said . . . I'll check it again and call you."

"Yeah, do that." He straightened and stretched; his smile became a grin. "The Queen of England said something about dropping in, but hell, I can always put her off. Need any help bringing the twins' stuff home?"

"Gavin's not coming, and Garland's roommate passes through here on her way home to Durango. They're planning on driving all night from Boulder. I don't like it much, but—" she shrugged— "you know how it is."

Jed, who had spent four years at the university himself, allowed as how he did. "What's Gavin up to?"

"He found himself a summer job. An opportunity too good to pass up— his words, not mine. A Denver-based bigwig acted as adviser to a campus political group Gavin's involved with. There's an election coming up in the fall; he asked for Gavin's help."

Jed pulled at his long Roman nose. "And he's being paid for this? I thought that sort of thing was strictly volunteer."

"Apparently Gavin's a lot better at it than most. Besides, it gives him a valid excuse for staying clear of the ranch."

"Hey, Tessa, that's got nothing to do with you."

"I know that," she said, thinking it helped to

hear him say it. "Actually, it *will* be a great opportunity for him . . . he has the interest, and what's more important, the knack."

"Ever wonder what it'd be like being the mother of the president of these United States?"

Turnip started at the sound of Tessa's burst of laughter. "Never thought you had such a lively imagination, Jed."

"Stranger things have happened, Tessa."

His expression, suddenly sober, unsettled her. "You mean like you meeting up with Scott Shelby in the town square?"

"God almighty, that Cottonwood grapevine sure beats a fax machine when it comes to speed! Nothing all that strange about me talking with Shelby, except it's usually over the phone."

"That's what I told Jeannie," Tessa said, "but one of Scott's wives, a regular customer of hers, lives on his Cottonwood ranch, so she assumed he'd lose interest in the property when he bought himself a showplace up in Telluride."

"Huh. If you ask me, Shelby would never turn entirely loose anything he might make a penny on. He used to practically invite my herd in to graze his land; now I'm paying top dollar."

"Worth it, isn't it?" Tessa asked. "Best in the county, Dad used to say. You should have heard Barry on the subject. Envious?" Her waving arm encompassed the hilltop. "I swear he was greener'n this new spring grass."

"Oh, I heard all right. From Barry, both his

brothers, and on one memorable occasion, old man Wagner, too. But you know how it is: who wants to pay top dollar for something you used to get at discount?"

They grinned companionably at each other. Ranchers came in two basic styles: feckless or penny-pinching. Jed and Tessa always tried to strike a happy medium, but when push came to shove, neither of them hesitated to make their pennies cry uncle.

"Jeannie said he's looking pretty good."

"Shelby? I wouldn't know about that. He must be, what, pushing sixty? Looks a whole lot younger though." Jed frowned. "Unnatural, if you ask me."

"Sensible living, maybe," Tessa suggested.

"You believe that, next you'll be telling everyone you saw Elvis flipping burgers at Nellie's Delly."

"No-o-o, because I'd be too busy reviving Nell." With the back of her gloved hand, she pushed away a lock of hair that had fallen over her forehead, and peered up at the sky. "What do you say we call it a day, Jed? Those clouds come down any lower, I'll think I'm at the seashore and start listening for foghorns."

"Quitter!" Jed jeered, but he wasted no time loading up the truck. "Call me about dinner with Garland, hear?"

"Will do. Say hello to your dad for me."

"Come by and do it yourself, why don't you?"

"One of these days. I'm waiting on a delivery

of feeder calves . . . Garland and I'll be taking them on up to the summer camp end of June. If I expect to get top dollar for 'em, they'll need all the fattening time they can get."

"That's only a couple of weeks away, Tessa. Snow's still clogging the forest service road a lot short of your cabin."

"Hot spell's predicted." She held up crossed fingers. "Maybe we'll get a nice even melt for a change."

Jed reached into the bed of his truck and pulled out a shovel. "If not," he said, brandishing it, "we'll be spending the rest of the spring digging out the ditches, as usual."

"Thank you, Mr. Bradburn," Tessa said. "That's just what I wanted to hear." She peeled off her gloves and thrust out her work-roughened hands. "You know those hand cream commercials on TV? I've been thinking of hiring mine out for the 'before' sequence."

"C'mon, Tessa. You look great, always have. Why do you suppose Scott Shelby plastered your photos all over creation?"

"That was then, Jed. I doubt he'd pay me so much as a plugged nickel now."

"You made the man a damn fortune! I just hope you got to keep some of it." She avoided his eyes, her lips tightening. She reached for Turnip's reins, yanked the startled horse towards her, and swung into the saddle. "What I got paid and what I do with it is none of your business."

"No, I guess not." He threw the shovel back in the truck. "Don't know how I could have thought different."

Jed climbed into the cab, gave Tessa a perfunctory wave, and drove off down the hill.

Turnip plodded in the truck's wake between the silvery ribbons of tire-flattened grasses, his briefly aroused spirits dampened by the thickening drizzle. Knowing the horse could make his way home unaided, Tessa allowed the reins to hang slack along Turnip's drooping, extended neck. She pulled the poncho from the bag hanging from the saddle horn and fumbled into it, swearing as her hair caught in the grippers. One end of the cord securing the hood had disappeared into its tunnel, forcing her to hold the flapping ends in one hand. She squinched her eyes against the rain the drizzle had become; the angle of her neck paralleled her mount's.

The year seems to have lost its way, she thought. Despite the sudden greening and the white cups of the marsh marigold starring the high meadow wetlands, despite the June-captioned page of the wall calendar in her kitchen, it felt more like March.

As if to confirm her doleful ruminations, a pellet of sleet stung the back of her hand. A moment later, assaulted by a blast of the tiny icy globules, Turnip snorted, tossed his head, and prodded by Tessa's impatient heels, bolted for home.

* * *

After turning Turnip into the corral— where he kicked back at her before galloping off to harass the other horses— Tessa started a fire in the kitchen's potbellied stove, switched the electric range on under the tea kettle, checked the notes penciled in on the calendar, and called Jed.

"Thursday still okay with you?" she asked.

"What time?"

"Well, if you want a beer first, make it five; if not, five-thirty or six. Garland always wants that pot roast of mine her first night home, so suppertime's flexible."

"You got anything to go with that beer?"

"You mean like munchies?"

"Yeah, like that."

"Pretzels, chips, nuts maybe. Nothing fancy."

"I'm not a fancy man, Tessa."

His tone was reproachful. She felt a flash of irritation. "You have to tell me that?"

"Hey, I just— "

"I've known you all my life, Jed Bradburn. 'I'm not a fancy man, Tessa.' " Her voice was a gruff caricature. "For God's sake."

Interpreting the ensuing silence as another reproof, she ended it with a muttered, "See you Thursday then."

"I could bring a bottle of red wine," Jed offered stiffly. "One of those Australian Pinot Noirs."

"And you say you're not fancy!" Her tone had lightened, reflecting no more than wry amusement.

"It'll be good to have Garland home . . . kinda calls for a celebration."

"It does, doesn't it?" she agreed softly. "Thanks, Uncle Jed."

Two

Jed replaced the receiver on the kitchen wall bracket and stood staring at it.

Uncle Jed.

"Hope that wasn't that durn life insurance salesman again," his father called in from the doorway. "As if I had a life worth insuring."

"It was Tessa, Pop, asking me for supper on Thursday, the day Garland's due home from college."

"Garland, huh? Hard to think of that little tyke all grown up— hard enough thinking of Tessa that way." Walter Bradburn wheeled his chair closer and peered up at his son. "They could've been yours, you know, Tessa and the twins both. But no, you and your ma— "

"Leave it be, Pop."

"Can't, Jed. Riles me everytime I think of that Barry Wagner, always thinking those muscles of his made up for his lack of brains. Never could, understand why Tessa— "

"There's no future in looking at the past. Barry's dead, and Tessa and me . . ." Jed wiped a weary hand across his brow. "The road the three of us traveled forked a long time ago. I keep telling you that, and you keep getting mad. No point to it."

"These days, getting mad's about the only thing that gets my juices flowing. That's point enough for me." He rolled closer; his rheumy eyes darted from the bare kitchen counter to the cold electric range. "You planning on skipping supper here tonight, too?"

It was a classic Bradburn double whammy, so blatant it amused Jed more than it annoyed him. "I have a couple of portions of that macaroni and cheese dish you like in the freezer. I thought I'd heat it up in the microwave."

"That all?"

"Iceberg lettuce wedges with thousand island dressing, fresh-baked rolls, and brownies from Nellie's Delly."

Mollified, the old man gave a grunt of satisfaction. "You buy those brownies?"

Jed laughed. "I sure didn't swipe them."

"I thought maybe that silly woman gave 'em to you. She's sweet on you, you know. Driving in here every two minutes with her baked goods, buttering me up, making goo-goo eyes at you."

"*Was* sweet on me, Pop. She finally realized it wasn't worth the effort."

"Durn silly woman. Be nice to have one around the place though . . . your hands ain't exactly soothing, you know."

Being an old man's handmaiden wasn't ex-

actly what Nellie had had in mind, but Jed knew
better than to say so. Walt Bradburn had always
perceived himself as the center of a universe;
the cruel accident that crippled him, robbing
him of his cherished physical prowess, had further limited his horizon. His universe had become *the* universe . . . or at least the only one
he gave a damn about.

After supper, Jed helped his father get ready
for bed. The routine never varied: off with his
clothes and leg braces, into a hot bath for a
ten-minute soak, then over to the bed for a massage followed by an application of a talcum pow-
der, the kind formulated for babies, whose scent
was the only one his father tolerated.

Some years back, another woman accused by
his father of making goo-goo eyes had brought
a gift-wrapped container of talc by Calvin
Klein— or was it Ralph Lauren?— in a mis-
guided effort to win him over. She departed,
fuming, after telling Jed not to bother calling
her until he cut himself loose from "that old
coot's" apron strings.

Once settled, Walter Bradburn switched on
his small color TV and zapped to the channel
celebrating John Wayne Week, and although he
frowned when Jed— having seen *Rio Bravo* three
times in the last two years— declined to pull up
a chair, the rousing opening theme soon distracted him.

Closing the door quietly behind him, Jed
walked down the hall and into the dark low-

ceilinged living room. Familiarity guided him
behind the shabby armchairs facing the stone-
faced fireplace, around the old black-and-white
television set to the window commanding in
good weather a partial view of Courthouse
Peak. If he had been given any say in the matter, he would have long ago replaced the
graceless double-hung window with a wide bay.

The peak was shrouded in clouds now, the
earlier drizzle having given way to a steady, sul-
len rain. Jed's well-muscled shoulders drooped
as he envisioned the muddy runoff from the
mesa behind the house swirling into the creeks.
He'd really pushed himself that week to free
up Sunday for trying his luck with the trout-fly
patterns he had dreamed up over the winter,
but he knew it would take three days for the
water to run clear again.

A couple of those flies were pretty fanciful,
but these days he got more pleasure out of fool-
ing trout than eating them. He'd even taken to
using barbless hooks. Trouble was, once school
let out for the summer, it was hardly even worth
the trying. *This weekend, it wouldn't be worth anyone's trying* . . .

Jed sighed. Each year saw more and more
out-of-state campers crowding the Forest Service
roads, parking alongside the newly stocked
creeks, the eager tourists throwing in worms any
which way, their kids following on behind throwing rocks.

There was still some posted water that held

wild cutthroats, but Jed figured their days were numbered, too, considering all the "no trespassing" notices that got ripped off over the summer. *Hardly worth the time and expense of posting 'em.*

Jed turned away to the fire-blackened hearth. He tossed in a couple of logs on top of the half-burnt remnants of last night's fire, twisted a few sheets of newspaper into spills, and clicked a wooden match into flame with his fingernail, a practice his mother had deplored.

"Leave the boy be, Aggie," his father would growl.

"How can he keep his grades up if he can't write?"

"Burnt fingers never kept a man from tending stock!"

Walter Bradburn had fought his wife's determination to send Jed off to college right down to the wire. Nothing he actually said could be singled out as proof that Jed's being adopted prompted his objections, but Jed couldn't help thinking it did.

"Your Pa don't mean nothing by it," his mother would say. "It's just his way."

He never had any such wonderings about her. No natural son ever had a better mother. Her rough hands, when she patted his, always seemed soft as silk. He'd won his scholarship for her, and although the years would prove her right about the many ongoing benefits a college education would bring him, she fretted until the day she died about his one regret, which at the time had almost overwhelmed him.

It happened the fall of his sophomore year. He'd come home at Thanksgiving, thinking they'd go together to the Cottonwood High's homecoming game as they always did: Barry Wagner, famed for his quarterbacking and flamboyant bulldogging; Tessa Hatton, former high-stepping cheerleader and present barrel-racing champion, and Jed Bradburn, whose outlandish devotion to book learning was generally agreed to be outweighed by his stand-out performance in bareback bronc-riding events, near and far.

The Trio Con Brio.

Jed settled back into one of the armchairs, smiling as he recalled the source of the nickname. According to Tessa, the director of her church's youth choir, frustrated by a particularly lackluster performance, had waved his arms and shouted, *"Con brio,* you turkeys, *con brio!"*

"We didn't know if we were being insulted or what!" she reported indignantly. "But I damn well wasn't going to give him the satisfaction of asking, so I looked it up later at school. *'Con brio,'* " she recited in her husky alto, " 'with vivacity, dash, and spirit.' Not bad, huh?"

"Like us," Barry said smugly.

"Trio con brio," Jed had suggested.

His reward had been Tessa's heart-stopping smile. Then, five years later, without warning, three became a crowd.

Tessa had entered a barrel-racing event down Albuquerque way, and Barry offered to drive the van. It was the last big rodeo of the fall season; the championship of the southwest division was at stake, and she had always depended on Jed and Barry's psyching-up to give her that extra edge. This time, Jed wasn't available.

According to Jeannie Disbrow, who came in second riding one of Tessa's horses, Barry followed up his pep talk with a whole lot of TLC at the super blow-out celebration of Tessa's big win.

"Bought her champagne, massaged her ego, and just about everything else he could get at in public." At that point, Jeannie had rolled her eyes. "No one saw 'em leave, Jed. Like that song says, they must've got married in a fever. Came trailing back to Cottonwood three days later, Tessa with this pukey little gold band— no wider'n horsehair— on her finger, both of 'em looking like something drug through a knothole."

Remembering, Jed got up to poke at the fire. Sparks popped and flew up the chimney. *Oh yeah, they got married in a fever, all right.*

Not that Tessa ever admitted as much. She was way too proud for that. She avoided him through the Christmas holidays; Jed avoided Barry— couldn't stomach his swaggering— and returned to Boulder before his vacation ended, pleading the need to study. And for the next two and a half years, except for working himself half to death on the ranch during vacations, that's about all he did. Hunched over his scarred desk, surrounded by teetering piles of paper-slipped books, dizzied by fatigue, and haunted by the memory of Tessa's smile.

In February of his last year at the university, his heartache was sidelined by tragedy. Walter Bradburn, driving back in early April from a cattlemen's meeting in Durango, got caught by a late-season run of the notorious East Riverside slide north of Silverton. His truck ended up in the ravine, half-buried in snow, unseen until morning. By the time the volunteer EMTs got him out, the damage to his spine was irreversible.

Jed's mother insisted he finish out his senior year. Assured by rancher neighbors of their help until he returned, he reluctantly acceded, but when she arrived in Boulder in May for his graduation, relieved from her nursing chores by sympathetic friends, he was shocked by her appearance. In early September she died of the cancer she never found the time to have diagnosed.

Jed slumped in his chair, assaulted anew by a wave of the guilt that over the years had become his closest companion; his sidekick; his goddamn shadow. Guilt he'd tried to drown in work, ease with caretaking, assuage through renunciation. . . .

Renunciation?

"Jesus!" Jed muttered. "Of all the self-pitying, self-serving crap . . ."

He shoved himself up and paced in front of the dying fire. *Why now?* he wondered. His father's rages erupted much less frequently than they once did— so did his own sexual urges for that matter.

He didn't much like being celibate, but the alternative— clumsy fumblings and couplings with lonely widows and desperate singles hoping for more— had even less to recommend it. There was a time when he'd hire a nurse and take off to Denver for a weekend with a woman— okay, a call girl, who accepted personally selected clients only, and only by appointment. But after the fifth weekend he decided the easing of his loins wasn't worth the drain on his wallet and the paternal complaints that greeted him on his return.

But that was, what, ten years ago? He'd come to terms with it long since. Sublimation, according to that psychology course he took. So why now?

Wind rattled the windowpanes.

The front must be moving out, thank God.

Jed thought of Tessa on Hayden's Bald. Wet, cold, miserable. Bitter. Barry's death hadn't seemed to help her any, cruel and crazy as it was.

He thought of Scott Shelby. *Pretentious s.o.b.* He'd never quite forgiven Tessa for her connection with him.

Forgiven? No, it was Barry who'd never done that.

Accepted, that was it.

Come to think of it, there was a whole lot he'd never accepted.

Jed peered out the window. Shreds of the earlier cloud cover, chased by the rising wind, scudded across a bright, high, full moon. A coyote's dolorous wail rose and fell in the dry wash-laced rough stretching behind the house into the juniper-studded foot of the high mesa that marked the northern boundary of the Bradburn spread. The familiar nighttime keening, as much a part of western ranchlife as the lowing of cows in more domesticated landscapes, struck a responsive chord in Jed's heart. Unthinking, he lifted his chin. His mouth rounded. Then, coming to himself, he shook his head in private embarrassment.

"Jesus," he muttered. "Next thing you know I'll be sprouting fur on the back of my hands."

He paused at the door to his father's room on the way to his own. A rumbling untroubled burr greeted his ears. Sleep was, he knew, the only place the old man found peace. The little death sought as temporary escape from his fierce, unyielding fight against the real thing.

"Sleep well, Pop," he murmured.

Three

"Mmm-mm, your pot roast smells just as good as I remember, Mom. Worth coming home to."

Tessa looked up from the black iron pot whose aromatic contents she was testing with a fork. "First it was your horse, now a hunk of meat. Where do I come in?"

Garland hooked a long tanned arm around her mother's shoulders. "Well, let's see now . . . next comes Uncle Jed, Miguel, Plume—"

"Oh, come *on*, Garland! Plume bites!"

"Yeah, but your bark—"

"Is worse than his bite," they finished together. "Very funny," Tessa said.

"Laugh-a-minute Wagner, they call me."

Tessa closed the oven door, tossed the fork and hot pad on the counter, and planted a kiss on her daughter's smooth cheek.

"Gorgeous, I call you."

Garland tossed her tawny blond head and affected a Miss America simper. "Oh, well, that, too." She grinned at her mother and began as-

sembling napkins and stainless steel cutlery on
a tray. "Wine glasses, you said?"

"Jed's bringing an Australian red— does Pinot
Noir sound right to you?"

"Sounds classy, but then he always was a
classy dude. Me? I'm strictly a California jug
wine girl— I offer two choices: red or white."

As Garland turned, tray in hand, towards the
table at the other end of the big kitchen, her
full flower-strewn cotton skirt swirled above her
fine-boned ankles.

Strictly thoroughbred, Tessa thought fiercely. *Jug
wine? Hell, champagne is the least she deserves!*

She recalled the first time she tasted champagne. It was at the big bash Scott Shelby threw
at his ranch to celebrate the first, over-the-top
sales reports of the Wild Westerns line. Tessa,
outfitted in the latest Shelby gear, was lavishly
toasted with a French champagne she overheard
someone say cost in the neighborhood of a hundred dollars a bottle. A lot of bucks for something that tasted to her like a slightly sour,
upscale soda pop, but she had to admit it went
down easy.

Too easy maybe, because afterwards she had
only a hazy memory of promising to go on a
nationwide department store tour to further
boost his skyrocketing fortunes. "I want every
woman in America yearning to look like you,"
Scott had said. How could she refuse?

For Barry, however, refusal had by that time
become second nature. They slept together less

and less, and when they did, his performance could be described as perfunctory at best. So it came as no surprise when, at the last minute, he refused to accompany her to the party.

"You want to show yourself off to your Los An-gee-leeze buddies, that's okay with me, but I'm not about to be your fancy-man escort."

By then she already knew that nothing about her involvement with fashion and Scott Shelby was remotely "okay" with Barry, but she never expected to come home that night to a dark house and locked door. *Her* door more than Barry's, actually. After her parents died in a plane crash, she and Barry had exchanged their mobile home on the Wagner homestead for the spacious log dwelling on the Hatton spread she inherited.

She recalled pounding on the door until her fists ached, then crunching through the frosty gravel out to the barn where she burrowed— mouth dry, head spinning— into the corner of the stall she'd earlier filled with fresh straw, taking some small comfort from the warm looming presence and inquiring velvet nose of the equine resident she'd raised and trained.

The following night was the last they spent together in the same bed. In those days, no one thought of forced marital intercourse in terms of rape, but afterwards, when her pregnancy was confirmed, Tessa couldn't help wondering if Barry's violence had given his listless sperm an extra jolt. Unable to appreciate the irony after more than ten childless years, Barry had assumed the worst.

"Hey, anybody home?"

Tessa looked up from the salad-cutting board. "God*damn*it!"

Jed hesitated in the doorway, shifting from one boot-shod foot to the other. "Wrong day? Wrong guy, maybe?"

"No, no . . . come on in, Jed. It's just . . ." She sighed, regretting she hadn't gone upstairs sooner to change. Her fingers brushed ineffectually at tendrils of hair that had fallen loose from the knot bundled at the back of her head. "Oh, well, it's not me you came to see, is it?"

Before Jed had a chance to answer, Garland raced across the room and plastered herself against him. He reeled back against the door-jamb and flung up the hand holding a paper bag. "Whoa, there, I promised your mother wine to drink, not marinate the floor with."

"Oooh, *mon cher oncle*, I'm so glad to see you!"

Tessa's cleaver whacked harder than intended into the head of cabbage she was holding. Bits of green flew up into her mouth, her eyes, her hair. "Seems to me, Garland, living where we do, Spanish would come in a lot handier'n French."

Garland's huge hazel eyes blinked. "I'm taking Spanish, too, Mom."

"So did I," Jed said. "Had to work at it—languages never came easy to me—but I've never regretted it, especially now, with NAFTA."

"I didn't think NAFTA had much effect on the ranching industry, Uncle Jed. According to Gavin . . ."

Tessa turned back to the severed cabbage. Lips tightening, she began slicing it into shreds. *Since when had ranching become an industry? Made it seem like one of those filthy, noisy, iron and steel foundries back East.* She tried to recall the name of the city she'd been whisked through on the way from Marshall Field's in Chicago to Cincinnati. *Had a man's name . . . Harry? No, Gary . . . Gary, Indiana. Couldn't see it for the goddamn smoke.*

She turned to her daughter, knife in hand. "I'm expecting the calves to be delivered in a couple of weeks, Garland . . . you want to help me take them up to summer pasture?"

Garland and Jed exchanged amused glances. "Sure, Mom," she said. "Fact is, I've been looking forward to it—" She broke off. "Just what were you intending to do with that knife if I'd said no?"

Tessa looked down at the brandished blade, then smiled sheepishly. "Lord, I don't know. Slice the buttons off that pretty blouse of yours, maybe."

Garland rolled her eyes and crossed her arms over her breasts. "What? And leave me naked as a babe?"

"Some babe," Jed said, winking.

"Nobody but me and your 'shir onkle' to see you," Tessa muttered.

Garland raised her eyebrows at Jed. "As I was about to say, Mom, it's nice to think of those little fellows fattening on our good green grass instead of in one of those ghastly feed lots. You planning on taking the Longhorns up, too?"

"I sold them."

"*Sold* them? But your plans— "

"For God's sake, Garland, that bull killed your father!"

"But it wasn't— " Garland caught Jed's warning shake of his head out of the corner of her eye. "I'm sorry, Mom. I wasn't thinking straight. You were right to sell them."

"If you'd heard the Wagners going on and on about it . . . kinda drove my plans for cross-breeding them out of my mind. Gram Wagner I can understand, but since she and your grandfather moved down to Brownsville, all I hear about them comes second-hand."

"From Uncle Lloyd and Aunt Pauline, you mean."

"Yeah. 'Course they thought it was a damn fool idea from the start. By the time the Wagners started ranching, at the turn of the century, Herefords were the way to go. But the Hattons— Lord, Garland, we go back to the days when Longhorns were the only animals hardy enough to travel a thousand miles and more to market!

"They prowled the gullies for water, browsed on brush when the grass gave out, rubbed the ticks off of their hides before anyone thought of dipping vats, and raised sturdy calves without benefit of vaccines. The Texas Longhorn kept more people fed—and more cowmen from going broke—than any other breed. I was just trying to help keep 'em from becoming forgotten."

"That's sentiment talking, Tessa," Jed said. "Sure, the Longhorns filled a real need in their day, but I remember your father saying, more'n once, that it was 'Hereford on the range, Shorthorn in the feed lot, and Angus on the table.' "

"That wasn't original with Dad, Jed."

Jed shrugged. "Doesn't alter the truth of it."

"Well, no point discussing it. The Longhorns are gone and so is Barry—that's a truth that won't be altered either."

Tessa's harsh statement discouraged further comment about her disposal of the small herd. While Jed fished in the pocket of his leather bomber jacket for the cork puller he had brought with him, Garland held the wineglasses up to the light and polished away a few water spots. Tessa, her head bowed, vigorously stirred a ranch-style dressing into the coleslaw.

Barry died early on a Sunday morning, two years ago. It was the Labor Day weekend, and on Saturday he had started drinking even earlier than usual. Although he drank too much every day come sundown, he confined his all-day bouts to the weekends. Not that it made any sense, given the seven-day schedule of a working ranch, but it allowed him to convince himself he could still control his growing habit.

The Labor Day rodeo was the biggest county event of the summer. Barry had tried to argue the twins into staying for it instead of heading back early to Boulder for the fall semester. But, pleading a sensible reluctance to buck the end-of-holiday traffic, they left as planned, which in Barry's disgruntled, already booze-hazed mind was yet another example of behavior unnatural to any gen-u-wine kin of his. He spent the rest of the day tipping a bottle to his lips, at first hiding the bottle in a paper bag; later, he didn't bother.

By the start of the bulldogging event— at which he had himself excelled long years before— he had become belligerent, shouting insults at the competitors, flailing out at Tessa when she tried to calm him. His brother Lloyd, alerted by pals that Barry had exceeded the bounds of locally tolerated macho behavior, marched down to his seat in the stands, manhandled him out to his pickup under cover of a boys'll-be-boys grin, tossed him in the back, and advised Tessa to get him the hell home.

By the time she did, he had passed out.

She covered him with a horse blanket; later, while she was washing her supper dishes, he swaggered in, stinking of vomit, and demanded she get him something to eat. When Tessa suggested he bathe first, he cursed her and stomped out to the barn and the cunningly stashed bottles she'd long since given up trying to find.

Disheartened and disgusted, she had taken a long hot bath and gone to bed. A single shrill scream roused her during the night, but thinking it was a bobcat, Tessa soon drifted back to sleep.

The next morning, alerted by the restiveness of the horses in an adjoining corral, she spied Barry's familiar figure sprawled in the bull pen. Above him, the big Longhorn trotted to and fro, huffing and pawing nervously at the blood-soaked earth, his neck still encircled by the braided bulldogger's rope Barry had somehow managed to secure around the animal's thick neck.

As she approached, the bull snorted, lowered his head, and warningly presented the long graceful curves of his red-stained horns.

Ride 'em cowboy.

At the time, the unfeeling sentiment, flashing unbidden into her mind, had appalled her; remembering it now, two years later, it merely seemed a fitting epitaph.

Jed raised his glass in a toast to Garland's return. Tessa sipped, then sipped again. It was lovely stuff, rich and fruity, yet dry.

"Yum-yum," she said.

"You're spoiling me, Uncle Jed," Garland lamented. "How do you expect me to settle for jug wine after this?"

"Gives you something to set your sights for, young'un. Speaking of which, what are your plans for the summer . . . aside from helping your mother with the calves and her horses, that is."

Garland's eyes lit up. "The horses'll have to wait their turn this summer, Uncle Jed, on weekends mostly. Mom got me a job up in Telluride."

"Is that so," Jed returned cautiously. "What doing? Not table-waiting, I hope."

"I could do worse—the tips are outta this world up there—"

"That's not the only thing that is," Jed muttered.

"I'm going to be working with the Chamber Resort Association, you know, on all those festivals they've got going? Probably more as a gofer than anything else," she admitted, "but if I get my toe in the door this summer, who knows?"

"This your idea, Tessa?"

"So what if it is?"

"I don't suppose hearing about Shelby being back had anything to do with it."

"Is that a question, Jed?"

"Not really," Jed said, "more like a comment." He popped a forkful of tender meat into his mouth and chewed thoughtfully. "Best pot roast in the San Juans."

"Scott's being here was just a coincidence. I still have contacts in Telluride . . . what's the harm in using them? After I gave the Chamber Garland's academic average, all they wanted to know was if she looked as good as me. Better, I said."

Jed frowned.

"C'mon, Jed," Tessa said, bridling at his obvious disapproval. "This is the real world we're talking about! So far, Garland's life choices have been limited to horses, cows, and Boulder's pizza parlors. She needs more'n that to base a lifestyle on."

Jed leaned back in his chair, raising the front legs off the well-washed vinyl tile floor, and folded his arms. "Sounds like you've been reading those magazines in the rack at the Cottonwood Mart's check-out counter. Life choice, lifestyle . . . next thing you'll be talking about is life *experiences*. Godalmighty."

Red flared in Tessa's cheeks. She opened her mouth to snap out a protest, but seeing her daughter's stricken expression, thought better of it. She took a slow sip of wine. "No-o-oo, I was thinking of *past* life experiences, actually."

Garland hooted at the look of shock on Jed's face. "Gotcha!"

He grinned sheepishly. "Yeah, I guess she did."

"Like another helping?" Tessa offered.

"Generous in victory, too," Jed said, lowering

the chair legs back to the floor. "What a woman."

Tessa arrowed a sharp look at him as she collected his plate. Although relieved for Garland's sake that open warfare with Jed had been averted, she sensed a quickening of the complex, ongoing undercurrent that had become all too familiar.

Jed's resentment had first surfaced the summer after she and Barry eloped. Aware by then that "happily" was the wrong adverb to apply to their married state, he had lashed out at her.

They were on Hayden's Bald, replacing fence posts. She'd carried over a preservative-soaked length of cedar bare-handed, driving a splinter into her palm when she set it down in the hole he had just dug. He'd stripped off his gloves, taken her hand in his, and deftly extracted the sliver with a single sharp tug. She supposed it was the touch of flesh on warm flesh that triggered his outburst.

"Damn it, Tessa! Why'd you want to run off with him like that? I thought we had an understanding!"

She remembered pulling her hand from his and licking at the trickle of blood. The sight of it seemed to inflame him further.

"Maybe you can fool everyone else into thinking you're happy, but not me." At that, she had turned away. "Look at me, Tessa! You never could fool me!"

She whirled to face him, eyes blazing. "*You* thought! All you ever did was think, Jed Bradburn, and whatever you thought was right, huh? Wrong! Barry's a doer, and what I wanted done had nothing to do with *thinking.*"

Jed was shaken. "I suppose," he muttered, "what you're talking about is a toss in the old hay— "

"Whoo-*ee*. Give that man a great big *see*-gar."

"But you didn't have to go and *marry* him! God, I'd've thought— "

"There you go thinking again, Mr. College Graduate." Tessa, finding herself on a roll, was relentless. "I imagine you've heard about the greater fool theory . . . well, okay, maybe I'm not sure about the theory, but I know a prime example of a fool when I see one! The only genuine understanding we ever had was about this fence, and even that didn't start with us. Tell you what, Jedidiah, from here on out you stay on your side, I'll stay on mine, and you can keep your damn *thoughts* to yourself."

In due course the wounds had healed— they shared too much history for them not to— but the underlying ache persisted. Ten sour, childless years later, too proud to admit she had made a wrong choice, Tessa grabbed the offer Scott Shelby held out to her, finding it as tantalizing as the carousel's gold ring that had glittered just beyond her six-year-old reach at the Colorado State Fair.

Her merry-go-round whirl with fame didn't last long: one heady year and a six-month phase-out to normality. But it was long enough to lace Jed's rankling hurt with disapproval.

Not that he ever said anything directly. It was the way he frowned when she resigned as coach of Cottonwood's barrel-racing hopefuls, even when she assured him it was temporary. Temporary for you, he'd said, but not for the current crop of contestants. And his reaction the next summer, when she sent her ranch foreman up to Hayden's Bald in her stead. She knew damn well Miguel would do whatever needed doing in the way of fence-mending better and faster than she could, but afterwards Jed just pulled that long nose of his and allowed as how it wasn't the same.

Remembering, Tessa glared at Jed. *Wasn't the same? Jesus! What the hell was?*

Jed, looking up from his bread-mopping-up operation of the gravy on his plate, was unprepared for the hot resentment he saw in her eyes.

"Tessa?" His voice was anxious, bewildered.

She scraped back her chair. "I'll get dessert. I found a jar of peaches left from that batch Jeannie and I got up in Fruita last summer."

"You gave Pop and me a half-dozen jars for Christmas . . . that and some apricot preserve."

"No wild raspberry?"

"Right! Raspberry! That was his favorite. He actually smiled when he tasted it."

"I'm sorry, Jed," Tessa said quietly.

"I'll come over for a visit real soon, Uncle Jed," Garland promised, apparently thinking it was Walter Bradburn's famous orneriness her mother was referring to.

"You do that, honey," Jed said, wiping his mouth. "Can I help clear?"

"Nope," Tessa said. "Let someone wait on you for a change."

Fifteen minutes later, Jed declined a second helping of peaches, pushed his scraped-clean bowl aside, and stirred his coffee. "So, Garland, decided what you want to do yet? Assuming, of course, that your summer of high-life in Telluride doesn't turn your head." He smiled broadly, defusing Tessa's defenses. "A couple of years ago you were talking about training as a nurse practitioner . . . that means graduate school, doesn't it?"

"Yeah, it does. But so does veterinary medicine. There's this whole new field of orthopedics focused on athletic injuries, and I was thinking, what about animal athletes? Why not a veterinary practice dealing with the treatment of physical stress peculiar to them? It could be combined with preventive medicine— Mom's been practicing that for years with her quarter horses."

Tessa looked at her, astonished. "Me?"

"Sure, Mom. A lot of trainers— and owners,

unfortunately— think only of the short term. You know, more bang for their bucks. They van their horses all over creation, competing the hell out of them, ruining their legs, and what's worse, breaking their spirit."

"A lot of that's the fault of the system, Garland," Jed said. "Too many dollars at stake over too short a season."

"Look, I know there'll always be greed and abuses, same way there is with human athletes and team owners, but maybe, with a little education— "

"You know what they say, honey," Tessa broke in. "A little education is a dangerous thing." Jed and Garland frowned at her. She threw up her hands. "Hey! I'm just quoting! Truth is, I agree with you."

"Of *course* you do, Mom— who do you suppose put the idea in my head?"

"Glad to know I'm good for something besides selling a line of clothing the world could very well have done without."

"Now, Mom . . ."

"C'mon, Tessa . . ."

"Gotcha!" she said, grinning wickedly. She got up, lifted the coffeepot off its hot plate and refilled Jed's cup. As she straightened, holding the pot out in one long-fingered hand, she tilted her head thoughtfully. "Actually, I sort of fancy myself as the Mother Teresa of American equines . . . God knows I'm old enough," she added, looking down at herself with a rueful eye.

There was no denying she was no longer as slim as she was at twenty, or even thirty, but Jed's brown eyes saw the generous curve of hip revealed by her jeans and the thrust of breast outlined by the soft drape of her silk shirt as appropriate to the handsome woman she'd become. Unfortunately, Tessa's blue eyes did not.

Sure, Jeannie Disbrow could disguise the gray in her sun-streaked hair, but she had yet to find a foolproof way to mask lines gained through fifty years of squinting against a summer sun untempered by city haze.

Twenty years ago, Scott Shelby had hailed those lines as a rancher's badge of honor. *Real and honest and true,* Tessa recalled him saying, but then Scott always did tend to repeat himself. Today they were deeper, longer, wider . . . pleasing only to a cosmetic surgeon.

Jed looked up at her, smiling. "Can't say I've ever thought of you as a Mother Teresa type, Tessa . . . fact is," he added with a nod towards Garland, "despite this beautiful, intelligent, all-grown-up evidence to the contrary, I still have trouble thinking of you as any type of mother."

"Oh, yeah?" Tessa declared, planting her fists on her hips, "Dare I ask what you *do* think of me as?"

Jed's smile faded. He spread his fingers out on the red-and-white checked tablecloth; his eyes dropped to study their drumming tips. "As just Tessa, I guess," he murmured.

He raised one finger and slowly rubbed the tip of his nose. His eyes, solemn now, lifted to hers. "Just Tessa."

Four

Late on Sunday afternoon, as Jed poured the shot of whiskey his father looked forward to at the end of each day, he heard Tessa's truck drive in. He went to the door and peered out through the screen door. It was Garland.

He screeched the door back on its dry hinges and waved her in. "To what do we owe the pleasure?"

"I start work up in Telluride tomorrow, Uncle Jed. My hours are ten until five, so I thought I'd better come visit with Pop before I started. Mom says he goes to bed right after supper."

"And Mom, as always, is right."

"Always? C'mon! You've been friends too long to believe that!"

"Usually?" he offered. She shook her blond head. "Sometimes? Now and then? Once in a great long while—"

Garland threw up her hands, laughing. "Actually, she's right more often than I wish she were." She looked askance at the bottle clutched in Jed's hand. "Am I interrupting anything?"

"Like a bit of solitary boozing, you mean?

This is for Pop, Garland. I stick pretty much to beer before dinner. Care to join us?"

"Yeah . . . beer for me, too."

A moment later, in obedience to an internal clock Jed often wished was more fallible, Walter Bradburn rolled in. Seeing Garland, his usual querulous expression gave way to a playful smile and lovable-old-codger-type comments about her pretty face making him wishing he were young again. Garland, too sensible and nice to take offense, told him he still had more ginger than most of the young guys she knew.

The old man preened, hoisted himself higher in his chair, tossed off the shot of whiskey Jed had handed him and held out his glass for more.

"Pop, I really think— "

"You think too damn much, Jed. This is still my house, ain't it?"

Jed's lips tightened and thinned; Garland, embarrassed for him, studied the foam-speckled surface of the beer in her mug.

Jed opened his mouth to refuse, then thought better of it. He went to the kitchen, splashed a token thimbleful into his father's glass, and grabbed another can of beer for himself from the fridge, tearing back the tab so fiercely he slashed his finger on the jagged edge.

Shit!

He stared out the window above the steel sink as he sucked at the cut. The view wasn't as spec-

tacular as it was from Tessa's kitchen— the Bradburns had elected to build down in a cottonwood-
fringed hollow, protected from the winter blast
of winds spiraling down from the high peaks.

The house did indeed still belong to his father. So did the barn, the sheds, the land, and
the cattle grazing on it. Forget the fact that it
was his training and knowledge and hard work
that made the Bradburn ranch a model admired
and emulated, not only in Ouray county, but
beyond. Not that anyone put it in just those
terms, but the awards won and the invitations
to speak to cattlemen's groups amounted to the
same thing.

And what did he have to show for it?

Hardly more than your common or garden
saddle bum: one horse, a set of worn leather
tack, and a beat-up truck.

Granted, the horse, bred by Tessa, was a
damn fine one, and the saddle and bridle were
silver mounted, won bareback bronc-riding the
next-to-last time he competed. That was the
glory year; the year after, as Pop never tired of
reminding him, had been a disaster. Why, Jed
had yet to figure.

As for the truck . . . what was it Joe Higgins
said when the left fender rusted out? "Well,
boss, it still runs pretty good."

Garland's laughter drifted in from the living
room. It was good for Pop, seeing her, Jed
thought. Helped the old man forget for a little
while how much he had lost. Which was why,

of course, he clung so hard to the things he had left. *Including himself.*

Jed bowed his head over the steel sink. *It wasn't right, a grown man living this way.*

He guessed he would someday inherit everything, but that really wasn't the point. He closed his eyes, trying to remember the name of the Dickens novel assigned in high school. Everyone had seen the movie on television at one point or another; yet they found, via the dismal grades on their returned papers, that it wasn't quite the same as the original.

Great Expectations, that was it, and he was an overage Pip.

"Hey, Jed! You brewing that whiskey out there?"

"Distilling, Pop," Jed muttered under his breath. "Only beer and ale are brewed." He walked into the living room and handed him his glass.

"You sure you didn't pour too much in?" his father asked sourly, eyeing the minuscule portion.

Jed winked at Garland and raised his second can of beer to her. "I thought I'd have another, too, seeing as how this is a special occasion."

Walter Bradburn grunted in recognition of his son's oblique warning. *Try this tomorrow night and see how far you get.*

* * *

Jed walked Garland the few steps out to the truck. It was very still. They could hear peepers shrilling down in the stand of cottonwoods.

"The sound of spring," she said softly.

"Yep. Before long it'll be too dry for 'em there." He opened the cab door for her. "Thanks for coming, Garland. There's not much that makes him smile these days."

"Glad to be of help, Uncle Jed." She sighed. "I wish I could say it's because he's a dear old thing, but . . ." She hopped up into the cab, avoiding his eyes.

Jed leaned against the doorframe. "Honey, you're not telling me anything I don't already know."

"Well, damn it, why do you put up with it? I mean, ranch boss all day, nursemaid at night . . . it's not fair!"

"Fairness has nothing to do with it, Garland. Besides, what's my alternative? Pa tolerates nurses only in a crisis, and the last time, when one of them was dumb enough to tell him her hourly rate, they could hear him clear out in the bunkhouse."

"Well, it seems to me . . ." She faltered and cleared her throat. "Seems to me you're a pretty nice-looking guy with, you know, good prospects." This time the words tumbled out.

Amused by Garland's earnestness, Jed watched her pick at a frayed spot on the edge of the beaded belt he'd given her for Christmas the year her father died. He bought it in New

Mexico, at Gallup's Intertribal Indian Ceremonial. Nell Lewis had helped him select it. *Bad mistake, taking Nell* . . .

"You keep doing that," he warned, "and we're going to have us a bead shower. I really don't want to spend the rest of the night here on my hands and knees."

She looked up at him, her eyes tender with concern. "Oh, Uncle Jed."

"I know what you're thinking, Garland, but I think maybe I was destined to be a bachelor."

"Nonsense! Why, you're— "

"It's not for want of thinking about it," he broke in. "Or even trying to do something about it," he admitted, "but somehow it just never worked out. There was this one girl— this was years ago, mind you, when a man could still get away with calling a woman a girl— pretty and smart, nice as could be . . . we got along really well. Then I brought her home to meet Pop, and, well, it kind of reminded me of Red Riding Hood and the wolf. Have to give her credit though, she told me straight out a package deal like that wasn't what she had in mind."

Garland huffed indignantly. "If you ask me, you were well rid of her . . . probably would have made a lousy mother."

"Now, Garland."

"Okay, okay . . . so was she the only one?"

"There were others; none I thought seriously about." He smiled wryly. "A couple, of 'em fig-

ured if they chased hard enough they'd eventually wear me down, but I got pretty good at
spotting dollar signs in a woman's eyes. I'd just
tell them the truth of the matter, that until Pop
died, he owned everything worth having around
here— "

"Except you, Uncle Jed."

He pulled thoughtfully at his long nose.
"Well, according to some, even that's a matter
of opinion. Anyway, that pretty well stopped
them in their tracks. Except for one, who'd been
twice widowed and left pretty well fixed. Her
idea of fun was a weekend in Vegas, so I allowed
as how gambling was against my religion . . . I
saw no need to tell her it was a religion of my
own devising." They grinned at each other. "I
heard later there'd been some question about
the naturalness of the death of both her hus-
bands."

"Yikes!"

"Yeah." He shook his head. "Good looker,
though."

"Speaking of good lookers . . . you and Mom
were pretty close once, weren't you?"

"Still are, Garland."

"I don't mean as *friends*."

"Look, honey, your mom and I . . . the time
when we might have been more than
friends . . . well, it's long past."

"But she's so *lonely!*"

Jed dropped his hand from the door. "That's
not a good enough reason, Garland. Not for

anybody. Your mother is a very . . . complicated person."

"Mom?" She sounded astonished.

"She's more than just your mom, you know. And one thing she's sure not doing is waiting around for me to sweep her up on a big white horse and gallop off into the sunset. For one thing, she's got better horses of her own at home."

"No she doesn't! She's always bitching about the deal she gave you on Bolt. Strange name, I always thought."

Jed laughed. "You can blame that on your mom. He's by Thor out of Zig-zag, and his full name is Thunderbolt . . . made me feel I ought to say something like 'Hi-yo!' whenever I got on him."

"Zig-zag! Gosh, remember the way she tilted when she rounded the barrels? I swear that mare defied gravity!"

"Passed the ability on to a lot of her off-spring, too."

Garland laughed. "Are you suggesting there's such a thing as a gene for tilting, Uncle Jed?"

"Well, all kinds of things can be inherited—some good, some not. Could have been a spontaneous mutation originating with Zig-zag."

"Hey, maybe that explains Gavin's and my hazel eyes," Garland said in a light tone Jed knew was forced. "Spontaneous genetic mutation . . . yeah, sounds real scientific. I'll have to try that one on Mom."

"You'll do no such thing, Garland."

"You know Daddy never accepted—"

"There were a lot of things your daddy never accepted. Growing up was chief among them." Jed reached out and took Garland's hands in his. "Look, honey, what happened . . . the kind of man he became . . . it wasn't all his fault. Sometimes I think God played a dirty trick on him."

Garland's eyes widened. "But you're the one always telling Gavin and me about what a golden boy he was!"

"He was! Good health, high spirits, looks . . . it sounds funny to say it about a man, but he was beautiful. If you'd seen him sailing down the football field— I swear his feet didn't seem to touch the ground. Lighter than air. Same on the cinder track at school and riding the bulls . . ."

His eyes drifted beyond her, linking as the present caught up with him.

"It was all just handed to him on a golden platter, Garland. He never reckoned on the years slowing him down, and later, when he saw others passing him by—"

"Are you implying Mom was one of those 'others'?"

Jed shifted uncomfortably. "You know, I really think she's the one you ought to be talking to about this."

"I can talk with her about most things, Uncle Jed, but not Daddy. Never could. I was only kidding about trying out that genetic mutation thing on her."

"Well, you know that Barry and I . . . we sort of shepherded your mom through her early barrel-racing days."

"Slave-drove, according to her."

"I wouldn't go that far," he protested. "Although I have to admit . . . you know about your mom's rivalry with Jeannie Disbrow?"

"Oh, sure, they laugh about it a lot."

"Yeah? Well, it wasn't always a laughing matter. Jeannie was good. Not quite in Tessa's class, but what really held her back was her horse. Your mom fretted about it; she couldn't help wondering what would happen if Jeannie had a horse as good as hers. Well, it so happened that Jeannie's horse went lame just before a rodeo they had both entered. Your mother insisted on lending Jeannie one of hers, and Barry just about went into orbit— accused Tessa of betraying him."

"*Betraying* him? I don't get it . . . seems to me Mom was just being incredibly generous to Jeannie. How could Daddy— "

"Don't you see?" Jed broke in. "He'd invested himself in her: his time, his energy— "

"But so did you!"

Jed shook his head. "Not to the same degree, Garland. Barry was strictly an all-out kind of guy. If she won, *he* won. No compromises; no second thoughts."

"Like yours?"

Jed's smile was rueful. "Yeah, like mine. But I seem to have strayed from the point I was trying to make. In fact, I don't even remember what it was."

"Something about genetics, Uncle Jed. Genetics and hazel eyes."

"Was that it?" He looked as if he wished it weren't. "Okay, let's go back to that. You see, the trouble with the science we had in high school was that we didn't get enough of it. It wasn't anyone's fault, there just wasn't enough time. But even if you paid close attention, oversimplifications were inevitable. I doubt if we spent more than two days on Mendel's law."

"Mendel . . . Mendel . . . Isn't he the guy who grew all those peas? God! Imagine spending your entire life messing around with pea plants!"

"He was a monk, Garland; I expect he had a lot of time on his hands. Anyway, the example our science teacher gave us had to do with eye color—I guess he thought we'd relate to that better'n tallness and shortness in peas. So, okay, brown is dominant, blue is recessive. That's a given. But, he added, since eye color is determined by a pair of genes inherited from each parent, the variance from brown to blue can be considerable, unless *both* parents' genes are exclusively of the recessive blue type. In that case, he told us, if the kids have brown eyes, you better check out the milkman."

Garland grinned.

"Yeah, it was a pretty funny line," Jed agreed, "and everybody laughed, but unfortunately, it was the only part of the whole damn lesson that stuck with your dad."

"Mom's are blue," Garland mused, "and so were Daddy's. Except his were gray-blue . . . sagebrush blue, Mom called them." She searched Jed's brown eyes. "Gavin's and mine are hazel. Are you saying Daddy thought that Mom and you— "

"He was wrong," Jed said flatly. "About her and me— about her and anyone else for that matter. Your mom's the type who lies in the bed she makes, no matter what."

Garland grimaced. "They didn't share the same room, let alone bed!"

"I didn't know that," he muttered. "But I know your Mom," he added fiercely. "She's the most loyal person I've ever known . . . out of sheer stubbornness if nothing else."

"Oh, Mom's stubborn all right, but she's also human. All those years! I can't *imagine*— "

Garland stopped short. She bit her lip and ducked her head in a futile effort to hide the flush suffusing her cheeks. Seeing it, Jed was made suddenly, uncomfortably, aware of her budding sexuality.

Budding, hell! It's already bloomed.

"You know, Garland, I used to think that if maybe . . . maybe if there hadn't been *twin* pairs of hazel eyes . . ." He paused to collect his thoughts, wondering if he should continue.

She's not a kid anymore, he thought. *Besides, she asked me.* "Along about your first birthday, I suggested to Barry that it might be a good idea if he took a good long look at the portrait of your great-grandmother hanging on the dining-room wall in your grandparents' house."

She frowned. "I don't remember seeing anything like that last time I visited them in Texas— 'course they don't have a regular dining room in their condo there . . . more like a dining alcove."

"Maybe they stored it away. You ask 'em about it next time you go. Anyway, she had hazel eyes, midway between brown and green, just like yours and Gavin's."

Garland gave him a funny look. "How come you noticed and Daddy didn't?"

Jed shrugged. "I've always noticed things like that, family resemblances in the way people look and move . . . maybe it's because of my being adopted. Not having any blood kin of my own, I feel as if something's missing, so I keep looking." His smile dispelled any sense of self-pity. "You know that way Gavin has of hitching himself up when he doesn't agree with you?" Garland nodded. "Pure Barry Wagner!"

"So what did Daddy say? she persisted.

Jed's eyes dropped. "Oh, just that his great-grandma's eyes didn't have those little gold speckles like yours and Gavin's. I told him the artist could've forgotten to put them in— the point being, they were hazel. But *he* said— you know, hitching himself up—maybe the artist forgot the color, too; maybe he should've painted 'em blue."

"And maybe, if you're right about what you said before," Garland murmured, "it gave him another way to justify his resentment of her . . . and you. Pairing you up would fit right in."

Jed raised troubled eyes to hers. "Not me, Garland." He shook his head. "Barry knew better. Those ten years after they got married and before you guys were born . . . me and Tessa, well, except for our business dealings on Hayden's Bald, things were kind of strained between us."

"Who, then, Uncle Jed?"

"Trust me, Garland, he had no reason!"

"Who?"

Oh God. Reason or not, once she started working up in Telluride those old rumors'd find her out. His eyes even had those damn speckles.

He sighed. "Shelby, Garland. Scott Shelby."

Five

Tessa was standing at the sink peeling potatoes when she saw the swirl of dust heralding the approach of a vehicle. She glanced at the clock on the wall. Four-thirty. Too early for Garland.

Tessa wiped her hands on the dish towel and went out on the long, wide veranda. She squinted against the long slanting rays of the sun, trying to identify the pickup nosing like a well-trained cow pony into the post-and-rail fence separating the narrow grassed yard from the sage-tufted land beyond. The bulky figure that stepped out of the cab was all too familiar.

"Hey there, Lloyd," she called. The man nodded and started towards her.

A second figure scrambled out of the other side of the cab and trotted up beside him. "Been a while, Tessa."

"Sure has, Pauline. Good to see you guys," she added insincerely. "Come on in!"

Tessa waved her brother-in-law and his wife into the house, wondering what had brought them unannounced to her door. She knew better than to think it was simple sociability.

"If I'd known you were coming I would have—"

"I told Lloyd he should have called first," Pauline broke in, flustered as usual.

Pauline was Lloyd's second wife. She meant well, Tessa reflected. Not a mean bone in her curvy little body . . . and not a thought in her pretty little head.

Lloyd frowned at her. "Tessa is family . . . no need for it." The last half of his sentence, delivered with a challenging stare, was aimed at Tessa.

Tessa smiled blandly. "All I meant was, if I'd known, I would have baked a pan of that apple cake you like, Lloyd. Matter of fact, the ingredients are all waiting to be mixed. Garland's back from college for the summer and it's one of her favorites, too."

Lloyd shook his big shaggy head. "I'll settle for a beer, Tessa."

"Pauline?"

"Tea, if it's not too much trouble, or coffee . . . or juice maybe?"

Lloyd snatched off his hat and wiped his beefy hand across his forehead. "For God's sake, Pauline!"

Pauline hunched her narrow shoulders. "Whatever, Tessa."

Tessa's smile was the understanding kind you

give an anxious child. "So sit, you two. I'll only be a minute."

Lloyd pulled a chair out from the kitchen table and whumped his bulk into it, rousing Plume, who managed a hoarse, token "woof!" from his basket before slumping back into sleep. Pauline slid into the chair across from Lloyd. Her tiny pale fingers fidgeted with the salt-and-pepper shakers. "Garland around, Tessa?"

"She started work today, up in Telluride. She may not get back before you leave." Lloyd eyed Tessa narrowly, suspecting a hint for a short visit. "Of course, that depends on how much time you have to spare for me."

Mollified, Lloyd grunted and popped off the tab on the can of beer Tessa handed him. "Telluride, huh? You wouldn't catch me lettin' my girls work up there."

You wouldn't catch anyone up there hiring them either, Tessa thought. "How are Sharla and Mandy? You must have almost enough grandkids for a baseball team by now . . . hard to keep track, the way they keep popping them out."

"Sharla's got three," Pauline volunteered, "and Mandy four, with a fifth on the way. They're the cutest things, Tessa! Full of ginger and curious as a litter of kittens." *In other words,* Tessa thought, *hell on wheels.* "The girls still work part-time at their hairdressing," Pauline continued, "so I get to see a lot of the kids.

Almost like having my own," she added wistfully.

"Almost never won no ribbons," Lloyd pronounced.

"Here's your tea, Pauline," Tessa said. "Do you want sugar with it? Sweetener? Honey?"

"Gawd! You're as bad as she is!"

"I can think of a lot worse things, Lloyd," Tessa said. *Like that first wife of yours.* She knew it wasn't nice to think ill of the dead, but in Rhonda's case, an alternative way of thinking never came to mind. "So how're things on the Lazy W?"

Lloyd shrugged. "Me and Jack aren't gettin' any younger and the land's sure not gettin' better. The Hattons and the Bradburns snatched up all the good grazing land."

As if it had been a conspiracy.

"They just got to Cottonwood first, Lloyd," Tessa said. "No crime in it; none intended. Pure chance."

He shot her a dark look. As far as the Wagners were concerned, the bad luck that had dogged them through the years— lack of water, stock killed on highways, barns razed by fire— hadn't a thing to do with their poor irrigation practices or neglected fences or carelessly discarded cigarette butts. Someone else was always to blame— she doubted if even God was exempted— and in the case of Barry's death, Tessa herself.

"Gavin come home, too?"

Tessa, alerted by Lloyd's elaborately offhand tone, paused before answering. "He's got a job up in Denver for the summer."

"Denver, huh? Those twins of yours sure seem to land on their feet." Tessa refrained from reminding him that a few minutes ago he'd derided Garland's choice of work sites. "Both on scholarship, aren't they?"

"Partial scholarships, Lloyd. Two kids in college at the same time is a huge financial drain any way you look at it."

"That so?" Lloyd's cat-ate-the-canary smile made Tessa realize she'd slid right into an artfully set trap. "Well, maybe I've got a way to help solve all our problems. That land me and Jack sold Terry Ballou up on the mesa?" Tessa nodded, not trusting herself to speak. "He sold the last of the lots in that subdivision he made out of it a coupla months ago . . . can you beat that? Rest of the country wrestlin' with a lousy real estate market and here we got folks trampin' around in snow up to their belly buttons payin' his asking price for land that didn't even have any water up to three years ago."

"Water he never should have gotten!" Tessa protested.

"He got it fair and square . . . no one forced Greta Larsen to sell him those rights."

"Forced, no, but he sure as hell didn't think twice about putting a lot of silly romantic ideas into her head." She shook her head. "Best water rights in the county."

"Terry didn't buy up all of them, Tessa," Pauline said.

"Enough to cut the value of her land in half . . . maybe more. Greta's ranch doesn't have a view, and the way things are going around here you need either a mountain vista or good water rights, preferably both." She sighed and pushed a stray lock of gray-streaked blond off her forehead. "Oh well, there's no fool like an old fool. I just hope she had fun while Terry's little dance lasted."

Lloyd chortled. "You gotta admit he gave her something no one else ever did. Can't put a price on that."

"Maybe not, but I'm betting you and Terry have put a price on the acres being held in trust for Gavin and Garland, right?"

"Hey, there's no harm in talking, Tessa."

"I didn't say there was. It's a waste of your time, though. As you very well know, Barry's will named me as trustee for his holdings until the twins' twenty-first birthday. I have no intention of making a decision like that for them. You'll just have to wait."

"That's a year from now!" Lloyd cried. He thrust himself out of his chair and began pacing, his face darkening with angry frustration. "Goddamnit, it's Wagner land! Bought by a Wagner, worked by Wagners— "

"And inherited by Wagners," Tessa hotly reminded him.

Lloyd stopped short, turned, and leaned towards her. "Wagners? Let me tell you, lady, those kids of yours missed being left out of Barry's will by no more'n this much!" He extended two stubby fingers held so close Tessa could barely see daylight between them. "It just about killed him, thinking about you and that fag Shelby. It was me, seein' how much it hurt him, that told him to forget it." He turned his fingers to stab at his burly chest. *"Me!* You owe me, Tessa!"

"You can't have it both ways, Uncle Lloyd." Garland's cool voice, addressing them from the living-room doorway, reduced her elders to startled silence. "If Scott Shelby fathered us, he's hardly likely to be gay."

Tessa was the first to recover. "Garland! We didn't hear you come in."

"Obviously," she said dryly. "I saw that the geraniums in the barrel next to the front door could use water, so I came in the company way. You're looking younger than ever, Aunt Pauline."

In fact, Pauline's stricken expression had added ten years. "Oh, Garland! Your Uncle Lloyd didn't really mean all that."

"Not to fret. We've all been tiptoeing around this for far too long."

Tessa reached her hand out towards her daughter. "Your father *was* your father, Garland. I want you to be sure about that."

"I am, Mom . . . always was. I just wish Daddy had been."

Pauline got up. "Lloyd, I think we'd better . . ."

"Yeah . . . yeah, I guess so." He scraped back his chair and looked from Tessa—no help there—to Garland. "One of these days, you and me and Gavin, we really got to talk—"

"Goodbye, Uncle Lloyd."

He opened his mouth, closed it, and nodded, for once lost for words.

After her in-laws left, Tessa stood at the screen door staring out at the departing truck's plume of dust, not trusting herself to speak.

"Tea, Mom?"

Taking a deep breath, she turned slowly. "You learn how to do that in college, Garland?"

"What's that, Mom?"

"Don't play the innocent with me!"

"Better a dropped bomb than one that lies there unexploded, biding its time. Tea?"

Tessa, distracted, nodded. "I don't remember ever saying—"

Garland turned from the stove to wave dismissively. "No one ever had to actually *say* anything. Gavin felt it sooner than I did. There wasn't as much . . . distance between me and Daddy as with him, maybe because I was, I don't know, more submissive?"

Tessa shrugged. "Cuter, I would have said." She responded to Garland's grin with a reluctant smile. They both knew it was a safe distinction. Even Jed had stopped well short of attaching the term "cute" to Gavin's fierce childhood expressions of independence.

Garland brought two steaming cups to the table. "Later, when Daddy started drinking so much, it got worse for both of us. Remember when Gav finally told him flat out he wasn't interested in becoming a rancher? Not that it could have come as much of a surprise."

Tessa closed her eyes, remembering.

You ain't no son of mine!

The more interest Gavin showed in book learning, the more Barry had resorted to deliberate lapses in proper English. Gavin's unerring eye for a promising colt cut no ice with him. "Where the hell is the surprise in that?" Barry had flung back at her when she faced him with it. "We *know* who his mother is!"

Tessa pulled the sodden tea bag out by its cardboard tag and dropped it in the saucer Garland held out to her. "Where did you hear about Scott Shelby? You've been in Telluride for only one day— hardly time enough to hear those old rumors."

"For heaven's sake, Mom! Everyone in the whole damn *country* knows about you being Scott Shelby's Wild Westerns girl."

"C'mon, honey, we both know this isn't about a fancy modeling job I had twenty years ago."

"I know Daddy was resentful of the money you made at it."

"Who the hell told you that!"

"Uncle Jed," Garland muttered, adding another spoon of sugar to her already sweetened tea.

Tessa cupped her ear with her hand. "Can't *hear* you!" she singsonged.

Garland sipped her tea, grimacing at the syrupy taste. She looked her mother straight in the eyes. "Uncle Jed."

"That son of a bitch."

"Mom!"

"He had no right!"

"He has more right than anyone but you!" Garland scrambled up from the table and dumped her tea in the sink. She stood for a moment, turned away, breathing hard. She turned back, head high. "A right, may I remind you, that you chose not to exercise."

Disarmed by her daughter's dignity, Tessa struggled to meet it. "Okay, so maybe I should have told you myself, but I was waiting for the right time and . . . well, it just never came along." Her smile was rueful. "Or maybe it got mislaid among all those other things I kept to myself, like keeping the Wagners out of bankruptcy court, and Pauline's abortion . . ."

Garland's eyes widened. "Aunt Pauline had an *abortion?* I always thought she couldn't have children . . . or that Uncle Lloyd couldn't—although knowing him, that's a possibility I bet nobody would dare mention."

"Lord, what a tragedy it was!" Tessa said. "They hadn't been married very long, and

Pauline, knowing how much Lloyd wanted a son to carry on the Wagner tradition— " She paused to grin. "He claims Jack's boys aren't worth feeding to the coyotes."

"Yikes! They may be flops as cousins, but I wouldn't have gone as far as that."

"Those were Lloyd's words, not mine."

"Flavored with sour grape juice maybe?"

"Probably. Of course in my opinion, the Wagner tradition's not worth much either. Anyway, once Pauline knew she was pregnant, she was so anxious to determine the baby's sex, that without telling Lloyd, she made an appointment for one of those ultrasound things. She asked me to drive her."

"Why you, Mom?"

"Her own family lived too far away, and I was the only Wagner she trusted not to tell Lloyd. What could I do? She's an awful wimp— probably couldn't live with Lloyd if she weren't— but she has this . . . this little girl *sweetness* about her."

"I know what you mean," Garland said. "So what happened?"

"Well, she learned she was carrying a boy, which thrilled her, of course, but the doctor saw something that bothered him. He advised amniocentesis, which confirmed his fear. Seems the fetus had a neural tube defect— spina bifida, they call it. It's always pretty bad, but she wouldn't know just *how* bad until the baby was born."

"Oh, Mom!"

"I drove her back to learn the results. There was this coffee shop, next to the hospital, where I waited for her. I remember I ordered a grilled cheese sandwich— you know, flattened and crispy, the way you can never do it at home?— but before it came she slid opposite me into the booth. Her eyes were red and puffy, and her face was this awful greeny-white. Well! It was plain the news wasn't good, and by the time my sandwich arrived I'd as soon've eaten a cow flop."

Tessa sighed. "Some families can accept whatever the good Lord chooses to send their way, but Pauline knew the Wagners, especially Lloyd, couldn't . . . not in a case like this, anyway."

"You and Aunt Pauline have never exactly been buddies, Mom. Didn't all this sudden togetherness of yours give Uncle Lloyd pause?"

"Pause?" Tessa gave a bark of laughter. "I can't imagine anything giving old Lloyd anything as la-di-da as pause, Garland. Besides, it was all over with that same afternoon. Pauline'd been too nervous to eat anything before we left home that day, so they just sort of fit her in. An abortion may be final, but unless you wait too long, it's not very complicated. On the way home she told me she had her tubes tied, too, even though her chance of conceiving another similarly affected child was only about two to five percent.

"To me that seemed like a pretty slim chance,

but I obviously couldn't say that to her. Ever since, though, I've wondered if she had waited—even a day or two—if she would've gone that far . . ."

Tessa pushed her fingers through her hair. "But, like they say, what was done was done. The hospital wanted to keep her overnight—she looked awful and felt worse—but what choice did we have? I called Lloyd to tell him Pauline wouldn't be back in time to fix his dinner, which didn't sit too well. He thought we'd gone to a swap meet, and I guess in a way we had." Tessa's smile was bitter. "When we pulled in, I just hustled Pauline upstairs into the back bedroom and told Lloyd something she ate had backfired on her. He spent all the next day looking for strays, and when he came in, she told him she'd lost the baby. I guess he had to get his own dinner that night, too."

"Didn't Uncle Lloyd wonder why she never got pregnant again?"

"Oh sure, but he never suggested getting medical advice. Pauline told me he finally decided it was one of those female things. Besides, knowing Lloyd, I imagine he wasn't keen on running the risk of being told he wasn't as potent as he once was." Tessa shrugged. "Blaming Pauline was easier."

"Poor Aunt Pauline!"

"The Wagner men aren't noted for their sensitivity to women's problems, Garland—in this case, that worked to Pauline's advantage."

Garland leaned forward. "Then why did you ever—" Her hands, clenching into fists, pulled at the tablecloth. "Damn it, Mom, you know I loved Daddy, but—"

"Why did I marry him?" Tessa reached over to smooth out her daughter's hands. "The Wagners were everything my sober, sensible parents weren't. My father never thought much of Boyd Wagner as a rancher, but my adolescent eyes saw him as larger-than-life, fearless, even a bit dangerous." She smiled at her daughter. "Your grandfather was in his mid-forties then, Garland, the prime of his life, and I swear the ground seemed to shake beneath his feet. And the boys! Oh my. Barry was the handsomest, Lloyd the strongest, and Jack the wildest, but all three had something of the others in him. They could have any girl they wanted . . .

"Which accounts," she concluded briskly, "for the Wagner look stamped on some of the first babies born to the Cottonwood girls of my generation."

"Including Gavin and me?"

"Yes."

"Despite our hazel eyes?"

Tessa's mouth thinned. "Yes!"

Garland grinned. "Like Uncle Jed says about cattle, I guess the Wagner bulls were prepotent."

"It's still family business, not Jed Bradburn's," Tessa retorted. "He shouldn't be talking with you about it!"

"I *asked* him, Mom! Besides, Jed's been more family to Gavin and me than the Wagners ever have."

Tessa looked pained. "Oh, Garland . . ."

"I'm not blaming you, Mom, I just think it's time we were straight with each other."

Tessa leaned towards her daughter and cradled her long fingers in hers. "Then believe me when I tell you that Scott Shelby is not only *not* your father, he couldn't have been. He's just about the most charming man I ever met, with a line strong enough to rope in the wildest range cow, but Hattons keep their promises, even those they wish they'd never made . . ."

Her voice trailed off; her eyes looked beyond Garland, through the window to the mesa looming darkly against the sunset sky. She took a deep breath and met her daughter's wide hazel eyes. "I never cheated on your daddy, Garland."

"That's what Uncle Jed said, too, Mom."

Tessa released Garland's hands. "My hero!" she sneered.

"C'mon, Mom. No point in blaming the messenger."

But Tessa did.

Pleading first-day-on-the-job fatigue, Garland went to bed early. Tessa tiptoed to the entrance of the bedroom corridor and waited until the narrow wedge of light under her door was extinguished. Closing the hall door behind her, she strode to the kitchen and dialed Jed's number.

"Who in the *hell* do you think you are?"

"That you, Tessa?" His voice sounded amused. "What have I done to rile you now?"

"Sure! Act as if I'm some silly, unpredictable female! You know damn well what you've done! If my children have questions about their father, *I'm* the one to supply the answers, not their uncle by . . . by . . ." She broke off, exasperated. "To tell the truth, I don't *know* what by!"

"Proxy? Long acquaintance? Propinquity?"

"Pro-*what?*"

"Pinquity. It means— "

"I don't care what it means, Jed! I only care about what you said to my daughter."

"In the first place, your children aren't children anymore; in the second place, I've never lied to them. Barry was never as hard on Garland as he was on Gavin, but she sensed the distance. Always had. She thought it was her fault." Tessa heard him take a deep breath. "Garland asked me a direct question, Tessa. I've always been straight with the twins; I'm not about to start changing that."

"You're saying I don't play it straight?"

"No, *you're* saying it, Tessa. I think that's what this call is really about. Your evasions are finally catching up to you."

"I never lied to my children, Jed." Her words were clipped, her voice taut with anger.

"Maybe not, but you sure are a champ at sliding around the truth, just like you were with barrels. Got to be a habit, I guess, with the twins, with me, with yourself . . . even Barry. You never loved him, Tessa."

"I keep my promises!" she cried.

"We all might've been better off if you'd broken that one."

"I probably wouldn't have been the Wild Westerns girl if I had— you're forgetting it was Barry who kept after me to do those barrel-racing invitationals."

"So? A little less fun, maybe."

"Oh, it was fun, all right, more'n you ever had or dreamed of! And I got paid damn well for it. How do you think the Wagners kept from going under when they hit that real hard patch twenty years ago?"

There was a long silence on the other end of the phone. Finally, Jed cleared his throat. "I didn't know about that, Tessa. . . . I guess sometimes things aren't quite as simple as they seem. Look, I— "

Tessa clunked the receiver into the wall fixture, cutting him off. *That's right, Mr. Propinkwhatever. Sometimes things aren't so damn simple.*

She knuckled the tears from her eyes. Jed had followed that straight and narrow path of his for so many years he no longer noticed the byways beckoning along the way. Maybe he never did. Maybe, she admitted reluctantly, his path never offered any. God knows Pop Bradburn was a far cry from Scott Shelby.

Special. That's how Scott had made her feel.

Barry had room in his world for only one special person: himself. He considered her barrel-racing ribbons as much due to his coaching as any talent of hers, and later, after they were married, his swaggering presentation to prospective buyers of the horses she had bred and trained made her seem hardly more than a glorified stable hand.

After the initial shock of Barry's senseless death wore off, Tessa had found herself reveling in the novelty of days spent blessedly alone, free from anxiety about his drinking and the occasional, stumblingly delivered, backhanded slap. But after a time that too wore thin, and the sense of something missing began to gnaw at her.

Gavin and Garland were settled, happily so, in college; Skywalk Ranch was widely acknowledged as a prime producer of well-bred and trained quarter horses. Great kids, fine horses: most women would be thrilled to death. So why wasn't it enough for her?

The answer had come, stunningly, on the heels of the phone calls telling her Scott Shelby was back in town. Suddenly, like a delayed tidal wave in the wake of an earthquake, that long-ago, never-quite-forgotten feeling of specialness rushed in over her, leaving her breathless and, yes, yearning.

She was probably too old now to inspire it, but her dear, beautiful Garland . . .

Barry had rarely been unkind to Garland, as he often was, sometimes cruelly so, to her brother. But he'd never made the slightest effort to make her feel special.

Tessa suddenly felt cold. Hugging her arms, she walked into the dim kitchen and turned the heat on under the kettle. The window over the sink framed a rectangle of darkening sky. As she watched, the evening star brightened above the shadowed, serrated edge of the mesa. Close by, a mule deer barked, followed by the flash of one, two, three white tails semaphoring through the fragrant tangle of sage and piñon. Her breath caught in her throat. How sweet and pure it was.

Special.

Just like Garland.

Please, God. Let her at least have a taste of it.

Six

"I'm a rancher, Jeannie, not Dolly Parton," Tessa said as she backed out of her friend's salon.

"I dunno," Jeannie said, frowning as the sunlight illuminated Tessa's just-completed color touch-up. "Seems a bit low-key."

"These days I'm a low-key kind of woman. Save the flash for your overflow trade from Telluride. Speaking of which—"

She caught the smile of greeting Jeannie beamed over her shoulder a moment too late. A jolt shivered up her arm as her elbow connected with the ribs of a passerby she had failed to notice. "Oh gosh! I didn't know anyone was—"

Seeing it was Jed she had bumped into, Tessa cut her apology short. Their conversation of a few nights earlier still rankled.

"Hiya, Jed!" Jeannie caroled. "Long time no see!"

Jed rewarded her trite greeting with a teasing smile. "Practically a lifetime . . . two weeks at least."

"Oh you," she returned. "When are you going to give me a chance at that unruly hair of yours?"

"Unruly but thinning, Jeannie. Thanks for the offer, but I guess I'll stick with Jake's barbershop and plain old haircuts. Salon styling's not quite my . . . well, style."

"I can do plain haircuts, Jed. Ask Tessa."

Tessa threw up her hands. "Hey! Leave me out of this! I have enough trouble with my own hair."

Jeannie looked hurt. "Trouble? I thought you just said you liked what I did."

"I did and I do, Jeannie. It's not your fault I'm going gray."

"I could do something more about that, if you'd let me."

"I like the way your hair looks, Tessa," Jed said. "Silver threads among the gold."

The two women stared at him.

He looked from one to the other. "You know, from that old song about— " Stricken, he pulled at his nose. "Oh, Jesus."

"Yeah," Tessa said dryly. "That old song about growing old. Thanks a heap, Jed."

"Would it help if I substituted platinum for silver?"

Jeannie giggled. "It might if she were Dolly Parton."

Tessa's wry smile widened into a grin.

Relieved, Jed asked, "I was heading to Nellie's Delly for a cup of coffee, Tessa . . . join me?"

Tessa's eyes narrowed. "You're buying?" He nodded. "Throw in a doughnut, and you've got a deal."

"Jeannie?" a distraught voice called from inside. "The bell rang two minutes ago!"

Jeannie rolled her eyes and hurried inside. Jed and Tessa walked the few steps to the deli in silence.

"Hey, Jed!" Nell called warmly. "Hi," she added coolly, as Tessa emerged from behind him. "Take whatever booth suits you. What'll it be this morning?"

"Two coffees, two doughnuts, Nell."

"I know you like yours black, Jed . . . how 'bout you, Tessa?"

"Milk and sugar, please."

"On the table," Nell replied briskly. "Be only a minute . . ."

"If it's on the table, why'd she ask me?" Tessa wondered aloud. Jed shifted uncomfortably. Tessa's eyebrows rose. "Oh, I get it."

"No, you don't," he said. "Let's just say hope springs eternal, even after the source has indicated itself as exhausted."

"Somehow I've never thought of you as a dry well," Tessa said, grinning.

Nell plunked a small tray on the table beside them. The coffee was rich, the doughnuts still warm.

Tessa munched hers thoughtfully. "I've got to admit she makes a mean raised doughnut. Do you suppose her hormone level has anything to do with it?"

He sighed. "You've had your fun, Tessa . . . happy now?"

"Yep," she mumbled through sugar-coated lips.

"What's this about Telluride?" he asked. She looked at him perplexed. "Just before you crashed into me— "

"Bumped."

"Okay, *bumped* into me, Jeannie was saying something about Telluride."

"Were you eavesdropping, Jed?"

"I was passing by, for God's sake. I just happened to overhear something about Telluride."

"I was about to tell Jeannie about Garland's job."

"So, how's it going?"

"Just fine. Busy as hell, but . . . well, there's a lot going on. Lots of interesting events and people. It's good for her. I'm going up myself this weekend for the Nothing Festival."

"The *what*?"

"It's one of those Telluride weekend events. I was really amazed when Garland showed me the schedule for this summer. There's a hot air balloon rally, poetry readings, a winetasting, hang gliding, and all kinds of music— the blue-grass concert is the one I really want to go to. They even have a Mushroom Festival."

"Suppose someone picks a Death Cap by mistake?" Jed asked.

Tessa laughed. "Well, that sure would make for lousy PR, but Garland says that since it's being held late in the season, the impact of anything like that on the overall tourist trade would be minimal. Hey!" she added, seeing the look on Jed's face, "that's the Chamber of Commerce's point of view, not hers!

"But to answer your question, the Nothing Festival offers a couple of days of doing whatever you want: hiking, shopping, hanging out—you know, unorganized."

"I thought you and Garland were taking calves up to summer pasture this weekend."

"Didn't work out, Jed . . . don't know why."

He looked at her in surprise. About things like that, Tessa always made it her business to know exactly why.

"They're being trucked in next week instead," she continued. "Actually, I'm sort of pleased. It's been a long time since I've been in Telluride."

"Didn't you go up there this spring to explore summer job possibilities for Garland?"

Tessa squirmed in her seat. "Well, yeah, but I didn't *stay* long— besides, now that she's working there, Garland can give me the grand tour. I thought I'd van our horses up, spend the day. It'll be fun!"

"Fun?" Jed muttered. He leaned back against the vinyl-covered seat back and crossed his arms. "I was just a little kid the first time Pop took me with him to Telluride. It was winter . . .

February, I think. I don't recall what took us there at that godawful time of year, but I know it wasn't fun. And cold? Lord, it was bad enough down here, but up there, two thousand feet higher, with those gray, stone-faced mountains looming above the town like the walls of a prison . . ."

"Parts of it were pretty even then," Tessa protested.

"Maybe so, but to me hell isn't a blazing inferno, Tessa; it's Telluride in midwinter, the way it was back then. Cold and dark and bleak. Empty stores with taped, cracked windows. Icy, rutted side streets lined with dilapidated houses . . ."

He sat forward and pointed a finger at her. "Back then, I bet half of the town could've been bought for back taxes! Today, painted up like the Victorian floozies that used to work at the Pick and Gad, each house goes for half a mil. It's all hanging ferns and boutiques now, and upscale guys like Scott Shelby instead of grimy miners."

"Are you saying that's bad?"

"I dunno, Tessa . . ." Jed shoved his hand through his hair. "The thing is, to me the difference is mostly surface . . . designer wallpaper pasted over a cracked and crumbling wall."

"It's given a lot of people pleasure, Jed, made a lot of other people money, and provided jobs in the bargain."

"It did back in its heyday, too. The mine owners lounged in offices overlooking the mountains while the miners slaved long shifts in dark tunnels to buy the bosses their fine cigars and imported whiskey. It didn't last, Tessa, and maybe this so-called rebirth won't either. Skiers are notoriously fickle."

"According to Garland, it's a popular year-round resort now."

"Maybe so," Jed conceded, "but to me it'll always be a semi-ghost town with a shameful history."

"Well, sure, that's all part of its romantic appeal."

Jed frowned. "Sorry, Tessa, I find it hard to think of misery and greed as romantic."

"You think on the past too much, Jed."

"And maybe," he retorted, "you don't think on it enough."

She narrowed her eyes at him. "Okay, out with it . . . just what in hell are you getting at?"

He took a last swallow of coffee and placed his brown hands flat on either side of the mug. "You really want to know?" Her impatient nod made her hair jounce on her shoulders. "I think you're looking for Scott Shelby to come to the rescue again."

Tessa stared at him, open-mouthed. "I don't believe I'm hearing this!"

"That first time . . . maybe you've forgotten how unhappy you were."

"I was restless, is all."

"You were miserable."

"I'd never met anyone like Scott before . . he thought I was, well, special."

"Other people did, too, Tessa."

"Yeah, sure. Special by proxy. 'Great little rider you got there, Barry.' But with Scott—"

Jed leaned towards her; a muscle twitched in his cheek. "He needed you!" Urgency harshened his voice. "You made him famous, and then he dropped you."

"No!" She scrubbed her palms with her napkin, sending sugar granules flying. "It wasn't like that!"

"Misery and greed, Tessa."

"My God. You sound like some Old Testament prophet." She flung the crumpled napkin on the table and slid out of the booth. "Thanks for nothing, Jed. As for helping with the calves next weekend, you'd be better off spending the time chiseling out a few new commandments, starting with Thou Shalt Mind Thine Own Business!"

Soon after Tessa strode out, Nell swayed up to the booth and slid the bill facedown towards Jed. "That Tessa. Still full of ginger. I remember her and Barry going at it hammer and tongs in here more'n once over the years." She leaned against the end of the booth and daintily swept a few loose tendrils off her neck into her upswept do. "But to tell you the truth, I'm kinda surprised Jeannie hasn't talked her into cutting her hair, them being such good friends and all. I mean, Tessa's getting a bit long in the tooth to be still wearing shoulder-length— "

"Put a cork in it, Nell," Jed advised as he slapped down four dollar bills, not bothering to look at the bill.

"Well *really!* I was only— "

But he was gone: across the green— ignoring the greetings of friends— and into his truck, fed up with Nell's obviousness, Tessa's prideful obtuseness, and most of all, his own self-righteousness.

He clanked the truck into gear, lurched away from the curb and steered around a startled dog that had paused to scratch an ear in the middle of the street. *Tessa was right,* he admitted to himself. *Whatever she was up to wasn't any of his business . . . Lord knows he had enough of his own to worry about.*

Jed was halfway home before he remembered he'd promised his father to bring him some of Nell's brownies. It was why he'd gone there in the first place.

Damn. He slowed to a stop, turned, and drove back towards town. Not to Nell's, though. The hornet's nest he set to buzzing there would hardly have settled down by now; no point stirring it up again. He, pulled into the Cottonwood market and emerged five minutes later, frowning, carrying a plastic sack containing a box of brownie mix, milk, eggs, and a bag of shelled walnuts.

"Planning on going into competition with Nell?" the clerk had teased him. Married to the town clerk, she was a notorious disseminator of information never intended for public distribution.

"Not hardly, Angie."

"Well, if they turn out good, I'll be calling on you come the next church bake sale."

Her loud-voiced commentary had attracted sniggering attention Jed could have done without. His father's opinion of the brownies he subsequently baked did nothing to improve his mood.

"These ain't Nell's!" he exclaimed accusingly "Not with all these walnuts."

"You always said you liked walnuts."

"*Some* walnuts, Jed, not a whole tree full. Durn near busted my dentures on 'em," he grumbled, reaching for another.

"Don't start with me, Pop!"

Walt Bradburn, startled by his son's growled warning, dropped the brownie from his unsteady fingers. "Now see what you made me do!"

"You said you didn't like them."

"Better'n nothing!"

Jed turned away, afraid of what he might say next. He knew he was being manipulated; he also knew there wasn't anything he could do about it. He noticed a scrawled-on piece of paper on the table.

"This anything I should know about, Pop?"

"What you talking about?"

Jed held out the paper. "This. Looks like a phone number."

"Oh, *that.*" Jed knew he wasn't about to admit he'd forgotten about it. "Gavin called . . . wanted to talk to you about something."

Jed felt a twinge of alarm. "Gavin called from Denver?"

"If that's where he's at, that's where he called from. Said he'd be at that number around five o'clock. Hope you ain't planning on talking long."

"I'll get you your drink first," Jed said dryly. "You want to go to your room now?"

"Don't fuss at me, Jed; I can manage on my own . . . uh, maybe I'll take another one of those brownies, just in case I get to feeling peckish."

Jed placed a brownie on a sheet of paper toweling, paused, then folded in another. Silently, he handed it to his father, who accepted it with a satisfied grunt.

Jed watched the old man spin his chair around and roll himself out of the kitchen and down the hall. Thank God he decided to go to his room, Jed thought. Without an afternoon snooze, he'd be hell on wheels by five.

Hell on wheels.

Jed gave an ironic bark of laughter as the

phrase's peculiar aptness to his adoptive father's situation struck him. He glanced at the clock. Two o'clock already. There'd be hell to pay if he didn't check to see if the heavier gauge fencing he'd ordered had been delivered. That damn Beefalo bull had already reduced one pen to shambles, thanks to the new hand thinking he knew all there was to know about wire versus an ornery two-ton animal.

But being the kind of man he was, Jed blamed himself for not supervising the kid more closely. *Cottonwood sure doesn't need another Barry Wagner-type tragedy.*

Just before five, Jed took the promised drink to his father in the living room before returning to the kitchen to put in a call to Gavin.

"Gavin? Everything okay?"

"Sure is, Uncle Jed. Thanks for calling back."

"Your mom told me about your summer job— sounds like fun."

Gavin laughed. "I wouldn't call it fun exactly— I've been working my tail off. Instructive, though. The guy who hired me is great . . . expects a lot of me, but always takes the time to explain why it's important. I guess you could call him a mentor. It's kind of nice being treated like a fair-haired boy."

Gavin's voice, although cool and controlled as always, held a note of pride.

"You were always fair-haired with me, Gav . . . well, most of the time, anyway."

"I know that, Uncle Jed. That's why I'm calling you . . . I wanted to ask your opinion."

"Seems to me, up there in big gun territory, you could get an opinion a lot more worth considering than mine."

"Not in this case. Uncle Lloyd called me yesterday. All bluster and a lot of stuff about blood being thicker than water . . . you know how he is. Well, these days the blood's running real thick apparently."

"How's that, Gav?"

"He'd like me to talk Mom into selling the part of the Wagner ranch she's holding in trust for me and Garland. Went on and on about it not being worth anything as grazing land. As if I didn't know, for God's sake! He wouldn't like to see Barry's kids wanting for anything— that's a direct quote— so he's ready to offer us more than a fair price for it. Pure, unadulterated bullshit. In the first place, this is the first time he's ever acknowledged his brother might have sired us, and in the second place— "

"He wants to develop it, along with Terry Ballou."

"You already know about this?"

"It's one of Cottonwood's more widely known secrets."

"Do you know if Uncle Lloyd's talked to Garland?"

"I suspect he knew that wouldn't work. Your

sister is the least material-minded person I know."

"You're right about that," Gavin agreed. He chuckled ruefully. "Not me, though, huh?"

"You're not as attached to the land here as she is."

"You're hedging, Uncle Jed."

Jed's reply was edged. "Don't sell yourself short, Gavin!"

"If I do, it was my daddy who put the idea in my head. Straight from the horse's mouth, you might say."

"Horse's ass is more like it," Jed muttered.

Gavin's shout of laughter made Jed pull the receiver away from his ear. "So, what you're saying is I should hang in for the long haul?"

"In a year you and Garland will be twenty-one . . . if that's what you interpret the long haul to be, then yes. You can't beat the view from that land, and these days a good view is money in the bank. Barring some worldwide catastrophe, its value can only go up."

"That's what I figured, Uncle Jed."

"Smartass kid," Jed said fondly. "If you know so much, why'd you bother calling me?"

"Because, like I said, I value your opinion."

"Well, I thank you for that," Jed said gruffly. "Tell Mom I said hello."

"Call and tell her yourself . . . but you needn't mention our conversation, okay?"

"Oh? Why's that?"

Thou shalt mind thine own business.

"I don't want Tessa to think I'm interfering in a family matter."

"But you *are* family!"

"Gavin, please."

"Okay, if that's the way you want it."

Jed, hearing the hurt in his voice, closed his eyes. "Good to hear your voice, Gav. Will I be seeing you this summer?"

"You'll be the first to know."

"After Garland, I bet."

"Oh, well, Garland." The smile was back in his voice. "Look after her for me, will ya?"

Jed agreed that he would, but after he hung up, he had a sudden vision of Garland, fleeing through the streets of Telluride, long legs flashing, blond hair flying, beset by sleek and savvy wolves of the species *californicus*.

I'll do the best I can.

Seven

Tessa pulled her pickup into the parking area adjacent to the big meadow that Telluride's town fathers had reserved in the laid-back sixties for use by its citizens.

At the time, when the valley's haze owed as much to marijuana as wood smoke, little more than informal gatherings of gently stoned guitar-strumming locals and their frisbie-chasing dogs had been anticipated. But the hippies were soon driven out by the tourist interests attracted by entrepreneur Joe Zoline's "winter recreation area second to none," and the summer season of festivals brought in headliners and leash laws.

"The park looks almost like I remember it," Tessa remarked to her daughter as they prepared to back their horses out of the trailer.

"Yeah, I imagine it does," Garland said. "Ordinarily, we'd be blasted out by now."

"Really?" Tessa murmured distractedly. She clucked reassuringly to the bay Appaloosa mincing backwards down the ramp. "Why's that?"

"Most weekends, Saturday mornings are given over to setting up stages and testing sound systems and crews yelling back and forth. Today the loudest sound is laughter."

The wide sunny expanse was dotted with strolling couples. A group of young kite flyers played out paper eagles and bright dragons that alternately soared and swooped above their families watching from blankets crowded with picnic paraphernalia. Beyond, a fisherman wading the shallows of the river that defined the park's northern border sent a long lazy cast into the sparkling riffles.

Garland smiled at her mother. "The usual weekend rumpus is, like, exciting, but this . . . well, it's kinda nice for a change."

Tessa returned Garland's smile, but she was secretly disappointed. Would a quiet family day like this bring Scott Shelby into town? Not the Scott Shelby she remembered. *Twenty years* . . .

"I still wished you'd worn my Wild Westerns gear, Garland."

"C'mon, Mom. I'd've looked like something out of one of those old cowboy movies."

Tessa turned to face her daughter. "What's wrong with that?"

Garland laughed. "You should see your expression, Mom. You keep forgetting I only *look* like you. I wish I had your get up and go, but I don't— " she shrugged— "and I never will."

Tessa's face softened. Dear Garland. Beautiful as the sunrise; sweet as mountain rain. "What you have is better, darling."

Garland eyed her warily. "Which is?"

"A level head . . . and the sauciest ass in Colorado," she added, reaching out to slap at the rear of Garland's well-filled jeans.

"Mom! You're scaring the horses!" Garland protested as the Appaloosa snorted and pulled back on the lead rope. After calming him, she stole a look at herself down over her shoulder. "You really think so?"

"Well, on the western slope anyway."

"Oh, you!" Mother and daughter grinned at each other. Garland stroked the big bay's arched glossy neck. "Why'd you want to bring this guy, Mom? He's practically shooting off sparks already."

"Zeus's owner is a local dignitary down Durango way. He wanted a flashy horse to ride in parades, and this keg of dynamite is what he came up with. Expects me to turn him into Mary's little lamb. Fat chance! But when he told me the fee he was prepared to pay, my better judgment took a hike. Actually, he's already improved some. First time I took him through downtown Ouray he got so lathered he looked like he'd been sprayed with shaving cream."

"Well, he'll sure liven things up on Telluride's main street today."

Tessa, unwilling to admit that was her primary reason for bringing Zeus, busied herself with backing his well-behaved quarter horse companion, Sunset, out of the trailer. Although Garland's chestnut mare was the better horse, Tessa was well aware that most eyes, including

Scott Shelby's, would be drawn first to the prancing white-spotted rump of the big gelding and the tawny-haired woman astride him in the silver-mounted saddle.

She tightened the cinch and swung herself up, unfazed by the big horse's wily attempt to pirouette himself away from under her. "Cut it out, Zeus!" Tessa remonstrated.

Sunset twitched her ears at the gelding's goings-on, but stood foursquare as her mistress mounted. Garland's easy seat in the custom-made saddle—her Uncle Jed's sixteenth-birthday companion gift for the horse her mother had bred and trained—belied her equestrian expertise. In fact, Tessa suspected that if their ribbons were counted up, her lead over her much less competitive daughter might be slimmer than she cared to acknowledge.

The women rode down Pacific and turned up Pine Street, with Zeus dancing a dozen steps for every one of Sunset's. By the time they reached the main drag on Colorado Avenue, each pumping action of the gelding's high-stepping legs was accompanied by a loud snort from his distended nostrils. As they rounded the corner, a pigtailed child bouncing up the sidewalk past the Flora-dora Saloon grabbed at her father's denim jacket and pointed.

"Ooohhh, Daddy! Isn't that the most beauti-fullest horse you ever saw?"

Grinning, Tessa swept her fawn Stetson from her head in acknowledgement of the compliment. Zeus, spooked by her gesture, tossed his head and sidestepped closer to the curb.

The father pulled his daughter back. "Hey lady! Watch that horse!"

"Maybe this wasn't such a great idea, Mom," Garland muttered.

But Tessa wasn't listening. Tourists alerted by the little girl's shrill voice, turned from shop windows displaying climbing gear and native American crafts to watch them pass. A clutch of burly college-age boys elbowed each other aside for a closer look. "Ride 'em, cowgirls!" one of them hooted through cupped hands. Welcoming the distraction, drivers of cars slowed by the noontime traffic smiled and waved. A black dog lumbered growling out of an awning's shade. A bicycle bell jingled a greeting.

Ahead, just past the New Sheridan Hotel, Tessa spied a bright gold head bobbing among a male trio emerging laughing from the San Miguel County Courthouse. The shape of it seemed familiar, and that brush cut . . .

"Whoa there, Zeus," she murmured, as she gently tightened the reins. *"That's* a good boy."

Garland rode up beside them. "What's up, Mom?"

Tessa didn't answer. Slowed almost to a halt, Zeus tossed his head against the bite of the bit.

"Tessa? Tessa *Wagner?*"

Tessa released the breath she was holding and arranged her expression into one of pleased

surprise. Turning in the saddle, she looked
down into Scott Shelby's face. His skin, still
youthfully taut, was evenly tanned. Not one of
those old hat, worked-at George Hamilton tans,
but just enough to lend an outdoorsy glow, even
if it was acquired in a salon.

"Hey there, Scott. I heard you were back.
Sure has been a while."

Jeannie was right. He still looked fabulous.
Trim as ever, easy moving as a good horse. Bet
he has one of those personal trainers, Tessa
thought. She eyed the lines of his coarse-woven
indigo blue linen jacket, pegging its price at
roughly six week's worth of her supermarket
tabs.

"Sure has, Tessie." *Tessie. Scott was the only person who ever called her that.* "But I'm not living
at the Cottonwood ranch anymore; in fact we've
just come from filing the deed for the new
place I bought up here . . ." He broke off; his
sherry-colored eyes shifted from Tessa to Garland and back again. "My God," he murmured.
"Déjà vu."

"I'm sorry . . . I'm forgetting my manners,"
Tessa said with an apologetic smile. "This is my
daughter Garland. Garland? You remember me
talking about Scott Shelby? The Wild Westerns
guy?"

Garland gave her mother a disbelieving look.
"Yeah, I think maybe I do," she remarked dryly.
She leaned down to shake the hand reached up
to her. Scott held it a bit too long, but his sud-

den smile was so mesmerizing neither of the women noticed.

There was no doubt about it, Tessa granted. Scott still exuded that lowdown charm, that straight-to-the-point sex appeal that made affection and love seem like female foibles. Frills. She wondered how she had managed to resist it.

"Garland is working here in Telluride this summer, Scott. With the Chamber Resort Association."

"Are you, now? Then you must be aware that Shelby Associates is the chief sponsor for this year's Bluegrass Festival."

"Well, no, I just started and—"

"I have some new ideas . . . maybe we could get together, discuss them over drinks?"

"I really don't think I'm the right person for—"

"I'll call you, luv. He turned his intense regard back to Tessa. "We were just going to the New Sheridan for lunch to celebrate my new acquisition. Why don't you join us?"

"It's not as easy to park a horse as it is a car," Tessa demurred. "Rain check maybe?"

"No maybe about it. I'm having a housewarming in a fortnight, Tessie; I've been feeling something was missing . . . now I know what it is. Please say you'll come."

"Fortnight?" Tessa repeated uncertainly.

"Two weeks, luv. From today. Sevenish?"

My God, Tessa thought. *It sure has been a long time since I heard that kind of talk.*

In Cottonwood, if anyone came for dinner at all, they arrived at five for beer and pretzels, expected to sit down at six, and were gone by eight-thirty in time to catch the nine o'clock movie on cable. Tessa suspected that Scott Shelby's housewarming would rival any made-for-TV production. *Probably have a better cast, too, considering how many Hollywood types were renting boxes in the Telluride Post Office these days.*

"Yeah, I'd like that, Scott. Could you send me directions? Everything's changed so much up here."

"I'll leave them with your daughter at the Chamber Association. You're included in the invitation, of course," he added, turning his high-wattage smile back on Garland. "And your father, too. I'm sorry, I've forgotten his—"

"Barry died two years ago," Tessa stated flatly.

"Oh. I didn't know." He didn't bother to say he was sorry; no reason he should be. "Oh, Tessie, you don't by any chance . . . could you possibly still have the outfit I designed for that first big promotion?" He turned to his companions. "You're probably too young to remember, but she just blazed out of those ads like a golden skyrocket—" he slanted an admiring smile at her—"and took me up along with her."

Except I came back down to earth a long time

ago, Tessa thought sourly. "What about it?" she asked.

"I thought maybe you could wear it at the housewarming." He held up his hand and drew his fingers across the space between them. "Then and now!" he pronounced.

He always did go in for dramatic emphasis, Tessa mused. She sneaked a speaking glance at Garland. *You?* Garland's blink was emphatic. *No way, Mom!*

" 'Fraid not, Scott," Tessa fibbed.

"No?" He seemed surprised, disconcerted, and a little hurt. He had expected her to preserve it, she realized.

"Those years . . . that time in my life . . . they're long gone. I'm not sure it's healthy, holding on to things like that."

"I suppose you're right." He sighed, then his expression gradually brightened. "Yes, of course you're right! It's not only unhealthy, it's tacky." He shook his head slowly. "God. I can't believe I suggested it."

He reached out to stroke Zeus's arched neck. She saw he still wore the handsome antique signet ring she had noticed at their first meeting—until then, the only rings worn by the men she knew were wedding bands. "Just proves how much I've missed you, Tessie," he murmured. "We had great times, didn't we? And we'll have more, you'll see!"

He threw back his head to blow a kiss at her, his brush-cut gleaming like gold in the midday blast of sun. He plucked a pair of sunglasses out of his breast pocket and slipped them on. Robbed of the intensity of his hazel eyes, his face seemed suddenly older.

Tessa blew him a return kiss—"Two weeks, Scott!"—and wheeled Zeus in a tight circle.

"Yeah. Whoop-te-do," Garland muttered as she urged Sunset to follow suit.

"What's your problem, Garland?" Tessa demanded.

"It's just that . . . well, I grant you he's a real attractive guy, but can you imagine anyone in Cottonwood saying 'sevenish' or blowing kisses?"

"No, but then I can't imagine Scott calling folks assholes or spitting in public. It won't hurt you to look at his world with an open mind, Garland. You might learn something." She gave her daughter a sharp look. "You might even gain something."

"Like what? Becoming a veterinarian to the stars someday?"

Tessa pulled Zeus up. "Have you taken a look at yourself in the mirror lately? I mean *really* looked?"

"Haven't the time, Mom. Besides, what's the point? Animals don't care what I look like . . . the people I care about don't either."

"For God's sake, Garland! Caring has nothing to do with what I'm talking about." Provoked by Tessa's snappish tone, Zeus snorted and side-stepped.

"Then what the hell *are* you talking about?"

Unprepared for her gentle daughter's challenge, Tessa found herself momentarily at a loss for words.

"Well, Mom? Enlighten me, please."

"Opportunity," Tessa finally said. "Unless Scott has changed a whole heap, there'll be a lot of famous names on hand to help him warm his house. Fashion types. Hollywood people. Think new frontiers, Garland. A chance to go—"

"Where no one's ever gone before? C'mon, Mom, I'm just an ordinary person, not a weirded-out character like those in that TV space series Dad was so crazy about—"

"'Star Trek,'" Tessa broke in. "Not all the characters were weird, Garland."

Sensing her mother's hurt, Garland's expression softened. "I know, Mom," she said gently. "But I'm not like you, either. 'Fess up now, was it really all that great being the Wild Westerns girl? There must have been a lot of pressure . . . and a lot of guys putting the make on you."

"Working under pressure teaches you a lot, Garland. You find strengths you never knew you had, and—" she shrugged— "you learn how to cope with your weaknesses . . ."

Her gaze drifted beyond Garland to the long lacy spill of water down Bridal Veil Falls at the end of the valley. "Your dad and I . . . it's no secret our marriage wasn't the greatest, but I never cheated on him, Garland." She turned in the saddle to look at her daughter. *"Never."*

"I know that, too, Mom." Garland tapped

Sunset with her heels, closing the gap between them. Her smile coaxed a reluctant one from Tessa. "But I gotta admit," she confided, "Scott Shelby sure must have put your moral fiber to the test."

Tessa's smile broadened. "You think so, huh?"

"Oh yeah. He's a seriously sexy guy. Not the soulful, hand-holding type of sexy . . . you know, the kind who takes you on long walks for meaningful conversations?" Tessa, not knowing, gave her daughter a blank look. "God, Mom, Boulder's full of them! Sure, they may bring a blanket along with the picnic basket, hoping for more than just talk, yet willing enough to bide their time. Nice boys at heart, you know? But that Scott Shelby!" She grinned and shook her fingers as if singed. "He puts a girl in mind of hotel rooms and rumpled sheets."

Her matter-of-fact delivery made Tessa blink. "I would have thought . . . that is, someone your age . . . I mean, he's not exactly a kid, sweetie."

"Look at the herd animals, Mom. It's always the mature bulls who dominate, right? Of course, it isn't as simple as that when it comes to the human species, but real sex appeal is timeless. Look at Sean Connery. Clint Eastwood. Uncle Jed."

This time Tessa couldn't hide her shock. "*Jed*? For God's *sake*, Garland!"

Garland looked at her mother in consternation. "I was speaking theoretically, Mom! I mean, Uncle Jed is . . . Uncle Jed."

Embarrassed, Tessa ducked her head. "Honey, I never thought— "

"On the other hand," Garland drawled, "if old Sean came to town, for a film festival, say, and we just happened to hit it off . . ." She rolled a roguish eye. "Well, now, in *that* case— "

"In that case," Tessa warned, "I'd nail your hide to the barn door!"

To emphasize her point, she gave Sunset a smart slap on the rump. The mare's suddenly quickened pace proved infectious. One after the other, the excited horses veered into the space between the crawling lanes of cars and, to the delight of the lunchtime crowd of tourists thronging the sidewalks, thundered in tandem down the wide avenue.

Eight

Monday morning, just after Tessa finished confirming the delivery of the feeder calves at the end of the week, the phone rang. It was Jeannie.

"So how was the Nothing Festival?"

"Not bad. Not bad at all. You might even call it a something festival."

"Don't play coy with me, Tessa Wagner. C'mon, give."

"Well, I saw Scott Shelby."

"Yeah? And?"

"You were right. He looks terrific."

"*And?*"

"He invited us, Garland and me, to his house-warming. In a fortnight."

"Fortnight," Jeannie repeated slowly. "Let's see now . . . is that four nights from now or forty?"

Tessa laughed. "Neither, you ignorant person. It means two weeks."

"Garland told you, right?"

"Damn it, Jeannie! You know me too well!"

"A fact of life I suggest you henceforth keep

in mind," Jeannie observed in a mincing tone. Their joined laughter resounded tinnily over the miles. "What are you planning to wear?"

"I *knew* you were going to ask that!" Tessa declared. "Either that or something about my hair. There's more to life than hair and clothes, Jeannie."

"Hair is my profession," Jeannie protested, "and clothes are Scott Shelby's. If I were a scientist, maybe we could exchange ideas about global warming, but— "

"Okay, okay. To answer your question, I haven't decided yet. Scott wanted me to wear my Wild Westerns gear. I told him I didn't have it anymore."

"Liar," Jeannie observed mildly.

"What else could I do? Admit flat out it no longer fit me? It was bad enough him seeing me side by side with Garland."

"Hmmm-mm. I see your point. What did Garland have to say about him?"

"She said, and I quote, 'he's a seriously sexy guy.' "

"No kidding? I'd've thought— "

"But she said the same thing about Sean Connery and Clint Eastwood," Tessa added with a rueful chuckle, deliberately omitting Garland's inclusion of Jed. "Anyway, Scott wants to meet with her . . . to discuss the festival he's sponsoring."

"Yeah, sure. In a rear booth in some dark bar, I bet. You didn't encourage it, I hope."

"No, I didn't . . . but I didn't *dis*courage it either. Why should I? It's like an open . . . open . . . Shoot! I can't think of the word! What are those little seeds they put on hard rolls?"

"Poppy?"

"No, no, the flat white ones . . ."

"Sesame?"

"Yeah! Open sesame! We're talkin' oppor-damntunity here, Jeannie."

"Are you sure that's what Garland wants?"

"She's twenty, for God's sake! Who knows what they want at twenty?"

"You did," Jeannie ventured.

"Oh no. I *thought* I did. I was wrong. If Scott can open doors for her like he did for me . . . Don't you see, Jeannie? By the time my chance came it was too late. I don't want that to happen to Garland!"

"She's not you, Tessa."

"I'm her *mother!*" Tessa cried. "It's what mothers *do!* Especially mothers of girls whose fathers abandoned them."

"C'mon now . . . Barry may have been a shit, but he didn't run out on his kids."

"It might have been better if he had. That way I could have made up some nice-sounding story about him. The way it was, he might as well have been a ghost. If it hadn't been for Jed—"

Reminded anew of how beholden she was, Tessa's lips clamped down, cutting her sentence short. The debt weighed on her like an ox yoke. She hunched her shoulders, unconsciously seeking relief. "Jeannie, I—"

"Gotta go, Tessa! Someone's rattling at my door . . . yeah, it's Angie. If I don't let her in quick, she'll panic. As usual, she's waited too long for a trim and touch-up. Not a pretty sight."

"Is she ever?"

"Meow, meow. Look, about that housewarming—you know, what you should wear? I'll get back to you. Coming, Angie!"

The receiver slammed down on the other end.

Tessa stared into the mouthpiece. She really hadn't had anything else to say, but the breaking of the connection spun her back into a whirlpool of troubled thoughts. She filled the kettle from the tap and dropped a tea bag in the Snoopy mug surviving of a pair Jed had long ago given the twins.

She had been looking forward to seeing Scott again. Had plotted it, in fact. Her very own scenario. It was fun. Harmless. And it worked: scene and sequel, playing out just like she remembered the process being described by a screenwriter she met during one of her whirlwind visits to Los Angeles back in the Wild Westerns days. Trouble was, it had brought back more than she intended, and this time there was no Barry to apply the brakes.

The kettle whistled. Garland was right, Tessa

conceded as she poured the boiling water into the cup. Sex was what Scott was all about. A woman didn't think of him in connection with walks in the park or dinner by candlelight or raising kids. Maybe, she mused, that's why his designs were so successful. Not that there was anything obviously sexy about them— no glitter; no satin; no slits up to here or down to there. The clothes Scott had designed for her had seemed straightforward enough— leather and suede, cashmere and silk, but while wearing them she had felt . . . what? Blonder? Prettier?

Yeah, but there was more to it than that . . .

Tessa frowned. She spooned the sodden tea bag into the sink, added sugar to the tea, and went to the refrigerator for a splash of milk. *Readier to take chances, maybe?*

She paused, milk carton in hand. *That was it!* He made a woman readier to take chances. All kinds of chances. And the effect was even stronger in the line that followed hers. Soft luscious pastels and clingy fabrics. Water Babies, he had named it. Not her type, really, but oh my . . .

As Tessa stirred the sweet milky mixture, she idly wondered who had given him the inspiration. She knew someone had . . . someone as slim as she had been. Younger, probably.

Sipping her tea, Tessa gazed out the window. A breeze stirred the pale grasses growing among the sage. Seeing the languorous bending of their tall stems, Tessa felt the sudden bite of envy. Why couldn't a person shrink-wrap her life, like a tube of glue or lipstick? A life, she reminded herself, she ought to be damn grateful for: ranch owner, breeder of good horses and great kids. No need for unsettling yearnings; no room for doubts and loose ends.

Tessa trickled the cooled dregs of tea into the sink. "Except," she muttered to herself, "the twins are grown, my brother-in-law's got his beady eye on my land, and horses don't keep a girl's bed warm."

Who am I kidding? I'm a woman, not a girl, and have been for a helluva long time.

"A grown-up, fifty-year-old woman," she continued doggedly under her breath, "plagued by doubts and the yearnings of a teenager. As for loose ends—"

A smart rap at the kitchen door rattled the glass panes, cutting Tessa's monologue short. She wiped her hands on the towel hanging under the countertop and narrowed her eyes against the light streaming through the newly Windexed rectangles. It was Jed. *Talk about loose ends.* She opened the door with a sigh.

"Hi, Jed."

He looked at her frowning face. "I can come back."

"You're here now." She stepped back. "You might as well come in."

"You took the storm door down, I see."

"Miguel said it was past time. He keeps me in line," she admitted. "If it weren't for him,

I'd probably spend my days squatting in here like a toad, slurping in flies the spiders I keep forgetting to dust out of the corners don't get."

"That's quite a picture," Jed said. "I guess you're feeling a little down this morning."

Tessa stared at him, first thinking of all the comparisons she might make— *down as . . . downer than*— then thinking, why bother? "What can I do for you? If you're expecting an apology— "

Jed threw his forearms up, palms out. "Hey, you were right. Whatever you and Shelby— " She thrust out her jaw. "I was just going to say I agreed with you, Tessa. It's none of my business." He slowly lowered his arms. "Friends?"

Tessa sighed. She clasped the blunt-fingered hand he extended. His callused palm felt rough and warm against hers.

He smiled. "I'll take that as a yes. The extended forecast is mighty nice for a change, so what I thought was, maybe you and Garland could use some help taking the feeder calves up into the high country this weekend."

"How'd you know I was planning to?"

"I figured since you didn't this past weekend— well, you've never been one to put your ranch plans on a back burner."

Not like Barry.

The unspoken words hung between them. Tessa glanced away. "No, I'm not," she murmured.

"So, how was it up in Telluride? Lots going on?"

"Not while I was there. Lots of people though. Nice for the merchants, I suppose, but too many for my taste."

"Turkeys by the flock, huh?"

Tessa smiled at his use of the local term for those who made the annual summer pilgrimage from the hot Texas panhandle to Colorado's cool mountains. "Not just Texans, Jed. Turkeys, chickens, ducks . . . take your pick. I never heard such a variety of accents . . . some of them foreign."

"C'mon, Tessa, to you anyone living east of Denver is a foreigner."

"Denver, hell! Anyone east of Ouray County!" They grinned at each other. "I'd appreciate your help, Jed. It'll be like old times."

"Not like all of 'em, I hope. Remember the time that crazy critter got himself hung up in a juniper?"

Tessa laughed. "I never could figure how he got that high. Must of been part kangaroo."

"Sure kicked like one . . . I have the scar on my thigh to prove it."

"Lord, I'd forgotten that!"

"You bound me up with a scarf of yours," he reminded her. "Blue and yellow, with a swirly kind of pattern. It got soaked with blood. Boy, you were fit to be tied!"

"I guess both of us were," she teased. She cocked her head to one side. "Oh yeah, now I remember. It was that paisley print . . . my favorite. I never did get your blood out of it."

"Like you said, Tessa. Old times."

His dark eyes smiling into hers, reminding her of what they'd shared over the years, warmed her like chocolate. Scott's scrutiny was more like a jolt of rotgut whiskey. Intense. Carnal. Nothing the least friendly about it.

"Yeah, Jed. Like I said." She looked beyond him through the window. "You're welcome to sit a while, have a cup of coffee if you'd like, but Miguel's waiting on me out in the corral. A guy's coming down from Montrose next week to pick up that buckskin you admire. He's paying top dollar for a good cutting horse, and I want to be damn sure that's what he gets."

"He's a grandson of Thor's, isn't he? Cutting horses don't come any better than that."

"Damn right, and in most ways this fellow's a genuine chip off the old block, except when it comes to backing. Then he turns balky."

"He's young, Tessa. Young fellers don't much like being asked to go back where they just came from."

"Older ones don't, either, far as I can tell."

"Maybe not, but us older guys are quicker to recognize when we don't have a choice in the matter."

Suspecting that Jed's observation wasn't as casual as it seemed, Tessa pursed her lips. "Well, in the buckskin's case, I don't have time to wait on wisdom."

"And I don't have time for coffee, Tessa, but thanks for the offer. I just stopped by on my way to the Shelby ranch. Turns out it's his ex-missus that wanted the grazing fee raised; Scott was just acting as a sort of go-between. I talked on the phone with her yesterday— nice-sounding woman— and she asked me over to see about renegotiating. Said that now she's lived here a while, she's learned that the reliability of the person you rent your grazing land to is as important as the money you get paid for the privilege. Seems I qualify."

"That hardly surprises me," Tessa said, "but why should her opinion matter? It's Scott's ranch, after all."

"Seems it isn't. Not anymore, anyway. The point is, I get the feeling she has money of her own. Talks like it, anyway."

"And you talk like a man fixing to set his cap," Tessa teased.

"According to the grapevine, she's more of an age for Pop than me."

Tessa stared at him. "Since when do you take Cottonwood gossip for gospel?"

"Shelby's not exactly a kid himself, Tessa."

"Well, no," she conceded, "but . . ." She hesitated. *Not exactly a kid* . . . hadn't she said almost the same thing to Garland? "If you knew Scott you'd know he was too . . . too— "

"Predatory?"

"It's not that . . . I mean he *is,* but if it were *just* that, anyone would be fair game, right?"

"What you're saying is he's hipped on youth."

Tessa felt herself flush. Unwilling to admit he might be right, she changed course. "Tell you what, instead of taking the grapevine's word, why don't you see for yourself?"

"That's what I'm about to do," he drawled. He walked towards the door.

"I'll be interested in hearing what you think," she called after him. "Well, not this very day," she amended. "I mean, I'm not about to stand here holding my breath."

He turned back, grinning. "Thought you didn't hold with gossip."

"An eyewitness report isn't gossip," she snapped.

"Whatever you say, Tessa."

"Damn it, Jed!"

"I'll call you about the weekend . . . and please, this time choose a decent-looking horse to ride. Turnip's a terrible advertisement for your business."

"Miz Wagner," Miguel called, "it's past noon. Maybe you take time now to eat something?" Tessa reined the buckskin up, pushed her straw hat off her sweaty brow, and gazed down into her foreman's narrow, deeply furrowed face. His taut brown skin looked tough as old boots, but his liquid eyes expressed concern. "Maybe a little siesta, too?" he added.

"I guess we could all do with a rest," Tessa said, correctly interpreting his tactful phrasing. "This fellow's so eager to work, it's easy to forget how young he is." She threw her leg over and slid to the ground. "So, what do you think?"

"He's coming along fine, Miz Wagner. *Muy bueno*. Still wants to throw his head up, but he's not fighting the bit no more, and he tracks back nice and straight. Good horse . . . best of your young crop."

"Good-looking, too," Tessa said. She patted the buckskin's sand-colored neck, sighed, and threaded her fingers through the coarse strands of his long black mane. "Lord, I hate to see him go. Hope his new owner appreciates what he's getting."

Miguel smiled. "You say that every time, Miz Wagner. My nephew know of this man, he say he'll do right by your little horse— and his friends, when they see what this *potro* can do, they will bring you more business."

"I just hope he keeps him whole. Cow sense like he's got deserves to be passed on."

"Like Thor did to him."

"That old boy sure grandfathered a lot of fine cow ponies, Miguel," Tessa said. "Remember the first time we watched him work? The way he sized up those calves, anticipating every move they made?" She laughed. "I swear I saw a smile on that horsey face . . ."

The three strolled together out of the corral,

boots and hoofs sending up little spurts of dust. Tessa squinted up into the sky. Squat white puffs had begun to form above the mesa, embryos of the cumulus clouds which would billow into towers by afternoon's end. She handed her foreman the reins. "Okay, Miguel, cool him down. He's earned a rest." She paused at the gate. "How's Chinook doing?"

He scratched his bony chin. "A little bit tetchy . . . off her feed some, too. She'll be dropping that foal any day now."

"You call me the minute she goes into labor, hear?" Manuel touched the brim of his sweat-stained hat. "I've got high hopes for this one." *Very high,* Tessa amended as she walked back towards the house.

She always did have, of course; that's what made it all so worthwhile. There was no such thing as a fully achieved goal. Perfection was God's province, not man's . . . or woman's.

A hot, dry breeze swept across her path, evaporating the moisture from her damp skin. She shivered, then stretched, hoping to work the kinks out of her back. The kinks came easier these days. Wincing, she hunched her shoulders back and forth. *Came easier; lasted longer.*

She paused next to the old windmill. Erected by her father a half-century ago, the tower leaned off-center now, but its rusty metal blades still creaked in response to every passing breeze, pumping water in fits and starts to the mossy wooden trough it served. The ranch had long since been equipped with more efficient systems, but Tessa knew it was the slow trickle through the trough's rotting planks that allowed the sunflowers ringing its base to flourish.

How her mother had loved their bright faces! *See, Tessa? They always face the light, keeping the darkness behind them.* "I know they're only plants," she had continued, "but I've always thought of them as . . . well, not a bad example for us."

"Out of sight, out of mind, you mean?" Tessa remembered scoffing. "That's not very realistic, Mom!"

"Maybe not, honey," her mother had replied, "but I've never seen much point in brooding about things you can't change."

Tessa figured she was in her teens by then, supposedly grown out of the childish sulks that had often sent her running away from home—usually no farther than the bridge over Houston Creek. A symbolic gesture, like Gavin stonefacing his father's verbal attacks.

She couldn't recall what had given rise to that particular exchange, but she was sure her mother's patience had, as always, put Job's to shame. *Let's see now, I was a late baby, so at that time Mother would have been . . .*

She idly counted it out on her fingers. *My God. About the same age as I am now.* It was a sobering thought. "And damn it," she muttered, "I *still* find that advice hard to accept."

Tessa snapped off one of the tough hairy sunflower stems and twirled the petaled head as she resumed her slow progress towards the house. She entered the kitchen, yawned, ran water into a tumbler, and stuck the sunflower in it. "Miguel was right," she murmured. "A sandwich and a little snooze will go down real nice right about now."

Yeah, too nice by half, an inner voice jeered. *Next thing you know you'll be dozing off in a porch rocker every chance you get.*

Jolted by a sudden mental image of herself rocking side by side with Pop Bradburn, Tessa threw water on her face, ran a comb through her hair, splashed on the rosewater she kept over the sink, applied a swipe of bright lipstick, and headed for her pick-up.

"I'm not out of the game yet," she confided to the dusty windshield as she wheeled out the front gate. "Nosiree*bob!* Not by a long sight."

Nine

"Was everything to your satisfaction?" the Silver Nugget's proprietor asked Tessa as she paused to pocket her change.

"Oh, yes," she replied. Too much fat and way too many calories, she thought, but that was her fault, not his. She pushed open the heavy door and narrowed her eyes against the mid-afternoon glare. "And every one of those lovely crispy French fries will stake out a new claim on my hips," she muttered as she strode out down the street, "but who the hell's looking?"

She exchanged nods with familiar faces spotted among the strolling tourists impeding her progress towards her parking slot. Ouray's main drag wasn't quite as trafficked as Telluride's yet, but just give the Chamber of Commerce time. The town's hot springs pool had always been a big draw, and of late just about every motel had its own spring-fed hot tubs to soothe guests after a day spent four-wheeling on the old mining trails or, in winter, Nordic skiing. Some even provided a European-style massage. Quite a change from the old boarding-house days when the only overnight guests were miners from Camp Bird seeking comforts of an earthier sort.

Tessa found herself yawning uncontrollably as she drove the ten miles north out of the narrow Ouray valley into the wide creek-fed meadows and piñon pine-studded foothills surrounding Cottonwood. She wasn't used to drinking at lunchtime, but an old friend from her high school days had joined her at the table, bringing with her a bottle of mildly effervescent white wine that they shared along with their reminiscences.

She circled the square, pulled up in front of Jeannie's salon, and walked in.

"Hey, Tessa!" Jeannie said, alerted by the jangle of the opening door. She eyed her friend speculatively. "Look, about this morning . . ."

"What about it?"

"Well, the way I cut you off. I didn't mean— "

"You've got a business to run, Jeannie. Deciding what I should wear to Scott Shelby's housewarming doesn't exactly rank up there with life and death."

"Or taxes," Jeannie added.

"Definitely not taxes," Tessa agreed, laughing.

Jeannie eyed the plump woman sitting under a dryer, deep in *People* magazine's rundown of the latest antics of the British royal family. She asked the blond operator washing a client's hair to call her when the bell rang. "C'mon back," she said to Tessa, leading the way through a curtained doorway. "Actually, I do have a suggestion for you . . ." She broke off, frowning. "Are you okay, Tessa?"

"Yeah, sure. Why?"

"You look as if you either just rolled out of bed or wish you could fall into one."

"Gee, thanks a whole lot. I had lunch at the Silver Nugget, which included Evelyn Lawson wallowing in sanitized memories of our dear old golden school days, ending in a long moan about how her life since high school had been all downhill— "

"I don't wonder," Jeannie cut in. "Those big boobs of hers have gone the same route. What was it the boys used to call her?"

"Awesome Lawson," Tessa supplied. "I didn't think she'd appreciate being reminded of *that.* Anyway, we shared this bottle of wine— well, not shared exactly, more like one-third for me and two-thirds for her. Tasted like a fancy soda pop, and it went down so easy I didn't think much about the alcohol content. I was halfway here when it hit me . . . damn near fell asleep at the wheel."

"Well, maybe what I have to tell you will revive you. Marion Shelby came in around noon for a trim and blow-dry, so I asked her opinion about it."

"About what, Jeannie?"

"About— " Jeannie took a deep breath— "about what she thought might be the right

kind of outfit for you. You know, for the housewarming? I mean, who would know better?"

"You did *what!*"

"Just hear me out, Tessa! It all started with
her telling me about Jed stopping in to see her,
how nice he is and all, and I happened to mention how you and Jed share a fence up on Hayden's Bald, and she thought your name sounded
familiar, and— " she shrugged— "one thing just
led naturally into another."

"Naturally?" Tessa challenged.

"Okay, so maybe I steered the conversation a
little. The thing is, she wasn't the least put out
or offended; if anything, she seemed . . . interested." They stared at each other. "So, do you
want to hear what she suggested?"

Tessa stuck her hands in her pockets and
leaned against the washer in which the salon's
soiled towels were noisily sloshing. "Yeah, I
guess so."

"Steer clear of glitzy. She was very positive
about that. She says go for trim and cool. Something you'll feel comfortable in, like pants and
a really good shirt. It could be silk, or even
satin, but understated . . . I guess that means
plain, right?"

"In other words, a dressy but tailored shirt.
No ruffles; nothing twinkly." Jeannie nodded.
"Hmmm-mm. Don't have anything like that, but
I've got those custom-made black gabardine
pants I use for exhibition riding— "

"Yeah, and the slick black alligator boots you

were awarded when you retired from barrel-racing after winning everything in sight." Jeannie slid an appraising glance at her friend. "That was a while back though . . . have you tried 'em on lately?"

"My feet are the one part of me that's stayed the same," Tessa said. "They may be flatter," she added with a wry smile, "but not fatter." The washer began to vibrate beneath her as the load entered the spin cycle. "Whoa!" she exclaimed as she shifted to the dryer. "Ever thought of renting these out as Cottonwood's answer to that fitness center up in Montrose?"

"Now *there's* a thought. Not a very good one, but— hey!" she protested, as Tessa lightly cuffed the top of her head. "What was that for?"

"For not minding your own business." Tessa leaned down and planted a kiss on Jeannie's cheek. "And so was that. The question is, where do I find this cool, trim, tailored and no doubt, very expensive silk— "

"Or satin— "

"Shirt."

"Telluride, probably," Jeannie suggested. "Ask Garland. Or we could look in those upscale catalogs I sent for last Christmas . . . the kind with clothes in colors like aubergine and celadon?"

"You're a regular font of couture wisdom today, Jeannie."

"Someone has to play fairy godmother to your Cinderella, Toots."

Tessa laughed. "Who have you cast as the wicked stepmother? Marion Shelby?"

"No way! She's a nice lady, Tessa. Though I'm damned if I can figure what the attraction was— his to her, that is. I can't see Scott Shelby being turned on by nice."

"According to Scott's peculiar value system," Tessa observed dryly, "niceness in a woman is a fault that can always be compensated for by good looks."

Jeannie stared at her. "You don't know then."

"Know what?"

"Marion Shelby must be at least sixty-five."

So Jed was right, Tessa thought. *I should have known; he usually is.*

"Oh, she's trim enough," Jeannie continued, "and she's funny and smart and up on everything, but she's let her hair go white, and sometimes she has that perky look of women in those awful TV commercials about denture cleaners . . . that I-may-not-be-a-kid-anymore-but-don't-count-me-out look?"

"There but for the grace of God, Jeannie."

"Hey, there's no call to start throwing scripture or whatever at me. I'm just stating an observation, not passing judgment. Besides, it's Father Time's grace we oughta be worrying about, not God's."

Tessa favored Jeannie with a goofy grin. " 'What, me worry?' "

"Ohmigosh!" Jeannie exclaimed. "Alfred E. Neuman! Remember the time my homeroom teacher found that copy of *MAD* in my desk? Lordy, how I loved that magazine! I wonder if it's still being published."

"Probably not in the same form. According to Gavin, PC has pretty much discouraged anyone from making jokes at anyone else's expense."

Jeannie looked baffled. "What do personal computers have to do with jokes?"

"I'm talking about political correctness, Jeannie. Look, suppose all the Alfred E. Neumans in the world got together and brought one of those class action suits against the editor."

"About what, for heaven's sake?"

"For holding them up to public ridicule. Gav says college newspapers really have to watch it these days. You can be hauled into court for being racist and sexist, even ageist . . . so why not nameist?"

Jeannie shook her head. "That's crazy, Tessa."

"Hey, it's a crazy world out there."

They heard a faint bell, followed by a shout for Jeannie.

"Duty calls," she said.

"Me, too," Tessa responded. "I told Garland I'd have homemade pizza for dinner tonight . . . which in my case," she confessed, "means adding stuff I haven't bought yet to the ready-made I've got in the freezer." She hitched up her shoulder bag. "Could I borrow those catalogs you mentioned?"

"Sure . . . they're in that box next to the washer, Tessa. Feel free to rummage."

Tessa emerged from the back room a moment later with an armful of glossy booklets. "Thanks, Jeannie!"

"Hope you find what you want, Cinderella. Just don't count on you-know-who to come up with the glass slipper."

"He did once," Tessa protested.

"Maybe so, but if he's the prince you've been waiting for all these years, I think you'd be better off with the frog . . . or is it the beast?" She pushed up the hood of the dryer to release her heat-flushed client. "Hell, Tessa, I never could keep those old fairy tales straight."

Fairy tale? Tessa mused as she wheeled her cart through the Cottonwood Mercantile. *Was that really all it was?* She added a package of sausage to her basket. *And if it was,* she wondered as she searched through the green pepper bin for one with no flaws, *what harm could a revival of it do?*

She suddenly recalled her high school English teacher's droning discourse about the use of *would, could* and *should.*

What harm would *it do?* Should *it do?*

She couldn't decide. *And I don't really care,* she thought as she counted out eight of the biggest mushrooms and plopped them into a plastic bag.

If I should die before I wake . . .

"God!" she muttered. "What left field did that sneak in from?"

Must be all that talk of aging, who is and who isn't . . .

"I feel just fine, damn it!" she assured the dairy case. "I still put in long days and I drop off to sleep the minute my head hits the pillow. Okay, so the head's going a little gray now, but what of it? Old is a state of mind; a state that hasn't shown up on *my* license plate yet, and I'm nowhere *near* cashing in my chips!"

"What chips are those?" a teasing voice inquired behind her. "Cow, poker, or potato?"

"None of your damn business!" Tessa snarled.

"Well! Excuse me for living!"

Tessa blinked and whirled. "Oh Lord, I'm sorry, Angie . . . my mind . . . I was. . . ." Her fingers fluttered, signifying general confusion. "Wow, look at your hair!" she blurted.

Interpreting the exclamation as a compliment, Angie simpered. "Jeannie did it yesterday. You don't think it's, uh, too much?"

Tessa eyed the towering platinum bubble. *Too much? It was monstrous.* A perfect match for the biggest mouth in town. "Suits you, Angie."

The rest of the week suited Tessa. On Tuesday she helped Miguel deliver Chinook's foal, a bay and white skewbald colt, rambunctious from the word go; by Friday, when the calves arrived, the buckskin was backing as if he'd decided it was his favorite direction. The week before, she wondered if she was asking too much for him; now she regretted letting him go for so little.

Saturday morning, Jed arrived with Bolt, already saddled, in his trailer.

"Who did you get to stay with Pop?" Tessa asked.

"I called an agency in Montrose. They sent down a woman who looks as if her last employer was the federal prison system— Pop was still asleep when she arrived, thank God. I gave her a list of Pop's likes and dislikes—there were more of the latter, as you might imagine—and his doctor's telephone number. I waited until she read it, then left. I don't recall either of us saying goodbye."

"Oh Jed," Tessa said. "Look, if you feel you ought to— "

"I'm here and I'm staying, okay?"

"Okay."

Tessa and Jed stood silently side by side, watching as the stocker calves milled in the corrals, rolling their eyes and bawling.

"Not very promising, are they?" Jed offered.

"Downright scrawny," Tessa said.

Garland, who joined them in time to hear this last exchange, said, "That's why they're here, isn't it? If they were already fat, what would be the point in going to all this trouble?"

"True," Tessa admitted.

"Very true," Jed agreed. "And if they have decent breeding— "

"Of course they do!" Tessa declared. "Like

my dad used to say, a low-grade calf, no matter what you do for 'im, is going to grow into low-grade beef. These are all purebred-cow and hybrid-bull crosses, Jed. For this purpose we want vigor, not breeding potential."

"Can't quarrel with that either." He tipped his hat off his forehead, exposing a brow creased with puzzlement. "So why are we standing here with long faces?"

"Because that's what we do every year, Uncle Jed," Garland said, grinning. "It's part of the ritual."

Jed exchanged a sheepish look with Tessa.

"Okay, I grant you that," he conceded, "but now that we've got that part out of the way, what d'ye say we get this show on the road?"

After Jed unloaded Bolt, Tessa handed him a pair of packed bags, like the ones already secured to her own saddle.

"Enough food in these to last us through, I reckon. Nothing fancy though."

"You still keep a supply of canned goods and biscuit makings up in the cabin, don't you?" Jed asked.

"Sure, but I never know if some poor lost soul hasn't needed it. I'm usually left a thank-you note, but grateful words won't fill our stomachs."

"I'm sure we'll do fine, Tessa. It's not as if we were back in the greasy-sack days, with dried fruit and beans in one sack and sowbelly in the other."

"Not hardly," Garland chimed in. "Mom found these new packaged meals in the supermarket. All you have to do is stick the container in a pan of boiling water. Tonight we're feasting on beef stroganoff."

"Shoot!" Jed declared. "If I'd known that, I would have brought along a bottle of one of those good California cabernets."

Tessa swung up into her saddle. "Will you listen to us?" she said as she gathered up the reins. "I swear, Jed, our fathers wouldn't have believed their ears!"

"No point in suffering discomfort out of loyalty to the good old days," Jed retorted. "Most of them were anything but good, and all the modern conveniences in the world can't spare today's pampered ranchers some hardship along the way."

"I was just commenting," she said blandly, "not judging."

Jed slanted a wary look at her as he recalled using those same words in a different context a few days earlier.

"Considering that Mom bought a designer silk shirt last night with her credit card via an eight-hundred number," Garland said, "I don't think she's all that hot about returning to the good old days herself."

Jed grinned up at Tessa. "Silk shirt, huh? Doesn't sound like something you'll be wearing around the old campfire."

"I wanted it for Scott Shelby's housewarming next Saturday. Satisfied?"

"You don't really expect me to answer that, do you?" He hoisted himself effortlessly into his saddle, every hard lean inch of him a cowboy for all times, all seasons. He grinned at Tessa. "You want to do the honors?"

Tessa grinned back and nodded.

"Oh God," Garland groaned. "Not the Clint Eastwood bit again."

"He wasn't *the* Clint Eastwood then, Garland. Just that real cute sexy young guy on 'Rawhide' who always said—"

"'Head 'em up, move 'em out!'" the three chorused.

Even though the herd was small, Tessa knew that the calves, still scared and confused by their long trucked-in journey, would tend to scatter like beads from a broken string upon release from the enclosures. Banking on their instinct to follow mature animals, she added a few cows to preserve order, and sure enough, after two easily foiled attempts to bolt back to the railed safety of the corrals, the youngsters fell into line behind the large plodding shapes they dimly perceived as Mother.

Jed, Tessa, and Garland urged their horses into a long familiar pattern: Tessa to the left, Garland to the right, pressing the lead cows forward and chivvying the bawling babies into a compact column behind them. Jed brought up the rear, checking any impulse to break away.

Jed watched admiringly as Tessa's horse, a gray mare named Mackerel, urged a balky youngster back into line. His own horse, Bolt, was one of her last foals, and since he was going on seven, Jed knew Mackerel must be in her late teens by now. Still had plenty of ginger, though.

Jed recalled how puzzled Barry had been by the name. "Why'd you want to name a nice horse like that after a smelly old fish?" he had complained. Tessa had patiently explained that in this case *mackerel* meant a cloud pattern, not a fish. *You know, Barry, that dappled look telling you bad weather's on the way?*

All of Tessa's horses had sky or weather-related names: Bolt, the horse she all but gave Jed; Garland's chestnut mare, Sunset, and Rain, the buckskin she was finishing up now for his new owner.

"See the way his dark mane streams against his sandy hide?" Jed remembered her saying. "If you look at it a little squinty, it's like the showers you see streaking down out of distant thunderheads." She had a poetic streak, Tessa did, even though she'd be the first to deny it. She was like her mother that way, Jed thought.

When the Hattons first came to Cottonwood, looking for land they could afford to buy with their precious meager savings, they had spent days in the saddle criss-crossing the valley. One day, lured into the high basins by the drifts of blue and white columbine they could see from the valley floor, Tessa's mother had looked from the thirteen-thousand foot pocket of bloom-blanketed green to the snowy peaks jagging up around them and said it was like walking in the sky.

By then, although they had already chosen a parcel of prime grazing land below, Tessa's father, moved by his wife's wondering remark, impulsively extended his purchase to the skyline at an additional cost worth no more than a moment's hesitation. In those days, the local cattlemen still considered the high grasslands fit only for sheep.

The Hattons named their spread Skywalk. Some of the old-timers sneered when they heard it, thinking it more suited to the dude ranches that even then were springing up down Durango way, but no one was foolish enough to say so in Amos Hatton's hearing. Walt Bradburn might have, but by then the two men had already shaken hands on the sharing of the fence on Hayden's Bald.

The riders wound their way through a rush of spring color. Blue iris spread like spilled sky across the valley's damp flats; Indian paintbrush had begun to polka-dot the foothills with red, and the yellow flowers of Oregon grape-holly shone through sheltering clumps of sage.

Wild roses clambered on the banks of irrigation ditches, which by midsummer would be massed with watercress. Fruit-bearing shrubs added a froth of bridal white. Pointing to them,

Garland smacked her lips noisily at Jed, panto-miming her anticipation of late summer berry-picking forays. Thinking of the sweet wine the berries would make, he winked and tipped an imaginary glass to his mouth.

They climbed steadily, hour after hour, twisting through the tormented trunks of piñon pine and juniper that studded the foothills' flanks, into high meadows ringed by groves of arrow-straight aspens, whose pale leaves trembled in response to breezes the riders could barely feel. Although spring was less advanced here, the sun was hot. Melting snow water chuckled down the rocks and across the trail, leaving broad stripes of greasy scum that the calves had to be urged to negotiate.

Above them, the deeply drifted snow had already begun to shrink back against the cliffs, and in the distance splintered peaks jutted above basins so newly and brightly green, their eyes narrowed against the impact.

To the first settlers arriving from the east, the grass on the Great Plains had seemed limitless. But by the late 1880's, the nearly five million head of longhorns driven north from Texas into Colorado had overgrazed the grasslands into desert, and ranchers again began looking westward toward the Rocky Mountains.

Walt Bradburn's father had been one of the first ranchers to venture into the well-watered foothills, but as the population grew, attracted by reports of the scenic wonders and the tuberculosis cures effected by the clear dry air, he once again picked up stakes. Ignoring the pleas of his weary family, he set a merciless pace up the treacherous ridges, through the first snows of autumn and across to the western slope, where a lifetime of hardship was at last rewarded by Cottonwood's lush meadow pasturage.

Jed suspected his adoptive father would have happily settled for his inherited lowland bonanza if it hadn't been for Amos Hatton's radical departure from the strongly held local cattlemen's opinion that the high mountain grazing season was too short for anything but sheep.

Walt Bradburn knew it was unlikely Hatton was right, but once doubt intruded, it began nibbling away at him, and there was nothing he liked less than uncertainty. Besides, the high land was rock cheap and the Bradburns' needs were few— Walt's were anyway; Jed doubted he gave much thought to his wife's. Years later, when the fattening of calves became a profitable sideline, the investment— which by then he attributed to his own foresight— paid off handsomely.

For Tessa, whose father's purchase was larger to begin with, the return was even better. "Assuming we get the little buggers up there in one piece," Jed muttered as he started after a calf who, deciding he'd gone high enough, began a stumbling descent into a rockfall.

Jed unhitched his rope, and with the easy

skill born of long practice, sent a loop soaring down to settle over the startled youngster's head. Knowing Bolt would keep the rope snubbed around the saddle horn taut, Jed made his way through the unstable shale, secured another rope around the calf's hind legs, and with Bolt's assistance hauled him back up to the trail, bones and fuzzy hide intact.

"Way to go, Jed!" Tessa shouted at him, punching her gloved fist skyward.

All in a day's work, Jed thought as he coiled his rope back into a series of neat loops, but if Tessa wanted to make something of it, well, hell, who was he to complain?

The midday sun scorched through his jacket. He rolled the rope up, tied it behind his saddle, and rode on, trying to ignore his hunger pangs. Just about the time his stomach decided to call a strike, Garland rode back beside him. "I'm the lunch wagon, Uncle Jed. You've got two choices: ham and swiss or roast beef and nothing. Both are on those nice big deli rolls."

From Nellie's Delly? Jed wondered. Somehow he doubted it. "Hard to choose . . . they both sound mighty tasty to me."

"Why not one of each?"

"Don't mind if I do," he said, snatching the offered packets before she could change her mind.

Garland fished in her backpack for a can of iced tea. "To wash them down with. I'm afraid it's not cold anymore."

"Long as it's liquid." He popped the tab and took a long gulping drink. "Ahh-h-h, just what the trail boss ordered. Thank you, honey." He snugged the can into his shirt pocket. "Enjoying yourself?"

"Oh yeah! This is my favorite event of the year. Gav might have bowed out a couple of years back, but I just keep on counting the days. I think of it as a sort of ceremony, you know what I mean?"

"The turn of the ranch year?" She nodded. "I do, too, Garland, but what I was asking about is life in general."

"Oh. Well, working up in Telluride is, uh, I don't know that I'd call it fun, exactly, but it sure is eye-opening. Promotionwise, it's pretty disorganized. I mean, people keep getting these *ideas*, but the events seem to come off okay, so who am I to criticize?"

"You see much of Scott Shelby?"

Garland dropped her eyes. She traced her finger around the saddle horn. "Some. He's been very, uh, helpful, but . . ." She shrugged. "No, I can't say I've seen him all that much."

Jed couldn't tell whether that meant she wished she'd seen less of him or more of him. From the way she sort of oozed around the subject, he suspected— and regretted— the latter.

Tessa's yell drew their attention. They couldn't make out the words, but her rolling of eyes and rubbing of her stomach vividly conveyed the message.

"Uh-oh, Mom's chomping at the bit. You got a place to stow your sandwich wrappings?" Jed nodded. "See you later then!"

Jed extracted a generously stuffed roll from its plastic baggie and watched, munching, as Garland guided Sunset slowly through the herd, clucking reassuringly at the calves as she made her way towards her mother. Their hat brims touched as, heads bent, they discussed sandwich and beverage choices. Serious business concluded, they smiled and parted, the two bobbing heads serving as place markers— one covered in fawn-colored felt, the other in airy straw— on either side of the herd.

Jed swiped the back of his hand across his mouth. *By God, they could have been mine.*

It wasn't the first time he'd thought it; he knew it wouldn't be the last. But was it what he really wanted? About Garland and Gavin he had no doubts: he'd been more of a father to them than Barry ever was, but Tessa?

It wasn't a question of whether he loved her or not, that was a given in his life. He always had; always would. But at fifty, she still didn't know what the hell she wanted, and he wasn't sure he had the patience to wait her out. He wasn't even sure he still had the inclination.

The trail steepened and narrowed. The calves, expecting disaster to overtake them at every corner, rolled their eyes and edged unreasoningly towards the steeply receding hillside. Knowing their horses could not follow if they bolted down it, the three riders worked in concert to contain them, their grim silence broken only by yowls of frustration as one calf, then another, made a break for it. Jed leapt off Bolt and scrambled down after them, falling, swearing, and finally waving the spooked youngsters back up into the herd with wide sweeps of his hat. Two long hours later, as the late-day light slanted into their bleary eyes, they reached the wide gate marking the boundary of the Hatton high pasture lands. A mile or so beyond it, nestled into an aspen grove rimming the largest of the basin's meadows, Tessa's cabin beckoned.

"None too soon," Jed muttered to himself as he paused to secure a second, smaller gate behind him. In truth, it had been an easy day as cattle drives go, the calves being too small and too few to present major problems, but the responsibility he felt for the women weighed on him more than he would ever admit. Sure, they were strong and healthy, and as skilled riders as any man he knew, but as he unsaddled Bolt and turned him loose into the meadow, he felt contentment flow through him like a golden stream.

He stretched, then flicked his hat up from his forehead with his thumb and forefinger. "Well, whadaya know," he said to no one in particular, "we made it!"

Hearing him, Tessa paused on the second of

the three log steps leading to the wide rustic porch. She turned, eyebrows raised, jaw thrust out. "Did you have any reason to think we wouldn't?"

The memory of other drives, other riders, flashed through Jed's mind. Choking dust and jostling red backs. A brassy sun assaulting them by day; cold night winds knifing through their mackinaws. And in the lead, always in the lead, Walt Bradburn, hunched stiff and stolid in the saddle. A human metronome swaying hour after hour to his pony's plodding gait, alert to the first whiff of impending danger. He never expected more of his riders than he did of himself, but for most— *including me, sometimes*— that was more than they could deliver.

"Well? Did you?" Tessa demanded.

Her imperious tone riled Jed some, but he was damned if he'd give her the satisfaction of showing it.

Should he tell her this was more like a day's outing than a cattle drive? Ten easy hours in the saddle, with a cozy cabin and two good-looking women to keep him company at the end? He met her impatient blue eyes. *Uh-uh.*

"Why no, Tessa," he drawled, "no reason at all. Just glad to be here."

Ten

The kerosene lamp cast a golden glow on Tessa's face as she leaned back against the pillows propped against the slatted wooden frame of her armchair.

She's still beautiful, Jed thought. More than ever, in fact. Was it because life's trials had honed her girlish softness into intriguing planes and hollows? Hadn't he always found the stark lines of winter trees more interesting than summer's bland, billowy greenness? *More interesting, yes, but not as comforting.*

They sat, all three, in companionable silence, drinking coffee from the crudely glazed mugs that Garland had made years before in a summer art program given by an eager but not very talented potter.

"Wow," Garland said, running her finger around the chipped rim, "they really are ugly, aren't they? No wonder you snuck them up here."

"Now, Garland," Tessa reproved. "I love them because you made them for me. Besides, they serve a good purpose up here. Sort of like your

Uncle Jed," she added slyly. "Him and his secret thoughts."

Jed grinned, feeling much too relaxed to protest. The packaged beef stroganoff had been surprisingly good, and Garland had brought dessert from a Viennese bakery newly opened in Telluride.

"I've heard about puff pastry," Tessa said, popping a last bit of it into her mouth, "but this is the first time I've actually experienced it. What did you say this was again?"

"Strudel, Mom. This one's apple, which Scott says is sort of the standard. They also have almond and apricot, and when I told the proprietor about our August crop of wild raspberries, he got very excited."

"Just thinking of them makes me feel faint," Tessa admitted. "Is there anything as wonderful as our native raspberries? That and the mushrooms."

Garland frowned. "I really wish you'd leave the mushrooms be, Mom. That botany course I took last semester? I learned enough about fungi to make me vary wary. In their immature stages it's really very hard to distinguish between some of the edible varieties and their poisonous look-alikes."

"I know all about that," Tessa replied. "If you know what to look for— "

"Those word-of-mouth guidelines of yours allow about the same chance as Russian roulette."

"I'm still here aren't I? But just in case . . ." She knocked on the chair's wide arm.

"I wish you wouldn't make fun of me like that," Garland muttered.

"I'm not!" Tessa exclaimed, sitting up straight. "No more than you do of me, anyway. It's called tit for tat."

"Me make fun of *you?* Why, I never— "

"All the time, Garland. It's Boulder this, and the university that— "

"If memory *serves,"* Garland broke in, sounding haughty but looking hurt, "you're the one who was so all-fired anxious for me to go, and— "

"Hey, hey, hey!" Jed exclaimed. "Seems like what we've got here is a classic bit of generational conflict."

"C'mon Jed," Tessa said, "give us a break."

"No, give yourselves a break." He looked sternly from one to the other. "Now, I want you to say you're sorry, then hush up and enjoy this nice fire I made for you." He waited for the exchange of reluctant, sheepish smiles, then rose, tossed another log onto the dwindling burning pile, and inhaled the fragrant smoke that curled out into the room. "I swear, I'll take piñon pine smoke over pot any day."

Garland laughed. "What do you know about smoking pot, Uncle Jed?"

"You're forgetting I was at the university in the anything-goes sixties, young lady."

"I tried it," she admitted. "A couple of times.

I didn't like the swimmy way it made me feel. I like being in control of myself, and," she shrugged, "I wasn't."

"Same with me," Tessa said. "Well, it never came up before," she added, seeing the astonishment in Jed and her daughter's eyes. "Scott Shelby runs with a fast crowd. He stayed clean himself— he couldn't afford not to— but some of the people I met back then . . ." She shook her head. "Pot was the least of it. I know what you mean when you said you felt swimmy, Garland. It's . . . well, *scary.*"

"Exactly," Garland said.

Pleased to see his two favorite women back in tune with each other, Jed settled himself down again in the chair next to Tessa's.

"Speaking of piñon smoke," Tessa said, "if you could bottle it, wouldn't it be a terrific men's fragrance? To give city guys the illusion of being outdoorsmen? These days the big-name designers— Bill Blass, Ralph Lauren, Calvin Klein— they all put out toiletries under their own names."

"Sheets and towels, too, according to a newspaper article I read a while back," Jed said. "Anything they can turn a buck on."

Tessa ignored him. "What do you think, Garland? Might be worth mentioning to Scott . . . might even earn you a few brownie points."

"I don't know about that, Mom," Garland said slowly. "I think that could have been a great sideline for Wild Westerns, but Scott's gone beyond that. He doesn't much like to look back."

Jed was aware of Tessa stiffening beside him. "Well, there sure isn't much he can do with that Water Babies line," she said curtly. "I can't see a cologne made from seaweed having much appeal."

"How about fish heads?" Jed suggested.

Garland grinned at him. "Water Babies is old news, too," she told her mother. "Scott's working on a new line now— in fact, he's using the Bluegrass Festival to promote it."

"Oh?" Tessa said. "What's the theme?"

"Wildflowers," Garland replied. "He says he got the idea from the flowers he's seen here in the San Juan mountains. They'll be the line's starting point, but before it runs its course it will include violets and lady slippers and trillium from New England; azaleas and jessamine from the south, and California poppies from the West Coast."

"Hmmmm-mm, not bad," Tessa said. "What's he calling it?"

Garland stared down into her mug as if amazed to find it empty. "More coffee?" she asked. Without waiting for an answer, she busily set about filling the expected order.

"Garland?" Tessa said when she returned with the coffeepot, "I asked you what Scott is calling his new line?"

"I think that maybe he's decided on Wildings, Mom."

"Why maybe?" Tessa said. "I think it's great. "Flowers and wild things. Appeals to both sides of a woman's nature. I wonder where—" Her eyes widened. *"Now* I get it. All this 'I think' and 'maybe' stuff . . . it was your idea, wasn't it?"

Garland sighed. "Look, it's no big deal, Mom. We were talking over lunch, and I just happened to mention— I don't remember in what connection— that sociologists have given the name wildings to those gangs of homeless kids in places like Buenos Aires and Rio." She shrugged. "Scott's the one who clicked on it."

"Some click," Jed murmured. "Vagrants to *Vogue.*"

Tessa wasn't listening. Her blue eyes narrowed speculatively. "Has he found a model yet?"

"Please, Mom. I'm not the type, and anyway I look too much like you."

"No one remembers me, Garland— like you said, I'm yesterday news." Jed detected an undertone of bitterness. "And what do you mean you're not the type?"

"I'm too healthy. These days the wan look is in, and you must admit that suits the wildflower image more than I do. Besides, Scott has already chosen a model. She's a country-western singer with huge hungry eyes and a long way short of well-rounded."

"Sounds anorexic to me," Tessa said. "Suppose she lands in the hospital and Scott needs a substitute? Would it kill you to go on a diet, just in case?" she persisted. "Do us both good. I'll just cross some stuff off my list of staples . . . peanut butter, those shortbread cookies we both like, sardines— I've been buying them for the calcium, but considering the calories in those little suckers . . ."

Seeing Garland's look of desperation, Jed could no longer contain himself. "Tessa, listen to yourself. You sound like a stage mother. Garland looks fine just as she is."

Tessa's jaw tightened and lifted. "Butt out, Jed."

"The hell I will. Garland has obviously been seeing something of Shelby— on business I presume?" Garland nodded. "So by now we can assume she knows what the situation is and whether she wants to be further involved."

" 'We can assume,' " Tessa repeated in a sneering tone. "Garland doesn't know what she wants— how can she? Sure, she's smart, she's got a 3.8 average after all, but she's still a kid when it comes to the ways of the world. At her age, I was already married, remember?"

Oh, yes, Jed thought, *I remember.* "What's your point, Tessa?"

"My *point?*" She grimaced and dug her hands through her hair. "She doesn't even have a boyfriend, for God's sake!"

The expression Jed saw on Garland's face over Tessa's shoulder was a dead giveaway. *She*

*not only lunches with Scott Shelby but has a boyfriend
Tessa doesn't know about? Oh boy.*

". . . I'm not trying to pressure you, darling," Tessa was saying. "I just thought a little,
you know, guidance? Look, I'm sorry if I came
on too strong."

"That's okay, Mom." Garland's smile was
forced. "Gav always said he'd have better luck
at teaching a muley-head steer to roll over than
taming your maternal impulses."

"Steer, huh! He could've at least called me a
cow!"

Garland and Jed gave a shout of laughter.
After a moment's bewilderment, Tessa added
her low, throaty chuckle. "Have you talked to
your brother lately?" she asked. "Every time I
call the number Gav gave me I get one of those
damn machines."

"I got a letter from him last week but— " Garland stopped short and caught her lower lip be-
ween her teeth. "He really didn't have much
to say."

"A letter? I got that jokey postcard from him,
but I don't recall any letters coming for you."

"He sent it to Telluride," Garland admitted
reluctantly. "Care of the Resort Association office."

"Why would Gav send you a letter that 'didn't
have much to say' to Telluride?" Tessa inter-
cepted the look of appeal Garland sent Jed. Her
hand shot out to circle her daughter's wrist.
"What is it I'm not supposed to know?" Winc-

ing, Garland pulled away. "Jed? What's going on here?"

"I imagine," he began slowly, "although I'm not sure, mind you— "

"For God's sake, Jed!" Tessa blurted. "I'm not asking you to predict the end of the world. Throw caution to the winds and get on with it!"

"I *imagine*," he repeated deliberately, "that Gav wrote Garland about the same matter he phoned to discuss with me."

"He called *you* instead of *me*?" She thrust her head towards him; her lips thinned to an angry slash. "Of all the disloyal— "

"Calm down and let me finish, damn it. If you do, you might understand."

Tessa slumped back and crossed her arms over her chest. "Try and make me."

"Well, it started with Lloyd calling Gavin, then Garland. I assume Gav wanted to compare notes with her, but he didn't want to call home because he knew how you'd react."

"Compare notes?" Tessa repeated, "About what?"

"About Lloyd's offer to buy the land Barr left them."

"That bastard," Tessa murmured. "That sneaky son-of-a-*bitch!*" she continued in a rising voice. "I *told* him that land wasn't for sale. Especially not to him and that real estate creep he's gotten so cozy with."

"You mean Terry Ballou?" Jed asked. "Th

guy Lloyd's gone into partnership with to develop those acres of his up on the mesa?"

"You got it. Knowing I was the twins' guardian, Lloyd came to me first— you came in on the tail end of that conversation, Garland, remember? I thought I'd left no doubt in his mind— of course with someone like Lloyd, you have to practically hit him over the head with a brick before he realizes you mean what you say. He's like that pit bull Barry had when we were kids, Jed."

"Old Gooch? Lord, I haven't thought of him for years! Crazy dog, Garland. Never let go of anything without being knocked silly. I kind of liked him, though."

"Yeah, me too. I can't say the same for Lloyd."

"That's why he tried his luck with us, Mom," Garland said. "He knows we'll turn twenty-one next year. I guess he was hoping to sow the seed of temptation in soon-to-be-fertile ground. Can't really blame him for trying."

"I can," Tessa said. "I trust you turned him down."

"Of course we did! How could you think otherwise?"

Tessa turned to Jed. "It's easy enough to think all sorts of things if no one tells you anything." Her voice was subdued. "These are my children, Jed. Surely you could have told me Gav phoned you."

Jed leaned forward to study the tips of his

fingers. His eyes flicked up. "He asked me not to."

" 'He asked me not to,' " she mocked. "Is that the best defense you can come up with?"

Jed straightened. "It's not a defense, Tessa. I didn't realize our relationship required one. That's just the way it is between Gavin and me . . . and Garland, too. They trust me to keep my word, and I always do . . . even if sometimes I have my doubts about it."

"So you've had your doubts. Wow. Am I supposed to be grateful for that? I can't help wondering what else you've kept from me. Considering the number of years that have come and gone since the twins were born, I imagine quite a lot. Didn't it ever occur to you I might not agree with your judgment?"

"I'm not about to give you an accounting of my actions, Tessa."

"Actions?" she cried. "That's the trouble with you, Jed Bradburn! You don't act, you just accept, sucking everything in like a . . . a human vacuum cleaner."

"Mom! Please!"

Heedless of her daughter's anguish, Tessa swept on. "When Barry and I got married, you never said a word. Just suffered in silence, passive as a fence post."

Jed's eyes narrowed to slits. "No moaning and groaning and— how does the Bible put it— no rending of garments? Is that it, Tessa? You always did enjoy playing Barry and me off against

each other, and year after year we reacted pretty
much as expected. You must have found it very
entertaining. By the time we got to high school
it had become a conditioned reflex: Barry'd
jump in that old heap of his and roar through
the town, scaring dogs and missing old ladies
by inches, and I—"

"You'd go all broody," Tessa cut in. "Like a
hen in a chicken coop."

"When I was a kid, showing my anger earned
me nothing but Pop's belt across my backside!"
They glared at each other. "As I remember it,
the odds had begun shifting in my direction,
when with no warning, whammo! 'Didn't anyone tell you, Jed?' " he said in a mincing fal-
setto. " 'Why, Tessa and Barry just up and
eloped!' " Recalling the moment, he slowly
shook his head.

"The way I saw it," he continued, "the game
was over before I even had a chance to place
my bet. If the situation had been reversed,
Barry would have hurled the cards in your
face . . . maybe even shot you. But me? I just
evened up the deck, tucked it in my pocket, and
walked out. Not much fun for you in that, I
guess."

"*Ran* out, you mean! Back to Boulder and
college without so much as a word."

Jed, who had gotten up to poke at the fire,
peered back at her. "Is that what's been eating
you all these years? That I went on with my
life?"

"Some life," she sneered. "Nursemaid to a zillion brainless Herefords and one cranky old man."

He turned. "Don't know as I would have put it quite that way, but I guess, from your point of view, that about sums it up." His sad, somber expression caused the challenge in her eyes to falter. "You know, Tessa, in those first few years, I spent a lot of time trying to figure out why you did what you did, but to tell the truth, I no longer give a damn."

Jed yawned, dusted off the pale flakes of strudel clinging to his long denim-clad thighs, and ambled across to the small bunk room always assigned him. He paused in the doorway. "Sorry you had to hear all that, Garland."

Tessa got up and walked quickly towards the closing door. "Jed? Look, I said things I shouldn't . . . things I didn't even— " The door latch clicked quietly into place. *"Jed?"*

It was too late.

"Mom, how could you?" Garland murmured.

Tessa couldn't bear to meet her eyes. "Oh Jed," she whispered. "I'm so sorry . . ."

Eleven

A bright scallop of sun had already flared above the highest peak when Tessa emerged, sleep-flushed and puffy-eyed, from the larger of the two bunk rooms. She sniffed the aroma of bacon and fresh-brewed coffee appreciatively.

"Sorry I'm so late . . . I had trouble getting to sleep."

Garland didn't bother turning from the basin in which she had set dishes to soak. "I'm not surprised," she muttered.

Tessa arched her eyebrows. "Good morning to you, too, Miss Grumpy." She yawned and surveyed the dim room, still redolent with the fragrance of piñon pine. "Where's Jed? Out rounding up the horses? He always did like to get the jump on everyone."

"He left about an hour ago."

"Left? Without saying goodbye?"

Garland slapped the dish sponge on the scarred wooden counter and faced her. "What did you expect, Mom? That he'd hang around so you could kick him some more?"

"Hey, I admit I went a little far but . . . well,

that's the way it is with me and Jed. You've seen it before.

"Not like last night I haven't. Maybe if you could come up with a sensible answer . . ." Garland's words trailed off uncertainly.

"Answer to what?" Tessa prompted irritably.

Garland took a deep breath. "Why you didn't wait for him." She ducked her head. Her unbound hair slid down to veil her face with gold. "Instead of, you know, marrying Daddy."

Tessa felt her insides clench. "Oh for God's sake, Garland! There's no single, simple answer to something like that. It has to do with a whole lot of things I don't expect you to understand."

Garland picked up the sponge and began scrubbing furiously at the iron frypan. "I understand a lot more than you think," she mumbled.

"Speak up, Garland!"

"It's not important, Mom," she said stiffly. "Which would you prefer, coffee or tea?"

"Coffee, I guess. We've got a good eight hours in the saddle ahead of us, and I could sure do with an eye-opener. Is any of that bacon I smell left?"

Seeing her mother's wistful expression, Garland relented. "I cooked up the whole package. Enough for breakfast, and the rest for sandwiches I'll make with what's left of the bread."

"After I have toast."

"After that," Garland agreed.

Tessa fried an egg for herself, toasted two

slices of bread over the two-burner gas grill, and poured herself a mug of coffee dark as sin. By the time Garland finished making the sandwiches and joined her at the roughly cobbled table with her own mug, she was feeling more ready to face the day.

"I gather from what you said last night that you're seeing something of Scott?"

"Strictly on business, Mom."

"But with a little fun thrown in, right?"

"Well, you know how he is." Tessa grinned and nodded. "I swear, he can put a sensuous spin on just about anything. Take last week, when the posters for the Bluegrass Festival were delivered. Remember the singer I told you and Uncle Jed about?"

"The waif with the big greedy eyes?"

"Hungry, Mom. I don't recall saying anything about greed."

"C'mon, honey. She's young, probably ambitious, and she's got a shot at hogging Scott Shelby's very powerful spotlight."

"Okay, greedy," Garland conceded. "Be that as it may, the poster photo makes her look more like a hooker than a folksinger, and when I took Scott to task about it— "

"Did you really?" Tessa broke in, chortling. "I sure wish I'd been there."

"Well, I did, but Scott just laughed at me, sort of the way you did now, and told me that was his intention. He wants guys to want more than just hear her sing— "

"It was the same with me, Garland. Of course I never sang anything . . ."

"I should hope not, Mom. Not in public anyway."

"Smarty-pants," Tessa said, thumbing her nose at her. "For Wild Westerns, what I did was ride around, usually very fast, looking, well, wild."

"Figures. But to get back to the poster, the festival has a featured male singer, too. Now I've seen that guy up close, Mom, and the hunk look he's got on the poster has nothing to do with reality— unless your notion of hunkiness includes guys with bellies swelling out over their belt buckles."

"That's the way publicity works, Garland. Surely you knew that."

"Yeah, I guess. It's different when you're part of it, though."

Tessa took a sip from her mug. She looked at her daughter speculatively. "Ever thought of going brunette? With your sparkly hazel eyes it might be— "

"Forget it, Mom! Sure, I'm flattered by Scott's attention, and I appreciate his admiring words even when they're not entirely sincere. When they are," she added thoughtfully, "I suspect it's because when he asks me to do something for him, I get it done on time. You'd be surprised what a rarity that is up there."

"Then why not build on it?"

"Earlier, when you asked me if Scott wasn't

fun to be with?" Tessa nodded. "Well, his idea of fun seems to center on raising the pulse rate of every female he comes in contact with. He's damn successful at it, too. Take Mona, the Chamber's festival manager— she gives me my assignments, oversees what I do, and rates my performance."

"In other words, your boss."

Garland nodded. "She's brisk, no nonsense, and very professional, right down to the tips of her polished black kid pumps— which look kind of weird up there in hiking-boot country, but Mona's more a woman of the eighties than the nineties. You know, success-oriented. She must be in her late thirties."

"Oh my," Tessa said. "Practically ready for the boneyard."

"The point *is,*" Garland continued, ignoring her mother's wry comment, "within days of meeting Mona, Scott reduced her to a simpering schoolgirl. She's a big woman, Mom. Not fat, but tall and solid. Statuesque. Anyway, Scott would saunter in, settle on the corner of her desk, lean real close, and talk to her in this sort of purring voice, all the while gently stroking her wrist with his fingertips."

"The old talking-and-touching routine. Works wonders. I use it with young horses all the time."

"Exactly!" Garland said. "I keep expecting him to arrive with a bag of oats and a hackamore. Not that he needs it. He just stares into her eyes,

smiling that big sex smile of his— you know how
a deer freezes when it's picked up by car headlights?" Tessa nodded. "Like that. *God*. It's embarrassing . . ."

Garland rolled her eyes. "And the *time* it
wastes!" she added. "Mona keeps insisting it's
all in the service of festival promotion, except
the only festival her fevered mind has room for
right now is Scott's. She might as well be wearing blinders. If she doesn't pull herself together
right quick, she'll be out on her generously en-
dowed behind."

"Hindquarters, dear."

"It's not funny, Mom."

"Scott never means any harm, Garland."

"Isn't that what they say about rattlesnakes?
So, okay, Friday afternoon, I'm getting my desk
in order to leave, and Mona wanders in, dazed,
wearing this white, drapy, pleaty *thing*. Not her
style at all, Mom. She looked like one of those
big puffy summer afternoon clouds, frazzled
edges and all.

"She'd gone to lunch at The Peaks with Scott—
a long, obviously wine-lubricated lunch— in the
course of which she apparently agreed to a lot
of special favors for the Bluegrass Festival he's
sponsoring. Expensive, precedent-setting favors,
like an augmented sound system, that she belatedly realized the Chamber's director will not be
at all happy about.

"She wasn't complaining or blaming, mind
you— she just couldn't understand how it hap-

pened. I didn't know *what* to say— I couldn't very well tell her she was a jerk— so I just smiled sympathetically, and after a moment she just— " Garland fluttered her fingers— "drifted out."

"She's a grown woman, Garland. If Scott shook her up some . . . who knows? Might do her some good."

"I'm not so sure. Face it, Mom: he's a predator."

"He always was, darling . . . although I admit it sounds as if he's settling for easier game now."

"Easy is right," Garland agreed. "He just swiped Mona in with those soft paws of his"— she growled softly and made a swift cuffing motion— "more or less in passing."

"Well, I was too quick for him," Tessa said, "and you're a lot smarter than I was. Let him play his little games, but lead him a merry chase. That way you'll both have fun."

"Yeah, but I'm the one taking up the slack at the Chamber as well as acting as Scott's gofer, hotel liaison, and whatever else he and Mona dream up for me."

"Maybe so, Garland, but I hear opportunity knocking in the background. If you play your cards right . . ."

Tessa's words drifted off. She cocked her head and reached out to touch Garland's sunstreaked blond hair, so like her own, save for the gray. "How about going redder? Chestnut, or maybe auburn . . . I don't think Scott's done auburn yet. In fact," she added with a puzzled frown, "after Water Babies, I kinda lost track of what he was doing. He married the Water Babies' model, but the ex-Mrs. Shelby living in Cottonwood sure isn't her."

"I imagine having twins to raise had something to do with your lack of attention to Scott's career, Mom."

"Yeah, I imagine so." *That and trying to keep Barry from drowning himself in the bottle and the Wagner spread from going bankrupt.* Tessa's smile was crooked. "Double the trouble, huh?"

"But a little bit of fun, I hope," Garland said. "Even if not of the Shelby variety."

"More than you can know, darling." Tessa leaned across the table, gripped her daughter's wrist, and searched her wide-set hazel eyes. "I've never regretted for one single minute suffering the way I did to bring my babies into the world."

Garland's eyebrows shot up. *"Mom!* You never said . . . no one ever—"

"Gotcha!" Tessa exclaimed, laughing. She patted her daughter's arm, got up, and slid her plate into the dishpan. She peered through the small dusty window above the counter. The sun, which had earlier shone so brightly above the mountains, had dimmed. "As soon as I wash these up, we'd better get going. The way those clouds are moving in, we'll be lucky to get home in dry weather."

Garland looked up from the heavy frypan she was wiping out. "Was it bad, Mom? Gav and me being born? I mean, it's hard enough having one, but two . . ."

Tessa smiled into her daughter's anxious face. "Piece of cake. You guys popped out like muffins out of a greased tin."

"Cake . . . muffins," Garland repeated as she shelved the clean dishes, "methinks you're hoping there's some of that strudel left to have with our lunch, right?"

"Well, now that you mention it . . ."

"Already packed, Mom. I just have to add the bacon sandwiches."

"Sounds as if we'll be having one of those greasy-sack rides Jed talked about yesterday. You about ready? I just have to roll up my sleeping bag."

"I've already done that, so yeah, I'm ready, but I sure hate to leave this place."

"Me, too. Always have . . . and unless something better comes along, I guess I always will."

Garland stared at her. "Something *better*?"

Tessa's smile was shaky. She hadn't meant to say that; she didn't even know where it came from. "Just an expression, Garland. Typical of persons— okay, of *women* of a certain age. What are they calling it now? Midlife crisis? Forget it."

"That's not the sort of thing I can use the delete tab for, Mom."

"I don't know what that means, but I assume

it has something to do with computers." Garland nodded. "You see?" Tessa complained. "It's no wonder I'm having a midlife crisis!"

By the time Tessa secured the gate behind them, closing the calves and the chaperoning cows in for a summer of grazing bliss, the cloud cover had reduced the sun's shine to a faint glow. Everything seemed grayer: the lush grass, the snow melt, and their spirits. They rode on in silence. When they reached the breaks above the foothills, the high peaks were shrouded by the lowering clouds, and condensation droplets began to drip from their hatbrims.

The two women took refuge in the last, lowest, stand of aspen to eat their lunch. Remaining in their saddles, they chomped resolutely on bacon sandwiches to whose excess of cholesterol the morning's ride had added toughness—or as Tessa quipped, insult to injury. She glumly finished her limp portion of strudel, but Garland distributed most of hers to the Stellar's jays hip-hopping through the branches above them.

A steady drizzle slickened the steep descent into the sage-covered foothills. Sunset and Mackerel, their necks extended, picked their way cautiously, almost daintily, along the boulder-strewn trail. Tessa, knowing a faster pace could end in broken bones or worse, vented her frustration via a string of explosive expletives.

Garland, who tended to keep her discomforts to herself, hunched her shoulders and pulled her hatbrim lower.

By the time they reached home, they were soaked through. Miguel offered to see to the horses' well-being, and after gratefully relinquishing their reins to him, they slunk inside.

"I guess Jed won this round," Tessa grumped as they trailed into the kitchen. "Leaving when he did, he probably beat the rain home."

"I doubt he'd think of it in terms of winning or losing, Mom," Garland said as she helped her mother off with her boots. "Life is more than a game to Uncle Jed," she admonished. "You're confusing him with Scott Shelby."

"Huh!" Tessa grunted, upending one of her boots. "Not hardly likely." Water dribbled out onto the floor. Holding up a pale wrinkled foot tinted blue by the chill, she exclaimed, "Looks like it belongs on a corpse, doesn't it?"

"That's disgusting!" Garland protested.

"Age is disgusting."

"It has nothing to do with age," Garland said, thrusting out her own foot for comparison.

"Well, okay," Tessa granted, "but practically everything else about me does. Sagging boobs and butt and dewlaps— "

"And morale," Garland cut in. "You look great, Mom."

"Yeah. For my age."

Garland gave an exasperated huff. "Of *course*

for your age. What did you expect, to be miraculously exempt?"

Tessa looked up at her daughter, her expression suddenly sober, almost somber. "As a matter of fact, that's exactly what I expected. Homecoming Queen. Barrel-racing champ. Daddy's darling— hell, everybody's darling. Oh, and the Wild Westerns girl. Mustn't forget that."

"Woman, Mom, not girl. You were thirty, as I remember."

"But you can't remember how it *was* back then— you weren't even born yet! I was a *girl*, Garland. I looked like one, felt like one, and Scott promoted me as one. Wild Westerns *woman?* Sounds ridiculous!"

"That's because you've got your eyes fixed on the past. How about the years since? How about the woman renowned as a quarter horse breeder and trainer? Loyal wife? Cherished mother?" The last was offered in a whisper. "Like that slogan says, 'You've come a long way, baby,' and you've still got a third or more of your life ahead of you."

"In other words, buck up, old girl, the best is yet to be?" Tessa's chin came up. "Bullshit."

Garland looked pained. "The clock's ticking, Mom. Denying it just makes you seem, well . . ."

"Foolish? I know that, but that's the way it is. I see Scott, still taking the world by storm at sixty— and according to you, still turning women's heads— "

"Mom."

"Success after success— "

"Mom!" Tessa blinked and paused. "I'm not so sure those successes have followed one after the other the way you seem to think."

"Nonsense. First there was Wild Westerns. When you add in the variations and spin-offs, that ran another good two years after I left the scene. Then Water Babies, another three if you add in the beachwear, which was a terrific success of its own, and then he branched out into menswear— "

"Which, according to the talk in Telluride, he quietly dumped after a dismal couple of years. Add 'em up and you've got ten years. If you want to be generous, make it twelve. What happened to the other eight?"

"Well, like Jed said last night, there were all those other things, linens and toiletries, scarves and pocketbooks— I even seem to remember pantyhose with his name on it, though why anyone would care— "

"Humdrum stuff, Mom. Hardly home-runs."

"How come you suddenly know so much?"

"Mona. Before she met Scott she used to talk a lot about stuff like that, and I'm pretty good at listening."

"Why do I get the feeling you're suggesting I try it for a change?"

"The thing is, there's a big gap in the Shelby

success story, starting with the first wife. We know who she is—"

"Yeah, the Water Babies girl . . . sorry, woman."

"How about the second? Where did she come from?"

"I haven't a clue. Jeannie knows her some . . . so does Jed, come to think of it."

"He does?" Garland said. "How come?"

"She's living on Scott's ranch— what used to be his, anyway— and he's renting the grazing land from her. Actually, he only met her last week. I meant to ask him what his impression was. Jeannie says she's older than Scott."

"*Older?*" Astonished, Garland shook her head. "I can't imagine Scott marrying someone older than himself without a damn good reason."

Tessa, lost in thought, didn't respond. "Eight years you said? Subtract one for getting geared up for Wildings, and there's still seven—"

"At *least* seven, Mom."

"— unaccounted for." Tessa got up and hooked her arm through Garland's. "All those years . . . I just assumed . . . I mean, I was raising you and Gav and working at getting the horse business on a paying basis, and what with one thing and another"— they both knew that meant Barry's drinking and the problems related to it— "well, like you said earlier, I guess I just lost track of Scott's fashion fortunes."

"Or lack thereof," Garland said, as they walked together into the living room. She moved to the big stone fireplace, crouched, and rearranged the partially burned logs. "Got any newspaper, Mom?"

"Should be some in the cupboard." Tessa curled herself up in one of the big easy chairs and watched as Garland tucked the newspaper spills under the blackened logs and touched a match to them. The tiny curls of fire twisted from one side to the other, fingering up between the logs, seeking the oxygen needed to sustain them.

"I suppose," Tessa murmured, her eyes narrowing as the fledgling flames grew brighter, "it wouldn't cost me all that much to go up there hat in hand."

Garland, who stood bent, her hands extended towards the flaring tongues of fire, turned her head to smile at her mother. "To Scott? For not keeping up your subscription to *Vogue?*"

"No, to Jed. For being such a . . . a . . ."

"Shit?"

Tessa winced. "Don't know as I would have put it quite like that." She shifted uneasily. "Of course, he might just slam the door in my face . . ."

She sighed. Apologies had never been easy for her. As a child, she would sit hour after hour in her room, denied the companionship of a visiting playmate she had somehow offended, rather than say she was, sorry, even if, deep down, she was.

But in this case . . .

Her eyes closed. How did that song go? Something about woman being invincible?

Yeah. She could do it.

"What'll you bet me," she drawled, "that if I mix up a loaf of your grandmother's famous never-fail pound cake, throw in some extra raisins and a bag of chocolate bits, and announce in a real loud voice I brought a sweet treat for his dad, Jed won't have any peace till he let's me in. I swear, Garland, that old coot can smell sugar a mile off!" She flashed her daughter a smugly triumphant look. "If it works for Nell and her damn brownies, it ought to work for me."

"That poor old man!" Garland wailed. "I know you treasure that recipe of Grandma's, but haven't you ever wondered if you left something out when you copied it? Something *crucial?* I mean, face it, Mom, your pound cake is dreadful."

"Shoot, I know that!" Tessa's evil chuckle bubbled up into a wide grin. "But so is Pop Bradburn."

Twelve

The old Wagner homestead, reached by crossing the busy highway connecting Cottonwood with Ouray, lay four miles east of Skywalk Ranch at the end of a mile-long access road corrugated by ranch vehicles and the motorcycles that had always been the Wagner boys' favorite mode of transportation.

Barry, thanks to numerous DUI citations, had been forced to give up his bike years before his death. In Lloyd's case, it was a bloody collision—the pal joyriding with him was decapitated—that persuaded him, as Pauline's pleas never had, to trade in his big Harley against a used, stripped-down, four-by-four. He still had a lead foot on the pedal, but since he drove it more off-road than on, fewer innocent people were at risk. Jack, who required neither alcohol nor buddies to fuel his recklessness, continued to scorch the highways, an accident waiting to happen.

Jack Wagner disdained the hog bikes so dear to Lloyd and his late brother's hearts. His sleek black machine of Japanese manufacture had been customized by a Grand Junction shop to Jack's exacting requirements for big bucks his family could have put to better use. Local guys familiar with such matters pronounced it the sexiest bike in the county— maybe the entire state. Tessa, seeing it parked Tuesday morning in front of the old ranch house where Lloyd and Pauline now lived, knew it as the noisiest.

Many a tourist's car had swerved perilously near one or another mountain road's edge as Jack came snarling out of nowhere, long hair streaming back from his unhelmeted head as he rocketed past. A mean, lean machine, just like his precious bike.

Tessa slid her pickup in next to it, swirling dust over its immaculate surface. As she tucked her sunglasses back in the case clipped to the windshield visor, she caught a twitch of the kitchen curtain out of the corner of her eye. A moment later, Jack ambled out into the porch. As usual, his bike, even when dust-covered, looked cleaner than he did.

"Hey there, sister-in-law. Seeing you makes this fine morning we're having even finer."

Tessa closed the truck door behind her. "Jack," she said curtly. She drew back as he came down the steps towards her.

He grinned as he pulled a faded red bandanna out of the back pocket of his grimy jeans and wiped the dust from his bike's jet surface. "That wasn't very considerate of you, Tessa."

Over the years, Tessa had perfected the trick

of projecting bland innocence when dealing with Jack. He liked nothing better than a betraying flush of color or suddenly averted gaze. Give him the slightest hint of a hit, and he'd keep at it and at it.

She looked up at him, wide-eyed. "I'm sorry, Jack, what wasn't?"

"C'mon, the way you wheeled in just now."

Her brow knitted with puzzlement. "I can't imagine . . . Oh my *gosh,* I didn't scratch your beautiful bike, did I?" She moved towards it solicitously, scuffing up a new cloud of dust in the process.

"Shit, Tessa!"

"Looks okay to me," she said, smiling sweetly up at him. He scowled back, blocking her path. "If you don't mind, Jack— this *is* Lloyd's house now, not yours."

Poor Jack, she thought as he sidled reluctantly to one side. *A has-been at forty-six.* A lifetime of unrealized hopes and brutish toil had soured and scoured the sensual features that had symbolized youthful rebelliousness and daring for a generation of Cottonwood teenagers. The James Dean of the western slope.

Girls had thought his insanely defiant exploits romantic; the paler versions copycatted by the guys had cost several broken limbs and at least one life. It never occurred to them that Jack's risk-taking had more to do with a lack of imagination than courage; it never occurred to him there might be more interesting or rewarding ways to pass the time. It still didn't.

Pauline appeared in the doorway, wiping her hands on her apron. "Tessa! What a nice surprise! I just this minute took a pan of sticky buns out of the oven. Come on in and visit with us, have a cup of coffee."

Damn it, Tessa thought, *how do you tell a person to lay the hell off your kids over a sticky bun?* Forcing a smile, she accepted a cup of watery coffee and followed Pauline into the dining room. Although his smile lacked warmth, Lloyd made a stab at a friendly greeting. Jack's wife, Patty, didn't bother to try.

"Don't see much of you anymore, Tessa," she twanged. "Forgotten the way?"

"I'm not in the habit of visiting without an invitation, Patty."

"Coulda fooled me," she heard Lloyd mutter.

"Since when does family need an invitation?" Patty asked, rolling her eyes towards the ceiling.

"I've been busy. I've got a ranch to run."

"Are you saying we don't?" Patty challenged.

"Of course not, but I'm on my own. It's easier with another pair of hands."

"You could have 'em, too, Tessa," Jack drawled from behind her. "All you got to do is ask."

He slid slowly by, his thighs brushing her bottom, confirming that a hand with her ranch work wasn't what he had in mind."

"I'm sure Tessa's already getting plenty of

that," Patty hissed at her husband. Her brassy blondness— once a natural pale silver, but blatantly fake now— drained her sallow skin of what little color it ever had. "And if you ask me, considering what Barry left those kids of hers, they all got a lot more'n they deserve to pay for any work that needs doing."

"Who's asking you, Patty-cakes?"

Jack's remark seemed off-hand, but Tessa saw the threat in his eyes. The only questions allowed in Jack Wagner's family originated with him. Her attention returned to Patty. It was amazing, she thought, how much her younger sister-in-law had managed to imply in that one sentence. *One, that my sex life is not only active, but probably scandalous; two, that the twins are* my *kids, not Barry's; and three, none of us are entitled to what he left us. Not bad for a woman never thought overly bright.*

"I hardly know how to respond to that, Patty," Tessa said evenly, "but as it happens, you managed to hit on the reason I came here today."

"Sit down, Tessa!" Pauline said, all but forcing her into the chair she brought in with her from the kitchen. "Have a sticky bun," she urged, trying the only way she knew to keep the situation from slipping further out of control.

"Thanks, Pauline, I know they're delicious— everything you cook is— but I think I'll pass this time."

"What does she mean by that, Pauline?" Patty

demanded shrilly. "Have you been entertaining her behind our backs?"

"Hush up, Patty," Lloyd said, a broad smile plumping his cheeks. "I swear, when you set those pearly whites of yours into something, it's getting harder and harder to shake you loose . . . worse'n one of those yappy little terrier dogs. No, we ain't been seeing her. Missus High-and-Mighty hasn't got no more time for us than you. You was saying, Tessa?"

Oh God. "What I was *trying* to say was that under the circumstances, I don't think I should accept your hospitality."

"Seeing as how you're sitting at my table and drinking my coffee, I'd say you'd already accepted it, but these circumstances you mentioned— just what are we talking about here?"

"About you calling Gavin in Denver, trying to buy the land Barry left him after I told you it wasn't for sale."

Lloyd spread his big hands and gazed in amazement at his brother. "How old do you reckon that boy is, Jack?"

"Must be all of twenty," Jack drawled, "and coming up fast on twenty-one."

"There you go! That's what I figured, too. I sure didn't think he still needed his mother speakin' for him." Lloyd's face worked hard at expressing his bewilderment to his family, but the look he directed back at Tessa was shorn of pretense. "That son of yours— "

"And Barry's," Tessa said.

"That boy's made it plain as plain he don't want no Cottonwood dirt soiling his college-boy shoes. I was just providin' him a fast and profitable way to shed it."

Tessa's eyes darkened. "You presume too much, Lloyd Wagner."

Lloyd guffawed. "Pre-*sume?* I'm not sure I take your meaning, but I'll take it as a compliment and thank you kindly for it."

Jack grinned; Patty giggled. Pauline, who was twisting her pretty embroidered apron into a mass of wrinkles, was the only one unmoved to mirth. Lloyd leaned forward. The shift of his bulk underscored the threat implicit in his grim expression.

"Now you listen to me, missy. Jack and me, we've always had our doubts about those twins of yours. Never had none in our family before, and in all those years you and Barry was married up till then— ten, wasn't it?— you never got the least bit pregnant with one, let alone two." He slowly shook his big head. "It just don't add up, Tessa."

"Seems to me it added up all right until a land sale depended on the bottom line."

"Now you wait just a damn minute!" Lloyd said, jabbing a beefy finger at her. "Maybe you and Barry never had much of a marriage, but I wasn't about to unhorse his widow, grieving or not. Things have changed since then," he added settling back into his chair. "Now I got to think of my own family."

"Same with me," Jack said.

Tessa rolled her eyes. "And here I was thinking nothing you guys could say would surprise me."

"She might not be a widow if she'd called 911 sooner," Patty offered.

"Bite your tongue, Patty Wagner!" Pauline cried. "You know what the coroner said!"

"He admitted he couldn't be absolutely sure, hon," Lloyd said. "Didn't he say his conclusions were based on the evidence made available to him? We'll never know what wasn't," he added solemnly. "No offense, Tessa."

Tessa scraped back her chair. "Well, it's been real interesting talking with you, but I think I'll leave now. I've had enough stimulation for one morning."

"Yeah, you do that," Lloyd said. "And while you still are— stimulated, that is— why don't you think on that land a little more? We'd sure hate to haul you into court, stir up all that old gossip, maybe add some more . . ." He snapped his fingers. "Hey, that reminds me! You been seein' much of that Shelby feller? I saw him in town a week or so ago. Passed right by— " he spread his hands about eighteen inches apart, like a fisherman bragging on a trout he'd caught— "about *this* close. You know, I never set much store on what Barry used to say, him being so jealous and all, but I swear when I saw his eyes— what do they call that color again, Tessa?"

"Hazel," she snapped.

"Yeah, hazel." He smiled. "I was pretty sure you'd know, the twins' eyes being such dead ringers. Can't help but put questions in a person's mind . . . maybe even Judge Colby's."

Knowing that Ben Colby's court had to do with the settlement of estates, Barry's among them, Tessa froze in her tracks. Her hands fisted. Then, recalling what Jed had told her about the portrait of the Wagner brothers' great-grandmother, her fingers uncurled.

"You think so, Lloyd?" she said. "Well, I guess you'll just have to take me to court to find out. Gosh, think of the lawyer's fees! Maybe even the court costs when I win."

Pauline scrambled up after her. "Tessa?" She thrust a packet of sticky buns into her hands. "For Garland," she said. The paper napkins she had hastily wrapped them in were gummy, and shreds of them would probably be found adhering to the contents, but the bravely expressed sentiment touched Tessa's heart.

She leaned to kiss her cheek. "Thank you, Pauline. Next time I'll call first."

Tessa had just plopped Pauline's offering on the kitchen counter together with the bag of groceries she picked up in Cottonwood on the way home, when Miguel burst into the kitchen after her.

"*Madre de Dios!* I been calling everywhere,

Miz Wagner. The man from Montrose, he's coming this afternoon. No one seen you . . . no one know where you could be."

"I was up at the Wagner ranch, having coffee with my in-laws." Miguel's eyes opened wide. "Yeah, I know. That's the last place anyone would have figured. So when's he coming?"

"Hour— " Miguel rocked his hand— "half-hour . . . maybe less by now. He called just after I saw you leave."

"Jesus!" Tessa jammed a quart of milk, eggs, and a package of chicken thighs into the refrigerator. The rest could wait. She wiped her dusty boots with a paper towel, poked her loosened shirt back down into her waistband, and peered into the mirror next to the sink. "He wasn't scheduled to arrive until tomorrow," she muttered as she smoothed her windblown hair back into a ponytail. After securing it with a rubber band, she rummaged in her purse for a lipstick, swiped it across her lips, and blotted them with the dust-grayed toweling she still held in her hand. *Eeccch.*

Grimacing, she balled the paper and lobbed it into the trash bin. "What d'ye think, Miguel?" she asked, turning to face him. "Will I pass muster?" Never having been asked for a judgment of that kind before, his mouth worked uncertainly before he settled for a wordless nod. "I imagine he'll want a final demonstration before he antes up," Tessa continued. "You got

Rain saddled up?" Miguel looked hurt. "Dumb question. Sorry, Miguel."

A glint of light drew Tessa's attention to the window. "He's here," she muttered. She took a deep breath, fixed a smile on her face, and strode out to greet him as Miguel scuttled around behind her to the corral. *Showtime.*

He turned out to be the kind of customer she liked best. Apologized nicely, but not too much, about arriving a day ahead of schedule— business reasons; didn't specify; no need to— and watched attentively, making intelligent comments as she put the buckskin colt through his paces. Rain's responses to neck-reining were split second, and the pivots and short stops on his haunches impeccable. He even passed the backing test with flying colors, despite the short-circuiting of Tessa's plan to run him through it once more that very afternoon. By the time Tessa finished demonstrating Rain's cutting prowess, she knew he'd be leaving in the silver horse trailer hitched to the big Mercedes of the same color drawn up to the corral gate.

"He looked as if he were playing a game with those Herefords," Rain's buyer said in her kitchen as he made out his check. "Didn't seem like work at all— in fact, I'd swear he was getting a kick out of it."

"Not literally, I hope," Tessa said. She held her breath as he scrawled his signature. "But you're right about his enjoying it. All good cut-

ting horses do, and Rain comes from a long
line of the best."

He gave her the check. No flourishing gesture, no regretful sigh, just casually handed it
over as if he were paying for a couple of tickets
to the 4H barbecue.

Twenty thousand dollars.

"You're sure, now." *He'd better be . . . he'd sure
have a hard time prying it out of my fingers.*

"Oh, yes," he said without hesitation. "My
doctor told me I had to find something to take
my mind off work. My wife figured he had
something like stamp collecting or model building in mind, but we agreed I'm not a sitting-
around kind of guy." He got up from the table
they shook hands. "You might say that for me
Rain is . . . well, right as rain."

Tessa laughed. "Call me if you have any problems. I don't think you will, though. For all his
coltish energy, Rain has the temperament of a
seasoned campaigner." She accompanied him
back to the corral. Miguel had already loaded
the colt into the van. She tugged his black tail
he turned his head and whickered. "Be a good
boy," she said.

Rain's new owner touched his hat brim to her
then shook hands with Miguel, who swallowed
hard as his senses registered the amount of the
greenback left in his palm.

As he tucked it into his pocket, Tessa
glimpsed the three numerals. One hundred dollars. Added to the bonus she had already de

cided to give him, he'd finally have enough for that big screen TV he'd been saving for.

Miguel straightened, his natural dignity restored. *"Gracias, señor,"* he murmured.

Standing side by side, they watched the van leave, dutifully waving as the Mercedes turned out onto the county road, silently tracking its diminishing silvery gleam until only a plume of dust could be seen.

"I'm gonna miss that colt," Tessa said.

"There's the bay," Miguel reminded her. "He could be as good."

"He could be even better," Tessa said. "Raw as fresh-caught fish, though, and he sure has a mind of his own."

"But a brave heart," Miguel reminded her.

"Like his sire," Tessa agreed, brightening. "And then there's the palomino mare, but she doesn't have the fire for cutting work."

"Real steady though, and very pretty. She will make a good pleasure horse for a child or lady."

"Trail horses suitable for children and ladies don't bring in the bucks, Miguel. You're right about her looks, though. She's pretty enough to have her picture on a calendar . . . but not as pretty as the girls on yours, I bet."

Miguel's lips tightened. As she well knew, he favored pious representations of brunette Madonnas and plump dark-eyed infants, both equipped with extravagantly gold-rayed halos.

"I was teasing, Miguel." She placed her hand

on his bony shoulder. "I only tease people I like."

She felt his muscles tense; then, after mulling over what she said, he nodded. His mouth bent in a shy smile. "I like you pretty good too . . . we make a nice team, *si?*"

"The best."

The sun had begun inching down towards the western horizon by the time Tessa turned up the road into the Bradburn spread. The foil-wrapped pound cake, still warm from the oven, jounced on the seat beside her; the check for Rain crackled in her pocket. She pressed her hand against it. Even the cake had turned out right, she silently exulted. Well, maybe not *right,* but a whole lot better than usual.

She peered through the screen door into the gloom. "Jed?" she called. "Jed, you in there?"

"Hold your damn horses!' Coming fast as I can."

Walt Bradburn's high cranky voice was accompanied by the hiss of his wheelchair's tires as he rolled in from the living room to peer out at her. "Tessa? Garland? Maybe if Jed'd clean this fool screen I could see better."

The screen was cleaner than most—cleaner than hers anyway—but Tessa knew he'd rather blame Jed than his failing faculties.

"Got it right the first time, Pop!"

"Well come on in!" he said, rolling back

enough to allow her to enter. "No need to stand on ceremony." She crossed in front of him into the kitchen, the old man following so close behind her she dared not slow her pace for fear of being bowled over. "I was beginning to think you'd forgotten the way, young lady."

Oh boy. Here we go. "I was getting a colt ready for sale, Pop. Can't train a good cutting horse overnight, you know."

"Never thought the day'd come when I'd take second place to a horse." He sniffed the air and wheeled closer. "I smell something sweet . . . what you got in there?"

Hoping to distract him from his complaints, Tessa had unwrapped the loaf pan. "I remembered how much you liked my mom's pound cake, so I thought I'd bring you one," she said, flourishing a scalloped-edged knife above it. "I put chocolate chips and extra raisins in this batch, especially for you."

He all but snatched from her hand the slice she offered him. "Wouldn't mind a glass of milk to wash it down," he mumbled as she hastily spread a dishtowel across his lap to catch the crumbs.

"Another piece?" she asked a few minutes later.

"Don't mind if I do." He thrust his glass out for a refill. "I sure do like cake that's got a little body to it. Most of the stuff Jed brings me just falls apart the minute you look at it, but this," he said, grabbing it up in his fingers, "this is real springy."

Springy?

Tessa, who had begun to think she'd finally made it in the baked goods department, had to laugh. What was it her father used to say when she got a little too big for her britches? *Remember, honey, pride goeth before a fall.*

Hearing Tessa's chuckle, the old man beamed a crumb-rimmed smile up at her. She leaned back against the table, crossed her arms, and sighed. As a child, uncertain if "fall" referred to a physical tumble or the season of the year, its connection with pride escaped her. Over the years, however, her many falls from grace had provided ample clarification. She sure didn't need any more courtesy of Walter Bradburn.

Tessa peered out the kitchen window, hoping to see Jed's battered pickup rattling up the drive. But the rutted road was empty, and the only sound she heard was Pop slurping his milk. She sighed and drew one finger down the dusty pane. *I may owe you an apology, old friend, but unless you get home pretty damn quick, the only thing you'll get from me is a view of my tail pipe leaving.*

Thirteen

Put on notice by the sight of Tessa's pickup parked in the turn-around, Jed entered the old house with mixed emotions. Hearing voices in the kitchen, he approached warily, holding the bag of groceries bought at the Cottonwood Mercantile in front of him like a shield. He pulled a white waxed bakery sack from under his arm and handed it to his father. "The brownies may be a little dented. Sorry."

Walt Bradburn peered into it. "Squashed is more like it." He looked up, frowning. "Took you long enough."

"I had other things to do, Pop. I told you that. Afternoon, Tessa," he said as he began unloading the groceries onto the table between them. "What brings you here?"

"I stopped in at Lloyd and Pauline's this morning. Jack and Patty were there, too— an added bonus, you might say— and, well, a cup of coffee and a chat with my wonderful in-laws was enough to remind me what a nice person you are."

Knowing that was as near an apology he was

going to get, Jed allowed a smile to relax the stiff set of his mouth. "That must have been some chat."

"Let's just say that by comparison, that little, um, exchange we had up at the cabin Saturday was positively lovey-dovey."

Jed considered this. "You want to tell me about it?" he asked quietly.

Tessa slid her eyes toward his father. "Not just now . . . maybe later?"

"Maybe later what?" the old man demanded. "No one tells me anything anymore."

"I asked Tessa if she'd like to see the Beefalo bull we bought."

"*We* bought? Hell, that was your idea, and a damn fool one if you ask me. Ain't natural mixing animals up like that. He's turning my spread into a goddamn ark, Tessa. Who does he think he is, Noah?"

"Have a brownie, Pop," Jed suggested.

"Thanks to Tessa here, don't need 'em now," his father said smugly. "She brung me some pound cake she made. Best I ever ate."

"Tessa made it?" Jed's eyebrows shot up. "Is this it?" he asked, reaching towards the demolished loaf.

"He says it's springy," Tessa warned.

"Oh." Jed's hand hesitated, then fell to his side. "Well, maybe later."

Maybe never, she mouthed.

"I wouldn't say no to another piece," Walt said, obviously fearing from their conversation that the cake might soon be snatched away from him.

"It's going on half-past four, Pop," Jed said. "Don't you think you ought to save room for supper? I've got some fresh lettuce and a couple of nice ripe tomatoes— "

"Rabbit food! That cake suits me fine for supper, and for lunch and breakfast, too."

"You know what Dr. Strunk said about eating too much sugar," Jed reminded him.

"Mind your own business, Jed. That goes for Doc Strunk, too. Tessa?" He thrust his plate toward her like a demanding child.

"It's for your own good, you know," Jed persisted doggedly.

"No, it ain't," the old man snapped. "It's for *your* good. He doesn't want the bother of tending me when I'm feeling poorly," he told Tessa, "but he'll be getting his reward soon enough. Not in heaven neither . . . he's seen to that."

Tessa looked at Jed, who shrugged in answer to the question in her eyes. She breathed a resigned sigh and picked up the knife.

"Not one of those stingy little slices, honey. I want something— "

"You can sink your teeth into. Okay," she said, plopping a hefty slab on his plate, "this should hold you for a while." She crossed to the refrigerator for the milk carton and refilled his glass a third time, hoping to provide him with at least a token amount of nutrition.

Ten minutes later, after promising to return

at six with his daily shot of whiskey, Jed wheeled his father to his room for a brief rest.

"Is he okay, Jed?" Tessa asked on his return to the kitchen.

"As okay as he ever is. His degree of complaint is directly related to how tired he is, and since I wasn't here to insist on it, he didn't have his regular two-hour after-lunch nap today. He'll probably spend the evening fussing about heartburn."

Guilt made Tessa drop her eyes. "I never should have given in to him. A goat would have trouble digesting that stupid cake."

"If you hadn't, he'd've fussed about *that*. This isn't a game you can win, Tessa. God knows I've tried often enough."

"At least Nell's brownies wouldn't give him indigestion, not to mention an overload of cholesterol. There are nine eggs in that pound cake, Jed!"

Her earnestness tickled him. "Springy, huh?"

"I never could bake to save my life."

He smiled. "Can't fault your intention, though."

Tessa heaved a vast sigh. "Well, we all know where good intentions lead." She sat down in one of the straight-back wooden kitchen chairs, tipped it precariously back, and folded her arms across her breasts. A crackling sound, issuing from her pocket, brought her upright. "I forgot! How on *earth* could I have forgotten something like that?"

Jed waited patiently as she fished in her pocket, extracted a folded rectangle of paper, and held it up to his eyes. "There! What do you say to that?"

"Maybe, if you held it steady— " he squinted— "and a little farther away . . ." He reached out and circled her slender tan wrist with his fingers. "Twenty thousand dollars? Jesus, Tessa, for what?"

"For Rain. You know, the buckskin colt I was training for that fellow up in Montrose?"

"Oh, yeah," Jed murmured, inspecting the signature. "Never heard of him. I could have sworn I knew all the ranchers up there."

"He isn't one— not an honest-to-goodness, fourteen-hours-a-day rancher, anyway."

"Sixteen hours," Jed said.

"Okay, sixteen. I gather he's one of those fast-lane type entrepreneurs. Nice guy though . . . not the type to blow his own horn. He said he bought Rain to help him relax. Doctor's orders."

Jed's eyebrows soared. "I know prescription medicine has gotten expensive, but that's ridiculous. Take two rides and call me in the morning?"

Tessa laughed and tucked the check back in her pocket. Seeing a corner of it peeking out, Jed advised her to button it in. "And for God's sake, remember to take it out before you throw that shirt into your Maytag. In fact, if I were you, I wouldn't waste time with me when you could be depositing it."

She smiled into his dark eyes. "Time with you is never wasted, my friend." She pushed back the chair and got to her feet. "Now," she continued briskly, "you going to show me that bull Pop's so sore about?"

Jed and Tessa stood side by side at the bull pen's stout fence, their forearms resting on the top rail, elbows touching.

"Doesn't look much like a buffalo," Tessa mused, "and he's a lot furrier than any beef cattle I ever saw. What made you decide to get your own bull? Isn't that kind of a pricey way to go about it?"

"Lacking twenty-thousand-dollar checks to deposit, sure, but the banks have always been good to me. Credit on my signature, that sort of thing. The breed's still in the experimental stage, and I have some notions of my own about the best way to go. This fellow's got a lot of the traits I need to build on."

"Hey, you *are* playing at Noah, aren't you?"

Jed turned his head to grin at her. "Noah, or maybe God. I'm not sure which. The thing is, Tessa, Beefalos are fantastic foragers. One of the problems with most of our modern breeds is that they want easy living, and we've just about run out of easy grazing land in these parts. That's why Lloyd's so sore about my getting the lease for the Shelby spread."

Tessa rested her cheek on her arm and gazed up at him. "I've been meaning to ask you about that . . . what do you think of her?"

"Marion Shelby? Interesting woman. Older than you'd expect."

"That's what Jeannie said. Older'n me even."

"Good God!" Jed clapped a hand to his forehead. "I didn't think that was possible."

Tessa swatted him. "Cut that out. All I meant was . . . well, it kind of throws a different light on Scott. Makes me wonder if he's the predator Garland seems to think he is."

"He is."

"C'mon, Jed, how can you sound so certain? You don't know him that well."

"Well enough."

"So how do you explain him marrying this old broad?"

"For one thing, she's not a broad. And there's something about her . . ."

"Money, maybe? Of course that would make him a predator of a different sort," Tessa admitted.

"There's more to it than that . . . more to her, too."

"You sound almost . . . interested."

Jed looked at her, startled. "Me? In Marion Shelby?"

"Yes, you. And I bet if you played your cards right, good-looking guy like you, upstanding, hard-working . . . a woman couldn't ask for anything more."

You did, he thought.

"An easy-keeper with no bad habits," Tessa elaborated. "Why, she'd have you coming to heel in no time."

"For God's sake, Tessa. You make me sound like a French poodle."

"Oh, no," Tessa protested. "With those sad brown eyes of yours, you're more the golden retriever type."

"For God's sake," he repeated in a mutter. "Speaking of cards," he countered, "what game are *you* playing these days? Unless you've got strip poker in mind, I sure wouldn't think you'd want Shelby to do the dealing."

Tessa laughed, as he expected, but she avoided his eyes. "Time was, you'd be right, but like I said, he's not quite what he used to be . . . not what I remember, anyway. So, what game am I playing, you ask? Let's just say I'm still shuffling the deck."

It wasn't really an answer, Jed realized. Maybe she didn't have one yet. He looked at her strong profile etched against the sky. She never did like dancing to the tune others settled for, he thought morosely, and nothing he could think to say would change that.

The bull, who had been eyeing them warily, ambled closer to the fence. He extended his thick shaggy neck to snuffle in their scent with his moist nostrils. Tessa reached over to scratch the broad flat spot just above them.

"Put this fellow in a plaid flannel shirt," she mused, "and you'd have a Lloyd Wagner look-alike."

Jed chuckled. "I'm not sure whether that's an insult to Lloyd or the bull. Speaking of Lloyd, what made you brave that den of bears this particular morning?"

"Bulls, bears, what's next?"

"Clowns maybe?"

Tessa's blue eyes sparkled. "Shame on you! Although I must admit Pauline did act sort of like a ringmaster. Every time things got a little testy, she'd rush in with her sticky buns."

"As a peacemaker, I'd say sticky buns beat a Colt or a whip hands down. Aside from gummy fingers, what was the problem?"

"The usual one where the Wagners are concerned: m-o-n-e-y. Their lack of it, and their schemes to make some. The latest of which involves getting their greedy hands on the land Barry left the twins. After serious reconsideration, Lloyd has decided Barry was right. Scott Shelby *did* sire them. And— surprise, surprise!— Jack agrees with him. Patty always did think so, of course. Pauline is the only holdout, but she's not about to say so where Lloyd can hear her."

"Why now, two years after Barry's death?"

"Well, call it a delayed time bomb. For some time now, Lloyd's been trying to find a way around our refusal to sell that land to him. If it had just been me standing in his way, he might have bided his time until the twins reached their majority, but no, he had to go wheedling and prodding at Garland and Gav— you know how Lloyd is, about as tactful and subtle as a bull elk in rut— and they set him down hard. He didn't like that much.

"Then last week, he happened to pass Scott Shelby down in Cottonwood. Passed real close, he said. Close enough to see his eyes square on. 'What do they call that color again?' he asked me."

"Jesus," Jed said. "I thought that foolishness had been laid to rest with Barry. I guess he wasn't the only paranoid member of his family."

"This has nothing to do with paranoia, Jed. Lloyd's just using it to pry me loose from my responsibilities as the twins' guardian. He knows damn well a juicy story like that'd spread like mustard on a hot dog, and if people buy it—"

"Your friends won't."

"It's not my friends I'm worried about. At this point, with the twins grown and all, it doesn't much matter if they do or not, but suppose Judge Colby does?"

Jed regarded her through narrowed eyes. "That bastard really got to you, didn't he? You just say the word and—"

"I don't need you to fight my battles for me, Jed," she said crisply. "Look," she added in a softer tone, "it's not that I don't appreciate your volunteering to be my knight in denim armor, but if push comes to shove, what I'll need more is your help in finding an expert to back up what you told me about genetics and eye color . . . you know, how it's not as simple a matter as most of us think? And there's that portrait you told me about, the one Barry's parents took with them down to Texas."

"The one of his hazel-eyed great-grandmother?" Tessa nodded. "You think it could really come to that?"

She shrugged. "Maybe not. Lloyd looked a little sick when I mentioned lawyer's fees and court costs. I'd be very surprised if there's much more coming in from the Wagner ranch than it takes to meet loan payments and put food on the table. Old man Wagner knew more about cattle on his off-days than those boys of his ever did all put together."

But Lloyd had Terry Ballou as a partner, Jed recalled, and shrewd developers like him equated view property with money in the bank. Considering how spectacular the land the twins inherited was in that regard, Ballou would probably be eager to supply whatever funds might be needed to snare it. "I'll do whatever I can, Tessa."

She laid her hand on his. "I know that, and I thank you for it. God knows you have enough troubles of your own."

"Nothing new about mine."

"You think so? Remember me saying I was

still shuffling my cards? Seems to me you've already thrown in your hand."

He frowned. "I'm not good at riddles, Tessa."

"Well, look at your situation here. You're the one who built this spread into a whole lot more than just another break-even operation."

"Pop had enough foresight to buy up whatever high basin land your dad didn't."

"Foresight, hell! He bought it because he didn't want my father to have it all."

"C'mon, Tessa, that's not the whole story. He was a different man before his accident. Hard, yes, even mean sometimes." *A lot of the time.* "But I don't remember him scheming and complaining the way he does now."

"Maybe so," she conceded, "but my point is, *you're* the one who put it to profitable use, and that makes the hat-in-hand routine he expects of you all the more demeaning. When are you going to sit that old man down and tell him what's what?"

Jed bit back the angry retort that sprang first to his lips. *She means well,* he told himself. "As a matter of fact, I already have."

"You *what?*" Tessa, turned to face him, her blue eyes wide.

"It happened after I came down from your cabin Sunday morning. I wasn't in the best of moods, and something he said or did—I don't recall just what, but I doubt it was anything worse than usual—made something crack inside me."

"The last straw breaking, maybe?"

"Could be," Jed acknowledged with a wry smile. "Anyway, one thing led to another— you know how that sort of thing goes— and finally I told him that unless he agreed in writing to make me his sole heir, I was going to clear out."

He took off his hat and blew the dust off the brim. "Well, you can imagine how he took *that.* Called me an ungrateful bastard— I couldn't deny the latter description; I probably am— and went on from there, ending with accusing me of blackmail. I swear, Tessa, there was enough steam in him to drive a locomotive." He put his hat back on and tapped it into place. "I told him, considering the hints he'd taken to dropping, I felt I had to protect myself."

"What hints, Jed?"

"For it to make sense, I have to go back a bit. You see, the feebler he gets, the craftier he becomes, and it pleases him to keep me off balance. A few months back, about the time I started talking about buying this bull, he asked me to bring his family albums down from the attic. They were covered with dust, pages scalloped by mice— he hadn't looked at them, hadn't even mentioned them, for as long as I can remember."

Jed paused. "When I was a kid, I used to sneak up there, look at those cracked and faded photos, and pretend those strangers were my family. He'd never bothered to write any captions, so I made up names for them— borrowed them from characters in books. For the children, I chose everyday names, the kind kids I might actually know would have. Tom and Becky and Nancy and Frank . . ." He smiled, remembering. "Some of the grownups were pretty fancy, though. Guinevere and Ivanhoe, for example.

"What, no Lancelot?"

"Nope. Seemed too sissy."

"I never even *heard* of Ivanhoe."

"It's the title of a novel by Sir Walter Scott— a romance, really. My mother read her copy over and over. She didn't have many books, but kids who like to read— not that I was allowed much time for it— aren't choosy. Actually, it was pretty exciting. All about castles and tournaments, knights and fair ladies."

"Ick."

"Horses, too, Tessa." They grinned at each other. "As I was saying, all of a sudden Pop put real names to the people in those faded old photographs. Aunt this and Uncle that, and he starts pointing out little boys in short pants who were his cousins, and girls with pigtails who were the sisters he bought out years ago and hasn't seen since.

"He doesn't know them, Tessa, and God knows he never cared about any of them— why, they don't even exchange Christmas cards! But now he wonders if they have kids. Kids that would be about my age now. Blood kin." He hesitated. "He's never made a will, Tessa. Do

you realize what could happen if he died intes-
tate? That's the whole point of what he was doing, of course, making damn sure that *I* did."

"Oh Jed," Tessa breathed. "How could he do
that to you?"

"He figures the uncertainty will keep me tied
to him. Never occurred to him it might do the
opposite. I told him the head wrangler could
manage the spread just fine without me and
that he could hire a woman to come and look
after him. You should have seen the expression
on his face when I said *that!*" Remembering,
Jed shook his head. "So, working on the prin-
ciple of striking while the iron's hot, I called
his lawyer— our lawyer, actually— day before yesterday."

"Owen MacHarg?" Tessa asked. Jed nodded.
"Good man, Owen. Only charges an arm."

"He's known about our situation for years,"
Jed said, "so when I told him what was up, he
said 'Godalmighty, pigs can fly after all!' He
drove up from Ouray late that same afternoon.
I don't know how he got the papers ready so
fast, but he said it was mostly boiler-plate stuff
and that he and his wife always welcomed an
excuse to ride up into our valley at that time
of day. Like you said, a good man.

"His wife and his secretary witnessed Pop's
signing of the will, and afterwards, when I
walked them out to the car, Owen said he
hoped Pop wouldn't have a change of heart.
Then he winked. I'm pretty sure that was his

way of telling me he'd let me know if that should happen."

"So the bluff worked," Tessa said. "I never would have thought you— "

"It wasn't a bluff, Tessa."

"My God, Jed!" she cried, searching his somber eyes. "What would you have done? Everything you've worked so hard for all your life is here!"

He tapped his head. "I can always take what's up here with me. I don't believe I'd have much trouble finding myself a good berth. It wouldn't be like having my own place, but at least I'd feel like a man again."

Tessa reached a hand out towards him. "In my eyes you've never been less than one . . . more than most, in fact."

As he looked into her blue eyes, soft with concern and affection, his earlier hurt and resentment melted away. His arms ached to hold her. "Thanks, Tessa," he said, taking her hand. "It's good to hear you say that."

"Surely you never doubted it!"

He gave her a crooked half-smile. He thought of the choice she'd made thirty years ago. "I'm a man beset by doubts," he said lightly.

" 'Beset by doubts,' " Tessa repeated musingly. "That's the story of my life these last couple of years. God, to be eighteen again! I thought I knew everything. . . . I knew I could do anything. The only thing I know now for sure is that I've got a yen for one of those

brownies you brought home. I can even over-
look the fact that Nell made 'em.''

Jed grinned, pushed himself off the fence,
and turned to stroll alongside her back to the
house. "She may have a tongue like an ice pick,
Tessa, but she sure has a light touch when it
comes to baked goods."

"Not like some, huh? That's right, laugh!
You've never been on the receiving end of
Nell's nasty little jabs. She practically purrs
when she looks at you."

"I require more than a talent for brownie-
making in a woman, Tessa. Which reminds me,
I'm thinking of taking Pop to the 4H barbecue
this Saturday. Why don't you come with us?
Once he gets jawing with the other old codgers,
we can join Jeannie and Art and the rest of the
crowd."

"Whoop-te-doo. Pop and his cronies will complain about our generation, ours will moan and
wring their hands over the younger one, and
the kids themselves will be too hyped on hor-
mones to do anything but breathe hard on each
other."

"C'mon, Tessa! I don't recall you ever passing
up the barbecue, even those years when Barry
was too pissed to get there under his own
steam."

"Sorry, but Saturday's the night of Scott
Shelby's housewarming up in Telluride— look,
forget what I said. It would have been fun."

"Oh sure. Put them on a scale and I can see how they'd weigh out real even."

Tessa sighed. "Give me a break, Jed. Scott asked Garland and me two weeks ago . . . this is the first time you've so much as mentioned the barbecue."

Jed didn't think he had needed to. Everyone went; it was a Cottonwood tradition. His gaze fell to his toes. They scuffed along in silence.

"I know!" Tessa said, grabbing his arm. "Why don't you ask Marion Shelby?"

Jed stared at her. "Somehow I can't see her licking barbecue sauce off her fingers."

"From what you and Jeannie say, she sounds equal to just about any occasion. Besides, if she's planning to stick around, run her ranch like an honest-to-God business, folks'll be interested meeting her."

"Well, you're right about that. I got the feeling she doesn't know many people here aside from those she has business dealings with." He chuckled. "She's not exactly the Sunday-go-to-meeting, shake-hands-with-the-preacher type. Yeah, I might just do that. All she can do is say no."

"But if she says yes," Tessa said, looking up at him through her lashes, "and if you hit if off," she added, all big blue eyes and tremulous smiles, "you'll still keep my name on your list, won't you?"

Damn you, Tessa.

Jed, determined not to give her the satisfaction of seeing him teetering off balance, took his time answering. "Probably," he drawled. "Old habits die hard, you know." He relished her startled expression. "But I can't promise which list it'll be—the short or the long."

She didn't care for that. "Then I'll just take the rest of my cake home with me . . . Pop won't like you for that!"

"I'll tell him it was your idea."

"He won't believe you."

"Oh? How come?"

"Because I'm on *his* short list. Always have been."

Tessa stuck out her tongue at him and darted away up the path, her litheness giving a lie to her age. She tap-danced up the steps and across the porch, arms extended, a watch-me grin on her face. Showing off, springy as her failed pound cake.

Damn you, Tessa.

But this time he smiled.

Fourteen

Thursday night, pleading fatigue, Garland called it a day before she had a chance to get caught up in the TV movie scheduled for nine o'clock. Tessa followed her upstairs to ask her to look at the outfit she planned to wear to Scott's housewarming.

"Now, Mom?" she said, pausing before her bedroom door. "I'm really beat. Today was frantic and tomorrow promises to be more of the same. The Chamber's sound system broke down, and I spent the entire day trying to find a replacement. Besides, I already know what you've got in mind— I can't imagine that seeing the sum of the parts will do anything more than confirm your original concept."

"*Concept?* Wow. No wonder I'm nervous. And here I thought I was just putting a nice shirt together with pants and boots."

"Sounds pretty foolproof to me."

"The thing is, I feel ready to celebrate, and looking good is part of it."

"Considering the price you got for the buckskin colt, you're due a celebration," Garland said. "Twenty thousand. That really smokes me out."

"He's worth every penny," Tessa maintained stoutly. "The bay colt I started working with this week is going to be a winner, too. Even Miguel says so, and you know how cautious he is."

Garland laughed. "I never knew a person less willing to count unhatched chickens."

"Yeah," Tessa agreed, "and after the hatching, he always looks twice before admitting that's what they are." They grinned at each other companionably. "How about tomorrow evening? I just want you to tell me that what I have chosen really does go together. I don't want to commit some terrible sartorial mistake, not in that crowd anyway."

"I think the word *sartorial* applies to men's tailoring, Mom."

"So? The pants and boots qualify; the only thing that doesn't is the silk satin shirt, but considering what some men are wearing these days, I guess that could, too. UPS delivered it this morning. Pure luxury. Wait'll you see it!"

"I'm afraid tomorrow's out, too. I won't be home until late. Why don't you give Jeannie a call? She has a good eye."

"How late is late?"

"I don't know. It depends."

"On what?"

Garland twiddled the knob on her bedroom door as if reluctant to pursue the subject.

"Garland?"

"If you must know, Scott wants me to take him on a wildflower hunt."

"You must be kidding," Tessa said. "Sounds like something you do with city kids to bring them in touch with the environment. Hands-on, they call it. In my day it was nature study."

"This new line of his, Wildings?" Tessa nodded. "It's one thing to have an idea— realizing it is a lot more complicated."

"He's got designers and an office staff for that, Garland."

"I know that, but he wants to choose the flowers himself . . . the shapes, textures, range of colors. Even though the final version of them will be, like, fantasies, he wants them grounded in reality."

"Are you planning to look for them with flashlights?"

"What? Oh, you mean the late part. He's taking me to dinner at Campagna afterwards."

"Sounds Italian. I wouldn't have figured Scott as the pizza type."

"It's Tuscan Italian, Mom. Not a pizza in sight, or if there is, I can assure you it would be topped with something more interesting than pepperoni."

"You used to like pepperoni."

"I still do." A frown creased Garland's smooth brow. "What's with you, Mom? You're the one who pushed this association."

"Because of the doors it could open for you!

I wasn't thinking in terms of dates . . . especially dates having anything to do with hands on," she added in a mutter.

"Men like Scott Shelby don't have *dates*, Mom. Relationships and affairs, yes . . . but dates?"

Her knowing smile put Tessa's back up. She knew she was no longer savvy about Scott's world, but there was no need for Garland to act so damn superior.

". . . Tomorrow is strictly business," her daughter was saying. "After dinner, we'll go back to my office and draw up a list of the flowers he's chosen and mark the location of the plants on a topo map for his photographer."

"Seems to me it'd be a whole lot easier— not to mention cheaper— to buy one of those big fancy wildflower picture books," Tessa grumbled. "I trust he's paying you for your time?"

"Of course he is."

"So, how late is late?"

"I don't *know*," Garland snapped. She walked into her room and started undressing, effectively ending the conversation.

Tessa stood in the doorway. Her gaze drifted beyond her daughter's slim figure, half-hidden now in the deep closet, to the dimness beyond. The room looked much as it always had, except that the posters Garland had tacked up in the late eighties— one of a rock group, U2; the other of Prince, rouged and eyeshadowed— had been replaced by a single larger one. The highlighted hawkish profile of the late Leonard

Bernstein, gray hair flying, his arms and baton waving, now dominated the wall over her bed. *That's what college does for a girl,* Tessa thought.

Blue satin award ribbons— the cheap dye long since bleached to a pale streaky tint by the sunlight that flooded the room by day— still hung in a long neat row beneath a bookshelf tightly packed with titles ranging from *The Black Stallion* to *Wuthering Heights,* which at fifteen Garland had pronounced the most romantic story in the whole wide world. Tessa smiled wryly. Despite Garland's breathless description, Heathcliff had sounded to her like a real loser. *Sort of like Barry on a grand scale.*

A bright scarf lay across the faded quilt on Garland's bed. The old patchwork, made from scraps of clothing surviving from her Great-grandmother Hatton's family trek by wagon from the Missouri River to their Nebraska homestead, had been too narrow for the water-bed Barry surprised Tessa with five years into their marriage. Eight years later, to mark the occasion of the twins' graduation from cribs in a shared nursery to real beds in rooms of their own, she presented the quilt, along with its story, to Garland. It became her most treasured possession. Determined to arrest its fraying, she insisted on doing the required repairs herself, her chubby fingers plying the needle more dexterously as she grew. Looking at it now, Tessa knew that nothing, not even a loving heart, could stay its increasing fragility.

The passing years had taken a toll of more than horse show ribbons and treasured quilts. Garland was no longer the university-bound teenager who, when her last duffle had been loaded into the pickup and Gavin had shamed her into leaving her favorite stuffed horse behind, had suddenly panicked and run sobbing back into the house.

That first semester, Tessa had agonized over the pleading letters and teary phone calls. But for once Barry had been right, even though she suspected his reason for wanting Garland to stick it out had more to do with his relief at having the twins out from underfoot than concern for her character development. Be that as it may, Garland began her second term stoically— departing after the Christmas vacation with hardly more than a martyred sigh— and by the end of the summer, restless and disenchanted by the local teen notions of entertainment, admitted she was looking forward to returning as a sophomore.

Last summer, Tessa recalled, she left for Boulder and her junior year two weeks early. To settle in, she said. *Don't make such a big deal out of it, Mom.* But Tessa had sensed the beginning of the process of making a life of her own as Gavin already had. Consciously or not, Garland, too, was moving on.

As if on cue, she emerged from the closet wearing a blood red oversized T-shirt that doubled as a nightie. The big black blocky letters marching across Garland's chest urged Tessa to Remember Tiananmen Square. It didn't say why. Garland picked up the scarf splashed across the quilt and carefully folded it. Tessa couldn't remember seeing it before. It looked expensive.

Had someone given it to her? Was she moving on with someone else?

"It's not big enough for two," Tessa murmured, fingering a corner of the patchwork.

Garland turned. "Did you say something, Mom?" Her voice was cool.

"Nothing important, darling. I was just thinking of the tribulation that old quilt has witnessed."

Garland draped the scarf over her sunflower-decorated rocker— Tessa recalled them painting them together. *The sloppy ones are mine*— and folded down the quilt. "Happiness, too, Mom," she rebuked gently.

"Yes. Yes, of course. And, darling? I'm sure you'll have a grand time tomorrow. Scott always did work hard at making things seem special . . . not that he ever let on he was making any particular effort."

Garland looked up from setting her Mickey Mouse alarm clock. "He makes *me* feel special," she said, smiling, "yet he doesn't make demands. Boy, I like that in a man." She yawned. " 'Night, Mom."

Tessa hesitated. "I guess I won't see you until Saturday morning then."

"You'll see me at breakfast tomorrow," Garland said patiently, "unless you're planning to sleep in."

"Sleep *in?*" Tessa had never "slept in" in her entire life. "What I meant was, I won't wait up for you tomorrow night."

"Glad to hear it, but can't this wait until morning?"

Tessa's hands came up. "Absolutely. I just thought I should tell you that, because sometimes I forget you're not a kid anymore. Maybe not quite a grown woman either, but— "

"Mom, *please?*"

"Okay. Enough said. Sweet dreams, darling."

The next morning, after Garland left, Tessa phoned Jeannie.

"Hey, Tessa!" Art Disbrow's hearty voice greeted her. "You calling to say you've decided to run off with me?"

"You've asked me that every time I've called for the last twenty-five years. Suppose I said yes?"

"Then I'd let you be the one to break the news to Jeannie."

"She'd beat me up, Art."

"Yeah, I guess she would," he said smugly. His voice, as always, sounded on the verge of laughter. "Imagine, the two best-lookers in town mixing it up over a fat old geezer like me."

"You're neither fat nor a geezer. Just well-fleshed and mature."

"My, my, Miz Wagner honey, how you do go on. You want Jeannie? She's just about to leave."

"If you can catch her, I'd appreciate it."

"I've never had a problem with the catching, Tessa; getting her to cooperate's the tricky part. *Jeannie?*" he bellowed, "pick up the phone, will ya?"

"Oh shit!" Tessa heard faintly, followed a moment later by "Tessa, that you?"

"Shit yes, Jeannie."

"You weren't supposed to hear that. What can I do for you?"

"Look, if you're in a hurry—"

"No, it's okay. The cat had kittens under the kitchen table last night, and believe me, that wasn't in my game plan. Hey, you want one? They're real pretty. At least I think they are . . . actually, it's a little early to tell."

"Ask me again in six weeks." Tessa hesitated. *Do I really need Jeannie's approval?* It wasn't as if she was thinking of wearing an ostrich boa and sequined shoes . . .

"Tessa? I don't mean to sound impatient, but—"

"I know. You've got a business to run. I just called to tell you that Jed may be taking Marion Shelby to the 4H barbecue. I thought if you and Art could save a place for them at your table, introduce her around—"

"Does that mean you're not coming? Shoot, Tessa! Everybody will be there . . . last I heard there'll be enough of us to fill a couple of those long tables."

"Garland and I are going up to Scott Shelby's housewarming in Telluride. I told you about it, remember?"

"Went clean out of my mind. Well, obviously the 4H barbecue's pretty tame stuff compared to hobnobbing with the rich and famous."

"You're as bad as Jed. Talk about sour grapes."

"Not sour, Tessa, just dangling out of reach. So while you're up there hip-hopping with Shelby, Jed'll be down here square-dancing with his ex-missus?" She chuckled evilly. "Is that ironic or what!"

"I can't see me hip-hopping with anybody. In fact, I don't think anybody does it anymore. And to set the record straight, Jeannie, I suggested Jed ask her."

"Did you now?" she drawled.

"You said she was a nice person . . . Jed thinks so, too. Where's the harm?"

"Don't know as there is any, dearie. But I do know Miz Shelby's coming in tomorrow to get her hair and nails done. It's not her regular day . . . in fact she called me here at home last night to ask if I could squeeze her in. Her voice sounded real urgent. I couldn't help wondering what was so all-fired important."

Knowing Jeannie was hoping to get a rise out of her, Tessa held her tongue.

"Damn it, Tessa," Jeannie complained, "you're no fun at all! Tell you what, I'll call you Sunday morning . . . we'll compare notes. You can brag on Shelby's guest list, and I'll tell you how the date you set up worked out."

Tessa frowned, wondering if what Garland had said about Scott could apply to Jed. Relationships and affairs sounded a lot more open-ended than a simple, old-fashioned, one-time date. "Yeah," Tessa muttered, "you do that."

"From the tone of your voice, a person might think you've been sampling some of that sour grape juice yourself."

"I imagine Scott's champagne will take care of that," Tessa countered.

Jeannie's sigh whispered through the receiver. "I can't top that, Tessa, and I've run out of time to try. Have a real nice day!"

Fifteen

Tessa couldn't resist a last look in the mirror. She tightened the narrow black grosgrain bow gathering her shoulder-length hair into a neat ponytail and plucked a couple of Plume's long beige hairs from her black pants. "I swear, Garland, the way this gabardine picks up stuff you'd think it was magnetized."

"I think your eyes must have built-in magnifying lenses, the way you keep fussing about things no one else can see." Garland's long sun-streaked hair swung in a gleaming arc as she turned towards the door. "Can we go now? We'll be a good half-hour late as it is."

Tessa eyed her daughter's pale turquoise washed-silk tunic and billowy ankle-tied pants. "I don't remember seeing that outfit before. You look," she added sourly, "like a damn water nymph."

"I bought it in Boulder this spring. The minute I saw it I thought of the necklace Uncle Jed gave me." She fingered one of the turquoise-studded silver squash-blossoms. "What do you think?"

The necklace was an old and very beautiful Navajo pawn piece Jed's mother had wistfully admired when she saw it hanging, dusty and forgotten, in a Utah trading post back in the thirties. Worth a chief's ransom in today's market, at the time it was too much of a bargain for even tight-fisted Walt Bradburn to pass up. Considering the enduring gratitude it earned him, it would have been a bargain at ten times the price.

After Aggie died, Walt took it into his head to sell it. To help pay the funeral expenses, he had said, and why the hell not? "There ain't no other women in the family," he complained to Jed, "and far as I can tell, none in sight neither."

So Jed offered, tight-lipped, to pay his father the price he would have gotten from a dealer. It took five years' worth of installments, plus interest, subtracted monthly from his meager token wages. The next time anyone saw the necklace was when Jed presented it, polished to a soft luster, to Garland the day she graduated from high school.

She had, of course, protested being given such a valuable family heirloom, but Jed just smiled and slipped it over her head. "You're the only family I'm ever likely to have," Tessa recalled him saying.

"It's beautiful, Garland," she murmured. "And so are you. I just hope you won't be embarrassed to be seen with an old lady like me."

We've got your authors!

We have 4 FREE BOOKS for you
as your introduction to
KENSINGTON CHOICE
To get your FREE BOOKS, worth
up to $23.96, mail the card below.

FREE BOOK CERTIFICATE

As my introduction to your new KENSINGTON CHOICE reader's service, please send me 4 FREE historical romances (worth up to $23.96), billing me just $1 to help cover postage and handling. As a KENSINGTON CHOICE subscriber, I will then receive 4 brand-new romances to preview each month for 10 days FREE. I can return any books I decide not to keep and owe nothing. The publisher's prices for the KENSINGTON CHOICE romances range from $4.99 to $5.99, but as a subscriber I will be entitled to get them for just $4.20 per book or $16.80 for all four titles. There is no minimum number of books to buy, and I can cancel my subscription at any time. A $1.50 postage and handling charge is added to each shipment.

Name _____

Address _____ Apt. _____

City _____ State _____ Zip _____

Telephone (___) _____

Signature _____

(If under 18, parent or guardian must sign)

Subscription subject to acceptance. Terms and prices subject to change.

KC0495

We have
4
FREE
Historical
Romances
for you!

(worth up
to $23.96!)

Details inside!

"C'mon, Mom, you look great," Garland said, swatting her mother affectionately. "Especially considering your advanced age," she added, earning a swat in return.

As they drove up the gravel road winding across the valley floor, the slanting rays of the setting sun tipped the meadow grasses with gold. Mule deer trailed out of the scrubby oaks to join the grazing cattle in the cottonwood-fringed meadows. Larks soared and dipped above the creek, feasting on a cloud of gauzy-winged flies flitting just above the water rippling alongside the road.

"Must be a new hatch," Garland said. "That means there'll be a lot of well-fed trout by morning. Maybe I should string up my rod this weekend, catch us a panful."

Tessa laughed. "Remember that contest you and Gavin had one summer? Don't recall how old you were, but I doubt this valley ever saw two such determined fishermen before or since."

"We were ten, Mom. Ten-year-olds are like that—fixated, they call it now. I know I gave Gav a run for his money, but when it came to snaring nightcrawlers for bait, he won hands down."

"Maybe so, but I seem to remember that Gav always tried to set the hook too soon. Not that it mattered much. I never thought I could get tired of trout, but that summer . . ." She shook her head.

"It got so we could hardly give them away," Garland agreed, laughing. "Once, when Gav made a third delivery to Uncle Jed in the course of one week, he suggested we might consider releasing the fish."

They came to the bend crossed by a narrow plank bridge. The loose boards rumbled under the wheels. "Do you suppose any of those trout we released could still be alive?"

Tessa reflected on the possibility. "They'd be real lunkers by now."

"Yeah. Lurking in the deeper pools, surfacing like submarines to slurp in those flies— "

"I bet it'd take more'n flies to satisfy *them*," Tessa said.

Garland's fingers beat a nervous little tattoo on the steering wheel. "Gawd. Imagine if you fell in . . ."

They looked at each other, made faces, and rode on in silence through the deepening summer twilight.

They gained the highway a little after eight with, according to Garland, a good half-hour still to go.

"Strikes me as just about right," Tessa said. She pointed to a narrow gravel road leading off to the left. "Hey, didn't you say Scott's new place is just off the Last Dollar road?"

"On the other end, Mom. We take it from this side and God knows when we'll get there."

"Too bad. Prettiest road in the county."

"Can't get much prettier than this," Garland said, nodding towards the wide sweep of snow-tipped peaks, crimsoned now by the setting sun.

"No," Tessa agreed. "It can't.

The private road Garland finally turned into wound up and up through mature stands of aspen and spruce. The grade was steady and the surface smoother than the usual quick-and-dirty bulldozer job standard in less prosperous towns in the county.

"What are you peering at, Mom?"

"I'm looking for catch basins."

"*Catch basins?* Whatever for?"

"Drainage. This road is a lot better engineered than you might think at first glance, Garland. Ah! There's one!" she exclaimed, pointing. "They cost big bucks to install, and I bet Scott spent another small fortune for a top-of-the-line four-wheel-drive vehicle he won't even need to get up a road as good as this."

"Boy, nothing escapes you, does it?"

"Not when there are price tags attached."

The road emerged from the dim forest into a lush meadow commanding a spectacular view of Sunshine Mountain and Mt. Wilson. Ahead of them sprawled a log-and-stone structure punctuated with long inset rectangles of glass. Bright shafts of light beamed across a low wide terrace hung with glowing lanterns. Tessa's voice hushed. "And speaking of price tags . . ."

It was too dark to make much sense of the

design of the house, but it was big. Very big by
Cottonwood standards; too big by Tessa's. *My
God, imagine trying to keep it clean.* They parked
in a mowed clearing, and as they approached
on foot, the laughing people glimpsed through
the tall windows seemed more like midgets than
normal-sized adults.

"Wow," Tessa murmured.

"It's like never-never land, isn't it?" Garland
said. "Although I imagine most of the people
in there have long since forgotten what childhood's all about."

Tessa gave her daughter a sharp glance.
"You've been here before, have you?"

"In and out, almost as fast as that. Just to
double-check the newspaper ad copy for the festival Scott's sponsoring— Shelby Associates, that
is."

"Same thing, isn't it?"

"I guess."

"Look, I'm not passing judgment. You're a
big girl; you can learn a lot from Scott."

Garland fell silent. Tessa chose not to notice.
Besides, there was too much else to occupy her
mind. As they mounted the single wide step to
the stone terrace surrounding the house, Scott
came forward to greet them.

"Garland," he said, taking one of her hands,
"and dear Tessie." He leaned forward to lightly
kiss her cheek. "Now the party can begin."

"Nonsense, Scott," Tessa said. "It's in full
swing already."

He grinned at Tessa. "Same old down-to-earth Tessie. God, it's good seeing you again."

"I could do without the 'old' part."

"Now, Tessie," he chided, "I meant old only in the sense of familiar. You brought me good luck, you know."

"I'd say you've made plenty of your own since. I mean, look at this place!"

His shoulders lifted in a deprecating shrug. "You remember Sam Englehardt, Tessie?" She nodded. "He talked *Architectural Digest* into giving it some space in their November issue."

Garland gave him a knowing look. "Which means it will coincide with the introduction of Wildings, right?"

"Smart as she is beautiful," Scott said as he opened the door.

Tessa marched in, her long-legged stride faltering as the din of talk and laughter gusted towards her. Then, as Scott and Garland came up beside her, there was a sudden hush. She became aware of speculative eyes taking their measure. Her chin came up; her blue eyes issued a challenge. *We're every damn bit as good as you are!*

Tessa turned to bolster her daughter with an encouraging smile, but found she needn't have bothered. Scott had bent close to murmur something that brought a slow smile to Garland's lips. His long fingers rested on her shoulder; his breath stirred the gold tendrils that wisped around her ears, and when she nodded, his hand slid slowly down to take hers and bring it to his lips. Garland turned towards him, her silk tunic undulating around her slim hips, to touch her head to his shoulder. Her cheeks, Tessa noticed, were suffused with color.

Tessa felt a sudden sharp pang.

Envy?

How could that be? Garland was her daughter, for God's sake, and Scott was old enough to be her father.

But as he moved jauntily forward, Garland's hand swinging in his, he seemed ageless. He reached out to pull Tessa along with them with his other hand, then slipped it familiarly around her waist to rest in the small of her back. The breath caught in her throat as she felt the warm pressure of his fingers.

"People? May I have your attention please? Some of you already know that this gorgeous woman on my left was the inspiration for Wild Westerns, the line that launched me into fashion's big time. I know Sam Englehardt does, because he's the genius who dreamed up the ad campaign.

"Tessa Wagner and I met by accident. It all began at a rodeo in Cottonwood, that little cow town just over the mountain from here, more years ago than I care to acknowledge."

"Twenty," a gruff voice supplied. "More or less."

"Thank you so much, Sam," Scott said. "I'll

take less, if you don't mind . . . how about you, Tessie?"

"Me, too," she muttered.

"My muse agrees with me," Scott said. His hand firmly propelled her forward. "Tell them how it was, Tessie."

She stared at the sea of faces. Amused faces; doubting faces; young faces. My God, but they were young. Why would they care how it was back then? Most of them would have been in grade school twenty years ago. What the hell did Scott expect her to say?"

"Was that meeting really accidental, Tessa?" a throaty female voice inquired.

The woman's obvious skepticism rankled. "Sure was. I had other things on my mind that day, and even if I'd wanted to strike up an acquaintance, I wouldn't have known what to say. The guys I was used to . . . well, they weren't much like Scott." She turned back to face him. "Come to think of it, you never did say why you were there that day."

"I suppose I could claim it was fated," he said, "but the truth is I'd never been to a rodeo. Oh, I'd seen them in movies and on the tube— who hasn't? But actually being there, hearing the shouts and the bellowing, seeing the broncs twisting and plunging and the dust swirling up in choking clouds . . ."

Scott's left hand dropped away from Garland's and spiraled into the air. "It was all very strong, very elemental stuff. Very Hemingway.

Then at intermission time, the ring was cleared, some battered barrels were brought in, and there was a garbled announcement over the loudspeaker about an exhibition. Some circusy sort of trick riding, I assumed. I had already started down the rickety grandstand when this girl of the golden West gallops in, riding hell-for-leather.

"One look at that blazing smile, that mane of gold hair bannering in the breeze as she leaned her horse around those barrels, defying gravity and loving every minute of it— " He cast his eyes upward. "My God, who wouldn't be inspired? So I waited for her by the exit gate. The rest, as they say, is history."

"Not quite," Tessa drawled. "For one thing, my horse damn near bit his fingers off." She grinned at the shout of laughter her words provoked. "That little horse could pivot on a button, but he had a mean streak. Never did take kindly to strangers."

"Neither did Tessa's husband," Scott confided in a stage whisper.

"What other part of your anatomy did *he* threaten, Scott?" It was the same throaty voice, which Tessa identified as belonging to an attractive thirtyish brunette snuggled against a large jowly red-faced man in his fifties.

"I'm happy to say I survived intact . . . as you, dear girl, have very good reason to know."

Her companion grunted and started forward, but was quickly discouraged by nearby guests.

Ignoring him, Scott turned his attention to Garland. "I had also hoped to introduce to you the talented young singer who will be representing my new line, Wildings, inspired by the colors and textures of Colorado wildflowers. Kayla Farrell will be the featured artist in the upcoming Bluegrass Festival Shelby Associates is sponsoring, but she was unable to join us tonight due to previous concert commitments. However, my lovely assistant, Garland Wagner, will be happy to answer any questions you may have . . . probably better than I, because she is more intimately involved with the day-to-day details." Smiling, he swung her to face him. "In fact, I'm hoping I can persuade her to make our successful summer relationship a permanent one."

Relationship? Tessa frowned. A day spent scouting for wildflowers wasn't her idea of a relationship. *What the hell was going on here?*

"They keep getting younger and younger, don't they?" she heard someone murmur near her. Tessa turned angrily but was unable to determine the source of the insinuating comment.

". . . While I've been chattering away here," Scott was saying, "I see the tables have been transformed into veritable groaning boards, courtesy of Philippe Boucher, with whose culinary expertise I'm sure most of you are familiar. Tables have been set up on the terrace, where braziers have been lit to provide warmth on this cool night, and servers will soon be passing among you with a selection of wines. The house is open for your inspection—"

"Including the closets, Scott?" a snide voice inquired.

"Closets, too. If you're expecting skeletons, I fear you'll be disappointed," he added in a tone whose lightness Tessa suspected of being somewhat forced. "As you know, this isn't a new house. In fact, some of you may already be familiar with it, but I've done things, added things, you might find interesting. As I said, please feel free to roam, and thank you for coming!"

Tessa moved forward, hoping to snare Garland, but Scott had already taken her with him into the crowd.

Unused to neglect, Tessa regarded them sullenly as they bent smilingly to answer questions with a practiced ease that in her daughter's case Tessa found astonishing. "My God," she muttered, "you'd think they were royalty."

She felt suddenly queasy; the palms of her clenched hands became moist with sweat. She hadn't felt this way since her teens, before she had established herself as a winner; long before her biggest challenge was finding a spot to jam in the latest blue ribbon or an uncrowded shelf for another silver cup. But once experienced, the symptoms were unmistakable.

Envy.

This time there was no doubt about it.

When she gave up competing after winning

the Western states championship, Barry had accused her of complacency, but Tessa had known the only place left to go was down, and she liked being a winner too much to risk that. Like the time Jeannie's horse went lame and Tessa loaned her one of her own horses— a much better one. When the story got out, her selflessness had been widely hailed, but Tessa knew Jeannie didn't stand a chance of beating her time, no matter what horse she was riding. Where was the sacrifice in that?

Tessa groaned. Garland was her *daughter,* for God's sake! What place did envy have in regard to a relationship she herself had encouraged?

Is it because, after all these years, I again see myself as having nowhere else to go but down?

"Hey, there, Tessa Wagner . . . are you really the small-town girl Shelby made you out to be?"

She looked up, startled. The man wheezing alcohol-laden breath down at her was the same one who had taken exception to Scott's comment to his brunette companion. A temporary one, apparently, since she was nowhere in sight.

"I am," Tessa said, drawing back, "but in case you hadn't noticed, I'm a woman, not a little girl."

"Oh, I noticed all right," he said. Her skin crawled as his bloodshot eyes toured her from head to booted toes. "I like a female with a little meat on her bones. What do you say we go riding together sometime? I can make it well worth your while . . . ask anybody."

His leer left Tessa in no doubt of his meaning. "Well, I dunno about that," she drawled, moving round behind him. "I like my mounts to have well-muscled hindquarters, and it appears to me you have a way to go in that department." She picked up the tails of his cashmere jacket. "A *long* way."

His lumpy face reddened. "Bitch," he muttered.

Tessa thumbed her nose at his wide retreating back. Feeling more like her familiar cocky self she started towards the buffet table. "Excuse me, excuse me," she murmured, smiling and nodding, wishing that people who had already filled their plates would get the hell out of the way.

"Ms. Wagner?" A hand gripped her elbow, abruptly halting her forward progress. She pulled away, whirled, and stumbled. The man who had spoken reached out to steady her. "Sorry if I startled you. We met in town a couple of weeks ago?" Tessa looked at him blankly. "The day you were riding that big horse with the spotted rump? Scott introduced us."

Tessa's confusion evaporated. "Now I remember. You were on your way to lunch to celebrate the recording of his deed to this house. I'm sorry, I'm afraid I don't recall—"

"Alan Baumgartner," he supplied. "Have you eaten?" Giving him a mournful look, she shook her head.

"Neither have I. Look, if you'll let me in ahead of you, I'll clear the way."

Which he did, blandly ignoring the glares of those he displaced. He handed Tessa a plate and a linen-wrapped package of cutlery, and they began inching their way along the table, selecting from the opulent array of delicacies.

"That horse of yours really caught my eye," Alan said, adding a trio of prosciutto-wrapped chicken livers to his plate. "My wife likes to ride, and now that we've settled here . . . well, I'm wondering if maybe you'd consider selling— "

"Whoa," Tessa said, holding up one hand. "That wasn't my horse. In fact, I wouldn't give him stable room. The guy who owns him wanted a flashy horse to ride in parades, but he didn't reckon on him going into orbit when faced with more than two or three people at a time." She shook her head. "A real knothead. I did what I could with him, but I'd as soon train a donkey for dressage. Sorry, Alan."

He sighed. "No more than I."

Tessa added a selection of exotic-looking olives— a nice change, she thought, from the standard pimento-filled green ones— to the slice of poached salmon on her plate. "Is your wife an experienced rider?"

"She rode a lot in her teens back East— that's where she is now, visiting her family. She did some show riding and jumping, but mostly on a fairly local level of competition. I don't think she's ever done much trail riding . . . certainly not in rugged country like you have here."

"Has she ever owned a horse?"

"Not that I'm aware of. Would that make a difference?"

"Well, starting out, it would be best if you could find what we call an easy keeper . . ." Tessa added shrimp salad and tiny dill-seasoned new potatoes to the salmon and balanced a couple of flaky spinach-filled pastries on top. "Do you suppose Scott will supply us with doggy bags if we ask real nice?"

"Hey, that's a thought! It'd sure make my meals easier while Betsy's away," he added wistfully.

Nice guy, Tessa thought. Not like that creep with his let's-go-riding routine. "You know, I do have this palomino mare. I had high hopes for her as a cutting horse— Lord knows she has the bloodlines for it— but I'm thinking maybe she's a little too placid to ever be top rank. The really good ones have the same urge to win that top human athletes do."

Alan's expression brightened as she spoke. "Palomino? Golden coat and cream mane and tail? Like Roy Roger's horse?"

Tessa laughed. "Yep, just like Trigger. Except my mare is smaller and prettier. She's not cheap, though. I've already invested a lot of training in her, and as I said, her bloodlines are the best."

"Good enough for breeding?"

"Absolutely."

"Betsy might like that. When you say not cheap. . . ."

This guy's a lawyer, Tessa reminded herself. "Twenty thousand," she said, crossing her fingers behind her back.

"That much," he murmured.

Tessa looked him straight in the eye. "You could find a nice horse for a lot less."

They fell silent. Alan pointed to a crystal bowl cradled in ice and filled with small black globules.

"Is that what I think it is?" Tessa asked.

"The real thing," Alan said. "It's not cheap either."

"I've never had any," Tessa admitted.

"Alan?" a vaguely familiar-looking man called across the well-laden table. "Can we talk? Something's come up."

"In a minute. My partner," Alan explained. He spooned some creamy cheese onto Tessa's plate and topped it with a generous portion of the caviar. "Eat them together," he advised. He closed his eyes and kissed his fingers to his lips. "Perfecto."

"Hey, Alan!" The partner was losing patience.

"Look, I've got to go. You're in the Ouray book?"

"In the Cottonwood section," Tessa said. "If the pages stick together, you're liable to go right past it."

"I'll give you a ring next week when Betsy comes home. If anyone else expresses interest in your mare in the meantime—"

"I'll put them on hold," she promised. It was a safe enough pledge. Buyers of twenty-thousand dollar horses didn't come along every day.

She eyed a silver platter heaped with little cheese biscuits. *Was there room enough on my plate?* Deciding there wasn't, she turned into the path of a young man intent on reaching the buffet table. The dazzling straight-arrow smile he flashed her in apology put her in mind of whatshisname, the lead actor in that movie about the Southern law firm fronting for the mob. Quite a look-alike, she mused. Just then, a lovely red-haired girl moved in beside him. Look-alike, hell! That *was* Tom Cruise, and the redhead was his wife. Nicole? Nicolette? Something like that. She'd read about them being married on the slopes here, three, four years ago.

Awestruck in spite of herself, Tessa shifted uncertainly from one foot to the other, trying not to gawk. Snatches of conversation about people and events she knew nothing of swirled around her, and as she searched in vain for Garland's familiar face, the falsity of the Southwestern ranch decor became more and more apparent. For one thing, it was too clean and simple. The decorator of choice for genuine ranch people like her in-laws was Sears, a prime source for the voluminous ruffled window treatments favored for Cottonwood's master bedrooms. Here, there were no drapes or curtains of any sort, nor was there any furniture remotely resembling the leatherette-covered Barcaloungers favored by Lloyd and Pauline. Instead, the vast living room's soaring stone fireplace was flanked by couches that were obviously custom-made, each large enough to comfortably accommodate the theatrical gesturing of a half-dozen chattering guests. The museum-quality Navajo chief blankets carelessly draped across the oatmeal-linen upholstery had little in common with the garish Taiwanese knockoffs stocked by local gift shops. It pained Tessa to see them misused this way. Envisioning the smears of food and spills of wine the light of day would reveal, she wondered if she should say anything to Scott.

"Keep it to yourself," she muttered.

She'd been away from this scene too long, she decided. Resolutely turning her back on it, she collected a glass of wine from a tray offered her in passing, and wandered into the wide corridor leading off from the living room, in search of a quiet place to enjoy her supper.

The contrast between the delicacies on her porcelain plate and the spicy sauce-slathered beef being served up in Cottonwood that evening made her smile. The annual 4H barbecue was a local tradition dating back fifty years. Observed on the second Saturday after the Town Hall thermometer first hit seventy degrees, it was the way Cottonwood folks told themselves summer had finally begun.

It didn't take much imagination to picture the crowded village park, the laughter, and the cries of distress as wandering dogs, lured by the heady aroma, snatched tidbits from the hands of wide-eyed toddlers overwhelmed by their first encounter with this crowd of large, noisy people.

The ranchers contributed the meat, the firemen did the cooking, the women brought the rest. Tessa closed her eyes as she mentally ticked off the list. Homemade breads and biscuits; baked beans and pickles; fresh sweet corn—the first of the season—trucked in for the occasion; more kinds of salads than one could dream of, and enough pies and cakes and cookies to ensure a weekend-long, sugar-induced high.

By six, the long tables were filled; after the blessing, the mayor delivered a few words of welcome, ignored by everyone except for the ritual closing phrase, which was taken up in a full-throated roar.

. . . And as usual, folks, it's all you can eat!

The room Tessa wandered into, cool, quiet, and dim, was a far cry from that Cottonwood mob scene. A drafting table stood uptilted against the wall, flanked by matching stands holding an impressive array of electronic equipment. She recognized a computer and printer; the rest of it, much of it blinking, confounded her. She reached out a tentative finger, then

withdrew it, fearing erasure of . . . well, whatever could be erased. Financial records. Business phone numbers— scratch that, *fax* numbers.
Design notes. Maybe even the designs themselves.

Dear God.

Tessa backed off and headed across the
gleaming plank floor for the softly lit leather-
upholstered couch at the other end of the room.
The cushions creaked disconcertingly as she sat,
but the freshly saddle-soaped smell of them—
*Scott must have had an army in here yesterday get-
ting this place ready—* made her feel at home.

Not that anyone could feel like really kicking
back in a showplace like this. It was the spickest
span she'd ever seen. The drafting table was
bare save for sectioned containers of sketching
materials neatly sorted according to general
type— pencils, pens, and colored markers— and
further sorted by particular function or color.

What was that disgusting term Gavin had
used to describe a compulsive fellow student?
Anal-retentive. Tessa idly wondered to whom that
applied here. Scott? His housekeeper? She reminded herself to ask Garland.

Above the table was a long shelf of reference
books whose spines had been rigidly aligned,
and the magazines on the low table in front of
her were stepped, one atop the other, according
to size. She peered hopefully over the rolled-
back top of the couch. Not a dust bunny in

sight. Scott's cleaning crew had done its search-and-destroy work well. Too well, for her taste.

Tessa's stomach gently rumbled. She circled her fork above her laden plate as she tried to decide what to try first.

All you can eat.

When you came right down to it, she reflected soberly, the same policy applied here, despite the differences in the setting, the menu, and the diners themselves.

Except no one here would be willing to admit it.

Sixteen

Tessa looked up from her plate to see a trio of young faces peering in at her, obviously weighing the advantage of a place to sit against having to make nice with a middle-aged stranger. Not feeling in the mood for forced chit-chat herself, she met the inquiring eyes with a hostile glare that elicited a huffy "Sorry!" and the desired retreat.

Tessa leaned back, eyes closed, the better to savor the last morsel of caviar. A moment later she heard a sigh, followed by a shifting of the cushion as someone settled in beside her.

"I'd just about given you up, Tessa. Had about as much as you can take?"

Tessa opened her eyes to see Sam Englehardt's hound-dog face turned towards her. The pouches under the sad brown eyes contemplating her were new since she last saw him twenty years ago; his hair—what there was left of it—had gone gray, but his expression remained that of a man who, having seen everything, is surprised by nothing.

"I could sure take more of those little black fish eggs, Sam."

"Considering that the going price for Beluga caviar is in the neighborhood of fifty bucks an ounce, I don't think Scott would appreciate your calling it fish eggs." He grinned. "Sounds like something your good ol' boys use to bait a hook."

"If they're after carp or catfish, that's just what they do, except the eggs *they* use are big and red and strictly domestic. Been a while, Sam . . . how's it going?"

"Not bad, Tessa. Yourself?"

"Not bad. I think I sold a horse tonight. Alan Baumgartner? For his wife."

"Nice kid, for a lawyer. Smart, too. He can handle just about anything and is good about supplying referrals when necessary, but he specializes in entertainment law."

"Isn't Telluride a little far from where the action is?"

"Not anymore it isn't. The ski slopes and summer festivals are star-studded, and faxes and E-mail fill in the gaps the rest of the year. I understand he's drawn up some very creative contracts for his clients." He skated a shrewd, heavy-lidded glance at her. "He can afford to pay a good price for a good horse."

Tessa laughed. "That's what I figured, so that's what I asked. Didn't seem to faze him none. Course, it won't buy me a place like this."

Sam turned to look at her. "I wouldn't have

thought you'd want one, Tessa. On the other hand, that blow-hard husband of yours—"

"Barry died two years ago, Sam."

He grunted. Back in the Wild Western days, Barry had tried passing himself off as Tessa's manager when Sam came with a camera crew to take some footage of her on her home ground. Angry words were exchanged, and Tessa finally had to step between them.

"You're right, though," she added. "I can't imagine wanting a house this big. For one thing, I could never keep up with it. Why, I bet changing the bed linen takes Scott a whole morning." Sam hooted. "What's so funny?" Tessa demanded.

"The thought of Scott making hospital corners."

"Yeah, I guess that is pretty silly. With the money he's piled up over the years, he must have an army of bedmakers."

"He hasn't got all that much, Tessa. Besides, by Telluride standards, this is hardly more than a pool house."

"God, has he got a pool, too?

"Hasn't everybody?" he said dryly. "But that's not my point . . . you've heard of Oliver Stone?"

"Well, I know he's a hot Hollywood director," she said, "but I'm not into that kind of thing these days. In fact I never really was."

"I know that, Tessa. That's one of the things I liked best about you. I think you're the only woman Scott never managed to charm into his bed."

Tessa turned to stare at him. "How in hell would you know that? Did Scott— "

"No, no. Scott probably thinks he did. He's very good at altering past realities to suit his present needs. Some of the big names you see here came tonight because, well, Scott's a charmer and people like him, but unless he makes it big again with Wildings, Scott Shelby will soon be very old news. That's where Oliver Stone comes in. This house is, what, five thousand square feet? Stone's is sixteen."

"Sixteen *thousand*? You've got to be kidding! Nobody could possibly use that much space."

He reached over to pat her hand. "Bless your innocent heart. Bigness is what counts. Being bigger than anyone else counts even more."

"But that's so . . . so *dumb.*"

"Sure it is, Tessa, but that's show biz! Hot-cha-cha." He flashed her a big Jimmy Durante smile. "And these days the fashion business is part of it. Hot rock groups set the beat for the models on the runways, and it takes a lot more than a good design to sell a line to the fashion press. This Bluegrass singer Scott signed for Wildings?" Tessa nodded. "She's a greedy, self-absorbed little slut, but she projects like gang-busters, and that's what it takes now. If it works, the first thing he'll do is triple the size of this place and throw another party." He tapped the back of her hand gently. "But if I were you, I wouldn't count on being invited. Once he recoups, he won't need you to remind people how good he was."

Tessa blinked at him. "Wow. You sure don't beat around the bush."

"I can't afford to, Tessa. I have a knack for persuading people to part with their hard-earned money to buy my clients' products. I work my aging tail off to earn some of it for myself, and I'm damn good at it, but I'm a realist. What I do may *look* arty, but basically I'm a pitchman and the bottom line is sales. Aesthetic inspiration is only one means to that end, and a minor one at that— people in my game can't afford to loll around waiting for the muse to strike." The lines curving from his nostrils to the corners of his mouth deepened to furrows. "It takes a toll, Tessa. Someday, when I've finally run dry, I'm going to write a book." He yawned and stretched. "But right now I think I'll crawl off to bed. I wasted most of the day with a difficult client in LA, and by the time I got here I didn't even have time for a reviving shower." He lumbered to his feet. "Good to see you, kid.

"Sam?" He turned back. "That singer you mentioned? She wasn't here tonight . . ."

"So?"

"You saw Scott introduce my daughter . . . do you think maybe . . . ? I mean, they've been working together on the festival and, well, Garland's a beautiful girl . . ."

Sam ran stubby fingers through his thinning hair. "Oh God," he sighed. "Yes, she's beautiful, very much so, but she's not right for this new line. She's too calm . . . too damn *nice.*"

Tessa's smile was wry. "I never thought of that as a bad quality."

"In a daughter or a wife, no. But it's not right for Wildings. Not for Scott either, Tessa."

His tone was gentle, but his eyes seemed to be admonishing her.

"Just what are you telling me?"

"I wouldn't presume to tell you anything. I'm merely suggesting you think twice before encouraging Garland to build on their present relationship . . . whatever that may be," he added in a mutter.

Tessa stared up at him, stunned. "For God's sake, Sam!"

"No, Tessa, for your daughter's sake."

After Sam left, Tessa continued to sit, numbed by Sam's insinuation. He had always seemed genuinely fond of Scott, in fact his tolerance of Scott's frequent, abrupt, and often irrational dismissals of advertising concepts he had hailed as "mahvelous!" only hours before had been damn near saintly.

What could have happened to change all that? Had Scott's enduring appeal to women finally gotten to Sam? The cult of youth had begun to apply to men as it always had to women, and here was Scott, ten years or more older than Sam, looking at least as many years younger.

It's not fair!

How many female voices had cried that since time began, Tessa wondered. Wasn't it was about time the boot was on the other foot?

She took her empty plate back to the thronged living room, relinquished it to a smiling server, and looked for Garland, hoping she was ready, or at least willing, to call it a night.

The crowd was quieter than it had been earlier in the evening. Less anxious to impress. Especially the ones who had been posturing on the couches. Their gestures were languid now; their eyes heavy-lidded. They looked what used to be called "laid-back."

Tessa frowned. No, that wasn't quite right. You didn't *look* laid back, you just *were*.

More likely, she realized belatedly, *they were stoned.*

Suddenly it became very important that she find Garland. She saw a flash of turquoise near the windows and a burst of applause as Garland was hoisted, laughing, into a chair set up on a low table. Tessa started forward.

". . . we picked the flowers yesterday," Scott was saying.

"Scott stuck them in the bottle of wine we were drinking," Garland broke in. " 'To help preserve them,' he said."

"Pouilly-Fuissé helps preserve *me,*" Scott protested, "why not wildflowers?"

"But I made him pour it out— " Scott rolled his eyes— "and refill it from the creek."

"Gorgeous place!" Scott exclaimed. "What's it called again, luv?"

He calls everyone luv, Tessa reminded herself as she neared the group.

"Yankee Boy Basin," Garland supplied.

"Don't you love it?" Scott asked, reaching for the white cardboard box one of the caterer's crew handed to him. He opened it, revealing a nest of pale green tissue paper. "Whichever is due the credit, the wine or the water, this is the result." Reaching in, he lifted out a wreath of pale pink sweetbrier roses starred with larkspur columbine, and yellow cinquefoil. Balancing it on the tips of his fingers, he slowly revolved it so everyone could see.

"Oh Scott . . . oh my," Tessa heard Garland murmur. "It's exquisite."

"So are you, luv."

Her sherry-colored eyes, a paler, brighter hue than his, widened as he reached up to place it on her head. Smiling tenderly, Scott gently settled it into the springy mass of gold hair. "There," he said. "A garland for Garland."

Stepping back, he smiled at their small but appreciative audience. "Ladies and gentleman," he said, making a graceful bow, "I give you Wildings."

"You mean stand-in for Wildings," Garland protested. "I wouldn't want to find myself accused of trying to ease Kayla Farrell out of her contract."

"Looking at you now," Scott said, "I'm of the

opinion that her loss would be a decided gain
for me."

Flushing, Garland scrambled down from her
perch and lifted her hands towards the wreath.
"If it's kept cool, this should last until Kayla
arrives back on Monday. Think what a super
photo opportunity it will make!"

In her haste to remove it, Garland scraped
the wreath's thorny base against her temple. A
drop of red swelled. Tessa moved forward in-
stinctively, intending to stem the scarlet ooze,
but Scott forestalled her. Intentionally? She
could not tell.

Garland stood, unprotesting, seemingly mes-
merized by his intense regard as he reached out
with one long finger to gently wipe the blood
from her cheek, and then, very deliberately,
raised the crimsoned tip to his mouth and
slowly licked it clean.

Tessa heard a gasp, followed by an excited
titter, as the sheer eroticism of the gesture registered on the spectators.

She felt again the caustic twist of envy.

Sharper this time. Hotter.

Oh dear God.

Irrational? She knew that. She didn't want
Scott; she never really had. But the knowledge
failed to dilute the bitter aftertaste. The only
thing she did want was to leave this place, these
people, as quickly as possible.

"Garland!" Her voice was hoarse, almost a
growl. Garland's face turned slowly towards her,

as if unwilling to relinquish the attention of the strangers clustered around her. "You ready to go? It's past two."

"I hadn't really thought . . ." Scott bent to murmur in her ear. "You go on without me, Mom. Scott says I can sack out here tonight. He says it would make things easier tomorrow."

"What things?"

"Oh. I guess I forgot to tell you. The guy who's going to photograph the wildflowers arrived today—he's here somewhere," she added, her eyes scanning the crowd, "and Scott thought my input would be valuable, so—"

"I thought you spent all day Friday providing Scott with your valuable input."

"For God's sake, Mom," Garland hissed, suddenly aware of the interest generated by their exchange. Brightly smiling, she broke out of the loose circle, grasped her mother's arm, and led her sputtering to the far corner of the room.

"What the hell do you think you're doing?" Tessa demanded, pulling her arm from Garland's clutch.

"What am *I* doing?" Garland threw up her hands. "You're the one embarrassing me in front of my friends."

"Friends? They sure look like strangers to me. *Fawning* strangers. Psycho-somethings."

"Sycophants," Garland supplied coolly. "An altogether different term, but just as objectionable."

"Yeah? Well, if you ask me," Tessa said, eyeing them scornfully, "in this case both terms apply."

"At the moment, asking you anything is the farthest thing from my mind. Frankly, I find your sudden switch from stage mom to nursemaid both bewildering and insulting. If you remember, all this was your idea!"

"Spending the night with Scott Shelby was never my idea. You two came up with that one on your own. I guess I don't know you near as well as I thought I did. Maybe virginity doesn't count for much these days, but I wish you'd saved it for someone more deserving. God knows Scott's had more than his share."

Garland paled. Tessa, immediately regretting her words, reached out. Her daughter winced away from her touch.

"I haven't slept with Scott and, so far at least, I have no intention of doing so. But if I did, it wouldn't be the momentous occasion you seem to think it would be. In case you haven't noticed, Mom, I'm not a kid anymore. Haven't been for some time. Tonight, when we arrived here, I compared this place to never-never land, remember?" Unable to speak, Tessa nodded. "At the time, I was thinking of the unreal celebrity world Scott lives in, where no one is allowed to grow older. But now I'm wondering if it doesn't apply just as much to you."

Defeated, Tessa's shoulders slumped. Her anger spent, Garland took her mother's hand. "Go home, Mom. Scott has an appointment in Cottonwood tomorrow; he can drop me off on the way."

"In time for supper?"

"I imagine so.

"I'll plan something that can be held over."

"Okay."

"Well, then. Thank Scott for me, will you? I really don't feel much like . . ." Tessa's words trailed off. She filled the void with a deprecating shrug, wanting to leave, yet finding it oddly hard to break away. She took a deep breath. *One, two, three, smile.* "Tell him I really liked the little fish eggs."

"Fish eggs?" Garland frowned. "Oh!" she said, her brow clearing, "the caviar!" Her eyes lighted with amusement. "Yeah, I'll be sure and tell him that. In fact, I bet he takes it up. He likes being thought irreverent."

"He does? He wasn't as sure of himself as that in my day."

As she said it, Tessa gazed earnestly into her daughter's hazel eyes, but if Garland understood what she was trying to say, she gave no sign of it.

"See you tomorrow," Garland murmured as she leaned to give her mother's cheek a dutiful kiss. "Drive carefully. And Mom? Watch for deer on the road home— you know the effect bright lights have on them."

Tessa nodded. *On people, too,* she thought.

Misinterpreting her mother's resigned expression, Garland smiled sheepishly. "Listen to me trying to teach you to suck eggs."

"I've never sucked an egg in my life, darling, but I appreciate the sentiment."

And she sincerely did. But as Tessa wound her way back down the road, her headlights throwing wide fans of light across the pale green trunks of the aspens massed along the verge, she wished the only thing she had to worry about was deer.

Seventeen

The morning sun slashed into Tessa's eyes. She moaned, rolled over onto her stomach, and tried to ignore the taste of bile that welled, bitter and acid, into her mouth.

She turned her aching head and cracked one eye towards the clock on the bedside table. Eight o'clock. *My God.*

"Wasn't it only the day before yesterday I told Garland I never sleep in?" she muttered, pushing down the covers. She sat up, immediately regretting it. She hadn't had that much to drink last night, certainly not enough to account for her aching head and this miserable queasiness. Just the thought of breakfast made her shudder.

It was the caviar, she told herself.

Tell him I really liked the little fish eggs.

Was Garland right? Would Scott really take that up?

More to the point, would he take Garland up? In either case, she could easily picture the little smile, smirky yet winning, that would accompany it. *The last of the red-hot charmers.*

No, she corrected herself, Scott was never that obvious. He was more the cool and lazy type. Feline. Crept up on you like . . . like hypothermia. Soothing, calming, insidious.

She struggled to her feet. The room tilted. Calm, she most definitely was not.

She forced down an austere breakfast of dry toast and tea. She snapped at Miguel when he phoned to ask when he should expect her at the corral. Then, in an excess of remorse, told him to take the day off.

Tessa had planned to work with the bay colt, but she could hardly expect balance and grace from the horse if she herself was incapable of it. Sure, bloodlines were important, but when it came to performance, the trainer makes the horse. Didn't she always say that bad results meant she should look to herself, not the horse, for improvement?

However, having long ago made it a rule never to work the horses unless someone else was at hand, she had, by giving Miguel the day off, denied herself the chance of working with the colt even if she managed to pull herself together.

Damn!

Knowing Miguel, he would probably make a beeline for St. Margaret's to confess sins hardly worth the cost of the gas to get him there, then stop off to visit with his nephew's family on the way back. Tessa would be surprised if he returned before sundown, and Garland wouldn't be home until God—and Scott Shelby—knew when.

Was Scott coming to Cottonwood to see his ex-wife? she wondered. She couldn't imagine what else would bring him down here. Except for his current interest in wildflowers, he wasn't the type to tour the highways and byways oohing and aahing. None of them were, she thought as she recalled her lame attempts at conversation with some of the guests at his housewarming. Especially the couple who suffered with fixed smiles her animated description of the spectacular drive from Grand Junction to Telluride via Gateway's red stone ramparts and the high green meadows below Lone Cone near Norwood.

We don't have a car, they told her. They flew in, they told her. In their own plane, they added. *Well, la-di-da.* It seemed to her that if they could afford their own plane, they could sure manage to shell out a few bucks for a car rental.

It was all very puzzling. All those people, spending more bucks to set themselves up in the mountains than most people earned in a lifetime, then not bothering to look at them. She wondered if any of them had ever risen early enough to see the peaks washed with the rising sun's clear yellow light, basked like lizards on a sun-struck slope above the high green grassy basins, and ridden through the twilight's deep purple towards home and the smell of piñon logs crackling in the fireplace.

Tessa shook herself. You can't have it both ways, she told herself. Ruled in the sixties by a moral code that in Cottonwood hadn't changed much since her parents' day, she married Barry instead of allowing the fever to run its course. Having made that bed, she remained mired in it, too proud to openly admit defeat. The yearnings of her starving spirit came later, when the dry spell showed no signs of ending.

In the beginning, she expected, *wanted*, little more than sexual gratification from her marriage. And in those first months, oh! what erotic bliss! Barry had been strong and hungry and untiring. She had luxuriated in the heat they generated— their friends, on seeing them, would elbow each other's ribs— but by the half-year mark she sensed a waning of her desire, and by their first anniversary, boredom had set in. From a few things Jeannie had let drop inadvertently— in those days, Cottonwood wives didn't exchange confidences about the marriage bed— Tessa suspected that even pudgy Art was more imaginative.

Was it the slow grinding-down sameness of domestic life after her teen years of triumph? she wondered, or was it simply that marriage wasn't good for your sex life?

She recalled Scott laughing when, in the face of his persistence, she resorted to using her wedding vows as a shield.

"Luv," he had said fondly, "no one will ever try to package a movie with a title like *A Marriage to Remember,* because everyone knows it would bomb at the box office. Marriage is about putting the cat out at night and bringing in the milk in the morning."

"Bring the *milk* in? Not even Cottonwood has a milkman anymore. Say, just how old are you anyway?"

Scott had scowled. "The newspaper then. Stop trying to change the subject, Tessie. All I'm saying is that at the heart of every unappreciated wife is a *fille de joie* longing to be set free."

Though Tessa didn't know French, she had figured out his meaning. "Well, you can look for your joy someplace else, Scott."

Convinced at last that she meant what she said; that she actually believed in the sanctity of the marriage bed, even one with Barry in it, he had rocked back on his Gucci heels, thrust his hands in the pockets of his creamy flannels, and smiled blazingly at her. "I get joy just from looking at you, Tessie."

Incorrigible.

And she had loosed him on her daughter. A daughter who last night had said that if she did sleep with him, it wouldn't be that big a deal, the implications of which didn't really sink in until three hours later when she heard a knock at the front door while she was preparing lunch.

No one ever came to the front door. No one she knew, anyway; no one, considering her still fragile state, she had any interest in seeing. She ignored it.

Another knock, louder this time. Followed, after too short a pause, by still another, louder and longer.

God*damn*. She stuck the knife in the peanut butter jar— she'd already spread the jelly side of the sandwich— wiped her sticky hands off on her jeans, and strode out of the kitchen to the front of the house. Brushing cobwebs from the space between the rarely opened wooden and screen doors, she cautiously peered out. "Yes?"

A man stood, faced away from her, leaning against the porch post, one hand curled around it. Lounging against it, actually, his long lean body bent in a taut curve, his shirt sleeves rolled high on tan, sleekly muscled arms.

He turned. "Miz Wagner?" he asked, taking off his hat. His hair was a straight fall of glossy black. His features were shadowed, but the smile rivaled Scott's. He was very tan.

"I'm Frederico Chavez."

That explains the tan, Tessa thought as she automatically took the hand extended to her, wondering why he seemed to think she would recognize his name. "I'm afraid Miguel isn't here . . . I gave him the day off."

"I'm sorry?"

So he didn't know Miguel. "I . . . we don't need any hands right now. Maybe if you come back in the fall . . ." Tessa retreated behind the screen door.

"Actually," he said, rotating the brim of his finely woven cream-colored straw hat in his hands, "I came to see Garland. I know I should have called first, but I was in Durango yesterday on business for my father, so I thought . . ." He hesitated. "I know her from the university, Mrs. Wagner." His tone was cooler, more formal. "Gavin and me, we hang out together."

Ah, Gavin. Tessa relaxed and moved out from behind the screen. "I'm sorry . . . Frederico, is it?"

"My friends call me Rick." Another flash of white teeth.

"I'm sorry, Rick. Garland's in Telluride on business." *Monkey business?* "She's been putting in a lot of overtime lately."

His dark slash of eyebrows elevated slightly as if wondering at the dry tone of her concluding words, but all he said was, "Yeah, Gav did say she was working up there this summer."

"I don't expect her back until suppertime . . . uh, you can wait if you like."

Sensing her reluctance, he shook his head. "Thank you, but I'd better be heading back home. My dad'll be waiting on me. Nice to have met you, Mrs. Wagner. Now I know where Garland gets her looks." This time the smile was an unsettling, sensuous curl of lip.

He slipped his hat back on, adjusted it to a rakish angle, then touched the brim and hop-skipped off the porch into the sunlight.

Tessa's breath caught in her throat. His rus-

set-skinned face tapered anvil-like, from a wide
brow and high cheekbones to a strong, clean-
shaven jaw. He ambled towards his car, his an-
gled nose preceding him like the prow of a
pirate ship. Halfway there, he plucked his hat
from his head and, with an almost impercepti-
ble twist of the wrist, sent it gliding into the
passenger seat.

Watching him, Tessa got a sudden mental picture of Garland nestled beside him in the sleek
gray convertible, her gold hair a bright banner
in the clear mountain air.

Dear God.

Jeannie used to say guys like that were bad
news. She meant just the opposite, of course,
but for mothers of beautiful daughters it was
the literal, unnerving truth.

He turned back towards her. "You wouldn't
happen to have a number where I can reach
Garland, would you?"

She considered saying no, then decided there
was no point to it. He'd know she was lying,
and besides, he didn't seem the type to be discouraged by delay or inconvenience. "I do, but
I think it would be better if you called her
here."

"I guess . . . especially if she's on overtime.
Yeah, I'll do that," he said, as if trying to convince himself. "Writing her sure hasn't gotten
me anywhere."

While Tessa pondered the significance of
that, he vaulted over the car's closed door into

the driver's seat— *like a goddamn deer,* she thought— and zoomed off, one hand upthrust in a gesture of farewell.

Tessa stared after him, her hand shading her eyes, until the plume of dust dispersed. Her first impression couldn't have been more wrong. Not only was he not an itinerant ranch worker, he projected the same strong sense of self as Gavin did, although in this case it seemed slicked with arrogance. And that car of his: late-model, probably loaded, obviously expensive. It looked foreign. So did he.

Drugs.

Unwelcome musings, the product of nightly news accounts of crack houses and Columbian drug rings, slid unbidden into her mind. *Rico— Rick sounded too boy-scouty— Chavez: university student by day, street-corner dealer by night? Uh-uh. He didn't look sleazy enough for that. Maybe a middleman . . . what did they call them? A connection?*

She pictured fast boats, dark nights, and poky little backwater docks on the Gulf. Or a small plane, flying low, again at night, landing on runways carved out of the brush. A dangerous business . . . but from the looks of him, so was he.

And from the looks of him, who could resist him?

This time, the twisting ache Tessa felt had nothing to do with caviar; in truth, it probably never had. In both cases— Scott's and this dark young stranger's— their vibrant presence conjured up the remembrance of past desire and the sexual longing that transforms everything associated with the beloved object into a precious symbol.

Those first heady months of her marriage, when she went upstairs after breakfast to make the bed, the lingering odor of their lovemaking would overwhelm her. Tessa remembered sitting and staring at Barry's discarded work clothes tossed over the bedstead and hanging from doorknobs, their pajamas— it was winter— jumbled together beside the bed, the sheets spilling over onto the floor. A mess, yes, but one that invoked a particular moment, a heady kiss, an intimate caress. For her, that sweet disorder was a still life more filled with meaning than the greatest painting in the finest museum.

It had all been so long ago . . . so very long ago.

But the memory persisted, and the little green-eyed monster that had moved in to tend it— dusting it off and polishing it up with a vigor Tessa could have done without— was growing stronger.

By the time Garland arrived home— Scott didn't bother to come in, just dropped her off and waved— Tessa's headache had returned. *That's what I get for thinking so much,* she thought.

"Did everything go well?" she asked with forced brightness. "Did the flowers smile nicely and show their best profile?"

"Scott seemed pleased enough."

"Does that mean you weren't?"

"Oh, the photographer was okay— I mean, he obviously knows his business— but you know how those guys are. Click, click, click," she said, pantomiming his actions. "Even if he were a total dork, he used enough film to guarantee good pictures just by the law of averages."

"Then what's the problem?" Tessa demanded. The ache was worse now; she could hear the strain of it in her voice.

Garland threw her mother a dark look. "Kayla Farrell showed up while we were off rattling around the countryside. By the time we returned— two hours after she arrived— she was way overdue for someone to unload on. She chose me."

"Why you?"

"Because it amuses Scott to play us off against each other. Apparently she called him last night, very late, and in the course of what I gathered was a rather heated exchange, he let drop— deliberately, no doubt— that I might be replacing her. She didn't care for that. Little bitch," she added in a mutter.

"If I didn't know better, I'd say you were jealous."

Garland raked her hands through her tousled hair. *God,* Tessa thought, *even her gestures are like mine.* "I just wish Scott would back off . . . give me some breathing room."

"That goes with the territory, darling."

"Homesteading it was your idea, not mine," Garland shot back.

Tessa winced. "I thought you were the one that said it wasn't as easy to fool little girls as it used to be."

"Fool them, no, but that doesn't mean they can't sometimes be confused as hell."

"No more than I," Tessa said. "You had a caller today."

"Really?" Garland's first reaction to the abrupt change of subject was a blink, followed by a wry smile. "A gentleman caller, I presume?"

"You tell me. Frederico Chavez," she said, rolling each syllable out with elaborately accented overemphasis.

Garland's hazel eyes widened with shock, then narrowed. "Rick," she said flatly.

"The same. Handsome brute."

Garland looked pained. "Handsome, I grant you, but he's no brute."

"Glad to hear it. Especially since I got the feeling he was surprised I didn't know about him. I thought maybe he was related to Miguel—another nephew maybe."

"Oh great, Mom. But then why not? One look at me, and a person could think I was related to Princess Di. I mean, we're both blond and fair-skinned."

"I can think of a lot worse things than having Miguel for an uncle," Tessa pointed out.

Garland had the grace to look shamefaced.

"True," she admitted. "Did he say what he wanted?"

"He asked for you; he asked where he could reach you; I assumed he wanted to see you."

Garland dropped her eyes. "He's more Gav's friend than mine."

"Really? Why did he come here then? He must know your brother's in Denver, seeing as how they're such good friends."

"For heaven's sake, Mom!" She hesitated. "You didn't give him the Chamber's address or phone number, did you?"

"No," Tessa said, "I didn't think I should without your say-so. . . . Is there any other reason I should know about?"

"No," Garland said, but her eyes slid away.

Tessa wasn't sure if that meant, *no, there isn't any other reason,* or *no, it's nothing I should know about.* One thing was sure, she'd had it with tiptoeing around. "Garland, what's with this guy?"

"What's that supposed to mean?"

"It means who is he? How come he can afford to drive such a flashy car—"

"It's not flashy, Mom."

"Expensive then," Tessa said. "His hat, too. Looked like a genuine Panama . . . not exactly the kind of thing you pick up for a few bucks at Wal-Mart. I can't help thinking—"

"I know *exactly* what you're thinking. Good-looking Latino, obviously not hurting for money. Drugs, of course. What else could it be?

Cocaine, marijuana . . . hell, why stop there? Why not heroin, too? Wha' better way to lead the leetle Anglo *muchacha* astray, no?"

"Garland, please," Tessa murmured, wishing the pounding in her temples would stop.

"For your information," her daughter said, staring her down, "Rick's family has been in this country a lot longer than ours. They were in New Mexico before it was a state . . . maybe even before it was a territory. Soon after statehood, they moved north with their sheep—"

"Sheep!" Tessa declared, automatically reflecting the prejudice of the cattlemen she grew up among.

"—to the Chama Valley," Garland continued, ignoring her mother's outburst. "Up there, west of the Rio Grande, good grazing land was still cheaply available. So, since the Chavez family has always been both hard-working and forward-looking, they bought up all they could afford. The majority of it is in the Permian basin." She paused to give her mother a significant look. It failed to register.

"So?" Tessa said.

"So the Permian basin contains oil. Quite a lot of it."

"Oh."

"Rick's particular interest is the family-operated greenhouses. They were his mother's idea. It took them a while to get them on a paying basis, but nowadays a lot of the fancy organic produce served in upscale restaurants comes with a Chavez label. Very fresh and very pricey."

"Salad greens you mean? Like that bitter stuff I always fish out?"

"Arugula. That, and more exotic veggies . . . Rick reeled the list off to me once but," she shrugged, "it didn't stick."

"For someone who grew up on iceberg lettuce, arugula seems exotic enough to me," Tessa muttered. She rubbed her temples. *Maybe tea would help*. She filled the pot and carried it back to the stove. "So. Sheep, oil, and salad greens." She put a tea bag in a mug and stared at the pot. Then without warning, she wheeled on her daughter. "Where do you fit in?" she demanded.

"*What*? I don't know what you're talking about!"

But it was plain from the way her voice rose and cracked that she did.

"C'mon, Garland, I wasn't born yesterday. Unless you bugged your brother's room, there's no way you could know what you just told me short of a lot of conversations. Private conversations. Either that, or your Rick— "

"He's not *my* Rick, damn it!"

"— is the most boring, self-absorbed person on God's earth. In my experience, a person learns things like that about another person in bits and pieces. Here and there. Now and then."

"I get the picture, Mom." Her tone was surly.

"Then why don't you fill it in for me?" Tessa

poured the boiling water into the mug. She carried it to the table, sat down, and blew on it. "It's easy," she said looking up at her daughter. "Just connect the numbers like you did when you were a kid. One, two, three— "

"Okay, so we slept together." Garland leaned over the table, hands gripping the edges. "More than once . . . quite a lot in fact. Satisfied?"

"Were you living together, too?" Tessa asked quietly. "It's obvious you think that's none of my business, but I feel I don't know you anymore. You may think I'm judging you, but I'm not. I know what it's like to be physically . . . obsessed."

Garland straightened and stared at her. "You mean you . . . and . . . and . . ."

"Your father," Tessa supplied. *Why was it so hard for children to accept the obvious?* "In the beginning, anyway."

"But I always thought . . . I mean, towards the end you didn't even share the same room."

"Things changed, Garland." She sighed. "Unfortunately, they often do. Your father was really something in his day, and from the look of him, Frederico Chavez is even more so. Scott Shelby may try to seduce you, but a virile young guy like that . . ." Tessa shook her head. "It's hard to describe, but it's like being under a spell. Hypnotized. Afterwards, you can't believe you allowed yourself to be so . . . so crazy. Like a cow that's gotten into locoweed." She paused and stared into space. "Actually," she murmured, "choice has nothing to do with it. It just . . . *happens.*"

Tessa sighed again. "In your case, looks to me as if the 'go-slow' signs are flashing, especially if Rick's not willing to make a commitment."

"But that's just it, Mom. He is. I'm the one who's not." Her chin came up. "Not to any man. The only commitment I'm willing to make right now is to my education. Just before I came home we had this terrible fight. We both said things . . ." Garland tossed her head back; Tessa saw tears glinting in her eyes. "It's over. I don't want to talk to him or see him again."

"If he's a buddy of Gav's, how can you avoid him? And if it's over, why should it matter? He wanted you to live with him, you said no, end of story."

"It's not that simple. He didn't . . ." Garland hesitated; she avoided her mother's eyes. "He can't understand why, if I loved him, I turned him down."

"Why did you?" Tessa asked. "Not that I'm questioning your decision— far from it— it's just that I'm, well, curious."

Garland avoided her mother's eyes. "You made a commitment, and it turned into a suit of armor. Gav and I used to say you exchanged it for a heavier one every couple of years."

Tessa cradled her aching head in her hands. "Oh Garland, I'm so sorry! I tried my best to protect you and Gav from the worst—"

"I know you did, Mom, but seeing you clunking around brandishing your shield between us and our father's indifference and alcohol consumption . . . well, let's just say it fell kind of short of a model for long-term relationships."

"Relationship," Tessa murmured. "In my day we called it togetherness."

"Anyway, as I said before," Garland continued, "the only commitment I'm willing to make right now is to finishing college and applying to veterinary school. Cornell, maybe."

Tessa looked dismayed. "But isn't that way back East someplace?"

"Way, way back, Mom," Garland teased. "Upper New York State to be exact."

"Upper, lower, or in between, there must be something closer."

"God, you sound like Rick!"

"Heaven forbid. So how does Scott fit into all this?"

Her expression hardened. "There's a new veterinary practice up in Telluride that might be wanting a partner in a few years. I'm sure it would help my chances if I could bring some well-heeled clients with me, so since Scott knows everybody worth knowing up there . . ." Her words trailed off; she gave Tessa a funny look, as if wishing she could take them back. "I guess I'll just have to wait and see what role, if any, he might be willing to play."

Tessa wondered if she was being deliberately evasive. Garland's admission of her relationship with the Chavez boy had cast everything about her in a different light. In Scott's case, the light was increasingly lurid. She hadn't anticipated that the widening of her daughter's horizons might include a detour through Scott Shelby's bedroom.

How could I have been so stupid? Tessa wondered. The scared kid who left for Boulder with tear-stained cheeks had spent three years in an urban university setting, exposed to experiences and temptations Cottonwood had little knowledge of. Just because Garland didn't dye her hair blue or wear rings in her nose didn't mean she hadn't changed.

My daughter is twenty, she reminded herself. *A year older than I was when I ran off with Barry; a grown woman with priorities all her own.*

Now I know where she gets her looks, Rick Chavez had said.

At the time, Tessa admitted to herself, she had wondered if he was coming on to her. Knowing what she did now, she realized he was probably just pushing dear old mom's buttons. *Maybe if I get the mother on my side . . .*

Garland's life was just beginning. She had two attractive men at her beck and call, and plans she wasn't entirely willing to share.

What was it Jed had said after observing one of their mother-daughter clashes? "Damned if she isn't as steely as you are, Tessa, except in her case it's sheathed in velvet." He thought it was funny; Tessa didn't.

Steel in velvet.

Unsettled by her mother's long silent scrutiny, Garland said, "What's on your mind, Mom?"

For some crazy reason, the line from an old song popped out of nowhere into Tessa's head. *Hang your clothes on a hickory limb, but don't go in the water . . .*

"I hope you know what you're doing," she said harshly.

Garland sighed resignedly. "Okay, let's have it."

"You're using Scott, aren't you?"

Garland gave a shout of laughter. "These days they call it equal opportunity, Mom. We're using each other, except he's had more practice at it than I have. Sometimes, like today, he comes out on top— no double meaning intended— but in the long run— " her eyes darkened with determination— "*I* will." She laughed again. "Of *course* I'm using him! Turnabout is fair play, right? Besides, it was your idea."

"I never said— "

"You said he could open doors for me, provide opportunities, useful contacts."

"Yes, but— "

"But you thought I'd just soak it up like a passive little sponge, say thank you to the nice man, then trot back home to mother. Enriched by the experience and no harm done."

Tessa's eyes fell. It was too close to the truth for comfort. "Well, I— "

"If I were really as naive as you seem to

think . . ." She hesitated. "Let's just say that *if* I were, and *if* I had been a virgin, I doubt I'd be one now. Scott is not a nice man, Mom. I like him . . . in fact, I like him a lot. He's fun to be with, and that cherishing act of his is a terrific ego booster— it's like being in therapy without paying the fees— but nice he most definitely is not." She laughed. "I had about as much chance of actually being his Wildings girl as you did."

Tessa winced. Seeing it, Garland relented. "I'm sorry, Mom. The thing is . . ." She paused and took her lower lip between her teeth.

"Might as well finish what you started, Garland."

"Look, Scott likes you . . . no, more than that, he's very fond of you, and grateful, too, but . . . well, he's no longer . . . *interested.*"

Tessa stared at her blankly, her eyes clear blue. The silence lengthened.

Looking anxious, Garland bent towards her. "Mom? You understand what I'm saying?"

"Oh, yes," Tessa said, slowly getting to her feet. "It came through loud and clear. Not that it comes as any surprise," she lied.

Actually, it was the difficulty in facing it that was the surprise, she realized. Like tripping a mine on your return across a field you had already scouted.

She crossed to the sink with an oddly stiff and uncertain gait, as if trying to avoid invisible hazards. After putting the mug carefully into the sink, she trailed back across the kitchen, pausing at the entrance to the living room. "I think I'll go to bed now," she murmured over her shoulder. "I've had this headache all day . . . I can't seem to shake it."

"But what about supper?"

Tessa turned to look at her daughter. Her blue eyes were darker now. Haunted.

"Fuck supper."

If she heard Garland's gasp, she ignored it.

Later, as she lay across her bed, her arms hugging her damp pillow, she heard Garland's car start, then drive off. *Back up to Telluride? To Scott and his cherishing?*

The trickle of tears started again. This time she didn't bother to try to stop it.

Eighteen

Tessa's first reaction the next morning on seeing Garland's breakfast dishes stacked and washed in the rack next to the sink was relief: she had come home to sleep. Then she became anxious.

Recalling her uncharacteristic use last evening of an outhouse expletive, she grimaced. Had Garland assumed it was meant to apply to her, too? Tessa prayed not, but it was unlike her daughter to rise before her— she usually heard the loud clatter of the Mickey Mouse alarm as she passed Garland's room on her way to the kitchen— and even less like her to leave the house without so much as an exchange of morning greetings.

Whatever Garland's reason, she was obviously avoiding her.

Should I apologize?

Not until she knew what to apologize for, and once started, where would she stop? God knows she must have piled up a lot of apology-worthy errors over the years.

Feeling herself blundering into a mental and

emotional thicket with no clear-cut exit, Tessa closed her eyes. *Take the easy way out,* she told herself. *Just pretend nothing happened.* Feeling suddenly better— temporarily at least— she put the kettle on to boil.

Tessa was mopping up the remains of her egg with a crust of toast and frowning over an article in the local weekly about a Zoning Commission hearing on a request for an exception to the local zoning laws, when the phone rang. "Shut up!" she muttered. The ringing obediently stopped, only to shrill forth again as she neared the end of the meaty part in which Terry Ballou's name and the adjective *alleged* appeared not once, but several times. She swallowed the last of her tea with an audible gulp, got up, and answered it.

It was Lloyd.

Speak of the devil, Tessa thought. "I was just reading about your partner in the *Cottonwood Chronicle,*" she said.

"Not a word of truth in it," Lloyd sneered. "That kid they've got doing the reporting these days thinks it's his God-given duty to supply a scandal, or at the least the hint of one, in every blamed issue. These last couple of weeks it's been quiet enough to hear the grass grow— except for the 4H barbecue. Too bad you couldn't be there."

"Why is that?" Tessa asked, then, guessing why, wished she hadn't.

Lloyd chuckled a deep, rich, rubbing-his-hands-together chuckle. "Didn't Jeannie tell you, Tessa? Jed took the ex-Mrs. Scott Shelby . . . Marion, I think he said her name was. Considering the way he was ushering her around, introducing her to everybody who was anybody, I'd say he *escorted* her more'n took her. Those tables at the park got benches, you know, so he couldn't pull out the lady's chair for her, but if he could've, he would've. You never saw such bowing and scraping! Laughing together, dancing . . . they even toasted each other with those paper cups like they had champagne in 'em, 'stead of that piss-cheap beer the 4H sells for what good draft costs down at the Ouray Elk's Club. I gotta tell ya, they was the talk of the evening."

Tessa waited him out. It wasn't easy, but it was worth it. "I suggested he take her, Lloyd."

"Oh."

Poor Lloyd. "I don't mean to rush you, but I'm sure you have more on your mind than a report of Cottonwood's social activities, and I've got a horse to train."

"Well, me and Jack've been thinking, Tessa— "

"Glad to hear it, Lloyd."

"I can do without your smart mouth, missy." The chuckle was long gone. "And we've decided, much as we hate to do it to one of our own, that Barry didn't take everything into account he should have when you pressured him into making that will of his."

"I *agreed* he should . . . it was your dad pres-

sured him— all of you, as I remember— just before your folks left for Texas. Don't you think
he knew about the wild oats you boys sowed?
He told me he was damned if he wanted the
land he'd worked so hard going to a bunch of
bastards no one had set eyes on until they
showed up in probate court."

"Well, you got a point there, Tessa. At least
we *know* your bastards."

"I think we'll end this conversation right
here, Lloyd."

"We'll just take it up again in front of Judge
Colby."

"Fine. I'm looking forward to it."

"Or we could come to a friendly agreement . . . a land swap, say. Keep the dirty linen
in the family closet."

"What? And me with a brand new washer I'm
dying to try? See you in court, Lloyd."

Tessa winced as he crashed his receiver down.
The moment she got the dial tone, she dialed
Jed's number.

"You said you'd help," she blurted when he
answered. "I hope you haven't regretted it."

He didn't have to ask who it was. "Help with
what?" he inquired cautiously.

"With Lloyd . . . and Jack, too. They've been
thinking. Lloyd told me so himself."

Jed laughed. "The Wagner boys thinking?
Well, well, that's a switch."

"That's more or less what I said. He didn't
care for it." Jed, still chuckling, said he guessed

not. "He's going to take me to court, Jed. The first time he mentioned it— at that kaffee klatsch I told you about?— I figured he was just bluffing. Now I think he's half-convinced himself that Barry was right, and the threat of exposure'll scare me enough to give him what he wants without all the folderol of lawyers and courtrooms and judges."

"I'd've thought he knew you better than that!" Jed broke in.

"Me, too, Jed. But even though I know he can't possibly win, the twins were hurt enough by Barry's stupid suspicions. They really don't need this. Especially not Gavin. I think he has political ambitions, and even the hint of scandal— "

"How can I help, Tessa?"

"Could we get together to talk about it? Plan some strategy maybe?"

"Today, you mean?"

"I know it's short notice. . . . I could come to you."

"I don't think that's such a good idea, Tessa. Pop's deafness has this miraculous way of clearing up when you're saying something you don't want him to hear." He thought a moment. "There's this woman in Ouray . . . she'd rather walk on hot coals than sit with Pop again, but she owes me a favor— I gave her son a character reference for a job he wanted."

"Did you now." She clicked her tongue reprovingly.

"It was a perfectly honest reference, Tessa. I didn't fire him; he quit. He was a good worker; he just didn't like cows much. Said he prefers clerical work . . . can you imagine?"

"Certainly not. I'd always choose stepping in cow flops over working in a clean, air-conditioned office."

There was a brief silence during which Jed pondered the point in continuing this exchange. Deciding there was none, he asked, "This afternoon suit you? Two, maybe three o'clock?"

"Thank you, Jed." Tessa's tone matched his. "I can't tell you what this means to me."

"I'm doing it as much for the twins as you. They mean a lot to me, too, you know."

While Tessa waited for Miguel to bring the colt out to the training corral, she reflected on Jed's concluding words. What had they meant exactly? Were they his way of keeping a safe distance between them? Of letting her know his love for her had cooled?

Friendly affection.

Yeah, she guessed she could live with that.

Sometimes, when she came upon him unawares, she'd glimpse the fire in his eyes when he caught sight of her. He always banked it down real fast— Jed was too proud to peg his desire out on a line for everyone to see— but it excited her to suppose that if she blew on those embers, just a little, she could coax them into flame. Not being a tease, she never did. But she enjoyed the temptation.

Tessa shivered. The sun was high and bright, but she felt as if a dark cloud had suddenly robbed it of its heat. Gavin was already gone; Garland pulling away, and now Jed . . .

"He's full of fire today, Miz Wagner!"

Tessa whirled, gaping, then smiled sheepishly. Miguel meant the colt, of course.

The dark bay gelding pranced at the end of the halter rope, ears pricked, nostrils distended, pretending he was a wild stallion. She had named him Reshabar, after a wind out of the high Caucasus described as "lusty and black" in the weather encyclopedia the twins had given her several years ago for her birthday. She had no idea where the Caucasus were, but the name, nicked short to Resha, seemed made to order for him.

"My oh my, aren't you a pretty boy," Tessa cooed as she reached out to stroke his satiny neck. He shied away, snorting, then, seeing the carrot in her other hand, came forward eagerly to alternately munch and nuzzle.

Tessa pulled a rag out of her back pocket to wipe off her slobbered-on shirt front. "God, what table manners," she said, tugging the colt's black forelock. "Don't you be expecting dinner invitations from me anytime soon!"

To her surprise, Miguel found her lame quip hugely amusing.

"You're sure in a good mood," she said. "Did you enjoy your day off?"

"Oh, *si!* My nephew's wife had three babies . . . this was first time I see them. She was expecting only two." He grinned, exposing the gold inlay his usual smiles— worthy of a Castilian grandee, Gavin said— never revealed.

Remembering how Garland and Gavin had run her ragged, the thought of triplets made Tessa shudder. Her own mother was long dead by the time the twins were born, and the wild aborigines masquerading as Jack's kids had soured Mom Wagner on any further grand-mothering.

But in Miguel's culture, extended families and lifelong loyalty to blood ties was a given. Fathers and uncles bounced the babies on their knees; aunts and cousins and grandmoth-ers took turns, not only oohing and aahing, but with the changing and feeding and cud-dling.

"Would your nephew be offended if I sent him a check? I'd like to give them something, but they know what they need better than I do."

Miguel considered this. "Not if he knows it is for the little ones." He favored her with a dignified smile. "That is a kind thought, my friend. *Gracias.*"

Friend.

Tessa's thoughts returned fleetingly to Jed. She sighed. *It could be worse.*

"You want a leg up?" Miguel was saying.

The colt was prancing again. Little playful catch-me-if-you-can steps. Tessa grabbed his bridle, pulled his head down, and rubbed her nose across his velvet muzzle. "You big goof! Cool it, will ya?"

Whickering softly, he stilled just long enough for Miguel to boost Tessa up into the saddle. She gathered up the reins, then leaned forward to riffle her fingers through Resha's long black mane. "Gotcha!" she crowed.

The training session went well. *Very* well. Very well *indeed*, Tessa told herself. For a young horse, Resha was already exceptionally well-balanced, and the already bulging muscles in his hindquarters would soon develop the power necessary for a top-quality cutting horse, further proof of the value of Tessa's careful breeding program.

Barry, who had wanted quicker returns, used to pressure her to settle for horses that were, as he put it, "good enough." Tessa had ignored him and gone about her business. If he didn't know without being told why only the best were good enough for Skywalk Ranch, why waste her breath?

Once Resha settled down, Tessa put him through a review of earlier lessons: walking, turning, stopping, and standing steady as she mounted and dismounted from both sides. It was easier now to keep him at a slow jog, and his lope was soft and easy from the beginning.

A smart horse, he resisted backing in the middle of the corral for what he saw as no good reason, but he did so readily when Tessa rode him up to the corral gate and Miguel opened it back against him. Unquestioning obedience would come in time.

By the end of the summer he'd be ready for bitting and more formal training in neck reining, and by late fall she could begin schooling him in the more strenuous maneuvers expected of a cutting horse: the pivots and roll-backs and short stops on the haunches he was still too young to safely undertake.

An hour later, Tessa slid from the saddle, sweaty from working in the midday sun, but elated. She invited Miguel to share a sandwich and iced-tea lunch with her, which she made while he cooled the colt down. She carried a tray out to the weathered table set under the big cottonwood that shaded the area between the barn and the first corral.

"Sit!" Tessa commanded when Miguel returned from cooling Resha down and turning him out with the other horses. After brushing a drift of the cottonwood's fluff-tailed seeds from the table, she put their plates at either end and placed a basket heaped with potato chips— one of Miguel's few weaknesses— between them.

Seeing the chips, his dark eyes lighted with pleasure. Before he allowed himself to indulge, however, he offered up a few words of grace in

Spanish. Tessa, caught unawares with her sandwich halfway to her parted lips, could only hope her hastily bowed head made up for her lack of piety. Miguel merely smiled tolerantly and popped a chip into his mouth.

Tessa sighed and leaned back in her chair, grateful for the cool dry shade. She lifted her arms to hasten the wicking of the moisture out of her sweat-dampened shirt. *Next best thing to an air-conditioner,* she thought contentedly.

During her one trip east with Scott twenty years ago, she had found the humidity blanketing the North Carolina seashore suffocating. The heat, too, had been unrelenting, never varying by more than a degree or two in sun or shade, day or night. The motel's bathrooms and closet floors were blotched with what one of the crew told her was mildew. Nasty-looking stuff. By the end of their three-day stay, she half-expected to find its greenish-blackish spores growing between her toes.

She leaned forward to take a swallow of tea. "I was thinking of breeding Sunset again this fall after Garland goes back to college. That foal she had last year shows a lot of promise."

Miguel chewed thoughtfully. "I think maybe it is too soon for her, Miz Wagner."

Tessa's brow knitted in thought. "You may be right about that, Miguel. She shouldn't be used as a foaling machine. How about Zig-zag? Maybe we can get another colt as good as Bolt out of her before I retire her from mother-hood."

Miguel nodded and reached for another handful of chips. "And maybe Thor could cover her, you think? He's not as young as he used to be, of course."

"Well, hell, Miguel, neither are we and we're still going strong! I say let's go for it." She leaned closer. "To tell you the truth," she whispered, "sometimes I wish I'd never let Jed have Bolt."

Miguel looked at her gravely. Unused to receiving confidences from anyone, much less this woman who employed him, he thought hard and long before he spoke. "Some people say lightning never strikes twice in the same place, but they are wrong."

"Let's hope so," Tessa said. She held out the basket of chips. "Here, have some more."

They sat talking and making plans, agreeing for the most part, but sometimes not. When it came to the horses, they operated as equals. Barry used to complain that she gave "that old Mex" too much power. Annoyed by having her judgment questioned— the horses were her domain— and knowing there was little point in again reminding Barry that Miguel was an American citizen, Tessa would merely say he had earned it. Which, she realized later, was the same as telling Barry he had not.

In fact, Tessa suspected that Miguel had forgotten more about horses than she would ever know. Unlike herself, who sometimes let her enthusiasm for a particular animal influence her opinion, Miguel never, ever, expected more of a horse than he judged it capable of doing by virtue of its breeding, confirmation, and temperament. Was it instinct? The end product of long experience? Probably both, but she really didn't care— she was just thankful to be receiving the benefits.

Tessa smiled at him fondly. An intensely private man, his solemn, almost stately demeanor discouraged displays of affection, but sometimes she couldn't help herself: Miguel was a treasure, and he had entrusted her with the key.

Disconcerted by the blaze of white teeth aimed at him, Miguel looked first this way, then that. "I must go now," he said, getting up from the table. "That new boy I hired?" he said, nodding towards the blue-jeaned figure watching them from the other end of the barn. "He's a hard worker, but not a . . . how you say, hustler?" Aware of their eyes on him, the young man shifted restively from one foot to the other, obviously at loose ends.

Tessa, sure that her notion of a hustler wasn't the one Miguel had in mind, suppressed a smile. "You mean he's not a self-starter?"

"*Si!*" Miguel pantomimed steering a car. "He still has to be shown how to go." He touched his hat brim. "Thank you for lunch."

"My pleasure, Miguel."

She watched his spare, upright figure move

sedately towards the new hand, who trotted forward to meet his mentor. They rounded the corner of the barn together, the younger man nodding as Miguel talked. Tessa left the hiring and firing of the hands who worked with the horses in Miguel's hands. He always made a nice little show of seeking her approval, but in thirty years she'd never even considered second-guessing him. Barry hadn't liked that much either.

Tessa had just finished dressing after a long cool shower when Jed arrived. He knocked, walked in calling her name, and met her at the foot of the stairs.

She wore slim tan chino pants belted tightly over a blue, sandwashed silk shirt. Her hair, still a little damp, hung loose on her shoulders; her face, except for lipstick, was as God— and time— had made it. She was barefoot.

Jed looked at her appreciatively. "You smell nice," he said. "Soapy."

"Soapy, hell. It's a very pricey cologne Gavin gave me for my birthday this year." She grinned. "He forgot to peel the price tag from the bottom of the box. It's got one of those la-di-da names, but it's basically carnation."

"Okay, expensive soapy. Spicy but sweet."

"If you were thinking of adding 'just like you,' you can forget it, pal."

Jed's eyebrows rose. "Never crossed my

mind." They walked into the living room. Tessa sat in one of the big easy chairs; he lounged, hipshot, against the stone fireplace, one hand resting along the edge of the mantel. "You're in a perky mood today."

"Have you a problem with that?"

"No, not really, not as long as it stops short of taking playful nips at anyone in your vicinity . . . like me, for instance."

She looked indignant. "Whatever makes you think— "

"I've known you a long, long time, Tessa."

"One 'long' would have been enough," she remonstrated. "But you're right," she said, her smile returning, "I *am* feeling good. That bay colt, Resha?" He nodded. "He's a real sweetheart. Our training session went extremely well, and afterwards Miguel and I had a meeting of the minds about the direction the breeding program should be following." Her smile faded. "It made me forget for a little while about the things that aren't going so well."

"Like Lloyd, you mean."

"Yeah. Among others," she added in a mutter.

"Well, after you called I did some phoning around. One of the guys I've kept up with since my college days tells me that another of our classmates, who majored in biochemistry, is now a well-regarded researcher in genetics out on the West Coast. I figured maybe he could tell us how the twins came by hazel eyes by virtue of legitimate inheritance. As I told you, I'm pretty sure I already know the answer, but who's going to listen to me?"

"No kidding! Do you think he might— "

"I called him next, Tessa. Caught him just as he was leaving for a conference in Chicago. He said he'll be glad to help. He'll even testify if need be, but that would probably mean paying his expenses . . . airfare, motel, meals . . ."

"No problem. He could stay here. Enjoy the view."

"Then, on the way over, I got to thinking. What if you took a couple of days off, flew down to Brownsville, called on your in-laws, and asked to borrow that portrait? A temporary loan, you could call it. One look at it should change Lloyd's mind . . . Jack's too, I reckon."

She thought for a moment, then frowned and shook her head. "It's a good idea, Jed, but it won't work. For one thing, although old Boyd kind of liked me— he liked blonds, anyway— Mom Wagner barely tolerated me. She thought *I* thought I was better than the Wagners— "

"Didn't you?"

"Well, yeah, but I tried not to show it too much." Jed grinned at her. "I really did try," she protested. "Anyway, feeling as she did, when Barry died it was easier to blame me for his failings than find fault with her boy." She shrugged. "In her shoes I'd've probably felt the same. So if I sashayed in on them after all this time . . . Hell, Jed, the only contact we have now is at Christmas! Old Boyd always sends Garland a check for her birthday, but *he* signs the card."

"Nothing for Gavin? He's blond, too."

"Yeah, but the wrong gender," Tessa said.

"Another dirty old man, huh?"

Knowing he meant Scott, Tessa narrowed her eyes. *Did he know something she didn't?* Deciding to postpone opening that particular can of worms, she said, "As I was saying, if I popped in on them, saying 'Hi, how you doing, mind if I borrow Gram's portrait?' Mom'd be on the phone to Lloyd the very next minute to see what was up. Might do more harm than good."

"Hmm-mmm. You may be right about that, Tessa. Damn. I'm sure there's a way . . . we just haven't seen it yet."

He came over to stand beside her chair. He placed his hand on her shoulder; hers came up to squeeze it. She looked up at him. Her eyes, he realized, matched the color of her shirt. Clear, vibrant, and very blue.

"Thanks for being such a good friend," she said.

Friend.

After all these years, that's still what it came down to. Could be worse, he thought wryly.

"Why don't you stay for supper?" she asked. "This woman you've got staying with Pop . . . would the favor she owes you cover that?"

He laughed. "That and then some. I'll give her a call," he said, turning towards the kitchen

"Garland doesn't get home until six, six-thirty," she called after him. "If you want a drink first, we won't eat before seven, so it would be at least nine by the time you got home."

Jed turned back, a sheepish expression on his face. "Damn. I completely forgot. Garland called me. She's staying in Telluride tonight."

"She called you?" Tessa's voice was harsh.

"She said she got no answer here."

She nodded, as if to herself. "Yeah, I was with Miguel and the horses most of the morning." She looked up at Jed, then immediately away, as if afraid her eyes might give something away. "Uh, did she happen to say where she'll be staying . . . just in case I need to reach her?"

Jed, knowing perfectly well the real reason behind her question, pretended ignorance. "With some woman she works with . . . Mona, I think her name is."

Under other circumstances, Tessa's expression of relief might have struck him as funny. She got up and began pacing back and forth. "I'm worried, Jed."

"I really don't think Lloyd's little blackmail attempt has much chance of succeeding, Tessa."

Tessa frowned and waved her hand. "Not that. It's Garland. We had a . . . disagreement last night. No, more than that, as near a row as we've ever had."

"Yes, I know." Tessa stopped pacing to stare at him. "She came to see me last night."

"So that's where she went! I thought she had gone—" She stopped abruptly. "Well, I didn't really know," she finished lamely.

"You thought she'd gone up to Shelby's in Telluride. That's what Garland said you'd think," Jed said. "She didn't seem to care," he added. "Why do you suppose that is?"

"How would I know?" Tessa snapped. "You sound like one of those damn psychologists! I hardly recognize Garland these days! My own daughter," she said in a faint, bewildered tone. She pushed her fingers through her hair. "Maybe that sweet, open, honest nature I've taken for granted all these years was just a false front."

"Come off it, Tessa! That's bunk and you know it."

She glared at him. "Why are you angry at me?"

"That broken blossom routine cuts no ice with me. I've known you, too long."

"I thought I knew Garland, too. Did she tell you about this boy she's been seeing?"

"*Had* been seeing," he corrected. "Although I'm not sure," he added dryly, "that 'seeing' is the right word for it. And he's twenty-one, Tessa. Hardly a boy."

"All right, *man!* God knows those tight jeans he was wearing proved that," she muttered.

Jed looked at Tessa curiously. It was hard to

be sure in the dim light, but she looked as if she were blushing. He knew that sometimes color rose in her cheeks when she was annoyed, but that was a flush, not a blush. He couldn't decide which this was; he wasn't sure he wanted to know.

"A *young* man," he gently amended. "And Garland's a young woman. If it hadn't been him, it would be someone else."

"Scott, maybe?" Her voice shook. "She told me she was willing to use him."

"I don't believe it," Jed said flatly.

"Then I guess you don't know her either! She's a schemer, that daughter of mine. She's not even finished college yet and she's talking about going east to veterinary school and joining a practice in Telluride. She's already researched it, for God's sake! So, since Scott knows everybody worth knowing up there, she figures he can introduce her around. If Sylvester Stallone and Tom Cruise keep horses, enter Miss Garland Wagner."

"That's planning, Tessa, not scheming. As for Scott . . . these days that's called networking."

"Networking? Hah! You should have seen him coming on to her the other night! Not in the usual way . . . Scott's much too smart for that. He doesn't go in for gold chains and shirts open down to there— he knows that would make him look pathetic. He comes across like . . . well, not so much like an older man trying to

look young as a man who's ageless. He's very good at it, him and his high-wattage smile." She looked at him earnestly. "Do you know what I'm trying to say?"

Jed nodded. "Sure. Don Juan in Ralph Lauren duds."

"A couple of weeks ago, I told Garland he meant no harm, but now I'm not so sure. He'll use her if he can . . . maybe he already has," she added bleakly.

"I think you're worrying unnecessarily, Tessa. Believe me, Garland's more of a chip off the maternal block than you give her credit for. *You* didn't succumb to Shelby's charm twenty years ago . . . I assume you haven't now, either."

Her eyes skated away. "This time around I wasn't given the opportunity," she muttered. "Garland told me he wasn't interested. Flat out, just like that."

Jed didn't know what to say.

"Did you hear what I just said?" She stood very close. Her anguished blue eyes, searching his, were filmed with tears. "Not. Interested."

The tears brimmed over and slid unhindered down her cheeks.

"Oh, Tessa," he murmured.

Meaning to comfort her, he gathered her into his arms. She clung to him, her hands clutching his shoulders, then slipping around his neck. Her tear-moistened cheek pressed hotly against his before sliding slowly, skin on skin, until her lips met his, joined with his, as if it were the most natural thing in the world.

Oh Tessa.

Nineteen

Jed returned the pressure of Tessa's lips, harder and more urgently until they yielded. His tongue met hers, teased, slid along her teeth, then thrust insistently beyond. He felt her body quiver familiarly against him, and the thirty intervening years vanished like smoke into a winter sky, spiraling away all the accumulated hurt and resentments.

Tessa clung, kneading the back of his neck as his hands moved lower to capture the rapid rise and fall of her ribs, the elastic softness of her rounded hips. She moaned. The sound was guttural, almost animal-like, and suddenly she was taking the lead. Breaking away, Tessa grabbed his hand and turned towards the stairs. Accompanied only by the sound of their quickened breathing— there was no need to speak— they stumbled up, one close behind the other, into her bedroom and collapsed entwined on the wide bed.

The room, its shades drawn against the afternoon heat, was dim. The kind light bolstered Jed's illusion of a return to their youth. He kissed her throat, then the hollow visible in the vee of her blue shirt. As he fumbled to open it, she lifted her hips. He freed the last of her shirt's buttons, heard the hiss of a zipper, then her whispered plea for assistance. He knelt beside her and eased down her pants— first one leg, then the other— exposing long white thighs smoothly muscled by years of riding, ankles as delicately boned as a thoroughbred's.

His eyes couldn't get enough of her. Still on his knees, he reached toward her plain white cotton panties— no-nonsense, just like her, he thought tenderly— and cupped the crotch with his sun-browned hand. It was damp against his palm.

"Jesus," he murmured.

Her hand reached out to tug at his belt, then grope for his fly. Frantic with desire, he stood only long enough to strip his long lean body free of jeans and shirt, tossing them into the room's shadowed recesses. Her eyes opened wide at the sight of his naked arousal. She shrugged out of her shirt and lay back again as he knelt above her, tracing the soft globes of her breasts with work-roughened fingers. He bent to nuzzle the hardened tips, first licking, then nipping them gently. She tossed her head from side to side against the pillow, shuddered, pushed him up, and lifted her hungry mouth.

Jed looked down in dazed wonder as she bent her head to attend to him, her hair a golden shawl across his belly and loins. He bared his teeth and threw back his head. *Oh God oh God.* The sensation rapidly became too intense to bear. Groaning, he eased her mouth away; then, aided by the eager lift of her hips, he peeled off her briefs.

"Do I please you?" she whispered.

"You do," he murmured. "You always have. But this . . ." His fingers teased through the gold thatch to explore the hot moistness beneath. The musky scent of her excitement intoxicated him. "I've dreamed of this many times, seeing you like this— more beautiful than I imagined— but I never thought— "

"Then shut up and love me!" she demanded in an exultant throaty growl. "Just love me, damn it."

A quick hard thrust and they were connected. Friends became lovers in a long, slow coupling that for Jed, hearing her little chirps of pleasure, became a dance of celebration.

The sweet chirping roughened into panting gasps— She came with a violence that astonished him, her body arching then slackening as wave after wave of tremors found release. Jed, who had been holding back, waiting for her, let go. Feeling himself pulsing deep inside her, he cried out. Adrift in sensation, he wound his fingers in her thick hair, using it to anchor him to a suddenly transformed life.

"Hey! That hurts!" she protested.

He released her, then lifted himself, smiling.

"My darling Tessa," he said. "I promise never to hurt you again."

"Never is a long time," she murmured.

"The rest of our lives," he said.

She pulled him down. They exchanged kisses. Soft, playful little butterfly flutters at first, but the urgency soon returned. Tessa exhaled explosively.

"I need air," she gasped.

Their bodies were slicked with sweat. She wriggled away from under him, sat up, lifted her hair off her neck, and turned to smile at him. "That was . . . wonderful. Is there no end to your talents, Mr. Bradburn?"

He smiled back. "That about does it," he said contentedly, "but I wouldn't say no to an encore, and maybe some variations. Assuming you're willing," he added.

"Right now I'd rather eat," she said, evading his seeking hand. She stood and pulled on her panties. "Sex always makes me hungry." She picked her silk shirt off the floor and slipped it on. "Doesn't it you?"

He watched her long capable fingers dexterously ease the buttons into their slots. *As dexterously as she eased herself away from me,* he thought.

"It's been a while," he said, frowning.

She stepped into her chinos and zipped them closed. "Oh? I thought maybe you and Nell— "

"Once. Big mistake." He watched as she snugged her belt tight around her waist, emphasizing the generous curve of her hips. He imagined them under his hands again. *Warm, soft, smooth* . . . "Tessa? We've got the house to ourselves, and it's still early . . . what do you say we—"

She plucked an elastic hair-tie from the dresser and secured her hair into a neat ponytail. "Don't coax, Jed," she said absently, looking in the mirror and smoothing her dark eyebrows. "It's not like you. Besides, I put together a beefsteak and kidney stew this morning, hoping to smooth things over with Garland. Not exactly a summertime dish, but it's one of her favorites. Of course I didn't know then she wouldn't be home for dinner, but if I remember correctly, you like it, too, right?" She turned. "Well, am I?"

Jed, who had dressed to the accompaniment of Tessa's chatter, found himself wondering what the hell was going on here.

"You're right about a lot of things, Tessa, but not that. Fact is, I don't like kidneys one little bit. Never have. You must be thinking of someone else."

"Can't imagine who that might be." She preceded him down the stairs. "Well, let's see, I may have another pizza in the freezer, or . . . I know, how about a Spanish omelet? If Garland takes up with that Rick Chavez of hers again— I hope she doesn't, but I couldn't blame her if she did— I'll need to add them to my breakfast repertoire."

"Handsome, is he?" Jed asked.

"Movie star caliber." Tessa shook her fingers as if singed. "I swear if I were younger . . ." Her blue eyes sparkled. She looked sleek, well-fed . . . *satisfied.* "So, what'll you have?"

Jed picked up his hat. *Old and dusty, just like me.* "You, Tessa, but apparently I'm not part of your game plan."

She stared at him. "What the hell are you— "

"You used me, Tessa." He laughed harshly. "Sounds like a damn fool thing for a man to say, but it's the truth."

"Jed, please!"

"It's not all your fault. I just wasn't listening carefully enough about how you suddenly realized Garland's not a kid anymore, and discovered that Scott Shelby no longer finds his exciting, gorgeous Wild Westerns girl 'interesting.'"

"Hold on there, you thought. There must be somebody out there who still thinks of me that way . . . somebody to give the old ego a boost. Hey! What about good old Jed?"

Tessa's eyes still sparkled, but with tears now, not excitement. "Oh, Jed."

"You made your bed a long time ago, Tessa. I should have let you lie in it."

Tessa flinched at his words. She stared at her toes for a moment, then her chin came up. "I wasn't looking to you to fill my bed, just warm it a little. If it's any comfort, you scored pretty high . . . maybe eight on a scale of ten. After the first few crazy months, Barry never made it much beyond four." She cocked her head. "Come to think of it, you always were a good kisser."

Jed's eyes darkened. "Go to hell, Tessa!" He jammed his hat on his head and strode past her, his heels rapping across the kitchen's plank floor like a tattoo on a kettle drum.

The glass in the kitchen door rattled as he slammed it shut behind him. Tessa's tears spilled over. Snuffling, she groped in her pocket for a tissue and ended up wiping her sleeve across her nose. Outside, Jed's truck roared into life. She ran to the door, pulled it open, and stumbled out barefoot into the cloud of his departing dust.

"You can go to hell, too!" she shouted after him. Then, she started to cry again. That, she realized, made three times in one day.

"It's too much, damn it," she muttered, rubbing the heel of her hand across her eyes. Her tears mingled with the dust, giving her the look of a pale raccoon. *Just too goddamn much.*

Tessa decided to save the beef and kidney stew for Garland's return the following day. After searching the refrigerator in vain for tomatoes, onions, and peppers, she fixed herself a plain omelet. After sliding it onto a plate, she regarded the pale half-moon of coagulated egg with distaste, thinking it looked more like a penance than a meal.

"So what if it does," she muttered. "I never claimed to be a saint." She poured herself a generous glass of jug white, carried a tray into the living room, settled into her favorite chair, and aimed the remote at the TV.

The atmosphere of near-hysteria that prevailed on the game show that flashed on to the screen contrasted stunningly with the blandness of her austere supper. Contestants dressed in blindingly bright clothes leapt about as if they had been basted with hot pepper sauce. Her omelet, which could have used some, tasted like the kind of food hospitals offer surgical patients just taken off a liquid diet.

A scream issuing from the TV speaker pulled her attention back. It had sounded like terror, but the emotion distorting the features of the plump female contestant being awarded a matched set of luggage in a hideous shade of pink was obviously meant to be an expression of joy. Tessa tapped the volume button down. It didn't help. If anything, the gestures and postures looked even loonier without sound than with it. If that was body language, Tessa thought, the woman was overdue for a stay in a mental hospital.

She irritably zapped the TV off, put the plate with the half-eaten omelet on the table beside her chair, then leaned back and closed her eyes. A moment later she heard Plume's claws clicking in from the kitchen. He paused to give her plate a surreptitious snuffle, followed by a cou-

ple of cautious slurps. *Better you than me,* she
thought.

*There had been no mistaking Jed's body language
either.*

His body was, she admitted to herself, a lot
better than she had expected. A hell of a lot
better. Barry had been well-muscled, too, but in
a different way. He'd been more compact.
More . . . meaty, like a prime feed-lot steer. Jed
had the rangy, long-legged look of a maverick.
He could use a few extra pounds, but no one
would ever mistake that taut hide for youthful
sleekness. It took years of hard physical labor
to produce corded arms like his, and the hat
brim stripe across his forehead, its pallor startling against the walnut-brown of the rest of his
face, told of long hours exposed to the ele-
ments.

Her father, Tessa reflected, as she drained her
wineglass, used to describe him as a long drink
of water.

Well, she'd been thirsty and she'd drunk her
fill of him. Her wry smile held little amusement. She knew Jed hadn't really minded her
seducing him; she also knew he didn't give a
damn about not being thanked for obliging
her—if anything that would have embarrassed
him all too hell. No, what had galled him was
her avoidance of a repeat performance. If not
later this evening, then tomorrow . . . or
maybe the day after. Soon. *Someday.* It hadn't
been her intention to treat him like a one-

night stand. She wasn't really sure what her
intention had been. It had all just sort of . . .
happened.

Tessa got to her feet with a sigh and carried
the plate Plume had obligingly cleaned out to
the kitchen. He whined at the door, shifting
from one paw to the other. She let him out,
then contemplated the pot of coffee left standing since morning. The wine, drier than she
liked, had left a sour taste in her mouth; the
strong dark acidic brew would only make it
worse. She poured it down the drain, then
washed her few dishes, grateful Garland wasn't
there to ask unsettling questions, or, even worse,
contemplate her sorrowfully with those big
golden eyes of hers. Anything or anyone that
hurt her Uncle Jed, hurt her.

Tessa slammed the washed pot down on the
stove, rattling the dishes in the drain rack.
"What about *my* hurts and *my* needs?" she demanded of the empty room. "Doesn't anybody
but me give a damn about them?"

Suddenly the house seemed hot and close.
She grabbed a flannel work shirt off the rack
on the back of the kitchen door and strode out
into the night.

It was very clear. The winking lights of a jet
crossing far above stitched a precise diagonal
line across a darkening sky speckled irregularly
with star shine. She heard the shriek of a rabbit.

Prey and predator. The natural order of things, she assured herself.

Could have been an owl, she thought. Or maybe the bobcats Miguel had reported seeing: one at dusk about ten days ago and a larger, darker one last weekend, both carrying prey. Probably taking food back to a hillside den, he said, to feed kits born of their late winter mating. She wondered if they mated for life, or if the tom would go his separate way as soon as the kits were able to fend for themselves.

"And if he does," she asked herself in a jeering whisper, "will a loyal and doting uncle bobcat rally round to fill the emotional gap?" *Not very damn likely.*

From the shelter of the sunflowers ringing the old water trough near the kitchen door, a single cricket chirped tentatively. It was too cool for a chorus. Tessa shivered and pulled the flannel shirt close around her. *If I'd asked Jed to stay, I wouldn't be out here freezing my tail off.*

Plume trotted out of the darkness, nuzzled his cool wet nose into the palm of her hand, and nudged her towards the house. She opened the door, intending to follow his waving tail in, then, at the last minute, pulled it shut behind him.

Not quite sure of her intention, she turned and walked, hands plunged deep in her pockets, towards the barn. A horse whinnied from the corral. It was Turnip's call: nervy and demanding. She quickened her pace, trotted into the barn, grabbed a bridle off the rack, and before Turnip knew what was up, she had eased it over his head, shoved the bit in his mouth, and fastened the throat latch. He allowed himself to be led the short distance to a mounting block— he was too tall for her to scramble on bareback— and grudgingly obeyed her murmured "Whoa, there!" as she leaned to open the well-oiled gate latch.

Tessa waited to hear it click shut behind them before pummeling his ribs with her bare heels. Turnip grunted. His ears came back and he plunged forward, yanking the reins through her fingers. Tessa recovered her balance, collected the reins before he could capture the bit between his large, yellow teeth, then leaned forward to give him his head, this time on her terms. The big horse's stride steadied, lengthened, then flattened into a gallop.

Tessa didn't see the light flash on in Miguel's quarters; if she had, she wouldn't have cared. The heady sensation of speed and the jarring impact of Turnip's pounding hoofs drove every consideration from her head.

Tessa sent a whoop echoing into the foothills. One of Turnip's ears flicked back; his stride faltered. She gave his flank a resounding slap with the flat of her hand.

"Go, you ugly bastard, go!"

He snorted, jounced up, skittered sideways. Then, with his ungainly head lowered, a blunt-ended arrow pointing the way, he hurtled down the ranch lane towards the forest service road, swung onto its roughly graveled surface, and up into the fast-approaching night.

Twenty

When Tessa returned home, she found Miguel waiting for her, pacing in front of the barn, muttering in Spanish under his breath.

"Madre de Dios!" he exclaimed as she slid off Turnip. "Where you been? When you go, it not yet dark; you come home, it past midnight. I think maybe, the way you leave, you run this horse to death."

Turnip nudged impatiently at Tessa's shoulder, smearing it with greenish slobber. "Don't you wish," she said, knowing Miguel shared Jed's distaste for the horse. "We left in a hurry, sure, but we slowed down when we got into the hills— lot of gopher holes up there. Then, after we topped the rise on Hayden's Bald, we headed for that little grassy mound about halfway along the fence on the Hatton side." She shrugged. "Once we got there, I kind of leaned back, doing nothing, while Turnip grazed. I just plain lost track of time.

"It's been a long time since I've done something like that, Miguel," she added, looking embarrassed. "It was real nice . . . the stars got so bright I almost needed— " She laughed. "Do you suppose there's such a thing as star glasses?"

Miguel's lips compressed. He looked very stern.

"I'm sorry I woke you," she said.

He stiffly waved her apology away. "I was *muy preocupado,* Miz Wagner."

"Well, I'm sorry about that, too, but there was no need to worry. I'm a big girl; I can take care of myself." Miguel rolled his eyes at Turnip. "He's not so bad, Miguel . . . and he sure can run," she added with a cocky grin.

Too tired to shower, Tessa dropped her chinos and slobbered-on shirt in the hamper and plopped herself into bed. She slept soundly and dreamlessly. Upon waking at seven, however, she felt as if she hadn't slept at all.

After a late breakfast, she worked the bay colt, but was too distracted to get the best out of him. Miguel didn't say anything; he didn't have to. When Garland returned that evening, she answered Tessa's provocative questions politely, but as briefly as possible.

"So how's the campaign going?"

Garland regarded her mother warily. "What campaign is that?"

"Scott. You know, getting something for nothing."

Garland looked away. "Not exactly nothing," she muttered.

Tessa cupped her ear. "I can't hear you," she singsonged.

"I *said*," Garland said with exaggerated distinctness, "he's not into giving free gifts."

"I could have told you that," Tessa said. "He's not a bank, after all, and banks haven't done it since . . . God, it must be the mideighties. That's how I got the microwave, you know, just by opening a second account up in Montrose. Closed it again as soon as I could get away with it."

"That's cheating," Garland said.

"Lighten up, Garland."

The two women glared at each other. Then, unsettled by this flare of hostility, they turned away and became busily engaged, Tessa in cooking supper; Garland in setting the table.

After about five minutes of working in silence— it seemed a lot longer, she thought— Tessa slowed her stirring of the warming beef and kidneys to look over her shoulder. "He came on to you?" Seen through the steam from the boiling pot of noodles, Garland looked wraithlike and vulnerable.

"Yeah."

"You want to talk about it?"

"I . . . I don't think so, Mom. We don't see Scott the same way."

"That doesn't mean I like the idea of him trying to seduce my daughter."

"I'd rather not discuss it."

"With me, you mean. Well, it won't take me

long to get supper on the table; afterwards, you can go cry on your Uncle Jed's shoulder."

"Please, Mom."

Just then the telephone rang. "Will you answer it please?" Tessa asked. "If it's Jed, take a message."

"The table's set, I can stir the— "

"Just say I'm unavailable, okay?" Garland hesitated; the phone shrilled on. "Garland, answer the damn phone."

Garland grabbed the receiver off the hook. *"Yes?"* she demanded. *"Oh.* Look, I— " Out of the corner of her eye Tessa watched her pace back and forth in front of the wall fixture, one hand twisting the cord, the other raking her loose blond hair. "Rick, I can't . . . I . . ."

Sensing her mother's covert scrutiny, she retreated into the living room, the long cord snaking behind her. "What? *No!* I've already told you . . ." Her voice lowered to an urgent whisper, the words undecipherable.

Rick Chavez.

Most women would find him impossible to resist. Tessa wasn't sorry Garland could, but the reason she gave for it, putting her career goals first, seemed mighty peculiar. Well, maybe not *peculiar* exactly, maybe more like taking practical logic a little far. *If I want to do this, I can't do that . . .*

That seemed like something Jed would come up with, Tessa mused. The adult version of not being able to have your cake and eat it, too.

The noodles bubbled louder. She stared at the pot. *God.* She hadn't the vaguest idea how long it had been on the boil. *Fifteen minutes, maybe?* They'll taste like mush.

Tessa upturned the pot over a colander, gasping as the steam rose scorching into her face. She grabbed the smallest of the wooden salad bowls from the shelf above the fridge and, as the pasta drained, tore lettuce into bite-sized bits, shook in a generous helping of garlic and cheese croutons, and laced the mixture with the olive oil and vinegar dressing she'd made for the dinner Garland had missed.

Tessa paused, the uncapped dressing bottle held tilted in her hand. *If Garland had come home, then Jed and I . . .*

Oil oozed between her fingers and dribbled onto the floor.

Garland returned to find her on her hands and knees furiously swiping a paper towel across the floor.

"Accident?" she inquired, as she replaced the receiver on the hook.

"Thanks to you!" Tessa snapped.

Garland, bewildered, threw up her hands. "Mom, I don't know what I've done, but whatever it is, I'm sorry."

Tessa sighed and stood up. "No, *I'm* sorry." She didn't say why; she wasn't sure she knew all the reasons. "Supper's ready . . . what do you say we sit down and give thanks for the good Lord's bounty?"

Garland's eyebrows shot up. Except for major holiday meals, her mother was not given to the saying of grace.

"That's a novel way of changing the subject," she commented lightly.

"No, I mean it," Tessa said soberly, deciding she did. "I sometimes think we take the good things of life too much for granted."

They ate in silence, but this time it was more like the beginning of peace than a temporary cessation of hostilities.

"Rick's coming to see me," Garland blurted.

Unprepared for this announcement, Tessa's eyes widened. Her fork tilted; the stew-laden noodles slid into her lap, offering a welcome distraction.

As she mopped the gravy from her pants, Tessa sorted through the responses that sprang to mind and as quickly discarded them, settling for a simple, "When?"

"I thought this weekend . . . I mean, he was so *insistent.*" Her choice of words expressed harassment; her expression didn't. If anything, she looked quite pleased with herself.

"Where will he be staying?" Tessa asked.

"A hotel in Telluride. He's offered to take us out for dinner Saturday. I'll pick something really nice and expensive. Campagna, maybe . . . he can afford it."

"Isn't that the restaurant Scott took you to in Telluride?"

Garland nodded. "I have to be in town all

day Saturday, seeing as how I'm practically
Scott's production manager for the festival. I
thought you and Rick could come and watch it
with me."

"This *is* the Bluegrass Festival you're talking
about."

"Yeah. You got a problem with that?"

"Me?" Tessa said. "I wouldn't miss it for the
world."

Instead of going out after supper, Garland
decided to stay home to watch the old Western
Tessa had chosen from that evening's TV line-
up. If Garland was curious about why, if Jed
had been the caller instead of Rick, her mother
hadn't wanted to speak to him, she didn't ask.

They exchanged amused remarks about the
parade of cowboy clichés, wincing when the
hero jumped from the roof of the saloon into
the saddle.

"If I were that horse, I'd've bucked him clear
up again," Tessa growled.

"Not me," Garland said. "Too much effort. I
would have just shifted one step sideways."

"Ouch!" Tessa said. "What a wicked girl you
are."

"Not wicked, Mom, just practical."

Tessa had cause to recall Garland's statement
the next day. She was working the bay colt—

Back, back, back . . . that's a good boy— when she became suddenly aware of Scott Shelby watching her across the cradle of his arms resting on the corral's top rail.

She walked Resha over to him and gazed down at him.

"Did I know you were coming?" she asked.

He lifted his gold head and turned the full force of his intense hazel-eyed regard on her. "I'm sorry if I disturbed you," he said. "Don't stop on my account. I like seeing you work."

"I can't work with you looking at me like that. Besides, I'm sure you didn't drop by just to watch your aging Wild Westerns girl put a horse through his paces."

His smile could have melted iron. "Like fine wine."

"Huh?"

"The aging part, Tessie. You still have that lush look, you know."

Tessa sighed, slid off Resha, and handed the reins to Miguel. "Take fifteen, okay?" Miguel scowled. He didn't approve of her breaking a training session, especially for a man he had always considered frivolous.

"Coffee?" she said as they walked towards the house.

"Thanks, but I just had some with Marion. My ex-wife," he added. "She's living here on the Cottonwood ranch."

"Yes, I know," Tessa said.

"You know her?" he asked warily.

"No, but some friends of mine do." She left it at that, rather enjoying seeing him wonder how well they knew her and what they might have said.

"What's on your mind, Scott? Anything to do with Garland? At your housewarming, you two seemed to be getting along real well." Her tone was dry.

"I get along with all the women I work with," he returned blandly.

"Speaking as her mother, I'm grateful for the doors you've opened for her up in Telluride."

"Oh?" It was clear from Scott's puzzled expression that he never consciously offered anyone anything beyond his own irresistible self.

"Very grandfatherly of you."

He didn't like that at all. He turned towards her, scowling. "Am I Garland's father?" he asked abruptly.

Tessa stood stock-still and stared at him. "You can't be serious."

"It's the eyes, Tessie. More than one person has commented about the resemblance."

You've sure got that part right, she reflected bitterly.

"So-o-o, I thought maybe she got them from me." He smiled winningly, stuck his long hands in the pockets of his linen trousers, and rocked back on his heels.

Tessa, unmoved by this display of Shelby grace, said, "Not likely . . . unless, of course, you believe I'm capable of an immaculate conception." He gaped at her. "For God's sake, Scott, we didn't ever go to bed together!

"But we saw each other on and off for almost two years! *No sex?*" He looked insulted. "Are you sure?"

"Very sure. None. *Nada*. Zip." She regarded him speculatively. "Would it have made a difference if we had? In regard to your . . . um, feelings about Garland, I mean."

He shrugged.

My God, Tessa thought. *Not even incest gives him pause*. "Good thing you didn't want coffee, Scott, because I'm not in the mood to give you anything but the bum's rush."

His expression conveyed no embarrassment; if anything it smacked of self-righteousness. "I could have lied, you know."

"You'd have to have a conscience for that." Tessa heaved a weary sigh. "Go away, Scott . . . there's nothing for you here."

"Does that include Garland?"

Tessa looked away. She wanted to protect Garland. Keep her safe and happy. Not tied to her apron strings, exactly, but . . . but *what*? A picture of a spider's web flashed into her mind's eye, an intricate pattern spun with a strong gossamer thread and decorated with struggling prey.

"It probably would, if I had the right to make that choice," Tessa said slowly, as much to herself as Scott. "But I don't . . . not anymore. My daughter is an adult; she can make her own decisions."

Scott's face brightened. She felt like smacking it.

"The Bluegrass Festival is this weekend, Tessie. I hope you'll come. Not for my sake," he added hastily, "for Garland's. She's worked very hard on it."

Tessa, recalling Garland's invitation to Rick Chavez, surprised Scott with a smile. "I wouldn't miss it for the world."

Tessa didn't bother walking Scott to his car. She returned to the corral where Miguel wordlessly handed her Resha's reins. The colt was unhappy about being asked to resume working, but Tessa, aware of Miguel's dark judgmental gaze following them, persevered. When they finished a half-hour later, even Miguel was pleased. They both knew that getting a young horse to accept being reined back was crucial to his development as a cutting prospect.

"*Bueno,*" he said.

Tessa grinned. From him, that simple "good" was the equivalent of "fan*tas*tic!" from anyone else.

The phone was ringing as she entered the kitchen. She grabbed the receiver off the hook and stretched across to the sink to get herself a glass of water. "Yes?"

"Hey there, Tessa." It was Lloyd. "I think maybe you better get yourself a lawyer."

"You're not actually planning on go ahead with this idiotic business, are you?"

"Yeah, I guess I am. Judge Colby seems to think I may have a case."

"I don't believe it," she said grimly.

"Oh, he didn't like the idea much, but the way Terry's— The way my lawyer put the, uh, situation to him, he didn't have much choice. You'll be hearing from his clerk about a date for the hearing . . . before the week's out, prob'bly." He paused.

Tessa, at a loss for words, gulped from her glass, grimacing at the water's lukewarm temperature.

"Be nice to get all this behind us without too much fuss," he continued in a low, ingratiating tone. "Whaddaya say we get together? See what we can come up with."

Realizing from his smarmy voice that what Lloyd really wanted was a fast, cheap, out-of-court settlement, Tessa set her glass down carefully. She gripped the receiver with both hands— "I say you're a lowdown scheming bastard, Lloyd!"—then slammed it back on the hook, but not soon enough to escape his jeering laughter.

I shouldn't have lost my cool, she thought. *I played right into those ham hands of his . . .*

She paced restlessly, trying to decide what to do.

Should she call Ben Colby?

Not without some kind of proof. And to get that, she had to call Jed. *Oh God.*

It was the last thing in the world she wanted to do, but what choice had she?

Tessa waited until after supper, when Jed would be more likely to be in and Garland had gone upstairs to do some hand laundry. The phone rang a long time. He answered just as she was about to hang up.

"I was helping Pop get ready for bed, Tessa." His voice was cold. "What do you want?"

"I'm sorry, Jed, I never would have bothered you except . . . well, it's sort of an emergency."

"Is it Garland?" His voice took on urgency. "Has something happened to her?"

"No, no, nothing like that. It's Lloyd. He called today to tell me Ben Colby has agreed to hold a hearing to reconsider the settlement of Barry's estate. I guess I'll be needing expert testimony from that friend of yours. I was wondering if you'd call him again for me."

He paused. "I'll get back to you."

"There isn't much time. A week maybe."

"I said I'd get back to you."

Tessa closed her eyes. She couldn't remember him ever being this angry with her before. "Jed? I . . . I don't know how to thank you for—"

"No need. I'm not doing it for you."

"No . . . no, of course not. For the kids." Her voice dropped to a whisper. "Good night, Jed."

His response was the drone of a broken connection.

Tessa stared dumbly at the receiver in her hand.

Goodbye, old friend.

Twenty-one

At breakfast the next morning, Garland regarded her mother thoughtfully. "How long since you've had a trim, Mom?"

Tessa raised a hand to flick her hair off her shoulders. "Lord, I don't know— a donkey's age. You think I need one?"

"Mmm-hmm. It's looking a bit, uh, draggy."

Draggy? Was that Garland's way of hinting that a shorter length might help her look less long in the tooth?

"I usually wear it pulled back into a club or ponytail, you know."

"Yeah, but not always. Trust me, Mom. Call Jeannie."

Tessa gave her a guilty smile. "I haven't done that in a donkey's age either— " She broke off, looking puzzled. "Why a donkey? Do they live longer than horses and mules? I've known some pretty old ponies, but donkeys?"

"I haven't the faintest," Garland muttered. "Have you seen my car keys?"

"I thought you were planning to be a veterinarian!"

"Aha!" Garland crowed as she retrieved the keys from the depths of her shoulder bag. "I am, Mom, but I've a way to go yet. I'll have to get back to you on that."

"Did I tell you your boss stopped by yesterday?"

Garland turned from the open door. "Mona came here? Whatever for?"

"Not that one, Garland. Scott. He wondered if you might be his daughter. The eyes, you know."

"Well, well," Garland said, raising her eyebrows. "It's nice to know he draws the line someplace. What did he say when you told him I wasn't?"

"Well, the thing is, when it comes to sex, Scott doesn't draw lines . . . in fact, I don't think he even sees them. If anything, he seemed kinda disappointed."

"I wish I could think you were wrong." She shook her head. "Lord. What a creep."

"A charming creep, though," Tessa said.

"Yeah, he is," Garland admitted.

"He told me you've worked very hard to make his festival a success."

"Not as hard as that little bluegrass singer has been working on *him,*" Garland said.

"Back in the picture, is she?"

"Is she ever! Looking sweet and fresh as morning dew, but if you ask me, she's got a lot of hard mileage on her." Garland grinned. "The old rascal may have met his match."

"My, my," Tessa said, knowing better than to express outright delight at Garland's disillusionment.

They smiled at each other affectionately.

"Everything okay with you, Mom?"

"Sure," Tessa said, not quite meeting her daughter's earnest gaze. "Me and that bay colt, we're a lot alike these days, both of us learning lessons that don't come all that easy." Her smile turned rueful. "Only difference is, backing up gave him the most trouble; with me, it's going ahead."

"And damn the torpedoes?"

"Haven't seen many of those around here, Garland . . . except maybe for your Uncle Lloyd. I mean, look at him: he's big and round and pointy-headed, too."

"Now that you mention it," Garland said, laughing, "there is a certain resemblance. Gotta go, Mom! Call Jeannie, okay?"

And Tessa did.

"Tessa *who?*" Jeannie said. "Golly gosh, that name sure does sound familiar, but I just can't seem to— "

"Give me a break, Jeannie. It's been kind of hectic around here lately."

"Prove it!" she demanded.

Tessa hesitated. *Garland's a lot more sophisti-*

cated than I was ready to accept? Lloyd's taking m
to court? Scott Shelby's a shit? Jed told me to go t
hell? She settled for her brother-in-law.

"Lloyd talked Ben Colby into reconsidering
the settlement of Barry's estate. I don't know
when the hearing's going to be, but Lloyd said
soon."

"But that's ridiculous! On what grounds?"

"The twins' paternity. Seems he passed Scott
Shelby in Cottonwood a while back, and those
hazel eyes of his got old Lloyd to thinking."

"Oh my God. That *bastard!*"

Jeannie's indignation cheered her. "Well, it is
an unusual shade of hazel, you know. Sure gave
Barry pause . . . probably others, too."

"Not your friends, sweetie!" Tessa suspected
Jeannie was shading the truth; her next words
confirmed it. "Not your *real* friends, anyway.
Does this mean Lloyd hired a lawyer? I thought
he hated to part with so much as a penny.
What's he after?"

"I refused to consider his offer for the land
Barry left the twins. He wants it in the worst
way, and so does Terry Ballou."

"Oh, well, that explains it. If Mr. Deep Pockets Ballou is involved, Lloyd'll have a free ride
for as far as he wants to go."

"Thanks so much for sharing that with me."

"Hey, I'm sorry, but—"

"It's okay, Jeannie. You're not telling me anything I didn't already know."

"Can't Shelby put a spike in his nasty little

scheme? I assume you've talked to him about
it."

"Well, the thing is, Scott says he doesn't recall
not sleeping with me. Considers it a blot on his
record, I guess. Anyway, that's one of the reasons you haven't heard from me."

"You mean there are *more*?"

"Oh, yeah. But that's not why I called now.
Garland says I need a trim. She says, and I
quote, 'It looks draggy.' "

"Mmmm-hmm. Sounds serious. Angie Lind-
blad canceled her regular ten o'clock. How
would that be?"

"Today?"

"Yeah . . . uh, Marion Shelby's coming at
eleven, would that matter?"

"Can't see why. I haven't met her yet and I'm
kind of curious."

"That's right! You missed the barbecue,
didn't you? Say, how was that housewarming
anyway?"

"Ancient history, Jeannie."

"Oh, like that, huh?"

"Like that," Tessa said firmly. "See you at
ten."

Jeannie studied Tessa's reflection in the mirror, hoisted a lock of hair, weighed it, shook
her head. "Garland knows whereof she speaks,
my dear. You need a trim, a shaping, a wash,
and a thorough conditioning." She cocked her

head. "Maybe just a little color this time, to sort of brighten things up? Give you a new lease on life, cross my heart."

"Forget it, Jeannie. The old lease hasn't expired yet."

"Well, when you decide what your next move is— "

"You'll be the first to know."

"Promise? You haven't been that reliable a communicator lately."

Tessa drew a cross with her finger on the plastic wrap Jeannie had tied around her. "Promise."

Jeannie tilted Tessa's head back into the sink, wet her hair, and worked suds through it, her massaging fingers eliciting a sigh of contentment.

"That feels so goo-o-o-d!" Tessa purred.

"Don't care how it feels," Jeannie said briskly. "It's how it looks when I'm finished that counts."

Tessa watched with a respectful interest approaching awe as her friend clipped and combed and deftly wielded the dryer. Even before they entered their self-absorbed teens, Garland and Gavin had refused to allow their mother anywhere near them with a scissors, and Miguel had prepared the horses for shows ever since she left one of them with a chewed-off stubble for a mane. She had told him she just couldn't seem to get it even.

But Jeannie had. She always did, Tessa thought.

as she turned this way and that, admiring the effect in the mirror. "I feel like a new woman!"

Jeannie crossed her arms, a smug smile on her face. "Well, at least it's not draggy anymore."

The bell over the door jangled, announcing a new arrival. The woman who entered, waving hello at Jeannie, was small, grayhaired, and plumply pretty. Calm assurance flowed from her, and as she approached them, her steps brisk and light in polished brown boots, Tessa noted the flattering line of her long-sleeved white linen shirt and tan twill pants. They looked simple enough, but given her figure and a fit like that, she judged them made to order.

"Be with you in a minute, Marion," Jeannie said. "Charlene wants me to check a color job she's doing. That blond vision I just finished with is Tessa Wagner, by the way. She's the horse lady Jed and I were telling you about."

Tessa laughed. "Vision? Wow. I think Jeannie better have her eyes checked."

"I heard that!" Jeannie called from the other end of the salon. "You should have seen her when she came in!"

Tessa laughed. "Nice to meet you at last, Marion. You're interested in horses?"

"I think so," Marion said, shaking the hand Tessa extended. "What I mean is, I've always liked horses— I used to ride a lot when I was younger, even owned a couple, but that's a long time ago. You haven't changed much."

Tessa looked puzzled. "Uh, have we met before? I'm sorry, but— "

"No, no. Scott had your picture"— she squared off a big rectangle with her fingers— "over his desk. His very own girl of the golden West. I was jealous as hell."

"No need to be. What kind of horse are you looking for?"

Marion Shelby looked amused. *About what?* Tessa wondered. *Did I come across as pushy?*

"Are you by any chance free for lunch?" the older woman asked.

"I guess so," Tessa said slowly. "Sure, why not? It's been a long time since I've been up your way. You've got yourself a real nice spread— I'll be interested to see what you've done with it."

"So far, not all that much; I've got ideas though . . . Jed Bradburn helped me sort them out."

I just bet he did, Tessa thought, knowing how much he valued the grazing land she'd leased him.

"Sorry for the delay!" Jeannie said as she bustled back. "What are you having today?" She eyed Marion's gray bob appraisingly. "That trim's holding up pretty good."

"Just a wash and blow-dry, Jeannie. Do you mind waiting?" she asked Tessa, as she settled into the chair.

"Nope," Tessa said. "Half-hour about do it?" Jeannie nodded. "Good. That'll just about give

me time to walk to the town hall, ask a question
or two, and walk back . . . maybe the long way,
around the square. I don't get into town much,"
she explained for Marion's benefit.

"Just think what she's missing!" Jeannie said.
"The once-over from the old geezers on the
bench in front of the hardware store and being
deafened by the noon fire whistle. I mean, who
needs New York City!"

"Hush up, Jeannie," Tessa advised amiably.

"Maybe you'll find that Lloyd's changed his
mind," Jeannie murmured, no longer joking.

"Yeah, and maybe I'm really the vision you
say I am."

By the time Tessa returned—she didn't say
anything to Jeannie, just frowned and shook her
head—Marion was ready to leave. Tessa followed her silver, late-model four-by-four— *big*
sucker; fully loaded—dropping behind to avoid
the dust when they turned off onto the gravel
forest service road that climbed up and up, bor-
dered by a small rushing creek that narrowed
as it neared its source.

Tessa's ranch, Skywalk, commanded from its
sprawling valley setting a panorama of the entire San Juan range. The house on the spread
Scott had bought twenty-three years ago hun-
kered in the shadow of the jagged fourteen-
thousand-foot upthrust of the highest peak.
People sighed covetously when they saw the Sky-

walk view; this one sent your heart into your throat.

"Awesome," Tessa said as they walked together up a path paved with rounds sliced from huge logs.

Over seventy years old when Scott bought it, the low sprawling ranch house looked much the same as it had after he restored it. The trees he had planted were bigger now, but there had been no additions. Even the color scheme— dark-stained logs; barn-red trim and front door— was the same.

"Isn't it?" Marion agreed. "Last February, when the snow got so deep, I jumped every time I heard a distant rumble."

"Never been any slides here that I know of."

"Isn't there always a first time?"

"Actually, no. Snow always chooses the easiest, fastest route down. This isn't one of them. Now, if the house had been built below that fissure— " Tessa pointed to a deep wide treeless gash on the mountain's west flank— "then you'd have something to worry about.

"I can almost guarantee your safety here . . . well, you could get struck by lightning, I suppose, but snow slides? Uh-uh."

"Glad to hear that. This house suits me just fine. It's old and weathered, but kept in good repair, just like me." She waved away Tessa's automatic protest. "I want to turn this place back into a real working ranch, Tessa. I really don't have any interest in making an architectural statement . . . I've got better things to do with my time and money."

Was that a backhanded slap at Scott's new Telluride digs? Tessa wondered.

Inside, the house looked sort of like a cross between hers and Scott's, Tessa thought. There were some good old Indian things— Navajo rugs; a couple of Apache baskets— and a very nice collection of much newer pots from the Pueblo of Acoma stood on the wide wood plank mantel over the blackened fireplace.

Tessa picked it up and peered at the bottom. "T. L.," she read aloud. "I have one of hers, too. Theresa something."

"Theresa Lukee," Marion said. "I have three." Aesthetic credentials having been exchanged, they smiled at each other. "So what do you think?" Marion said.

"About what?" Tessa asked.

"About this place . . . Scott told me you were at his housewarming."

"Oh, I like this much better," Tessa said without hesitation. "The only statement Scott's house made to me was that I'd better watch where I put my dirty boots."

Marion laughed. "Come out to the kitchen with me, Tessa. I asked you to lunch, but I'm damned if I know what I've got to give you."

They agreed on grilled cheese sandwiches and a green salad. Tessa mixed up a ranch dressing. "Cottonwood style," she told her hostess. "A lot zingier than the bottled variety."

Marion, watching her shake in Tabasco sauce, said she didn't doubt it.

Over lunch they talked of horses. Marion confessed to a weakness for Arabians; Tessa said she didn't blame her.

"They're beautiful animals. More elegant than quarter horses, but not muscled enough for competition-level cutting and barrel-racing. There are a couple of top breeders not too far from here— one is in Montrose, the other down near Durango. I'm sure either of them could fix you up."

"I really appreciate that, Tessa. Would you be able to do any training I might require?"

"Sure thing. I'd enjoy working with a good Arabian again. We could do it together, then next time you could get a green horse and do the schooling yourself. Lot of satisfaction in it."

Marion gave Tessa a searching look. "You know, I think we're going to be friends."

"Well, hell, so do I, Marion," Tessa said, grinning. "We've been getting along like a regular house on fire. You had doubts?"

"I'm a lot older than you are. You're what? Forty-five?"

"Now I *know* we're going to be friends. Fifty."

"I crossed over into Medicare land this spring," Marion said with a rueful smile.

Tessa shrugged. "Scott's the only person I know who puts much store on things like that." She bit her lip. "Oh dear. Forget I said that."

"Why? You're quite right." Seeing her lips

curve in a soft smile, Tessa thought how attractive she was. "Dear Scotty. These days he's his own worst enemy. He's playing a losing game, but can't yet bear to face up to it."

Tessa didn't have to ask what game she meant. "Do you think he ever will?"

"What choice does he have? He doesn't look as good as he does by the grace of God, you know."

Tessa's eyes widened. "My God. I'll admit I wondered, but there sure aren't any telltale signs."

"He's paid a very good cosmetic surgeon a lot of money over the years to make sure there wouldn't be. His grace and style are uniquely his, of course, but in time— two years, maybe three— that expertly firmed jawline will begin to sag again, and he'll come trailing back to me, sadder, but probably not much wiser. I'll have to find a tactful way to discourage him from having himself tacked up again. By then he'll be closing in on sixty-five; I don't want him to make a fool of himself."

"I know it's none of my business, Marion, but . . . well, I can't help wondering what you expect to get out of it."

Marion met her inquiring gaze directly. "Nothing. I love Scott, and he loves me, too, in his way. He's a vain man, but not an evil one. Success is very important to him, and sometimes this need for it leads him astray. You're aware that after his huge success with Wild Westerns, he had another triumph with Water Babies?''

Tessa nodded. "The girl who inspired that line was his first wife, wasn't she?"

"Lovely creature," Marion said. "Smart, too. She was a marine biologist working in San Diego. Sleek as a seal and a lot smarter. Scott met her by chance, swept her up in his whole 'I'll make you a star' routine, and married her. When the line ran its course, she found that as far as Scott was concerned, she had, too. She walked out. She took with her only what she had earned, returned to the work she was trained to do, and wrote a child's guide to marine life. Unlike Scott's next ventures, it was quite successful. Are you aware he had a breakdown?"

Tessa shook her head. "My daughter Garland told me he'd had a few bad years."

"Seven. It was very hard for him. He kept trying and failing, and eventually lost everything to his creditors. That's where I came in. I'd known Scott for years— he was very popular on the California charity circuit. Always willing to organize fashion shows to promote worthy causes."

"Including himself?"

Marion grinned.

"Are you saying you bailed him out?"

"That was part of the deal." Tessa looked shocked. "Scott never went so far as to propose a prenuptial agreement . . . let's just say I had no illusion about how it was between us."

"But I thought his folks had money . . . from things he let drop, I got the distinct impression he came from an old North Carolina family."

Marion pushed her plate aside and rested her chin on tented hands. "Scott's parents emigrated from Hungary in the fifties, settled in New York City on the lower east side of Manhattan, and opened a clothing store. They sold designer labels at close to wholesale prices a long time before factory outlets were ever thought of.

"Working in an atmosphere like that, you learn what women want, what they're looking and hoping for, very fast. Scott began buying for the store in his early twenties and celebrated his thirtieth birthday by moving to the West Coast, where the California fashion industry was just beginning to take off. It must have been about then that he exchanged his humble rag trade background for blue-blooded North Carolina forebears."

"But he was so convincing!" Tessa said.

"Wasn't he? I remember him apologizing for that magnolia accent clinging to his speech— I didn't know then how hard he worked at acquiring it— knowing full well it just added to his golden boy charm." Marion laughed. "He really is a rascal! I might never have tumbled to the deception, except that one day I came home early from one charity meeting or another and found him in his study— huddled in a chair beneath your picture, actually— weeping.

"He finally confessed that his mother was in a nursing home out in the valley— his father had died back East years before— and he could no longer afford the fees. I agreed to pay them, of course, but I insisted on accompanying him on his next visit, and met this wizened little old lady who had never mastered the English language. Listening to Scott trying to explain me to her in Hungarian was quite an eye-opener."

"So he's pure fake!" Tessa said.

"No, his flair for fashion is innate and very genuine."

"I meant as a person."

"I like to think of him as a romancer."

"But he just plain, flat-out *lied!* Nothing very romantic about that."

"Most people lie, Tessa . . . in Scott's world, most of the time."

"Jed Bradburn doesn't," Tessa mused. "Although," she admitted ruefully, "that's one of the hardest things to accept about him."

"Living with saints has never been easy."

"Good Lord, Marion, I'd hardly call Jed a saint!"

"Then it wouldn't be so hard, would it?"

Tessa shook her head. "I don't understand."

"Of course you don't. Beautiful women have no need to."

"You think I'm beautiful?"

Marion cocked her head consideringly. "You

were beautiful, now you're handsome as the devil. That's better, I think. Elizabeth Barrett Browning must have been pretty damn handsome, too, otherwise I doubt Robert would have asked her to 'grow old along with me; the best is yet to be.' "

"I beg your pardon?"

Marion smiled. "It's not important, Tessa. What *is*, is for you to enjoy your life as it is now. Today and all the tomorrows. Jed loves you, you know."

Tessa looked at her, surprised. "Yes, I do, but how did you?"

"That evening at the 4H barbecue? He must have mentioned you a dozen times, sometimes with good reason, more often not. If I were a different kind of woman, I would have been quite put out."

"Perhaps," Tessa began slowly, "you should have used the past tense. About the loving part, I mean. I hurt him recently . . . quite a lot, I'm afraid."

"I'm sorry to hear that. He has value, that man."

"I thought he might have gotten in touch with you since. He thinks you're quite a gal . . . I thought maybe you and Jed . . ."

"Oh, no," Marion stated firmly. "Once you've been made love to by Scott—but I don't have to tell you how good he is."

"Actually, you do, because I never did. Every-

body thinks I must have— even Scott— but I
didn't. Cross my heart!"

Marion threw back her head and laughed.
"You may be the only woman who ever said no
to him, Tessa. Poor Scotty! He'd want to forget
that. But tell me, why did you?"

Tessa hesitated. This woman came from a
much more sophisticated world . . . how could
she explain it without seeming a ninny? "I was
married," she said at length, "and I don't break
promises . . . not even those I wish I hadn't
made."

Marion leaned across the table to take Tessa's
hands in hers. "Before I met you, I thought Jed
was probably too good for you. I see I was
wrong."

Tessa ducked her head and swallowed hard,
not trusting herself to speak. She patted
Marion's hand, noticing the wide gold wedding
band for the first time. *They may be legally divorced,* she mused, *but she obviously hasn't given
up hoping he'll come back to her.*

She scraped her chair back and stood up.
"Well, I wish I could say the same about you
and Scott, Marion. He sure doesn't deserve you,
and frankly, I don't know how you can put up
with waiting for him."

Marion smiled up at her serenely. "You have
to decide what you want most. What you want
above all else."

Tessa sighed. "That sure isn't easy."

"No, it's not. But once you know, everything else is."

At the door, Tessa thanked her. For lunch and everything that went with it. "You've given me a lot to think about."

"You were going to give me the names of breeders?" Marion reminded her.

"Shoot! Went right out of my head. Got a piece of paper?" Tessa scribbled out the information Marion wanted. "I don't have their numbers, but the phone company will. Good luck!"

"If one or both of them have horses that sound promising, would you be willing to come along with me to look them over? Maybe take them around the ring a few times? On a fee basis, of course. I wouldn't expect to get your professional advice for free."

"You wouldn't get it for free," Tessa said briskly. "Sure, be glad to. Tell you what, though: I'll throw in the coming and going."

"It's a deal!" Marion said.

Tessa drove home slowly, pulling over to give impatient drivers room to pass. Marion Shelby had indeed given her a lot to think about.

Lose a friend; gain a friend.

Unfortunately, it didn't balance out. An interesting chat over lunch didn't quite match a lifetime of comradeship.

Her misery suddenly overwhelmed her. "Oh, Jed," she murmured. "What have I done?"

Twenty-two

Saturday dawned bright and clear and windless. *It's going to be a hot one*, Tessa thought, but she knew that Telluride, two thousand feet higher than Cottonwood, would be just enough cooler to take the edge off. A perfect day for Scott's Bluegrass Festival.

She hoped for Garland's sake, considering how much time she'd put into it, that it was a hit. *For Scott's sake, too,* she conceded grudgingly. He had worked hard for his successes; it would be nice if he could return to Marion's forgiving arms with his aging head unbowed. Nice for both of them, actually. Marion was too good for him, but love doesn't make judgments like that. She knew exactly what she would be getting, and if the prospect pleased her, what the hell difference did it make what other people thought?

When Garland told her the Chamber had received more inquiries about the Bluegrass Festival than all the others combined, Tessa had offered to make a picnic supper.

"Including Rick?" Garland had said.

Tessa, who had needed no reminding, assured her the invitation did.

"I told you he wanted to take us to dinner, Mom—I can assure you he can afford—"

"That's not the point, Garland. If the festival is as crowded as you anticipate, the restaurants will be, too."

"So he'll call Campagna to make a reservation."

"That won't stop people from waiting in line looking daggers at those of us lucky enough to have tables. Kind of takes the edge off a person's appetite."

At that, Garland threw up her hands. "And you sure have a way of wearing a person down, Mom. Picnic it is."

When Tessa returned to the house after a session working with the bay colt, she found Plume waiting for her at the cellar door, hoping for a cool place to escape the heat. Tessa knew the goblins she feared as a child no longer hung out in that dark, earth-floored cavern, but she wasn't all that crazy about the scuttling, all-too-real little creatures that did.

Garland had no such fears. "Since when are you afraid of a few itty-bitty mice and crickets, Mom?" she liked to tease.

Since never, of course— as long as she could be sure that's all that was down there in the damp darkness.

Tessa opened the door for Plume, who waddled down the wooden steps, the white tip of his tail disappearing in the gloom.

"Don't blame me!" she called after him as she placed his water dish on the lowest step she could reach from the top. About what, she didn't say. She'd ask Miguel to come in later to let Plume out.

Tessa had bought a family-size package of boneless chicken thighs to fry for the picnic. They would be messy to eat, but Garland was fond of the spicy coating Tessa used, and it would be interesting to see how Rick Chavez coped. Deviled eggs, sliced tomatoes, pickles, three kinds of cheese, sourdough bread, a tin of homemade pecan-studded brownies (okay, not as good as Nell's, but close enough), a bottle of pretty good white wine, and a big thermos of coffee rounded out the menu.

Not exactly gourmet fare, but instead of settling for the usual jelly tumblers and the supermarket's generic paper plates, Tessa had gone out of her way to a newly opened party goods store in Montrose for plastic wineglasses and fancy designer plate sets complete with matching napkins and hot cups.

Tessa could picture Garland's amused expression and speculative sidelong glance when she saw them.

Who are you trying to impress, Mom?

"No one, damn it!" Tessa muttered. Certainly not a lot of jumped-up Telluridians. But she didn't want the youngest member of an old and respected family of oil-rich New Mexican landowners to think she was some backwoods janey-come-lately, either.

Tessa's pickup, along with scores of other vehicles, crept along the road leading to the festival parking area. It was four-thirty, a half-hour before the event was scheduled to begin, and the jam was already in progress. Waved into a parking slot by a teenaged boy, Tessa despaired of ever finding Garland. But no sooner had she turned off the engine than Garland and Rick Chavez were smiling in at her. *Had he arrived today or yesterday?* Tessa wondered. Now that she thought of it, Garland hadn't said where she was staying last night.

It's none of your business, she told herself sternly. "Thank heaven!" she cried. "I thought I'd have to send up smoke signals. How did you ever spot me?"

"Easy, Mom. We just looked for the least glitzy vehicle in the lot. There was no contest."

"Here, Mrs. Wagner, let me take that." Tessa, who had automatically begun sliding out the hamper from the passenger side of the truck's bench seat, gratefully relinquished the burden to Rick Chavez. "Will we need a blanket to sit on?" she asked Garland.

"Not us," Garland replied smugly. "Today we're V.I.P.'s. Guests of both the sponsor, Shelby Associates, and the Chamber Resort Association."

"We have folding chairs," Rick added, "with arms and cushions."

"I supplied the cushions," Garland said. "C'mon, we're right up front."

"Oh my," Tessa said, slowing her steps. "Should I have brought earplugs?"

Garland laughed. "This is a bluegrass concert, Mom, not punk rock. No screeching amplification; no flying objects."

Once they settled themselves and finished with the initial amenities, Garland excused herself and Tessa had a chance to covertly study the young man sitting beside her interestedly observing Garland's participation in the setting-up activity on stage. He lounged, elbows on the armrests, fingers intertwined, his long legs stretched out and crossed at the ankles. His beautiful pale Panama hat, tilted forward on the black gloss of hair, shaded his eyes from the long slanting rays of the late afternoon sun.

Five minutes later Scott appeared, his golden head shining like a beacon. The sleeves of his indigo blue shirt were rolled up on his arms, and a long strip of braided leather secured vanilla linen trousers around his slim waist. He leaned close to Garland, his hand on her shoulder, then looked down at Tessa, smiled blindingly, and waved. His eyes then shifted to Rick Chavez, sitting beside her. His smile faded. Tessa wished she could read his mind.

"That Scott Shelby?" Rick asked.

"Yep," Tessa said. "In all his splendor."

"Quite a piece of work," Rick commented.

Garland kissed Scott's cheek and hastened back to the trio of chairs. *To Rick,* Tessa thought, watching her hunker down next to his chair. Their faces close, they murmured to each other. Now and then, he slowly traced with one finger the lovely arc of her cheek. Tessa glanced up. Scott, staring after Garland, seeing her sleekly paired, looked for one startling instant every one of his sixty years.

The moment passed. His shoulders straightened, the smile returned, and he extended his hand towards the young woman who glided up behind him. She had a willowy, almost ethereal look about her, too frail to bear the weight of the guitar she carried. Her dress was long and unbelted, made of a sheer, minutely pleated ivory fabric that drifted around her like mist. Tessa thought that Garland, a slim girl herself, seemed positively robust in comparison.

Scott escorted her to the high stool in front of the microphone and tenderly helped her up on to it, where she perched, light as thistledown, her long ash-colored hair flowing around her like watered silk. She snuggled the guitar against her like a baby, stroking it soundlessly as Scott introduced her with a few well-chosen words. She waited for the applause to die down. Her eyes, lifted now to her audience, were huge, and of so pale a blue they appeared otherworldly. Her face was very white, and except for the soft full mouth, her features were sharp, almost pinched.

When Kayla Farrell finally spoke into the microphone, introducing her songs, Tessa was unable to make sense of her soft twangy accent. But when she began to sing, her expressive bell-clear soprano drew a sigh from the assembled crowd, and for the next hour, as her voice switched effortlessly from high and pure and true to a lowdown, raunchy growl, the audience nestled, awestruck, in the palm of her small hand.

During the break, Kayla's male backup group—a tongue-in-cheek nod, Garland said, to the traditionally male-dominated bluegrass style—played as the audience picnicked, their hard-driving performance sound relaxing into down-home rhythms.

"What happened to the guy featured on the festival posters?" Tessa asked as she portioned out the chicken, eggs, and tomato slices on the fancy new paper plates.

"Kayla happened," Garland said, grinning. "You could call it the sing-out at the O.K. Corral. By the end of the first rehearsal, he knew he'd met his match and then some. So he went out, got himself falling-down drunk, and staggered back accusing Scott of trying to sabotage his career. A lot of the terms he used to describe him with began with *f,* the kindest of which was 'faggot.' "

"Scott may be a lot of things," Tessa said, "but faggot definitely isn't one of them."

"I doubt if accuracy had much bearing on the choice of words, Mom. Anyway, he was gone by nightfall, and no one seems to miss him much."

"Shelby least of all, I'd say," Rick drawled.

Tessa and Garland followed his eyes towards the cottonwood grove at the far left of the stage area. Seated in the shade were Scott and Kayla, she at ease in a director's chair, Scott lounging at her feet smiling up at her. As they watched, he reached for one of her hands, turned it slowly, and placed a kiss in its palm.

"Off with the old; on with the new," Garland murmured. She seemed amused.

Tessa, thinking of herself and Marion, wasn't. "Yeah, and there's no fool like an old fool," she said sourly. "If what you said about that girl is true, she'll strip him clean."

"Oh, I don't know about that, Mom. In this case I'd say they've both met their match . . . be sort of interesting to see how this turns out . . ."

Hearing her voice trail off, Tessa turned towards Garland, seeking the source of her distraction. Rick's licking of his fingers, like a fastidious tomcat, appeared to be mesmerizing her. Thinking that the heat in her daughter's sherry-colored eyes could damn near singe the moist pink tip of his tongue, Tessa realized the little scene provided the answer to both of her earlier questions: not only how Rick would cope with the chicken, but how Garland had spent the preceding night.

"I'll keep you posted, dear," Tessa said dryly.

"Did you say something?" Garland murmured.

"Not worth repeating, darling. How about another deviled egg?"

Tessa leaned back in her folding chair and sipped her wine, wishing she could talk to Jed. Suddenly the sense of loss hit her so hard her fingers clenched on the plastic wineglass stem, tipping the contents. Tears filled her eyes.

Garland looked up, smiling. "You sure make a devil of an egg, Mom . . ." Her smile faded. "Mom? Is anything wrong? You aren't upset about Scott and his new ladylove, are you?"

Garland's guess was so far from the mark that Tessa was able to laugh as she knuckled away the wetness. "Lord, no," she said, rummaging in her bag, "it's the sun slanting into my eyes. If I had any sense, I'd've put on my dark glasses when we first arrived . . . ah! That's better."

"Tessa? Tessa Wagner?" She peered up at a male face hovering above her. "Alan Baumgartner," he said, "and this is my wife, Betsy. We were wondering if you still have that palomino mare you told me about. I tried to reach you by phone."

Tessa pushed her sunglasses down on her nose. "Alan! Nice to see you again . . . and nice to meet you, Betsy. I've been in and out a lot lately," she said after introducing them to Garland and Rick. "I keep putting off getting an answering machine, but I guess I've put it off long enough. Yes, the mare still calls Skywalk Ranch home . . . if you'd like to see her."

They would, they said, and a meeting was arranged for the following Wednesday. After they left, Tessa turned to Garland for advice. "They don't know much about horses, and if they decide to buy her, I'll want them to have a veterinarian check her out, for my protection as well as theirs. It'd be best if it's someone up here they can turn to in case of problems. I wondered if the vet you told me about—"

"Matter of fact," Garland said, "I saw him again just the other day. Seems he started his practice here only two years ago. He got his training at Cornell, loves the mountains and skiing, and settled on Telluride because it offered the best opportunity for work and play. Trouble is, during the summer he's got almost more work than he can handle— especially with horses." She laughed. "You should have seen his eyes light up when I told him about my helping you at Skywalk. He wants me to work in his clinic during vacations. How's that for serendipity?"

Tessa, who didn't know what that was, merely smiled.

"This guy . . . is he single?" Rick inquired gruffly.

"He has the prettiest wife you ever saw, two picture-book kids—"

"And a great big beautiful golden retriever," Rick finished in a mutter.

Garland eyed him coolly. "Actually, the dog I saw sprawled on his front porch the day I interviewed him was an unattractive, very old mongrel who broke wind a lot."

"Interviewed?" Tessa said.

"Well, you know, like I told you last week, someday he might want a partner . . . and by then that dog won't be around anymore."

Rick Chavez frowned. "Garland, I really think we should talk—"

"Don't start, Rick." The warning in her eyes was succeeded by relief as applause broke out around them, heralding the second half of the concert.

At the conclusion, after two encores and a fruitless cry for a third, Garland left to help with the postconcert chores, telling her mother not to expect her until Monday.

"You're staying here again tonight?" Tessa asked.

"The festival isn't over until tomorrow evening, Mom. There are two more performances, and by the time we wrap everything up I'll be too beat to drive home, much less eat anything when I get there."

Rick stayed behind with Tessa to help her

back up the remains of the picnic. "Garland told me your fried chicken was special . . . I thought she was just being loyal, but she was right. She usually is," he added resignedly.

"But not always," Tessa said, thinking that maybe this guy had more to offer than a truly outstanding array of physical attributes.

Rick flicked a wary look at her as they walked towards the parking area. "No, not always." He adjusted his longer gait to hers. "Garland's boss is giving her next weekend off, Mrs. Wagner, and I thought . . . I'm hoping she'll agree to drive down with me to meet my folks."

"Yes?"

"Well, I'm also hoping that would be all right with you."

"Does that matter?"

Rick effortlessly lifted the cooler over the tailgate into the truck bed. He paused, staring at it, then turned to face her. "Not technically maybe, but yes, it matters. To me, anyway."

She thought a minute, then stuck out her hand and told him to call her Tessa. "Does that answer your question?" she asked.

He grinned at her, displaying an enormous number of enviably even, very white teeth. Tessa was glad she had put her sunglasses on. "Yeah," he said. "Yeah, I guess it does."

Twenty-three

Monday, Monday . . .

*Wasn't there a song by that name, somewhere back
in the sixties?* Tessa shook her head. Whatever it
was, Monday always signaled a return to worka-
day life, and this particular Monday started the
week in which the hearing on Barry's estate was
scheduled.

Jed said he'd get back to me.

But he hadn't. Not yet anyway.

Has he ever let me down?

No . . . but there was always a first time.

Tessa stared at the phone on the wall. Her
fingers itched to dial his number. Instead, she
snatched her hat off the peg on the back of the
kitchen door and strode out to the corral. The
Baumgartners were coming Wednesday to look
at Banner; she'd better make sure the little
mare hadn't forgotten her manners.

Jed parked his pickup near the kitchen door
knowing that if Tessa were home, that was the

door she'd come to first. He also knew he should have called first, which put him even more on edge. There was no answer to his knock.

As he stood wondering what to do next, Plume came trundling towards him from the vicinity of the barn, tail gently waving, which meant she was somewhere in the area. Jed walked towards the corrals, Plume at his heels, and as he rounded the corner of the house he saw Miguel's spare figure faced away from him near the training corral's entrance. Inside, cantering sedately around the ring, was a pretty palomino with Tessa astride, her streaked-blond ponytail jouncing gently against her blue-shirted back. Rounding the far end, she caught sight of Jed, slowly pulled the horse up, and stopped at the gate. Miguel stepped forward as she slid off.

"Perfecto," Jed heard her say to him. "For the Baumgartners, that is. For me, she's so placid and well-mannered she damn near puts me to sleep." Tessa handed the reins to Miguel and walked forward, eyes fixed on Jed, her steps oddly restrained, almost as if she were hobbled.

I'd forgotten how blue her eyes are, Jed thought.

"I'd about given you up," Tessa said. "The hearing's on Thursday."

"Not anymore it isn't."

"Rescheduled?" Tessa said in a despairing tone, wanting it over with.

Jed shook his head. "Canceled."

"What?"

"The hearing's been canceled . . . or rather, about to be. I've just come from Lloyd's."

"I don't understand. Are you saying he had a change of heart?"

"You could say that."

"Damn it, Jed, stop talking in riddles!"

He gestured with his head. "Come on out to my truck. Got something to show you."

She followed him, waiting silently as he reached into the bed of the battered vehicle and lifted out a large flat package wrapped in what looked like an old mattress pad. He carefully unfolded it and propped the revealed large rectangle of mounting board against him for her inspection. It was a portrait of a middle-aged woman, whose large head seemed at odds with the trim, mid-nineteenth-century garbed torso below.

"Hannah Comfort Wagner," Jed said. "Great-grandmother of Barry, Jack, and Lloyd, in all her hazel-eyed glory."

The grim-faced pioneer woman who stared out into the morning sunlight was hardly glorious, but there was no question about the color of the eyes.

"My God," Tessa murmured. "How on *earth* did you—" She broke off, leaned over for a closer inspection, then looked up at Jed. "It's not the original, I see that now, but how—"

"I took a couple of days off," Jed said. "Pop's been—" He clamped his lips shut. "Let's just say I wanted a change of scene. My geneticist friend sent me the information you wanted, but reading it over . . . well, it was so damn technical. Seemed to me that for someone like Lloyd, a more dramatic kind of proof was needed. I thought about your reasons for not going to see the Wagners, but I couldn't see how they applied to me, so I flew down."

Tessa gaped at him. "To *Texas?*"

"It's not like I was going to the moon, Tessa. A few hours down, an overnight stay, and a few hours back."

"But *this,*" she said, making a sweeping gesture towards the color reproduction. "How ever did you get them to loan it to you?"

Jed fell silent. He ducked his head to collect his thoughts. "Well, the first thing I did was phone them. I had the address— they're among the handful Pop sends Christmas cards to— and Information gave me the number. I told them Pop wasn't doing all that well, and I was thinking maybe it was time the town did something to recognize the contributions of the early Cottonwood ranchers." He cleared his throat. "I mentioned seeing this portrait in their parlor when I was a kid, and asked if they'd be willing to let me have a copy made for exhibition. They were, and I did, and this is it."

"But this copy is so *good*— how did you have time— "

"Had it done the same afternoon. First a color photo was taken, than reproduced to scale, then mounted on this heavy board. The best part is the other side— I hadn't noticed it, but the guy who photographed it did."

Jed turned it around. There, in precise copperplate script, was a description of the subject: name, address, approximate weight and height, hair (light brown, gray streaks), eye color (hazel with a dark honey tone), and brown mole next to the right upper lip.

"When I came back, I stopped in at the Montrose library to look the artist up. Seems he was journeyman painter from Kansas City who painted up a lot of torsos during the winter months— male and female, adults and children— then toured the west all summer drumming up commissions, making sketches and noting physical details. Then he returned to his studio in the fall and painted in particular heads on his generic torsos."

Jed paused and tapped the edge of the board. "It was this description more than the painted eyes themselves that took the wind out of Lloyd's sails."

"My God," Tessa said again. She shook her head, then looked up at Jed wonderingly. "You lied."

Jed started. "What the hell are you— "

"You *lied* to that old couple, Jed Bradburn! Cottonwood isn't planning anything in recognition of the early ranchers— I'd be one of the first to know if anything like that was in the works."

"What I said was maybe it was time we did, and if you ask me, it is. That's hoping, not lying."

"You misled them, then."

"That's still not lying, Tessa. How the Wagners chose to interpret it is their problem." He pulled his nose in frowning exasperation. "The *point* is— "

"That Lloyd's bluff was called and all those lingering suspicions finally put to rest," Tessa blurted. "I'm sorry, Jed. I should never have implied there was anything, you know, *questionable* about how you went about . . . it's just . . . well, you've always been so damn saintly it kind of took me by surprise— " She broke off in embarrassed confusion. "Thank you," she finished simply. "I know I don't deserve all you've done."

As she stepped towards him, Jed drew back, reached into his truck for the mattress pad, and draped it back over the Xerox copy of the portrait. "I did it for Garland and Gavin," he muttered, "not you." He thrust it at her. "Here, they might like to have it."

He wrenched open the door to the cab, jumped in, started the engine, and before Tessa could collect her thoughts, had clanged away over the cattle guard under the ranch gateway.

Tessa wedged the big rectangle under her arm and trudged back towards the house, a corner of the padding trailing unnoticed behind her in the dust. Inside, she propped the board against the kitchen table. She removed the pad and slung it over one of the chairs.

Should I return the pad to him? she wondered. No point to it, she decided, taking in the stains and rents in the fabric.

Did I really call him saintly?

She had told Marion Shelby quite the opposite. Recalling the feel of Jed's lean, hard, naked body against hers and the frantic, glorious lovemaking that followed, she closed her eyes.

Saintly? Hardly.

A quiver of renewed desire stirred deep within her. Why hadn't she recognized their fervent joining for what it was? As a beginning rather than an encounter; a long-delayed fulfillment instead of a sop to her injured pride. Jed was right; she *had* used him, only to find herself forever in his debt.

On Wednesday, the Baumgartners came, accompanied by the veterinarian Garland had recommended. He asked Tessa a number of interested questions about her breeding and training program, but although he was both pleasant and knowledgeable, one look at the slightly built, jug-eared young man told her Frederico Chavez had no reason to fret as far as Garland was concerned.

The Baumgartners adored Banner— even Miguel smiled at Betsy's unabashed delight in her lovely gaits and manners— and after she passed the vet's inspection with flying colors, they roared off in their snazzy little red convertible, leaving Tessa with another twenty-thousand dollar check clutched in her hand and a delivery date set for the weekend.

"You shouldn't have excused the first stud fee," Miguel said, wagging his forefinger at her in gentle chastisement. "If others hear . . ."

"This was a special circumstance," Tessa said. "Banner could never have been a top cutting horse, you know that."

"But shown as a pleasure horse?"

She threw up her hands. "You've got me there, Miguel. Why do I keep forgetting there's a lot more to successful showing than Western events?"

"Because Western events are what you're best at, Miz Wagner."

"What *we're* best at, Miguel . . . except that you have the good sense to take off your blinders occasionally."

Miguel seemed puzzled by the glum tone of her concluding phrase, but for Tessa it merely expressed the present state of her life: blind to its possibilities; deaf to the needs of others, and altogether dumb.

Friday morning at breakfast Garland reminded her mother that she would be leaving from Telluride after work that afternoon for

New Mexico and her weekend at the Chavez ranch.

Tessa eyed the small duffle Garland brought downstairs with her. "Doesn't look as if you're taking much more than a toothbrush and a change of clothes."

"I don't anticipate the need for a ball gown," Garland said dryly. She looked down at her mid-calf-length, silver-buttoned denim dress. "I think of this as all-purpose, Mom, and I've got jeans and a shirt and sneaks in the duffle. What more could I want?"

"A bathrobe, maybe?" Tessa suggested.

"Rick said the bedroom I'll be using has its own bathroom."

"Ah," Tessa said, inferring that Rick and Garland would not be sharing sleeping quarters.

"Every bedroom does, for that matter."

Tessa raised her eyebrows. "Nice what oil money can do for folks, isn't it? Too bad your grandfather Hatton didn't think of settling farther south."

"I'll take our mountains any day over all that greasy black stuff," Garland teased.

"Oh my, don't let your Uncle Lloyd hear you say that . . ." Tessa snapped her fingers. "Hey! I forgot to tell you! He decided not to challenge your dad's will after all."

"No kidding! Why the change of heart?"

"Heart didn't have anything to do with it, Garland. It was all Jed's doing . . ."

Tessa explained the circumstances as objectively as possible. "I have the copy he had made of the portrait upstairs. "If you'd like to see it—"

"Don't have time now, Mom. Besides, I think maybe Gavin and I should look at it together." She picked up the duffle. "Just think of it," she murmured, "no more questions. Wow." She smiled at her mother. "Uncle Jed to the rescue again, right?"

Tessa ducked her head to avoid meeting Garland's eyes. "Right."

"Uh, I drove Rick down to meet him last Sunday morning. They seemed to hit it off. Which is more than I can say for Pop Bradburn."

"Well, you know how Pop is," Tessa muttered, fidgeting with her napkin. "He probably thinks of someone like Rick in turns of someone you hire, not get . . . *involved* with."

" 'You' meaning who, Mom?"

"Us. Anglos."

"Bigots, you mean."

"C'mon, Garland," Tessa said uncomfortably, folding her napkin. "How was I to know?"

Garland dropped the duffle on the floor and put her fisted hands on her hips. "Don't tell me you—"

"Okay, so maybe I thought at first he was looking for work."

Garland glared at her.

"Look, Garland, I *like* Rick Chavez, and you know how I feel about Miguel . . . if he weren't so damn religious I'd ask him to marry me. Tie him up for life."

Garland burst out laughing. The crisis had passed. "Good Lord, Mom! Miguel will never leave you. If you ask me, what you two have is better than a marriage."

"I hope you're not saying you think he's in love with me, because that's a crock of—"

"Not that way, no. What you and Miguel have is better even than love . . . well, better than lust anyway. Lust sure has a way of doing a number on a person's thinking," she added in a regretful mutter. "You guys have what you could call a commonality of interest, but you know where to draw the line. You know where it intersects and where it diverges, leaving you as separate, private people. Same as you and Uncle Jed. I don't think you know how lucky you are, Mom."

Tessa darted a suspicious look at her daughter. *Was she being sarcastic?* No, Tessa decided. Garland just hadn't noticed the fracture in her relationship with Jed yet. Too much else on her mind.

"It's harder when you're young, Garland," Tessa said. "That old devil desire has a way of popping up when you least expect it."

Garland grinned. "My, what an interesting picture that conjures up. See you Monday evening, Mom."

"Monday?"

"Mona gave me an extra day off, remember?"

"To recover from her Shelby experience? How is she coping, by the way?"

Garland shrugged. "Mona's a survivor. She may still be crying into her pillow at night, but you wouldn't know it to look at her. One thing's for sure, she won't be doing old Scott any more special favors anytime soon." She leaned to kiss her mother's cheek. "S'long!"

" 'Old Scott,' " Tessa repeated after Garland left. She thought of Marion patiently biding her time. *Nice woman. I wonder if she's located a horse yet?* Tessa resolved to give her a ring Sunday evening after she returned from Grand Junction, where she was scheduled to judge Western classes at a big horse show being held at a ranch a few miles north of town. One of the horses she had bred was entered in the barrel-racing event.

It'll be interesting to see that one again, she thought. He was getting on in years, but from all reports still going strong.

Which is more than I can say for myself, Tessa thought as she sat musing over a second cup of coffee, her mind wandering morosely from her immediate commitments to a future that seemed to drift aimlessly towards a bleak and featureless horizon. She'd continue working with the horses, of course, that was a given. But other than that . . .

An occasional jaunt with a woman friend? Good works for the church? The western slope chapter of the Quarter Horse Breeder's Association was always after her to serve on the board, but she hated paperwork, and the office of secretary was traditionally reserved for female directors. Judged by today's standards, she wondered if that qualified as sexism.

Tessa drained her coffee and scraped back her chair. She rinsed out her mug and upended it in the rack next to the sink. *Maybe someday I'll have grandchildren to distract me.* Recalling the way Rick and Garland looked at each other at the Bluegrass Festival, she smiled wryly. *Maybe sooner than I'll be ready for 'em.*

She opened the door to call Plume. Looking south, her eyes skimmed along the familiar line of peaks that jagged up black against the sky. Who would ride up with her this fall to help bring the spring calves down from the high pastures? Calm her down when her Wagner in-laws riled her? Take her to next year's 4H barbecue?

Don't be silly, she scolded herself. She could always take herself to the stupid barbecue; sit with Jeannie and Art; flirt with the guys. Like Garland's boss, she was a survivor, too. She'd manage . . . with Jed or without him.

But without him, how will I mend the fence up on Hayden's Bald?

Twenty-four

Tessa drove west out of Grand Junction on old Route Six. She'd been to the ranch where the horse show was being held, a bit north of the city and a few miles short of Fruita, but that was at least five years ago, and she couldn't remember if the turn was off to the left or the right of the road.

The traffic had been very light on four-lane Route 50, thanks to the early Sunday morning hour; here it was virtually nonexistent. She drove slowly, a window cranked down the better to enjoy the fresh morning air. The sky was cloudless, the air very still. According to the weather report crackling on the car radio, it would be hot, climbing into the high eighties by noon, followed by scattered late afternoon thunderstorms in the mountains. The typical summer weather pattern. The only unusual thing was the slight bead of perspiration Tessa felt forming along the edge of her upper lip. The forecaster either hadn't said anything about an increase in humidity or she'd missed it.

Ahead of her was a grove of peach trees. The curve the road took around it seemed familiar, and as it straightened out, she saw a horse trailer braking to make a turn to the right. As it cleared the verge, a brightly lettered poster announcing the show was revealed.

The trailer slowed as it jounced along the gravel lane, then pulled off to the left into a large mowed field and eased into the long line of horse vans that had preceded it. Beyond was a large fenced ring and a small grandstand, temporary by the look of it. Overall there was a general air of bustle created by horses being led, ridden, or groomed by men and women— young for the most part— clothed in aggressively styled Western gear. It resembled, Tessa thought, pictures she'd seen of Gypsy caravan encampments.

"Hey there! Tessa Wagner! Long time no see!"

Tessa's blue eyes searched through the crowd. Spotting a waving hand and a familiar smiling face, she plunged into the milling scene, becoming happily part of it.

The events Tessa was slated to judge were scheduled for early afternoon, after the hour-long break for lunch. By then, the sky was dotted with white puffs rapidly building into towers on the heat-hazed horizon. The decorative cotton bandannas worn by participants and spectators alike had long since been pressed into practical neck and forehead-mopping service, and the phrase about it's not being the heat so much as this damn humidity was on everyone's lips.

The only people benefiting from the discomfort level were the sellers of cold drinks, especially a pair of enterprising preteens ladling out lemonade from behind a rickety, wildly busy, stand.

"Is it really homemade?" Tessa asked in a whisper, recalling Gavin and Garland's ventures at a similar age.

Recognizing her as sympathetic, the younger of the two pointed to the pile of opened cans of concentrate concealed behind the curtain, then put a finger to her lips.

"Well, you opened them and stirred in the water by hand," Tessa said, plopping down a dollar bill for the largest size, touted creatively as the Tyrannosaurus Rex. "That's good enough for me!"

Tessa recognized the horse she had bred— like Jed's Bolt, he was Thor's out of Zig-zag— the minute she saw him enter the ring. The name she had filed for him with the registry, St. Elmo's Fire, had been inspired by the white blaze streaking down his chocolate face, but he was Elmo to the man who bought him from her as a green two-year-old, and his daughter, who rode him to second place in the Barrel Racing event, called him Mo.

"Not bad for a fourteen-year-old horse,"

Tessa said to her afterwards. "Your dad trained him well."

"Mo and I were born the same month in the same year, Mrs. Wagner," the girl said, her cheek pressed against the horse's lathered neck. "We're practically twins."

Tessa looked them up and down. "Not quite identical, though," she pronounced solemnly. "For one thing, you don't have the same number of legs."

The ginger-haired girl giggled. "No, but we can practically read each other's minds, can't we, Mo-Mo?"

To their mutual delight, the horse vigorously bobbed his head.

"Can't quarrel with that," Tessa said. An announcement blared over the loud speaker. "Gotta go," she said, taking a tissue from her pocket to wipe lather from the girl's cheek. "These horses aren't used to working in humid weather like this," she cautioned. "Better put a cooler blanket on Elmo before you load him in the van, but be sure to walk him and sponge him down first."

"I always do!" the girl called indignantly after her.

By the time the contestants left the ring after the last event, the sky had taken on a queer greenish tinge and the cumulus clouds crowding the horizon began to flatten here and there into ominous anvil shapes. The crowd thinned rapidly. Horses rattled up into vans; gates slammed on fidgety hindquarters, and as the first drops fell, yellow slickers were pulled on over fancy show regalia. Tessa, having turned down several invitations for the night, nosed her truck into the line of vehicles crawling towards the exit.

As she entered the road back to Grand Junction, she turned her windshield wipers from the intermittent setting to low, switching them to high when she recrossed the Colorado, now running red and turbulent enough to make her wonder if she shouldn't have accepted one of those offers of hospitality. The river couldn't have risen that much since morning if it hadn't been raining hard in the mountains for several hours, and from the look of things— or rather the *non*look, considering the blinding slosh of rain defying the best efforts of the wipers— the storm would be her traveling companion all the way back to Cottonwood.

In Delta, deciding to call it quits, she turned into the first motel she saw and got the last available room.

"The road through Gateway's already been closed on account of flooding," the proprietor told her.

"Damn," Tessa muttered as she filled out the registration. "I was hoping to go home that way tomorrow."

"Where's home, ma'am?"

"Cottonwood, north of Ouray."

He shook his head. "They're saying this weather system's going to hunker down on the San Juans tonight . . . might not start moving out till midday tomorrow."

Tessa's supper, bought from a bank of machines accessible, thank goodness, from the interior corridor, was a stale candy bar, a bag of potato chips, and a can of soda which she consumed while watching on TV an old movie she remembered not liking much when she first saw it twenty-five years ago. After the third commercial break she abandoned it and turned in, her lullaby the relentless booming of thunder— only slightly muffled by the double panes of glass in the large window fronting the highway— accompanied by lightning flashing through venetian blinds she hadn't been able to close more than halfway. After about an hour spent fruitlessly worrying about things she could do nothing about— *Had Miguel thought to check on Plume's whereabouts before the storm hit? Would Turnip, notoriously thunder-shy, crash through the pasture fence and take everyone else out with him?*— she fell into a deep, blessedly dreamless sleep.

It was dark when she awoke, although her watch informed her it shouldn't be. She peered through the blinds. The rain had steadied into a leaden downpour. Tatters of dark clouds hid the sky above and to the east, but a band of paler gray on the western horizon widened and lightened as she watched.

By the time she finished breakfast— eggs,

toast, hash browns, the works—at a truckers'
café on the edge of town, the clear patch to the
west was wider still. The spectacular sweep of
alpine peaks to the south, however, could be
seen only in her mind's eye. A tourist driving
towards them this morning for the first time
could only wonder what all the shouting was
about.

The gravel-topped dirt road leading to Skywalk Ranch was a quagmire. "Skywalk, hell,"
Tessa muttered, trying to keep the truck on an
even keel. "Pond bottom's more like it at the
moment."

The sunflowers ringing the old trough trailed
tattered petals in the red mud. Some might revive when the sun returned; most of them, their
stalks twisted and bent, wouldn't. Tessa parked
as close to the kitchen entrance as possible,
pulled her slicker's hood over her head, tucked
her duffle under her arm, and scampered for
the door. Before she could turn her key in the
lock, it pulled open, sending her stumbling in.
Miguel's strong bony hands steadied her.

"Miz Wagner! I didn't know where you were,
who to call—"

"What's wrong, Miguel? Has anything happened to Garland?" He shook his head. "The
horses . . . did Turnip break out—"

"No. Please." He raised a hand high to stem
her questions. "It's Mr. Bradburn."

"*Jed?* Oh my God. What happened?"

"No, Miz Wagner, his father. He had a stroke . . . on Friday, I think."

"But I was here on Friday, Miguel."

He shrugged. "That's what Vince Higgins tell me when he call last night. He say now the phone to the house no longer works and the road is washed out. Yesterday, Jed went across the flooding road to move that bull— what you call him?"

"Beefalo," Tessa said.

"*Si*, Beefalo. Vince say the bull won't move for anyone else. Jed led him into the barn out of the storm, and afterwards the men watch him fight his way back across through the flood. An hour later, no one dares try. By now . . . who knows?"

Who knows indeed? Tessa wondered despairingly. But as she recalled one of Pop's more shortsighted economies, she knew on whom the blame should be placed.

A few years back, after the runoff from a hard rain gouged a whole new set of gullies in the ranch road, Jed had wanted to put in a culvert to divert future flows, then build a simple plank bridge across it to connect the barns and corrals to the house.

"Never cut us off for more'n a few hours in all the years we been here!" Pop stubbornly maintained when Jed tried to tell him about the drastic change in drainage conditions caused by Terry Ballou's wholesale clearing of brush on the mesa above the ranch for one of his vacation house developments. "You young fellers," Jed had mimicked with sneering accuracy. "Always in a hurry to get someplace other'n where you oughta be."

I bet Pop's not sneering now, Tessa thought. *In fact, he may not be doing anything now,* she suddenly realized.

"Did the doctor see Pop?" she asked Miguel. When he nodded, she reached for the phone. After telling Doc Strunk about the isolation of the Bradburn house and ranch road by floodwater, he expressed alarm.

"Walt's stroke was severe, Tessa. I told Jed he ought to be in the hospital, but he said he knew his father wouldn't agree to it. Stubborn old coot! He called someone— a woman up in Ouray, I think, but I never heard— "

"According to his foreman, Jed's holding the fort alone."

"Don't like the sound of that, Tessa . . . no way to get up there, you say?"

"Miguel says no. I gather the road in has turned into a river, and even when the rain stops they'll have that runoff from the mesa— " She stopped short. There was a way! Why hadn't she realized it sooner?

"Tessa? You still there?"

"Gotta go, Doc. Maybe I can't get over the river to grandma's house, but there's always the woods."

"Whose grandma? What are you talking— "

Tessa slammed the receiver into the hook and

turned to Miguel, eyes bright. "Miguel? Saddle up Mackerel. I'll throw a few things together and meet you outside the door here. Where did I put that duffle . . ."

"Miz Wagner? What you thinking of doing? You can't—"

"I can. Over Hayden's Bald. Jed needs me, Miguel. I don't have time to discuss it. Just bring those fence clippers with you."

Tessa pounded upstairs for a change of clothes and a dry pair of shoes. Returning to the kitchen, she zipped open the waterproof duffle she'd brought in from the truck, dumped her armload in on top of the stuff she'd taken to the horse show, and added a few staples— soup mix, canned tomatoes, peanut butter, crackers, powdered milk— from the kitchen cupboard.

She heard the mud-muffled clip-clop of hooves outside. She started to close the cupboard door, then, rising on her toes, she lifted down a bottle of bourbon from the top shelf. *Might come in real handy*, she thought grimly as she zipped it into the duffle. She dug in the twine drawer for an elastic cord and secured it through the canvas handles, praying Mackerel wouldn't get spooked by the feel of it thumping behind the saddle.

Tessa pulled on her slicker and tied the hood close around her face. Catching sight of herself in the mirror, she forced a smile. No point in

alarming Miguel any more than she already
had.

Miguel helped her fasten the bag to the saddle. He pointed to the leather pouch already in
place. "The clippers," he said. "Please, Miz
Wagner. I really wish—"

"Wishes aren't horses," she broke in. "How
'bout a leg up?" Sighing resignedly, he boosted
her. "I don't expect Garland home before this
evening, Miguel. Explain the situation. Tell her
not— repeat *not*— to follow me. I want her to
wait here until Jed's phone is back in service.
By then we'll be needing stuff, but at the moment I have no idea what it might be. Okay?"

It was clear from Miguel's expression that he
saw the situation as anything but okay, but knew
there was nothing he could do to stop her. His
lips moved in silent prayer.

Vaya con Dios.

Twenty-five

Jed sat dozing in Aggie Bradburn's old rocker, his chin touching his collarbone, when a noise, a faint tap-tapping, roused him. Thinking it a change in his father's labored breathing, he pushed himself up, suddenly awake.

"Easy, Jed," said a quiet voice from the doorway. "It's only me."

Jed settled back, but not for long. *Me, who?* he wondered, turning his head to blink at the figure walking towards him. Despite the rain he saw streaming down the window, it seemed enveloped in sunlight. He blinked again. "Tessa?"

"None other," she said, shrugging out of her bright yellow slicker. "Be right back," she added. "I'm dripping all over the floor."

By the time she returned, Jed was standing by the bed, staring down.

"How is he?" she asked

"Hard to tell. He can't talk. I'm not sure he recognizes me . . . or if he does, wants to. Doc Strunk wasn't encouraging, but you know Pop, he's what investors in the stock market call a contrarian." He adjusted the old man's covers. "I didn't think the road was passable."

Tessa hesitated before answering. "It's not," she said.

He slanted a look at her. "Then how in hell did you get here?"

"Hayden's Bald," she said. "I clipped the fence wire to let us through. I hope you don't mind."

"Not as long as I knew before I let any cattle graze up there." He led the way out of the bedroom, leaving the door slightly ajar. "Who's us?"

"Me and Mackerel. I put his saddle on your porch, but I had to leave him standing in the rain. He's not a happy horse," she added as they entered the kitchen, "but then these aren't happy times, are they?" Jed agreed they weren't. "I thought you might be running low on food," Tessa said, reaching into the duffle she'd left near the door. "I'm afraid I grabbed what was closest to hand." Packets and cans and small cartons cluttered the tablet top. "Kind of a strange assortment, now that I look at it."

Jed picked up the jar of peanut butter with one hand and the bottle of bourbon with the other. "Do we have these together or alternately?"

"Either way . . . whatever suits you." He was aware of her blue eyes searching his face. "You look like hell, Jed. When did you last sleep?"

He ran his hand through his dark hair. "Well, when you came in I was—"

"*Really* sleep, I mean," she said sternly. "A few winks and a catnap now and again don't count."

"They do if they're all you can get."

"Ah, Jed."

It was the softness of her voice that undid him. He took a ragged breath. "I don't know, Tessa. Two days . . . three, maybe."

"Go lie down. I'll call you when supper's ready."

He eyed the odd mix of foodstuffs on the table. "I can hardly wait," he said. His smile was forced.

Tessa smiled back, probably thinking any smile an improvement, and made impatient little shooing motions with her hands. Jed shuffled down the dark corridor to his room, too tired to lift his feet. The next thing he knew, Tessa was nudging at his shoulder.

"Rise and shine." He groaned. "Well, rise anyway. I turned on all the lights and started a fire in the stove." His protest was automatic. "I don't think this month's electric bill is going to matter all that much to Pop, Jed."

"No. Probably not." The sight of the warmly lit kitchen, a gentle fire glowing in its squat little potbelly stove, cheered him more than he thought possible. "It's summer, Tessa," he said, raising his hands to the stove's warmth.

"It's cold out there. The wind's come up since I arrived. Besides, it's August."

Weary as he was, Jed picked up at once on her sly reference to the classic description of Colorado weather. "Winter and July," he murmured, chuckling.

Tessa cupped a hand to her ear. "Is that a laugh I hear?" She slid a large soup bowl and small plate into one of the two places she had set on the old table. *"Bon appétit!"*

Jed raised his eyebrows but didn't say anything. Taking his seat, he picked up the wineglass. "My, my. All we need are some flowers and a couple of those little watchamacallem lights."

"Votive," Tessa said. She brought the open bottle of wine to the table. "I don't know about the wine, Jed. It was sitting in your fridge God knows how long."

"No need to bring God into it, Tessa. Three days. I opened it after the doctor left." He filled their glasses. "I found Pop sprawled on the porch, his wheelchair tipped over, when I came in for lunch Friday. For all I knew, he could have broken something. Maneuvering through the doorways . . ." He shook his head. "It took me and two of the guys to get him into bed."

"Why didn't you call me?" she asked in a low voice.

Jed sampled the soup. "Not bad. Should I ask what's in it?"

"I wouldn't advise it," she said. "Call it pot-

luck and leave it at that." She gestured to the
crackers. "I bought those for the picnic supper
I took to the Bluegrass Festival for Garland and
her young man, then forgot to pack them. They
were very expensive. The cheese is just plain
old rat cheese. You should have called me."

"Best kind, rat cheese. 'Her young man'? I
didn't know mothers said things like that anymore."

"This one does. Jed? Why didn't you? Call
me, I mean."

Jed carefully put his spoon down on his plate
and fixed her with a look of stunning intensity.
"I've never hit a woman," he said, "and I didn't
think I ever could, but I swear, Tessa, if you
dare tell me you owe me I'll smack you one."

"All right then," she said slowly, "I won't. In
fact, I hadn't been planning to. It's just . . .
well, that's what friends do. They call on each
other in times of trouble." She averted her eyes
from his, as if realizing how trite that sounded.

He looked at her thoughtfully. "We're not
friends, Tessa . . . not the way we were, anyway." He picked up his spoon and resumed eating. "I don't know what we are now, do you?"
Tessa shook her head fiercely, unable to speak.
"Then I guess we'll just have to wait and see."
He gestured at his empty bowl. "Good soup,"
he said. "Could I have some more?"

At six the next morning, when Tessa made
her hourly check of Pop Bradburn, his breathing seemed more labored than it had during

the night, and it was obvious he needed attentions of an intimate physical sort. When Jed came in, yawning, a half-hour later, she had just finished sponging the old man off. Together they disposed of the soiled sheets and rolled him onto padding made from paper towels. "Fortunately, you still have eleven rolls," Tessa said.

"I'm a coupon clipper," he admitted. "I'm not compulsive about it, but this was an offer too good to pass up."

"Relax, Jed," she said. "I took advantage of it, too. Together we have enough to supply an army barracks." They looked at each other, then quickly away. "That's one of the first things I'll ask Garland to bring," she added briskly.

Jed looked at her, astonished. "More paper towels?"

"No, silly. Absorbent bedpads."

They stood together by the bed staring down at the old man's slack, distorted face. Stertorous," Jed said.

"I beg your pardon?"

"His breathing," Jed explained. "Harsh and gasping. Doc said that might happen."

"Mmmm-mmm. He's not going to get better, you know."

"I know that, Tessa. The trick is to get nourishment into him for as long as—" Jed stopped abruptly. "For as long as I can," he finished. "About all he can take now is thickened liquids.

I prepared some yesterday." He looked over a
Tessa, catching her in the middle of a hug
yawn. "Go to bed, Tessa. The morning shift i
mine."

"Can I have breakfast first?"

"Sure. But leave some of that bourbon fo
me."

She cuffed him on the shoulder as she lef
the room. Breakfast consisted of a slice of pea
nut butter-smeared bread and a glass of mil
she took with her to Jed's room. The milk
made at the last minute with some of the pow
der she had brought with her, was lukewarn
and nasty; the bed, still warm from Jed's body
was delicious.

By noon, when Tessa woke, a watery sunligh
was making faint leaf shadows on the window
pane. Two hours later, Jed's foreman knocked
at the door, stumbling back astonished, like
someone in an old-time silent movie comedy
when Tessa opened it.

"How in hell . . . I mean how in heck— "

"Under the circumstances, Vince, hell seem:
the right word," Tessa said, grinning. "I rode
over yesterday."

"The Hayden's Bald way?"

"Only way there was."

"But there's a fence up there." Tessa's finger:
mimicked the act of cutting. "Well, I'll be. . .
Where's your horse, Miz Wagner?"

"Around here someplace . . . out in that long grass behind the house probably. Nice-looking gray . . . I'd be obliged if you'd take him back with you to the corral." He nodded and shifted uneasily from one muddy boot to the other. "You'll be wanting to talk to Jed, I imagine."

"Yes, ma'am. The boys and me . . . we was wondering how the old man is, and if there's anything we can do."

"Not much, I'm afraid. Right now it's sort of a waiting game. Jed? Vince is here." She stepped back to make way for him.

"Morning, Vince. Water down enough to get out yet?"

"Not yet, Boss. I waded through," he said, indicating his mud-caked jeans. "Maybe by the end of the afternoon, though. Leastwise that's what I told the girl what answers at the phone company. Told her we had a medical emergency up here," he added gruffly.

Deathwatch is more like it, Tessa thought.

"Do me a favor, Vince?" she interrupted. "Call Miguel for me. Ask him to get word to Garland about bringing us some things this evening. I'll go make out a list. And Vince? Tell him she'll need to stop off home for my pickup. Her little car doesn't have four-wheel drive . . ."

Garland arrived at seven. The doctor had just left, shaking his head, when she pulled in. Tessa's red truck was now an all-over rosy desert-sand color.

"Sorry about that, Mom. There's still a lot

of water out there, and I didn't dare slow down."

Tessa lifted two stuffed-full canvas bags from the bench seat. "Actually, it looks better that way . . . hides all those scrapes and rust spots." They carried their load into the kitchen. "Come see what Garland brung us, Jed!" Tessa crowed. "Steak! Fresh tomatoes! Tater-Tots!"

"I have a bottle of red wine in my shoulder bag," Garland said, "and there should be some brownies somewhere in there, too."

"Nell's?" Tessa asked.

"Not mine, certainly. I made it very plain to Rick that he wouldn't be getting much of a cook . . . not much of a bottle-washer either."

Before Tessa had a chance to digest that, Jed appeared.

"Did I hear someone mention steak?"

"Uncle Jed!" Garland whirled to hug him. "How's it going? With Pop, I mean."

"Not so good. He's not in any pain . . . at least that's what Doc thinks. Hard to tell, really."

Garland nodded. They all knew there was nothing to say. "Mind if I join you for supper? I brought enough for three."

"We'd have wanted you to even if you hadn't," Jed said. "I'm sure your mother would have been happy to sacrifice her share to you."

* * *

"So, Garland," Tessa began with elaborate ca-
ualness after they sat down. "What's this about
ooks and bottle-washers? She spent the week-
nd at the Chavez ranch in New Mexico," she
ded for Jed's benefit, who looked up puzzled
om pouring the wine.

"Well, I guess it begins with Rick's mother . . .
mean, *actually* it began with Rick, but I'm talk-
g about *after* that." Jed and Tessa exchanged
ewildered looks. "C'mon, guys," Garland pro-
sted, "it's *complicated*. For starters, I finally ad-
itted to myself that I'm in love with him."

"Surprise, surprise," Tessa murmured.

Garland thumbed her nose at her. "It was
at festival weekend that finally did it, Mom.
ut these days there's a lot more to a relation-
ip than just being in love."

"Just being in love?" Tessa blurted. *"Just?"*

"Please, Mom." Tessa said she was sorry and
pped her fingers across her mouth. "The
ing is, Rick had trouble understanding that
y wanting to be a veterinarian, and *his* wanting
e to be his wife needn't be an either-or propo-
tion. Not in my mind, anyway. So he came up
ith all these alternatives. I could look after the
havez sheep, he said. Help with the lambing
d keep the sheepdogs' shots up-to-date, he
id. So I told him I needed more than endless
ocks of black-faced Suffolks and a few ill-tem-
ered border collies. We'd have children, he
id. Surely kids would satisfy this ministering
gel urge of mine, he said. I swear, I felt like

socking him, only I didn't want to mar that go
geous olive skin."

"Isn't there a practice down there that mig
take you on?" Jed asked.

"Yeah, I thought of that, but it was Rick
mom, of all people, who told me to stand firr
God! You guys'll love her! She's this tiny, sle
der wisp of a woman, with long dark ha
wound up in a knot and skewered to the ba
of her head with this huge silver pin that mu
weigh almost as much she does. Her eyes a
big and black, just like Rick's, and boy, can th
snap when she gets her dander up!

"Anyway, she tells me Chavez men will stret
an inch to a mile in a second if you let the
so I told her what I had in mind after I get r
VMD— buying into that Telluride practice I to
you about, Mom?— and *she* said she bet that
then Rick could run the greenhouse busine
from up there, via computer. They already ha
the basic software, and as long as he has goo
people doing the growing and shipping, he
only have to come by every couple of weeks
so. Costing out the product and selling it
what he's best at, she says, and he'd be clos
to an airport and good contacts in Tellurio
than down at their ranch."

She beamed at them, and started clearing th
table.

"Good Lord, Garland," Jed said, as sh
drifted serenely from table to sink. "I hop

ou're planning to drop the other shoe some-
me this century."

She brought over coffee mugs, a plateful of
rownies, and an ear-to-ear grin. "We compro-
ised."

"Yeah?" Tessa said. "How?"

Enjoying watching them fidget, Garland
ok her time filling their cups. "We-e-e-ll,"
e said, sliding back into her chair, "we talked
d talked about it . . . argued a little, too,"
e admitted, "but for one thing, I'm not go-
g to apply to Cornell."

"Hallelujah," Tessa muttered.

"Rick's father suggested Colorado State at
rt Collins. He says it's first rate."

"I could have told you that," Tessa said.

"You did, Mom, but you know what they say
out familiarity. Anyway, I figure I could stay
Fort Collins during the week; spend my week-
ds at the Chavez ranch with Rick, then rent
place in Telluride summers, with me assisting
the clinic until I qualify for full partnership,
which point we'll move up there permanently.
hat'll give us lots of time to plan just the kind
f house we want."

"You plan to marry him, I assume?"

"Well, yeah, Mom. We thought next summer,
ter we graduate from the university."

"You're thinking of buying into this Telluride
eterinary practice *and* building a house up
ere?" Jed asked. "You're talking big bucks,
arland."

"We talked about that, too. As far as t[
house and property goes . . . well, Rick's gran
father left him pretty well fixed— "

"Oil money," Tessa interjected for Jed's ber
fit.

"But buying into the practice will be my r
sponsibility." She shifted uncomfortably in h
chair. "I called Gav from New Mexico, Mor
We talked over Uncle Lloyd's offer, and we
like to accept it. Gav's decided he's not cut o
to be a politician himself— too much glad-han
ing, he says— but he loves the process. He'd li
to open his own office as a consultant when l
has more experience under his belt, and h
share of the proceeds would give him somethi
to start building the capital he'll need.

"I know it's a shock, after all the rigamarc
you went through— "

Tessa stared at her daughter. "You two a
sure about this?"

"There's no access to that piece from the H₂
ton holdings, so selling it won't matter to us—
you— one way or the other." She reached o
to grasp her mother's hand. "Look at it th
way: the Wagners have never expended mu[
affection on Gavin and me, so why not ma[
'em pay for the privilege of seeing the last [
us?"

Tessa tapped the table with her fingers, tl
beat quickening as she considered Garland
words. "Yeah," she finally said, "why the h[

ot? But I hope you're not thinking of accept-
ıg their first offer."

"Hardly likely," Garland drawled.

Garland helped Tessa wash up the dishes and
dy the house. Not that there was much tidying
• do. The house was sparsely furnished—a
ouple of dark overstuffed armchairs and a
ıtty-looking braided rug in front of an ancient
·levision set in the living room; outdated photo
ılendars decorating the walls of the small, dim
·drooms—and the dust too ingrained to yield
• a casual once-over with a damp rag. It was
 depressing place, Tessa thought as she went
·om room to low-ceilinged room. She won-
·ered if Jed would get a dog after his father
ied. Something big and bouncy and cheerful.
ike me.

It was dark by the time Garland said her
oodbyes, promising to call in the morning to
·e if anything was needed. Jed and Tessa stood
n the porch as she carried the empty canvas
ırryalls back to the truck. The moon had risen;
ıe air smelled newly washed and fragrant with
•gebrush.

"I'm rested now, thanks to you," Jed mur-
ured to Tessa. "If you want to leave, too—"

"Do you want me to?" she asked. He shook
ıs head. "Then I'll stay for as long . . ."

As long as what? You need me? Want me?

Tessa wasn't sure she wanted to know the a
swer. "I'll stay," she repeated.

Jed looked in on Pop. "No change," he sai
then suggested they finish the wine. "Can't l
more than a half a glass apiece," he said, hol
ing the bottle up to the light. "Hardly wor
saving."

So they sat and sipped and talked. Jed ask
Tessa if she was comfortable with Garland's d
cision.

"Which one? Selling the land Barry left the
or marrying Rick Chavez?"

"Both, I guess."

Tessa twirled the glass between her finger
watching the liquid deposit red sheets of fil
that slowly slid back to replenish the dwindli
supply. "When I cut the fence up on Hayder
Bald— was that only yesterday?— I noticed th
the bark on that big cottonwood tree, the o
anchoring the fence where it turns back nort
has expanded over the wire you wound arou
it, almost burying it. I don't recall how lo
ago that was, but I remember you taking thr
turns on each strand— "

"— six strands, one foot apart," Jed said. "A
ready buried you say?"

"Pretty near." She took a sip of wine an
looked at him over the rim of the glas
"There's no way to put a stop to that expansio
Jed, or the force behind it. That tree just kee
on growing, going its own way. Just like Garlar
and Gavin. So you let 'em go."

"Whether or not you want to."

"Whether or not." She cocked her head, thinking it over. "I think mostly I do, but it takes a little getting used to." Her lips quirked in a half smile. "I just wish it hadn't happened so fast."

"And all at once," Jed said gruffly.

"You, too, huh?"

"Oh, yeah." He yawned and stretched. "Who wants to take the first shift?"

"I think you just answered that," Tessa said. "I'm not sleepy yet— too much to think about. It's going on midnight, Jed. Suppose I call you at— " she looked at her watch— "three o'clock?"

Two hours later, despite her best efforts, including repeated pinches on the tender underside of her arms, Tessa fell into a light doze from which— only moments later it seemed— she was aroused by a long, labored groan. She sprang guiltily to her feet and crossed the three steps to the bed, waiting for the creaking of the hastily abandoned rocker to subside before bending lower. The trite phrase that sprang horrifyingly to mind when she held her fingers to the old man's neck proved all too apt.

Silent as the grave.

Tessa stood quietly, staring down, a few moments longer, then drew the sheet up and over his face.

She tiptoed out— why, she could not say— and

closed the door behind her. In the dim light
the hall, she could just make out the flashir
figures on her watch. Ten minutes after fou
*Hadn't someone once told her that most natur
deaths occur at four in the morning?* That, to
seemed apt.

She entered Jed's room, quietly undresse
and slipped in beside him. The bed was narro
and hard. *The kind a monk would have,* sh
thought. She kissed his cheek.

He sighed and, gently grumbling, turned t
wards her. "Is it time?"

"It's over, Jed," she whispered. She felt h
lashes brush against her temple. "Ten minut
ago."

"Finally over," he muttered. "My God." H
arms came around her, hard. His hands, feelin
her nakedness, tensed. "Tessa?"

"Love me, Jed. Ever since that first time, I'v
thought of little else. You said we couldn't g
back to the way it was, and I no longer war
to. I may lose you, but that's a chance I'm wil
ing to take. Love me . . . *please.*"

He needed no further urging.

In daylight it might have been grotesque, th
juxtaposition of death and exuberant life. Bu
there, in the darkness before dawn, it seeme
right and good.

Their joining was gentle. His kisses were so
on her throat, teasing on her mouth. Then, a
his thrusts went deeper, his lips thinned an
hardened. He ducked his head and lifted on

full breast to catch the hardened nipple between his teeth. She cried out, arched up against him, and they climaxed together.

He fell back against the pillow and smoothed her hair from her brow. He didn't have to see her face to know the spacing of the eyelids he kissed, nor could darkness disguise the shape of the long legs, twined with his, that he'd known all his life.

Tessa fell asleep in his arms. When she woke— at what she estimated, by the stretch of the sunlight across the rumpled bedclothes, as midmorning— she was alone. Ten minutes later her teeth had been brushed, hair combed and tied into a ponytail, jeans, shirt, and shoes donned. The cloudy bathroom mirror told her she looked . . . well, presentable. But she felt great. Terrific in fact. A feeling hardly affected by the sobering sight of the closed bedroom door.

The kitchen was empty.

"Jed?" There was no answer. *"Jed?"*

She opened the door and stepped out on the porch. There, out in the long, storm-drenched grass, sat the old rocker from Pop Bradburn's room, a couple of big old suitcases, and a black enameled strongbox on top of which perched a cheaply framed snapshot of a smiling woman holding a small boy by the hand.

It looked, Tessa thought, like something assembled for an arty photograph.

Hearing a funny crackling sort of noise, she descended the porch steps and almost tripped over a bale of straw, one of several lined up along the front of the house. Peering cautiously around the corner, she saw Jed busily engaged in stacking more bales of straw against the weathered clapboards.

Tessa straightened. "What on *earth* are you doing? There's a dead man inside, in case you've forgotten."

Jed turned to look at her. "That's not something a person forgets." His expression was serious. Very intent. "I called Doc Strunk at first light; he's long since come and gone. He's probably at the town hall now, filing the death certificate."

"So what's all this about?" Tessa said, indicating the straw.

"I've already notified the guys at the firehouse."

"About *what?*"

"About burning the house down."

Tessa stared at him. "Jed, please. If this is your idea of a joke—"

"No joke, Tessa. What I figured is . . . well, I remember your dad saying once that for people like us the home place is as vital to the life we choose to lead as the beating of our hearts, and I believe that. I truly do. But for Walt Bradburn, this place was the *only* thing. He couldn't

get his own sisters off the ranch fast enough;
he had no love to spare for Aggie, the dearest,
bravest woman who ever lived; he treated me
like a hired hand at best.

"My God! Look at this sorry place!" he cried,
waving an impassioned hand at it. "There's no
love in it . . . never has been."

"But it's yours now, Jed. You could fix it
up . . . paint it, put in bigger windows maybe.
You could even plant some flowers," she finished lamely.

Jed reached her in two long strides. He
grabbed her shoulders; she winced as his fingers dug into her muscles. "It's *his* house, not
mine. Always was; always will be. I never want
to set foot in it again." He turned defiantly towards it. "*His* house, mean and cramped as his
heart, and now it'll be his funeral pyre."

She looked at him, aghast.

"They do this in India, you know, except
there the widow's expected to add herself to the
flames. At least Aggie was spared that." He resumed stacking the bales. "Only a few more to
go, Tessa. If you've got anything of yours in the
house, you'd better get it out."

Tessa swallowed the protest that sprang automatically to her lips. There was nothing she
could do, and the more she thought of it, the
more she had to grant the rough justice of it.

She stood a moment longer, allowing the ten-
sion to subside, then ran inside to collect her
things. She paused in the kitchen to grab a spoon

and the jar of peanut butter she'd brought with her. Okay, so her breakfast menu was peculiar; there was damn little about this particular morning that wasn't.

By the time she emerged, Vince Higgins and the other hands had already assembled. It was hard to tell from their expressions what they were feeling. Shocked? Curious? Excited? Maybe a little bit of everything.

She smelled gasoline. Turning, she watched as Jed sprinkled it solemnly, almost ceremoniously, on the bales. Setting the can aside, he stood quite straight. He closed his eyes for a long moment. He pulled a box of wooden matches from his pocket, struck one, then a dozen or so more, one after the other, and sent them spiraling into the waiting bales.

It didn't take long. The wood was old and dry and eagerly consumed. Tessa linked her arm in Jed's and pulled him back from the heat. "Where were you planning on living?" she asked.

"Well, I've got a place fitted out in the barn, with a desk and a fireproof safe I keep all the ranch papers in. It's sort of my hideaway. My books are there, a few nice paintings I've picked up over the years at the Ouray art show, a cot, and a big comfortable chair. It's nice. I'll manage."

His hideaway?

She slid a wondering look at him. His fine dark eyes were narrowed against the leaping flames. Getting to know this man she thought she'd known all her life might be quite an adventure.

She reached up to pull gently at the tip of his long nose. "What would you say to moving in with me?"

He hugged her tight against him and smiled down at her. "I was beginning to think you'd never ask."

Epilogue

A passing shower during the previous night had left a powdering of snow on the peaks jagging up beyond Hayden's Bald.

Seeing it, Tessa sighed. "Summer's almost over . . . Gav and Garland will be back in Boulder in a fortnight."

Jed turned in his saddle to look at her. "Fortnight?" he repeated, amused.

"A little something left over from Scott," she said. "The *only* thing, in case you were wondering."

"I wasn't, but I'm glad to hear it. Speaking of leftovers, what happened to that lump-headed brute of Barry's? I haven't noticed him giving the other horses a hard time lately . . . not that I miss him."

"Didn't I tell you? I gave him to Marion Shelby."

"Good Lord, I thought you liked her!"

"I do, Jed. In fact I spent most of a day with her looking at Arabians. She bought herself a couple of real beauties. They're pretty green though, so on the way back we stopped off at Skywalk for a tour of my training facilities."

He grinned. "Tour, huh?"

"Smartass," she returned mildly. "Anyway, Turnip caught her fancy. She said she'd never seen a horse who thought so much of himself. She says he reminds her of Scott."

"Except Shelby's not ugly."

Tessa, recalling Scott's blandly expressed willingness to pursue Garland whether or not she was his daughter, shrugged. "The way I look at it, everyone should have an ugly, ornery cuss like Turnip to cope with at least once in life."

"Not this cowboy!" Jed said.

"You had Pop."

"True," he admitted.

"And now you have me."

He laughed and guided Bolt close enough to Mackerel to give her an arm's-length squeeze. "Ornery, yes; ugly no."

"Give me a few more years and wrinkles."

"Never!"

She beamed at him. "As I was saying, the twins will be back in Boulder soon, and—"

"Have they given Lloyd an answer on his offer yet?"

"Well, I know they turned down the first two, and Gav persuaded Garland they should hold off on the third until he has a chance to consult with the guy he worked for this summer."

"Leaving Uncle Lloyd twisting in the wind."

"Uncle Jack, too. Gav's a strong believer in

equal opportunity.'' They grinned at each other. ''I was hoping Garland could help with the calves, but what with one thing and another— ''

''One thing being Rick Chavez?'' She nodded. ''Those calves must be strapping teenagers by now,'' Jed said. ''When were you hoping to bring them down?''

''Before we have any more snow up there . . . next weekend maybe?''

''Suits me. I'm not due for dinner at the White House until the following week.''

She gave him a startled, gape-mouthed look, then swatted him with her hat. ''Race you to the top!''

Tessa, having the advantage of initial intent, took the lead. She pulled up at the place where she had cut the fence three weeks earlier. ''What do you think?'' she asked when he joined her.

''Easy enough,'' he said, dismounting. He unstrapped the leather bag containing the coils of wire from Bolt's saddle. He held out his hand for the cable splicer Tessa was carrying. ''I'll splice the strands here, then reinforce it with added wire. Shouldn't take long.''

''What I meant was, what do you think about taking down the whole shebang— posts, wire, everything. Bradburn and Hatton,'' she cried, waving her hat in the air. ''All for one; one for all!''

''The two musketeers?''

Tessa, reminded of the absent third, sobered. ''Yeah. Better than one.''

Jed blew on his hands, rubbed them, then stuck them in the pockets of his flannel-lined denim jacket. "Look at me," he muttered. "It's not even autumn yet— not officially, anyway."

Together they gazed at the mountains' snow-freckled flanks. "Well, you know what the old timers always say about Colorado weather," Tessa said.

"Winter and July," Jed quoted, recalling the last time he'd thought of that, sitting across the table from her in the kitchen of the house that no longer was.

Grateful beyond measure for her ministering presence, unable to deny her connection to his heart and soul, he had found the old sham of fraternal affection impossible to resurrect. It was only later he realized that in the process of exorcising the pretense, the connection had strengthened.

Connection, he reminded himself, *not chains.*

He took a deep breath. "You know what else they say, Tessa." She looked at him questioningly. "Good fences make good neighbors. What do you say we just mend it and leave it be?"

"For old time's sake? she asked.

"No-o-o," he said slowly. "For all the times to come."

Coming next month
from *To Love Again:*

Something Wonderful by Martha Gross
and
For All of Her Life
by Heather Graham Pozzessere

WATCH AS THESE WOMEN LEARN
TO LOVE AGAIN

HELLO LOVE   (4094, $4.50/$5.
by Joan Shapiro

Family tragedy leaves Barbara Sinclair alone with her success. The fight to g
custody of her young granddaughter brings a confrontation with the determi
rancher Sam Douglass. Also widowed, Sam has been caring for Emily alo
guided by his own ideas of childrearing. Barbara challenges his ideas. And th
not all she challenges . . . Long-buried desires surface, then gentle affection. S
and Barbara cannot ignore the chance to love again.

THE BEST MEDICINE   (4220, $4.50/$5.
by Janet Lane Walters

Her late husband's expenses push Maggie Carr back to nursing, the career she
almost thirty years ago. The night shift is difficult, but it's harder still to ignore
way handsome Dr. Jason Knight soothes his patients. When she lends a hanc
help his daughter, Jason and Maggie grow closer than simply doctor and nu
Obstacles to romance seem insurmountable, but Maggie knows that love is alw
the best medicine.

AND BE MY LOVE   (4291, $4.50/$5.
by Joyce C. Ware

Selflessly catering first to husband, then children, grandchildren, and her agi
though imperious mother, leaves Beth Volmar little time for her own adventure
passions. Then, the handsome archaeologist Karim Donovan arrives and ca
paigns to widen the boundaries of her narrow life. Beth finds new freedom w
Karim insists that she accompany him to Turkey on an archaeological dig . . .
a journey towards loving again.

OVER THE RAINBOW   (4032, $4.50/$5.
by Marjorie Eatock

Fifty-something, divorced for years, courted by more than one attractive man,
thoroughly enjoying her job with a large insurance company, Marian's sudden r
lessness confuses her. She welcomes the chance to travel on business to a small N
sissippi town. Full of good humor and words of love, Don Worth makes her
needed, and not just to assess property damage. Marian takes the risk.

A KISS AT SUNRISE   (4260, $4.50/$5
by Charlotte Sherman

Beginning widowhood and retirement, Ruth Nichols has her first taste of freed
Against the advice of her mother and daughter, Ruth heads for an adventure in
motor home that has sat unused since her husband's death. Long days and lo
campgrounds start to dampen the excitement of traveling alone. That is, un
dapper widower named Jack parks next door and invites her for dinner. On
road, Ruth and Jack find the chance to love again.

*Available wherever paperbacks are sold, or order direct from t
Publisher. Send cover price plus 50¢ per copy for mailing a
handling to Penguin USA, P.O. Box 999, c/o Dept. 171(
Bergenfield, NJ 07621.Residents of New York and Tennes:
must include sales tax. DO NOT SEND CASH.*

Taylor—made Romance From Zebra Books

WHISPERED KISSES (3830, $4.99/5.9

Beautiful Texas heiress Laura Leigh Webster never ima
ined that her biggest worry on her African safari would
the handsome Jace Elliot, her tour guide. Laura's gua
ian, Lord Chadwick Hamilton, warns her of Jace's dang
ous past; she simply cannot resist the lure of his stro
arms and the passion of his *Whispered Kisses.*

KISS OF THE NIGHT WIND (3831, $4.99/$5.

Carrie Sue Strover thought she was leaving trouble behi
her when she deserted her brother's outlaw gang to live
life as schoolmarm Carolyn Starns. On her journey,
stagecoach was attacked and she was rescued by handso
T.J. Rogue. T.J. plots to have Carrie lead him to her bro
er's cohorts who murdered his family. T.J., however, so
succumbs to the beautiful runaway's charms and loving
resses.

FORTUNE'S FLAMES (3825, $4.99/$5.

Impatient to begin her journey back home to New Orlea
beautiful Maren James was furious when Captain Ha
delayed the voyage by searching for stowaways. Impatie
gave way to uncontrollable desire once the handsome c
tain searched *her* cabin. He was looking for illegal pass
gers; what he found was wild passion with a woman
knew was unlike all those he had known before!

PASSIONS WILD AND FREE (3828, $4.99/$5.

After seeing her family and home destroyed by the cr
and hateful Epson gang, Randee Hollis swore revenge.
knew she found the perfect man to help her—gunslin
Marsh Logan. Not only strong and brave, Marsh had
ebony hair and light blue eyes to make Randee forget
hate and seek the love and passion that only he could g
her.

Available wherever paperbacks are sold, or order direct from
Publisher. Send cover price plus 50¢ per copy for mailing
handling to Penguin USA, P.O. Box 999, c/o Dept. 17.
Bergenfield, NJ 07621. Residents of New York and Tenne
must include sales tax. DO NOT SEND CASH.